The Other Woman

Women of Colour in Contemporary Canadian Literature

edited by

MAKEDA SILVERA

Sister Vision
Black Women and Women of Colour Press

ISBN 0-920813-47-X
©1995 Copyright Makeda Silvera
Individual selections copyright by their respective author(s)

95 96 97 98 99 ML 0 9 8 7 6 5 4 3 1

All rights reserved. No part of this book may be reproduced or transmitted in any form or by any means without permission in writing from the publisher, except in the case of reviews.

Thanks to the following for permission to reprint copyright material in this book: West Coast Line *Colour. An Issue*, edited by Roy Miki and Fred Wah; "Going Home: Reflections on Issues of Colour, Culture, Gender and Exile," by Carmen Rodríguez; *Women Do This Every Day: Selected poems* by Lillian Allen, Toronto:Women's Press.

Canadian Cataloguing in Publication Data
Main entry under title
The Other Woman: Women of Colour in Contemporary Canadian Literature

Includes bibliographical references
ISBN 0-920813-47-X

1. Canadian literature — Women authors — History and criticism.
2. Canadian literature — Minority authors — History and criticism.
I. Silvera, Makeda

PS8089.5.W6074 1995   C810.9'9287   C93-095239-1   PR9194.5.W6074 1995

Published with the assistance of the Canada Council and the Ontario Arts Council

Editor for the Press: *Makeda Silvera*
Production and Design: *Stephanie Martin*
Pre-Production: *Leela Achayra*
Printed and bound in Canada by Metrolitho

Represented in Canada by The Literary Press Group
Distributed by General Publishing

Published by:
Sister Vision Press
P.O. Box 217, Station E
Toronto, Ontario

*For my daughters Keisha and Ayoola
and for the writers in this book who are
creating a dynamic upheaval
in Canadian Literature*

Acknowledgements

I wish to first thank the contributors, many of whom have extraordinarily hectic schedules but still found the time to be a part of this book. Their generous participation made this project a labour of love. I hope, in return, this book will contribute to dialogue and connections amongst women of colour writers in this country.

I thank Sister Vision: Black Women and Women of Colour Press — we've been part of each other since 1984 — for undertaking this book with me, for recognizing its importance, and for Sister Vision's continuing commitment to discovering and developing writing by women of colour.

Thanks and appreciation to Leéla Acharya for her expert job of transcribing and word-processing.

Thanks to Jane Greer for her continued support in assisting in pre-production.

Thanks to P.K. Murphy for always being up to the struggle, for meeting impossible deadlines as a copy editor and for doing so with her particular sense of humour.

My thanks to Agnes Huang for the West Coast connections and her enthusiasm.

I am also extremely grateful to Pamela Mordecai who, despite the "last-minute" call, brought her unparalleled proofreading skills to the manuscript.

And my special thanks to Stephanie Martin for understanding when creativity and production deadlines clash and for being the best friend a girl could ever want.

Contents

Makeda Silvera
    Introduction

Uma Parameswaran
    Names Resonant and Sweet — An overview
    of South Asian Canadian Women's Writing   3

Joy Kogawa talks to Karlyn Koh
    The Heart-of-the-matter Questions   19

Frederick Ivor Case
    Babylon and the Spirit Lash   42

Isabelle Knockwood
    I have to write whatever happened   63

ahdri zhina mandiela
    the true rhythm of the language   81

Ramabai Espinet talks to Elaine Savory
    A Sense of Constant Dialogue — Writing, Woman
    and Indo-Caribbean Culture   94

Rita Wong
    Jumping on hyphens — a bricolage
    receiving "genealogy/gap," "goods,"
    "east asian canadian," "translation" & "laughter"   117

Carol Talbot
    It's important to write from your soul   155

Himani Bannerji
    Writing was not a decision   180

CARMEN RODRÍGUEZ
    I live in a language that's not mine   208
LENORE KEESHIG-TOBIAS
    Keepers of the Culture   220
LILLIAN ALLEN
    Poems are not meant to lay still   253
MARIA CAMPBELL TALKS TO BETH CUTHAND
    It's the job of the Storyteller to create chaos   264
SALONI MATHUR
    bell hooks called me a "Woman of Colour"   271
AFUA COOPER
    If you're true to your voice   293
BEATRICE CULLETON
    I decided to go with reality   311
LIEN CHAO
    Constituting Minority Canadian Women and our Sub-Cultures — Female Characters in Selected Chinese Canadian Literature   333
DIONNE BRAND
    In the company of my work   356
SKY LEE TALKS TO C. ALLYSON LEE
    Is there a mind without media any more?   382
MAKEDA SILVERA
    The characters would not have it   405
ARUN P. MUKHERJEE
    Canadian Nationalism, Canadian Literature and Racial Minority Women   421

Contributors' Notes   446
Selected works by contributors   452

Forward

This book is a long-awaited celebration of the writing of women of colour in Canada and I am delighted to bring it to you. The voices in it speak not necessarily in unison but to and of a common interest.

The book's subtitle is *Women of Colour in Contemporary Canadian Literature*. "Women of colour" is a much-debated term. After all, names have been imposed on us, and since colonialism we have been fighting to name ourselves. Some think the term "women of colour" shouldn't exist, that people should be named specifically. I think that view makes it harder to wage common struggle. I think of the term as a large, colourful quilt, a resting place, a place to form alliances. I do not think of it as where we live, as really our home. But I also don't think that calling ourselves "women of colour" diminishes the identity or power of any of us or that it makes us invisible. We know who we are: women of the First Nations, South Asians, African Canadian, East Asians, Indo Caribbean, Afro Caribbean, Latin American, Japanese Canadian, Black, Chinese Canadian, African.

I am neither an historian nor a sociologist. I am a writer, a writer of short stories and essays, to be exact, and an editor. When I create characters, I must know their histories, the times and places that helped shape them, and I must know how they responded to these forces. Of course, I draw on what I see. And, of course, because I am a Caribbean woman of African descent, of working-class background, a lesbian, a mother, some but not all of my characters are too.

When I decided to work on this book it was because I wanted to hear the talk of other sister-women. I wanted to hear us talk about writing, our writing, and where and how we fill our characters with life and history. I wanted to say, "Here's a book with a lot of us. We're here, and we've been writing for years, and we're here to stay." I wanted to see us dance across the margin and into the centre of our lives. I wanted a book that looked back at us through our own eyes and not the eyes of white culture. But the one thing that soon became apparent to me was the near-craziness of doing this book. Crazy because there was a particular urgency to getting the book out, and, ironically, that urgency presents itself in our everyday lives, which leave very little time for interviews, far less for interviews across the country.

Even so, here it is. And it is indeed a fête to have so many writers from different regions, cultures, sexualities and classes talking about their work and what drives them to a life of writing. Wherever possible, I wanted writers in conversation with other writers. I wanted to read what other writers would ask each other, to see how smooth and easy such dialogues would flow. It was important that we felt at ease because this is our work.

It has not been possible to include the voices of all women of colour writing in Canada today, in the essays and conversations in this collection. Unfortunately, constraints of space, time and in some cases, distance, did not permit that. I feel however, that the voices here are representative of a substantial number of women writers, in addition to which the collection has opened space for writing critics like Dr. Fred Case to enter into the dialogue. It is my hope that these essays and conversations initiate important discussions, discussions that will continue in other collections like this one.

Make no mistake: this rich collection of work is our gift to you and to ourselves. In it we proudly lay claim to who we are and what we write about, and why and how we do it, and for whom. Here, we talk amongst ourselves and to you about the role of community and political activism in our lives and work. We talk about language, about our own mothertongue. We are dancing to our songs, our drums, our chants.

Makeda Silvera
Toronto 1994

Uma Parameswaran

Uma Parameswaran

Names Resonant and Sweet
An overview of South Asian Canadian Women's Writing

THE EFFLORESCENCE of creativity of South Asian Canadian women in the 1990s is breathtaking. Until 1990 poetry predominated, but in the last few years fiction has leapfrogged into prominence. Naming — oh, the wonderful feel of elation as one writes the list of names, women's names, South Asian Canadian women's names: Lakshmi Gill, Suniti Namjoshi, Uma Parameswaran, Himani Bannerji, Bharati Mukherjee — all who published good work through the '80s. Yasmin Ladha, Jamila Ismail, Ramabai Espinet, Nazneen Sadiq, Farida Karodia, Surjeet Kalsey, Tilottama Rajan, Nilambri Ghai, Maya Khankhoje, whose voices are now emerging. And others who are probably writing something new between the time this piece leaves my desk and the printed version rolls off the press.

The three Rs of feminist literary scholarship might be identified as the retrieval, recording and re-reading of women's works. Retrieval is the search, discovery and dissemination and storage for ready access of the writings of women of an earlier era. Recording is the search, discovery and documentation for ready access of the writings of contemporary women. Re-reading is the feminist critical analysis of women's published works. Together, these three steps could help us revise the literary canon that for centuries has been mainly patriarchal in content and viewpoint. In the context of minority literatures of Canada, the last sentence would need an added qualifier after "patriarchal": namely "and Caucasian."

The first two — retrieving and recording — are very important in the present phase of history. In areas of study that have been in existence for a long time, retrieval means revising the canon in order to give space and recognition to earlier works. In English and US literature, the work of Susan Gubar and Sandra Gilbert (the editors of *The Norton Anthology of Women Writers*, is a prime example of what needs to be and is being done. Similarly, in the sciences, Margaret Alic's *Hypatia's Heritage: A History of Women in Science from Antiquity through the Nineteenth Century (1986)* opens the door to a fairer understanding of women's contributions through the ages. It is exciting to see the effect of these opening doors on the younger generation. For example, my niece, a student of music, is studying the compositions of Hildegard of Bingen, who lived six centuries ago. Another young woman wrote of her lesbian awakening:

> I remember studying a short story by George Eliot called 'The Lifted Veil.' There is a relationship between two women in that story ... which I found puzzling — until it suddenly occurred to me that the women were lovers. I can remember my heart pounding ... when I went home that day, my heart was singing.[1]

And yet another woman, reviewing a recent anthology of South Asian Canadian writings, speculates how different her own education would have been if such texts had been available four or five years ago:

I often wonder what it would have been like had I seen the names of my people on reading lists, because it would not only be their work that would have been recognized as Canadian but also their names, their heritage, my name, my heritage.[2]

Ramabai's labour of love, *Creation Fire: A CAFRA Anthology of Caribbean Women's Poetry (1990)*, provides a similar source for Caribbean voices and readers.

These doors assume an even greater importance in the context of "productive" Canadian multiculturalism (and by that I mean interest in other cultures and imparting knowledge of them through the school system; there is a non-productive side to multiculturalism, ghettoization and xenophobia, for example). The other day, I met someone, a white woman, who had been a student of mine in the '70s. She said how excited she had been to have on my first year course a novel — Kamala Markandaya's *Nectar in a Sieve (1954)* — set outside the Western world, written by a non-Caucasian and most of all, written by a woman.

We have come a long way since then, and women writers are represented more frequently in university courses than was the case five years ago. In my university we have re-shaped our first year English course to accommodate a variety of foci and interests: female, feminist, multicultural, Native. Now that we have anthologies that can be used in schools and universities, Canadians such as Kalyani and this white student just might get to read and feed into a revised canon. Yes, we who are in any Canadian university, are living in an exciting time and place.

Retrieval, recording and re-reading. In the context of South Asian Canadian literature, each approach has its own distinctive area that needs to be covered. We need to retrieve the experiences of the first immigrant women that are surely somewhere in the form of letters, diaries, logbooks (and by these I mean the account books that Indian women often keep of day-to-day expenditures, which in parentheses include notations of events and experiences) and the memory banks of those who are still alive. There is urgency since these sources will soon be lost. We need interviews such as those that appear in Makeda Silvera's *Silenced (1983)*, interviews "of the lived experiences of the voiceless." The task of re-reading is ongoing: the theoretical approach most suited would perhaps be one which studies the intersections of race, class and gender as communicated through literature. Read Gayatri Spivak. Read Himani Bannerji, our own South Asian Canadian Himani. I could write odes! Here she is:

> I am very suspicious, not about naïveté, or revolutionary romanticism, but about the pragmatism of our 'postindustrial, postmodern, postsocialist, posthuman' world ... That's what kept me writing ... certainly about 'culture' and about 'discourse.' But whose 'culture'? 'Discourse' of what? And to what end?[3]

Discourse, theories, patterns. Yes, work that needs to be done. But for now, I focus on the second task of feminist literary work, namely that of recording. An introductory overview of what has been published so far is a simple but necessary task.

First, to define the parameters, by South Asian Canadian literature is meant the writings of Canadians who draw their ancestry from India, Pakistan, Bangladesh and Sri Lanka, and who have come to Canada either directly from these homelands or indirectly via Britain or one of the erstwhile colonies (for example, the West Indies, Fiji, African countries such as Nigeria, Uganda, Tanzania ...).

Though immigration from South Asia started in the 1890s,

literature in a published form by Canadian South Asians started only in the 1970s. There are several reasons for this slow blooming. The first Indians to touch Canadian soil were troops returning from Queen Victoria's Diamond Jubilee celebrations in 1897. Word of the new land spread on their return to India, and the first immigrants landed in British Columbia soon after.

They were not the first Asians to arrive. In the 1880s the Canadian Pacific Railway had hired about 15,000 Chinese labourers, 5,000 of whom stayed on after their contract. Another 11,000 Japanese and Chinese had entered by 1907. By 1907 there were about 2,000 Indians, almost all of them labourers and male. This degree of Asian presence was enough to set off a chain of hate and racism against the "brown plague" and the "yellow peril." There were race riots in 1907, mainly against the Chinese and Japanese.

Of the racist oppressions that flared up periodically, the *Komagatamaru* episode of 1913 is one of the worst in Canadian history. Three hundred and seventy-six immigrants from India, aboard the ship *Komagatamaru,* were sent back after being quarantined on the coast of Vancouver Island for two months.

Immigration from India came to a standstill after this; the 1951 census records 2,148 Indians, of whom 721 were female. It was only in the 1960s that immigration picked up again. The growth of any literature needs numbers since obviously only a small percentage of any population takes to writing as a career.

The second reason is that there is a pattern to an immigrant group. The first period is spent coping with the day-to-day challenges of orientation and settling down while memory and psyche dwell on the land left behind; the next period is spent looking towards and working within one's own ethnocultural community. Only then does the immigrant take his or her place in the larger community, and this is when writers come into their own. These periods are not necessarily as linear in the development of a community as in an individual because there is a continuous influx of new immigrants. The periods could be, and usually are, concurrent, but they occupy different spaces, as Julia Kristeva says, stages of development. The writings of the first period often look back: there was some literature written by west coast writers all along, but the setting was usually India and not Canada, and they were published in India. Also, they were written in Punjabi or Gujarati, and this placed them outside Canadian literature. One of the tasks that lies ahead is to get recognition that Canada's multiculturalism is functional only when Canada's other major languages are considered as Canadian as English or French.

Before moving on to an annotated recording of names and titles, I would like to make two points, the first about pioneers in South Asian Canadian literature who have made this movement possible, and the second about further studies in which I am engaged. In 1966 Stephen Gill edited and published the first anthology, *Green Snow*. Suwanda Sugunasiri compiled a resource volume in the early 1980s that was published in 1988, and along with its sister-business TSAR Books, has been the single most influential source of promotion for the writings and criticism in the diaspora.

My play *Rootless but Green are the Boulevard Trees* was the first full-length play to be published.[4] Arun Prabha Mukherjee's *Aesthetics of Opposition: Essays on Literature, Criticism and Cultural Imperialism*, published in 1988, was the first volume of critical essays on the diaspora and remains extremely significant. The work of the Ontario Society for Studies in Indo-Caribbean Culture is likely to be important, if its 1993 volume, *Indo-Caribbean Resistance*, is representative of its direction. Himani Bannerji's *The Writing on the Wall: Essays on Culture and Politics*, published in 1993, though not about Canadian writers, provides critical theories that are springboards for analyzing the literary works of the diaspora. My collection of reviews and critical essays over the years is being published in India, where Indo-Canadian studies are a growing area of interest.

One of the ideas that presently engages me is the exploration of Luce Irigaray's concept of "womanspeak" and Helene Cixous' *écriture feminine,* especially in the works of male writers such as Rienzi Crusz, Moyez Vassanji and Rohinton Mistry.

Lakshmi Gill and Dorothy Livesay were the first two women to become members of the League of Canadian Poets. Born in 1943, Lakshmi Gill was educated at Western Washington University, the University of British Columbia and Mount Allison. She now lives in British Columbia and is a "fiercely private" person, as the editor says in *Shakti's Words.* She has published four volumes of poetry. In her introduction to the literary section of an issue of *Asianadian,* she says,

> In January 1980 I discovered I could no longer read "White Literature."
>
> I was ashamed and angry that I had spent my entire life immersed in Western philosophies and ideologies.[5]

This is exactly what African Americans have said and what colonials have said about English Literature and what feminists have said about male-centred and male-authored literature. A sense of disillusionment and frustration is common to all groups unjustly unrecognized because of cultural imperialism.

While Lakshmi Gill's *During Rain I plant Chrysanthemums* (1966) is satirical and clever in its lampooning of Canada, for example, and holier-than-thou in reaction to Viet Nam in "Beneath the Purple Lantern," her *Novena to St. Jude Thaddeus* is complex in its introspective explorations and in its structure. Clustered under nine days, each segment is distinctive in theme and form. Anthologists would automatically single out the poems that deal with immigrant experience — "Coming out of a Canadian Winter," or the four line poem,

> Once
> Outside
> Canada
> Vanishes

or "Letter to a Prospective Immigrant" which has lines such as:

> "If you can bring blessings, come then
> (don't expect blessings in return); hell does not give
> but takes."

When I used the poems in *Shakti's Words* in a class, one of the students exploded at Gill's negative images of Canada. "Why doesn't she go back if she dislikes it so much here?" If one can keep one's cool, this could be a starting point for a lesson in cross-cultural sensitivity, but do we always have to keep our cool when someone reacts thus to Canada's first woman member of the League of Canadian Poets, a resonant Canadian voice probably even before this student was born? Perhaps anyone who reacts with such heat can understand only a response that slaps him or her in the face.

In our predictable search for immigrant experience, we often overlook poetry as it is. Gill has written many poems on alienation, isolation, winter at the literal and metaphorical levels, etcetera, but let us read a few of her poems as is and leave critical exegesis for another place, another time.

> The car ran over
> its entrails, killing it again
> proving you can kill the dead ....[6]

> My bed is a way station
> where the children bounce
> and wrestle
> in their pink and blue pyjamas
> after the long journey
> of night-sleep
> to gather their strength
> for one more day.[7]

> How sublime in its simplicity:
> this prime minister
> concerned with a drowning bird.[8]

"Light, not Fire," a poem for Milton Acorn at the 6th League of Poets meeting, ends with the intensely moving lines:

> some laughed, some ate their salad
> while I cried inside like a mother
> whose son grows away, must grow away
> as everything grows away
> beyond our reach.

The poems clustered last, under the ninth day, are contemplative:

> On the Ninth Day
> hanged
> from the world tree
> lakshmi to Lakshmi ....
> let us not disguise our mythologies.
> Let us not make mythologies.[9]

This refusal to make mythologies brings us to Himani Bannerji, our most articulate activist, author of two volumes of poetry, *A Separate Sky* (1982) and *doing time* (1986). Here are the lines I have probably quoted to others a hundred times, and will as many times over again:

> If we who are not white, and also women, have not yet seen that we live in a prison, that we are doing time, then we are fools .... I cannot write poems anymore because I don't know what language, what words, what metaphors or myths I could use to describe the world around me .... And I am not sure there should be any more of these metaphors around, or myths, of signs, or symbols, or whatever they call them.[10]

Rather than doing without metaphors and mythologies, Suniti Namjoshi reclaims some myths and subverts others. Certainly our most prolific poet, Namjoshi has published ten volumes, the most notable being *Feminist Fables* (1981), *The Authentic Lie* (1982), and *Conversations of a Cow* (1985).

> Consider next, if you will, what the embrace of Pygmalion must have felt like at first; he human and sweating, she, cold to the bone ... They loved one another, she this marble man, he this human woman. But he was a sculptor. He carved another stone, and she ran away with the man next door, who, as it happened, was a potter, and worked in mud.[11]

The same wit sparkles even more in *Conversations*, a poetic narrative about a cow that takes the narrator to a lesbian heaven. In

Feminist Fables she interprets the myth of Philomel being turned into a nightingale:

> She had her tongue ripped out, and then she sang down through the centuries. So that it seemed fitting that the art she practises should be art for art's sake, and never spelt out, no, never reduced to message — that would appal.[12]

Suniti moved to England in the 1980s, to live with Gillian Hanscombe. Their joint work *Flesh and Paper* (1986), a cycle of love poems that are refreshingly more about communication than lovemaking, is her most artistically beautiful work. Her move away from Canada gives rise to a recurring question that has no easy answer: Where does one draw the line for belonging? As of now, Namjoshi has lived more years in India than elsewhere, but soon she will have lived longer in England than in Canada.

Similarly with Bharathi Mukherjee: soon she will have lived longer in the United States than in Canada; also, she has consciously turned her back on a Canada that is crassly racist, she says, and claims she is American, that she was born "American" by virtue of her sensibility, which celebrates the American way of life.[13] If self-identification were the final criterion, Mukherjee is not a Canadian writer. However, to adapt W.B. Yeats, "though she has done most bitter wrong/ To some who are near my heart (Canada and Canadians)/ Yet I number her in my song" because her best works are set in Canada or were written when she was a Canadian. I certainly like her subversive attacks on the establishment. I like citing the comment she made in *Saturday Night* when asked why she had left Toronto and Montreal for New York: she said that she would be mugged in New York because everyone risked that in New York, but in Canada she would be mugged because she was brown.

The controversy-generating documentary, *The Sorrow and the Terror* (1987), that she wrote with Clark Blaise, is about the Air India crash of June 23, 1985, that killed 329 people, ninety percent of whom were Canadians of Indian descent. The research seems thorough and the book is engrossing: the conclusions drawn by the authors are that Khalistani extremists planned and executed this act of terrorism in Canada, and that despite many warnings and trails, the Canadian government had been too complacent to take pre-emptive action. Readers would be moved to sorrow by the interviews the authors have painstakingly put together.

Let us grieve for the victims and those they left behind, but let us never forget the first reactions of the Canadian government. Prime Minister Brian Mulroney telephoned condolences to Prime Minister Rajiv Gandhi of India for the great loss. The transport minister, Don Mazankowski, accused Air India of negligence in reporting that there had been three suspicious bags detained by security at Mirabel airport; the three bags turned out to be harmless. The transport ministry and Mr. Mulroney's office quickly worked on damage control, but let us never forget that our prime minister's first reaction to the death of 300 Indo-Canadians was to send condolences to India's prime minister; he was condoling the loss of the airplane, maybe?

Bharati Mukherjee celebrates the United States in *Jasmine* (1989), a story of a young woman who comes to the States as a stowaway, gets raped, kills her rapist, works in New York for an Indian family, moves west and *voilà* realizes the American dream. But let me leave a deeper analysis of this for another time, another place. Enough to say that Mukherjee's "The Management of Grief" in *The Middleman and Other Stories* (1988) is one of the best delineations of the tangled wires of cross-cultural communication.

Cross-cultural communication in its lighter form appears sporadically in Uma Parameswaran's *Trishanku,* her 1987 cycle of poems, spoken in about fifteen different voices. Her play, *Rootless but Green are the Boulevard Trees* challenges the tradition of having a single protagonist by centring a family on stage. I could comment on the use of humour in her stories and poems or the poignancy of her immigrant themes, but let me leave that too for another time, perhaps to another critic. There is a growing interest in her work in India, where Canadian Studies are expanding. No prophet is accepted, etcetera.

Among newer writers, Yasmin Ladha's *Lion's Granddaughters and Other Stories* (1992) shows the flowering of South Asian women's writing yet to come. The stories draw in the reader in several ways. The author's Tanzanian background expands our horizons to include a geographical landscape that is other than geographical Canada. As I have said in my essay "Ganga in the Assiniboine," though the landscape around me is spruce and maple, the landscape of memory is treed with mangoes and banyan. The contribution of South Asian Canadians is that we bring Ganga to the Assiniboine, not only for ourselves but for our fellow Canadians. Stories such as "Aisha" and "Lion's Granddaughter" bring alive East African landscapes and lives.

Especially in the title story, we hear tunes and tones that spanned the world through the mission school education that was the legacy of the Raj, taught by the authoritarian white or Anglo schoolteachers that we have seen in the works of Achebe, in the African stories of Margaret Laurence, in *Midnight's Children.* The Rushdie connection is established through the author-reader dialogue in the first story "Beena." The British 19th century apostrophe "Dear Reader" is replaced with "Readerji" and "Yaar Reader." I would like to note that the mark that South Asian Canadian women's writings have arrived is that Ladha's book has neither glossary nor explication of foreign terms; it is the reader's responsibility to work at the meanings. Ladha follows the Rushdie approach, combining it in the later stories with well-placed explications within the context. The first story works and makes the reader work a little too hard at these reader-author interactions and coinages, but I suppose it is necessary in order to set up the rest of the volume in context.

Ladha's voice is that of a feminist, of "my *shakti* power" as she calls it. "Giving up the Company of Women" is a fine example of Ladha's shakti power. I choose it over others because I am at a phase where I am drawn to Canadian connections, where I focus only on those facets of a work that address our Canadian links. This is a conscious reaction to the average Canadian critic's tendency to focus on the exoticism of South Asian Canadians' writings to the exclusion of our Canadianness.

Another recent novel is *The Deaths of Sullyman Rush-to-Die* (1991) by Memuna, about whom I know nothing except that she is an older woman and uses no last name. Many of the episodes in the life and lives of Memuna's Sullyman resemble Salman Rushdie's — but, of course, this is a work of fiction and we find the usual disclaimer "any reference to persons dead or alive is unintentional." Sullyman does die repeatedly in the volume — once shot by Priya, once in Tiananmen Square, once as he watches his grandmother's death, once buried alive by those who had never read his book but are convinced it is a Christian plot to undermine Islam.

New journals have recently appeared, including *Ankur* and *Rungh* from Vancouver, and at last non-South Asian Canadian magazines are giving space to writings by the Indian diaspora.

So they keep coming: names, women's names, South Asian Canadian women's names, resonant and sweet. Maya Khankhoje, Sophia Moustapha, Suniti Namjoshi, Kaushalya Bannerji, Lakshmi Gill, Uma Parameswaran.

Endnotes

1. Naomi Guilbert in *Contemporary Verse 2*, 12:3, 1989.

2. Kalyani Pandya, on *The Geography of Voice: Canadian Literature of the South Asian Diaspora* in *Contemporary Verse 2*, 16:2, 1993.

3. Himani Bannerji in "The Writing on the Wall", p. ix

4. First published in *The Toronto South Asian Review*, 4:1, Summer 1985 and later published as a volume in 1988.

5. Lakshmi Gill in *Asianadian*, 1981.

6. Lakshmi Gill in "Dead Skunk on TCH" (Trans-Canada Highway).

7. Lakshmi Gill in "My Bed."

8. Lakshmi Gill in "Pierre Trudeau and The Drowning Bird."

9. Lakshmi Gill in "On the Ninth Day."

10. Himani Bannerji in *doing time*, p. 9.

11. Suniti Namjoshi in *The Authentic Lie*, p. 44.

12. Suniti Namjoshi in *Feminist Fables*, p. 102.

13. Bharathi Mukherjee, interviewed by Bill Moyers on PBS.

Karlyn Koh

Joy Kogawa

Agnes Huang

Joy Kogawa
talks to Karlyn Koh

The
Heart-of-the-matter
Questions

Koh: I want to begin by asking you about writing and becoming a writer. When and how did you first start to write? Did you have any role models?

Kogawa: I think I probably wrote all my life. Right from very early childhood I loved stories. But if the question is when did I first start publishing, when did I become a writer seriously in that way, then I made the decision to start working on it when I was a young mother with two small children at home, and that would have been 1960. I published my first story in 1964, but before that my main love had been music. I guess it was a matter of filling in my time. After I had babies and I had to stay at home, and there was nothing much to do with my life, so I stayed home and wrote.

But there's another question behind that: why the pen, why not art? Why not something else? I think I always did love language and I loved stories and I loved reading. Maybe that's the way I was born, liking that kind of stuff and liking the rhythm of words. Then I was lucky in one sense that there was the King James Bible, which was a very rich source of language. I had a lot of that in my childhood, plus the encyclopedia — the Book of Knowledge — there was good writing in there. So it was that, plus my mother was a good story teller and she told me a lot of Japanese folk stories. I think all those things added up to my wanting to write. And my dad used to stay at home with his pen, sit at his desk. That was the thing to do, to sit at your desk with a pen, *(laughter)* so these are all models. But in terms of who my models were in the writing world, I don't think I had any.

In the 1960s, when I first started to publish, the things that were consuming me were moral questions, questions of ideals, so the things I read were on topics like guilt and love and will, and all those kinds of questions. So I used to read a lot of Rollo May. And having been raised a Christian and having a lot of questions about that, I read things like Martin Buber and Bishop Robinson, various things like that. But then when I first started to send things out to the publishers, I sent things to *The Ladies Home Journal*, to any magazines I saw in the stands, and they always came back with rejection slips.

KOH: How has being a Japanese-Canadian woman had an impact on your writing?

KOGAWA: I think in the very first years when I was publishing I was like the other people of my generation — I had virtually no consciousness, except in a negative sense, of Japaneseness. I would see myself as white. I wrote as a white person. I wrote, in fact, in a male voice initially. In that sense I was a mimic, I read and I wrote what I read. So my first short story was about a little boy called Jimmy Parkin and the Parkin family and his grandfather. Completely male story, completely white, male story. And that was my first published story — it was called "Are There Any Shoes in Heaven?"

It was about a family, the Parkin family, that had left the

mountains of British Columbia and were living out on the prairies of Alberta, and this little boy hated it, and he wanted to go back to the mountains. That was a Japanese-Canadian story. I didn't know it, I was just writing it. It was my story in as much as I loved the mountains, and I hated the prairies, and I wanted to go back, and I was always wanting to go home. So the themes were themes from my life, but they were transposed onto the people of my milieu, the people of my environment. Anyway, it didn't occur to me that anybody would ever publish a story about anybody that wasn't white, hadn't an Anglo-Saxon name, because those were the only ones I ever heard. So I continued in that vein.

I wrote poetry, but in poetry I didn't have to have a subject as such, I didn't have to have a name — it was just raw emotion and it just came out of me. And the struggles that I had were struggles with questions of love and evil and death, and those are universal questions, so I didn't have any particular consciousness, again then, of race. I didn't associate my suffering as the suffering of a person who was a minority human being. I simply attached it to all suffering. So I wrote like that, and I wrote about not being able to love and not being able to understand what the point of living was and things like that. And it wasn't until I had written that kind of poetry for years and years and years — it used to gush right out of me — it wasn't until much later, in the late 1970s, that I wrote a story called "Obasan," and then it started to become a novel.

But even at that point, I was not thinking particularly of writing about Japanese-Canadians, I was simply writing out of my own life and writing it in some of the way I wrote poetry. I would dredge things out of dreams and put them out there. When I was at the Archives, though, in Ottawa, that's when I became aware of another voice that I was not conscious of being within me — Muriel Kitagawa's voice. To me, it was a voice from the outside, one that

I had never encountered, and one that I could only report on. So Aunt Emily's voice was always outside of me throughout the entire writing of *Obasan*. After I wrote it, my life changed and Emily invaded me. But that came later.

Koh: So *Obasan* was started and then you encountered Muriel Kitagawa's letters?

Kogawa: Yes, it was the short story "Obasan" that was written first, and the letters were encountered after that. And it was after I encountered the letters that I decided really to write a novel. My initial encounter with Muriel's papers was to feel that they deserved to be a book of their own, and Roy Miki thankfully did that — I mean, it's Muriel's words. What I initially thought I should do was just take her words and edit them and put them as a book. But I'm not much of an editor, and I wanted to employ her words in the narrative of a story, so I picked and chose and used a lot of Muriel's letters to Wes Fujiwara, her brother, and some of her writings in other things. At first I used them verbatim, because I didn't want to alter the words. Later, I had to cut them and change them to make them fit a story.

Koh: Just to go back to the "Obasan," the short story, how did that evolve after writing stories in a white male voice?

Kogawa: Well, the sequence of events is this: first I had written my first chapbook, *The Splinter Moon*, then I wrote *A Choice of Dreams* after I went to Japan in 1969. After that I had a lot of poems about domesticity and just a constant stream of unhappy poems, which was what I was writing in those days. And they came out in *Jericho Road*. This is how affected I am by reviews: what happened was that *Jericho Road* was badly reviewed, that is, reviewed as not a great book in the *Globe and Mail*. And that made me think: well, I can't write poetry any more, I guess I'll quit.

That was when I stopped. I stopped this gush of poetry. I just stopped. I know that I ought not to be that affected by what other people say and what other people think and feel, but there's a part of me that is or that doesn't have proper boundaries. So what people say just comes in and becomes my point of view and I lose my own. I don't have a point of view in a lot of ways and that's a real problem for me in my life. But at any rate, I was that affected by that review and maybe at some inner level, I felt that I couldn't write poetry any more.

I had just applied to the Canada Council for a grant to go to the United States to meet some Asian-American writers. Now, I hadn't had any particular interest in meeting any Asian writers, but I had a desire to get a Canada Council grant. *(laughter)* I couldn't think of any other project at that point. And when I got this grant I thought, I guess I have to do this, and so I took off. I guess a lot of things happened that way. *(laughter)* I went to San Francisco, California, and there I had a dream. I had read Hisaye Yamamoto's short story "Yoneko's Earthquake." The dream said that I would meet no greater author than the author of "Yoneko's Earthquake." So I figured I'd better go meet her. I got on the bus one day and went down to Los Angeles, and I phoned up Hisaye Yamamoto and talked to her.

I was really a leaf in the wind being blown about by whatever dream came along and said do this or that, so I did. Then I eventually left and I went back to southern Alberta, where my parents were living, and again, I didn't know what to do next in my life. My kids were away at university and I was drifting and lost and sort of in an emotional mess. One night I was staying at my parents house — the house was attached to a church hall — and I had a dream again and the dream said I should go work at the Archives in Ottawa. So I went to Ottawa, and then of course I found the letters, but that was another story. I didn't intend to do that. But somewhere in there I was staying in a little room in Ottawa and I wrote — and I don't know why I decided to write this short story about "Obasan" but I wrote it. And I wrote it and rewrote it and finally it was okay and then I had that short story. And then when I saw Muriel's papers I somehow thought this short story "Obasan" should be the first chapter and I should just write some more stuff. Well, as it turned out, "Obasan" got shredded into about three chapters since that first short story and I just worked on it. Isn't this boring? *(laughter)*

KOH: I'm thinking about you making the connections with the Asian-Americans in California and about the recent Writing Thru Race Conference. What sense did you get from being with your peers in the writers of colour community?

KOGAWA: I felt so good. I felt so glad to see all those faces. You know, it was such a good feeling. I loved it. I have some of that feeling sometimes when I go to Hawaii and I look at all those people and they look so wonderful. And I know that they've had a lot of strikes against them — not in Hawaii but over here — everybody's had strikes against us. And there they were all together and then I listened to them. I went into some of those sessions and they were so articulate, and they were so bright and they deserve to be heard. It's so hard in a country where we're dominated by other sensibilities and other powers. So it's really hard and yet these were really worthy people.

I loved that feeling. You know, when I was a kid and I was made to feel that overall I was unworthy and inferior and ugly and so inadequate, and that was part of who I was for so long. That was just within me and I believed it all. I mean, you get a bunch of inadequate people together and you've got a lot of inadequacy, but what I felt at Writing Thru Race was that this is not a place of inadequacy, this is a wonderful community of people and there is power here, tremendous power. And it's not just the power of originally bright people, it's the power of people who have something extremely important to say and who have been through the crucible, they've been through the fires, and because of that there's something that has been purified.

Now, of course, we're all ordinary human beings. But I did get the feeling that out of a milieu like that could come a very special world that is really needed in this country. And that letting the life from that little group come forth could really be the sunlight that's needed. So it felt prophetic to me.

KOH: Did you get a sense of coming out of isolation as a writer of colour at the conference?

KOGAWA: I think that the kind of belonging I felt there was more political than literary. I think that writing is a very isolating thing. One has to be on one's own a lot of the time, almost all the time. Initially, when I was first starting to write, I would call up people and get together in groups and talk with people, but I didn't do a lot of that. And it was good during those phases when I was still crafting, when I was studying technique, and when I needed to learn discipline and to keep going — groups are useful for that. But when it comes down to the actual day-by-day discipline of working, nobody can do that for you and no group can do that for you. So my gladness in the group was not so much, as I said, for the crafting of work.

KOH: You've spoken powerfully in *Telling It* about the challenges and liberation of living in the grey areas, between identities and communities. Can you elaborate on these "identity haircoats," as you put it, and how you negotiate the grey areas between categories?

KOGAWA: That's a tough question. These days I'm thinking of "grey areas" in a different kind of way. So let me see now ... the different identities, the identity of woman, identity of Japanese-Canadian and Asian-Canadian, the identity of writer, the identity of mother, the identity of this or that or the other thing, all these different identities, how to negotiate them? I haven't thought about that. I think what happens depends on the people I'm with and on the situation. I can get polarized or I can get categorized within my own mind or within the minds of people, and so when there's a distinct classification ... then one either addresses that or escapes from one or the other. Certainly, if you're wearing a haircoat, and if ethnicity is uncomfortable, the thing one would want to do in such a situation would be to get it off as quickly as possible. Or one discovers that it isn't such a haircoat after all and that makes it more comfortable.

I can get easily triggered and enraged if I have experiences of racism, which I do from time to time, as I'm sure we all do. And then there are other times when the experience of being a non-white can be quite comforting, and there can be a lot of camaraderie and a lot of advantage, even, in it. So it depends a lot on the situation and the grey areas. In what I'm writing now the greyness and the fog and the confusion of not knowing very clearly can be a way to survive within a situation where the pain is too great, where denial is necessary in order not to be blinded by the truth of the sun. So these days I'm doing a much more in-depth exploration of the fog, the mist, the confusion. I've discovered a lot of things. One of the things, I guess, is *(laughter)* — it's an old adage — but ignorance can be bliss. Not knowing can be a way in which one not just survives but thrives.

KOH: This is in reference to the interview in *Sounding Difference* when you used the term "spiritual identification." I would like to ask you some questions because I was quite intrigued by that term. Could you elaborate on the connection between spiritual identification and your other identity, namely that of a woman of colour writing in Canada?

KOGAWA: Okay, to me the questions that are the questions of life, and death and meaning and hope are the spiritual questions — although they are also questions that you can ask within any other context. To me, they are the soul questions. The heart-of-the-matter questions, the bottom-line questions. The questions that feel ultimate to you or the questions that seem to be the questions that are beneath the questions, the ones that wake you up in the middle of the night. For me, the spiritual questions are questions about the existence of evil and so these questions subsume the others. They are the most primary questions and they inform all the other categories of being for me.

If I have a religious bent I take the stories that have been collected through the ages by the mystics and by the great religions — I happen not to know about many great religions, I only really know about Christianity, and I don't even know enough about that — but I will take those stories, I will assume that there is spiritual truth and relevance in those stories, whichever stories those are, and interpret or reinterpret them and use them like a grid, a grid of meaning. And I will place that grid of meaning onto my life's questions. And I look for direction for my life through that grid. For example, there's a story of Abraham and Isaac. That's a story of sacrifice that has been interpreted and reinterpreted, and people have criticized it, saying any god that will require his subjects to sacrifice has to be an immoral god, and therefore it can't mean that, so it gets reinterpreted to mean something else.

    I have used that particular story in what I am writing right now. And other stories of that kind, the stories of Jacob and Esau, these twins that are warring within the womb. One was a hairy fellow, Esau. And Jacob was smooth, Jacob was more loved. But Jacob was a rotten guy, he deceived his brother. And yet Esau sold his birthright. He was the first-born, he had the birthright, but he sold it for a mess of pottage. That's a terribly rich story. And how Jacob wrestled with the Angel until he got a whole new name for himself, "he who strives." I take stories like that and I wrestle with my angel until I become the striver, and until I become a warrior and then the woman warrior. The ways in which one becomes the warrior, what one has to do to be a warrior, the ways in which one has to go over the edge. To me, the spiritual dimension is simply something that infuses the rest of life, giving it direction and meaning.

KOH: And also to continue on the question, you noted in *Canadian Forum* that women are often "relegated to a spiritualized realm, disempowered from moving through other worlds." Can you comment on that?

KOGAWA: I think that a spirituality that stops a person from engagement with what is within one's environment, or one's world, is a strange kind of thing. It seems to me most infantile. I am not going to deny the virtues and the possible realities of mystics and hermits and various gurus who take their people away into their clusters or communes or places. I'm not going to deny that, but I think that to me the idea of a greater and truer spirituality is that which assists a person to be more fully engaged with the world.

    Now, what I think often happens with women is that there is a form of spirituality that is considered to be delicate, sensitive — and ultimately stultifying — and which says you're too fragile for the real world, you stay in your corner and say your prayers, that is your life. So that is a relegation to a prison, basically. That person stays there in quite a lot of agony, I think, not really being able to experience the joy of life. Although some people might prefer that because they find the world too hard. I think traditionally, in the past anyway, women were considered to be desirable when they were like that. Too weak to do anything.

KOH: Back to *Sounding Differences* again. You mentioned your loss of the body and you also noted that "In writing I keep breathing, I keep living and it feels so good when I've got that right word out." So do you then see writing as a way of reclaiming the body or a way of healing through memory? Could you elaborate on writing the body?

KOGAWA: Well, first of all, my body is practically non-existent in my mind these days — it's a terrible mess. All I can really say is when I pick up the pen I am picking up a tool. I am trying to come back to my body and I haven't done it yet, and maybe I never will because my body has been so far removed from me. I don't know what I'm going to do about that. But the pen for me is sort of my hope of getting somewhere. It's also maybe an admission on my part that I'm in a prison and I need to write my way out. I mean, if I found my body, if I were back in it, I might not write. I might not have to, I might actually be happy *(laughter)* and I'm not.

KOH: Much critical work on *Obasan* has pointed to the theme of silence. Would you say that in *Itsuka* a much more complex process is happening? In the second novel are you working on something more complex than the strict dichotomy between silence and speech that the critics focus on in *Obasan*, talking about the silenced history? It seems that *Itsuka* attempts to deal with listening. As one of the characters, Nakayama-sansei, puts it, "You will be told what you are made ready to hear."

Kogawa: Remember what I told you about my reaction to critics? *(laughter)* There was this one really devastating review in the *Globe and Mail* that said basically *Itsuka* was an unpublishable book and that it was published simply because I had had one successful book, and it said — this is the phrase I remember — "pages and pages of painfully embarrassing writing." That's what he said. It was really a devastating review, it just knocked me dead. Anyway, I tried to go back to rewrite the book and basically cut down as much as I could. The paperback edition is somewhat different from the hardcover. I've ended up hating the book as a result.

I was at one point going to write a trilogy and I was going to have the current theme that I am writing about in it with the same characters, but I'm not doing that at all. I'm doing an altogether different thing. I don't know what I was trying to do in *Itsuka*, but I think what I started off trying to do was to write the beginning of what I am writing right now — I wanted to write the precursor to what I am writing right now. I was struggling essentially with certain problems, which is why the character of Cedric could be somewhat problematic because he was going to be developed in a certain way. But when I got involved in the redress movement the book got hijacked, and I put it on the shelf, and by the time I was ready to start writing again, I was writing something else.

I was writing redress and the whole book got altered. The character then was forced to fit into *Itsuka*. Anyway, I think that what happened to me — speaking about silence and speech — is that after writing *Obasan* and in a way being forced into public situations, the

Naomi character that was within me, who basically could not talk, and which is really the way I used to be, got more and more transformed, and the Aunt Emily voice came out. I found myself being more like Aunt Emily. And I think in *Itsuka* I was much more like Emily, but since I was writing in Naomi's voice, I had a problem because I didn't want Naomi to be transformed too suddenly. I didn't know how to do that anyway because she didn't have a parallel experience to mine. I had had a public kind of attention that helped me to change and Naomi didn't have that. So Naomi had to remain the way that she was, more or less, although she could be changed a little bit through the redress activity. So there were a lot of problems in that book that probably did not get properly addressed.

And then I got fed up with trying to write it because of this exterior motivation. It wasn't so much an interior one, you know — attending to dreams, trying to discover what's coming forth — it wasn't that. It was just that there was a story I had lived through, and I couldn't write about it while I was living through it. And yet I knew it was an important story that had to be written in some kind of way. So using these characters I wrote it, but there was so much that had to be altered from reality in order for it to be non-libellous that it was very much hampered by the nature of truth and it was very much hampered by the nature of fiction. So those two things clashed in that book and it was just altogether a huge problem for me. Anyway, I didn't exactly answer your question. The question had to do with silence and whether there was another kind of speaking in *Itsuka*. Right, and I've never thought about that. It's a good question and I need to think about it.

KOH: Did you encounter many difficulties getting published as a Japanese-Canadian writer? If so, what were they?

KOGAWA: In the very beginning I was never aware of that. First of all, I didn't write in a Japanese-Canadian voice in the beginning. I wrote as a white voice, and so I just assumed if it was written well enough it would just get out there to the white audience for which it was intended. And then when the poetry started it went into these literary magazines, and I don't know that there was any barrier there. Then when *Obasan* went off there may have been people who dismissed it because it did go to more than one publisher. And it might have been for that reason, it might have been the story, it might have been any number of reasons, and I don't know what they were. But I didn't think about that. I only thought that if it was good enough it would get out, and that was the only thing I ever thought about. It's the only thing I ever still think about.

KOH: So what advice would you then give to Asian women who are writing and trying to get published?

KOGAWA: I think if her audience is primarily other Asian-Canadian people who are having specific experiences then I think the press she should go to should be one that distributes to that audience and to those people who are particularly interested in that kind of marginality and experience. I think there is a tremendous legitimacy to that because once it's out there it can then become part of the mainstream, if you want it. Some people don't ever want to be part of the mainstream. I know there are some times when one deliberately tries to stay away, like there are some presses that they really despise — the stuff that comes out like chips or junk food and they feel that it does not serve the real nourishment needs of people. And so there is sometimes a rejection of the mainstream for those good reasons. I do not consciously think of who my audience is. I just write without really thinking about audience.

KOH: My next question ties in with what you said about wanting to represent the "real," especially in the context of political struggle. Is it a constant struggle to represent the truth of experience in language?

KOGAWA: The fictional truth as opposed to the concrete real? Like the table real and the inner real? The fiction and the fact, the document and the fictionalized reality? We're talking about those two kinds of real? I remember Fred Cogswell saying at one point to me, when I was asking him that kind of question, that the truth of the fiction precedes the other truth. That the fiction has its own truth, and one has to be true to that. It has to work as fiction, and so the real facts of the matter get sacrificed for the fiction when one is working in fiction. If one is not working in fiction and one is working with document then that does not apply, then the fiction may not enter that.

But I have never been a documentary writer, except when I am writing articles, and when I do that I don't have this struggle. I did have this struggle in *Itsuka* because it purported to be about reality, and much of it was. So did *Obasan* for that matter. There was much of it that was real and much of it that was not. And it all had to work together somehow through some laws that made it work as art. And how to negotiate all that? Well, there were problems. I remember working on *Itsuka* and thinking: well gosh, you don't have the sequence right, that didn't happen in fact like that, it happened after that. Then this other voice said: what the heck, it's fiction, you know, so it doesn't have to. So then I thought somebody is going to see that, and it's going to bother them, then somebody else who doesn't know that is not going to be bothered by that. And at that point I was so exhausted with trying to fit it in to the right sequence that I left it where it was, knowing that it wasn't correct in terms of the events that happened. So there's a lot of license with fiction, but there is also that awareness that one is dealing with lies. So it isn't the same kind of lying. But the lie that is within fiction is known to be a lie, therefore it's morally acceptable. You can't do it with a document. Somebody said to me that they realized that *Itsuka* was *like* what it was, not *what* it was, and I think that's true.

The problem I have with trying to write The Truth, The Real Live Thing, is that I don't think you ever get it. You never get it. I think you can go on and on and on and on. Take *Now Let Us Praise Famous Men* by Walker Evans and James Agee. They did a book of photographs and text, and in the text there was sort of the itemizing of everything that was in the drawer, everything that was on top of the chest. And that was an attempt to try to say the truth about that. That is one way of trying to write the truth, saying that this happened on this date and so on. But that's not the truth. I don't know in how many years it's been that we have used the words "truth" and "fact" as if they were synonymous. Because truth is much more than fact, I think. And fact itself, I mean, who knows?

KOH: That's true. *(laughter)* What place does politics occupy for a writer in a context where facts are questionable and truth is never attained?

KOGAWA: I was thinking about the playwright who is also the leader of Czechoslovakia and about writers in certain countries in South America. I think art and politics invade one another, and they have to from time to time. I think that there are many, many writers who think that there's something very dirty about politics, and that it is good to stay away from it altogether and to occupy your minds with more private matters. I think that the boundaries between almost anything and anything else are pretty near gone, and I don't know where the dividing line is for me in art and politics, in my thoughts and in my life, in what I think, do or feel. I don't know where the lines are.

KOH: Do you see yourself as necessarily struggling against a language which is patriarchal? And is the struggle against and the re-invention of language a political act for you?

KOGAWA: I just want to go back before I answer that one to this political thing again. When I think about some of my friends who are very political I think that I'm such a novice that I need to be taught why they are where they are in their politics. And I look back at some of my own journey and I'm just astonished by my own naïveté in my journey thus far, that I had no awareness about things. It amazes me, especially when I think that I used to work in the prime minister's office, a very political place, obviously, without a clue about things. I just thought people needed to be nice to one another, people needed to cooperate. I didn't even understand how the parties worked, I didn't understand oppositions and things like that.

So I suppose there's a part of me that if I say that my art and politics are combined — I mean, I don't know what that means because I am still a novice at politics, way far behind the lines. So when it comes to this question you've just asked about reinventing language, the language of patriarchy and so on, I think that I'm behind the lines. I haven't come to the starting point. I think the structures of the language and the ways that they have structured my mind are not visible to me. I think they are much more visible to people who have been able to see much more than I do, and I need to be informed. That Mary Daly, who has written *Gyn-Ecology*, I have that book on my shelf, but I haven't read it yet. And I know that some of the poets, the feminist poets and the lesbian poets, who have written a counter-language of some kind, I don't know what it's about.

When I think about English and I understand that it's the language of control, and it's the language that is the most nominalizing language in the world. That is, that it takes verbs, takes action, and makes them into nouns and makes events and action into controllable things. And this all serves the agenda of patriarchy and it serves technology, so that we are within this language. At the same time, I have to tell myself Shakespeare wrote in this language. And there is poetry in this language. It's funny, it's a language that's taken over the whole world.

And this is one thing that excites me about Hawaii — it is the Pidgin there. It's the way a language can be subverted and used to be a language that speaks from emotion. And I love Pidgin, I love to hear it. And I think if one became a student of Pidgin, you escape *(laughter)* the language of technology, enter the language of poetry, enter the language of emotion. So I think that maybe the language can be altered and used. I think Chinese is one of the most advanced languages in its directness and its use of analogy. That's my understanding of it. I don't know anything about it, that's just something that I've read. So I think that English could be used that way too, that one could state an analogy and speak the language of emotion and get away then from the heavy demands of academe for example. *(laughter)*

KOH: So is there some way out when you write? Is there some escape, or re-invention when you pick up the pen?

KOGAWA: Out of the language that I use? Using the language I use to escape the language that I use? *(laughter)*

KOH: Yes. I was thinking of the ambivalent implications of using a language which one cannot fully own to write one's self, so to speak.

KOGAWA: I think that I am trying to escape. I think that the great motivating thing in my life is the need to be more free. I think that I am so constrained, I am so wrapped around with a very heavy conscience, with a very life-denying kind of conscience that just has me gripped. And I don't know how to get away. I want to get out. I want to be able to soar. Even in these last few years of my life, I still want to soar and dance and sing and shout and laugh. I have not done that in my life. And maybe I never will. I can weep.

KOH: I am reminded of Judith Butler writing, "... the taking up, reforming, deforming of one's words does open up a difficult future terrain of community, one in which the hope of ever fully recognizing oneself in the terms by which one signifies is sure to be disappointed." Is the frustration then in the impossibility of writing "to that point where it feels real," as in the *Sounding Difference* interview, of finding a spiritual clarity?

KOGAWA: I remember saying something about the light — the light in the bottom of the well and the light from the stars — clarity and the light. Yes, what is this thing about wanting to be clear? It's uncomfortable when you have all these questions, and there are no answers, and you keep wanting to know. Where does that come from? That need to know things? But I've always had that. Right from very early childhood. I always really wanted to know, and I think that wanting to know comes from suffering: that you know that things suffer and you don't want things to suffer. And the clarity is to be able to have the comfort of knowing that something has stopped suffering. Well, that's the way it was when I was a child, anyway. Who can stand suffering? Nobody can stand it. We're just built that way to want to get away from it.

It is terrible not to know. But when you don't know that you don't know, it's not so bad. When you're in denial you can go on with your life — it's a great survival tactic, I've discovered. And I look back and I see that I have lived my life in denial and that's what I write about. It enabled me to thrive to the extent that I did. But the fog is the denial, the fog is surviving. It's sort of like the atmosphere that surrounds the world: it keeps us safe, it keeps the sun from coming through and destroying us. The sun is like the truth. I mean the truth is what enables things to grow.

But too much of it kills us. And so although one wants the sun, one also — automatically, I think — puts up the show that protects us, that's denial. As soon as you see that, it's denial. You have to tear it away and that's the hard part. It means going in directly to the sun and / or into the flame and surviving that. Because another layer will come to protect you and that's the angel, that's the angel in the flame. You go into the flame and you will find that the safest place to be in a fire is to go directly into it, into the clearing where the ashes are. So that's what you do when you're no longer in denial: you go rushing into the thing, you get to the safe place.

KOH: It's like always living between paradoxes.

KOGAWA: Yes, but I guess that's one of those truths that people know about. And so the statement, "You will be told what you are made ready to hear." I think that's the way it works. Hear it little bit by little bit, and we become ready. After our journeys, our life journeys, after we confront one difficult thing after another, we don't run away from it, we stay with it until we confront it and go through it. And you get to the next one and the next one, and your journey continues. But at each stage you are protected from knowing too much. Each time you're protected a little bit.

KOH: Can you comment on the notion of the "mother tongue" and your relationship to the language in which you write, especially about expressing and exploring various identities?

KOGAWA: If I think about my own mother and her tongue — you know, she spoke Japanese, so her sensibilities were all Japanese. So I think that in my consciousness that is the very first experience, that's the deepest part of my unconscious. What I have from that language is sound, rhythm, feeling and very little in the way of intellectual construct. The language that I can express myself in is English. But I can hear Japanese and I can feel it.

KOH: Does it inform your writing at any level?

KOGAWA: Japanese? Not consciously. I'm not conscious of using Japanese. I'm so thoroughly at home in English. That's the only language I really know and I don't make any efforts to know any other. I get really embarrassed about my Japanese because it's so infantile.

KOH: I feel the same with my Chinese.

KOGAWA: Yeah?

KOH: Given your desire and need to write, do you feel there's a pressure to publish, especially after *Obasan*?

KOGAWA: Well, I don't know where it comes from but there's some great egocentric need to get attention too. I think there's a lot of egoism involved in it. I was thinking today: what if I didn't write any more, would that be okay? But why wouldn't it be okay, there are a lot of people who don't write. And they're living okay lives. So why shouldn't I? It really bothered me. *(laughter)* But I do feel a terrible compulsion, and sometimes I think if I'm not writing, I'm nuts. And it's a way to not be nuts. Because it feels so good sometimes when I'm writing. At the same time, it feels hard and I hate it. I really hate having to work so hard. For the longest time — when I was trying to write what I'm writing right now and I wasn't writing — it was really awful. I thought I'd never be able to write. Now I'm doing it and I can hardly wait till it's finished so I can move on to something else that's lighter.

KOH: What would you like to be writing?

KOGAWA: I've often thought I'd like to write fantasy and I'd like to write plays and children's stuff. I'd like to explode and just have fun, writing fun stuff for a change. So maybe I will. Oh, wouldn't that be great. *(laughter)*

KOH: So do you write full-time?

KOGAWA: I suppose when I'm not doing my zillions of other little things that I do.

KOH: So the present project you are working on, is it fiction?

KOGAWA: I think I shouldn't talk about that.

Koh: Okay. My last question is, do you have a vision for the future?
Kogawa: Any vision of the future?

Koh: Yes, because I'm thinking of what you said about the Writing Thru Race Conference — about the wonderful voices from communities coming forth and the power in that.

Kogawa: Let me see. A vision of the future, is that the question? That's such a huge question? Yeah, let's eat.

Bibliography

Telling It Collective, eds. *Telling It: Women and Language Across Cultures.* Vancouver: Press Gang Publishers, 1990.

Williamson, Janice. *Sounding Differences: Conversations with Seventeen Canadian Women Writers.* Toronto: University of Toronto Press, 1993.

Frederick Ivor Case

Babylon and the Spirit Lash

For the Rastafari and many of their sympathisers, the biblical Babylon is a metaphor for the moral degradation, poverty and humiliation of the industrialized and neo-colonized world. Though they live in Babylon, they attempt in every way possible to maintain social, religious and psychic integrity, struggling daily against the forces around them. The fundamental emotional reaction to their environment is the feeling of disharmony, of being in exile, of not belonging, of a deep and very real alienation.

In his 1979 song, "Survival" Bob Marley expresses it this way:

> Babylon system is the vampire
> Sucking the blood of the sufferers
> Babylon system is the vampire
> Building church and university
> Deceiving the people continually
> Me say them graduating thieves
> And murderers look out now
> Sucking the blood of the sufferers

Marley's rejection of Babylon was consistent in its condemnation of hypocrisy and exploitation. At the very centre of Marley's criticism is the institutional dynamic of governments, churches, financial and educational establishments that exist for themselves and for the personal interests of a very few. Bob Marley's courage in naming the evils of society and the perpetrators of a decadent humanism has encouraged the growth of an artistic climate of protest and revolt. His aesthetic accomplishments have also demonstrated an uncompromising commitment to perfection in artistic production.

The four poets whose works I discuss in this article also strive after artistic perfection. In addition, their works show very clearly that they have identified and rejected the metaphorical Babylon and its alienation. Dionne Brand, M. Nourbese Philip, Ramabai Espinet and Claire Harris have faced Babylon with the lucid consciousness of the artist. They have had to reject it to maintain their intellectual and social integrity. The literary work of these three writers is essentially about human dignity.

It would be facile and incorrect to speak of the universal appeal of their work, since there are many who would react sharply to the unambiguous ideological perspectives of their writing[1] and many who would have no sympathy with their affirmation of life as thinking and feeling women.

Their poetry lends itself very easily to thematic or ideological analyses. It is important to underline the pertinence of such studies, since there is little doubt concerning the poets' social purpose.[2] However, their work is also highly significant from an aesthetic point of view, and the ideological messages are somewhat weakened if the processes of their structuring are not closely examined.[3] In their struggles with and against Babylon the poets under discussion have seized what Nokan has called "des situations poétiques."[4] In many instances the poetic situation is an ideological contradiction projected into the lives of unwitting and often innocent subjects. The poets are committed to an honest intellectual exposition of disorder of various kinds that is given the appearance of order and civility. Their various poetic discourses are characterized by these preoccupations.

My analysis of poetic discourse will discuss the dialectical relationship between the aesthetic processes and the ideological discourse. In my references to literary critics and to other poets, I am seeking a deeper appreciation of the corpus and therefore I do not apply critical theories to the analysis of these works. I simply refer to ideas on poetic discourse that are pertinent to the work of Brand, Philip, Espinet or Harris.

In this context discourse analysis consists of the study of the semantics of the poetry and also of the structures which convey those words and connotations.[5] Though one may study these two notions separately, they are closely interdependent.

In my discussion of the expression of content, I am concerned with those surface structure elements which convey a message to us. I am concerned with what has been written and its sense implications and therefore tend to look for coherence and incoherence, consistency and inconsistency of ideological perspective. I also look for meaning, understanding and aesthetic appreciation. There is, in addition, a certain preoccupation with the poetic narrative as it unravels the theme of the poem.

In the case of the poetic structures that convey the substance of the poetic discourse, I examine the stylistic methods of arriving at meaning and aesthetic expression.[6] I therefore analyze the structure of the poems, the semantic devices and the semiotic principles that give them their final form. It is from the aesthetic structure of the poem that the reader derives both emotional and intellectual appreciation of the work.[7]

Social Comment and Poetic Structures

Dionne Brand's poetry is primarily an ideological discourse in which the social messages are explicitly conveyed. Throughout her work there is a preoccupation with those who have been systematically subjected to institutions beyond their control but who manage to maintain some degree of hope and optimism.[8] Her work is an intellectual exploration of oppression in which she analyses the micro-cosmic and macro-cosmic aspects of socio-economic and political exploitation. There are consistent attempts to adapt the poetic expression to the narrative voice and it is in this factor that one sees the versatility of Brand's work.[9]

The stylistic simplicity of "Eleven Years Old" in *Earth Magic* is deceptive. The first stanza reads:

> I'm old enough
> to work in the fields,
> my grandmother says:
> your limbs are young
> and strong,
> your mind won't rust,
> we need the extra hands
> to tend the crop
> and feed the goats
> and till this ungrateful land.[10]

The reader does not know whether the declaration of the first two lines is the direct speech of the eleven-year-old girl or the reported speech of her grandmother. The punctuation deliberately leads us into the ambiguity and to the realization that over the three generations represented there is a commonality of labour. The implicitly missing generation also produces a questioning in the mind of the reader who is no further advanced by the end of the poem. However, the circumstances of the poetic discourse lead to the conclusion that the missing generation must also have fallen victim to deprivation. The rest of the stanza is devoted to the words of the grandmother. The focus of the grandmother moves from the affirmation of the potential for physical labour to a negative qualification about the mind and returns to the physical attributes of the girl, symbolized by her hands.

The image of "the extra hands" is at once metaphoric and direct in its realism, but what is most striking is the use of the definite article, which depersonalises the owner of these limbs. This is in sharp contrast to the use of "your limbs" and "your mind." Furthermore, in lines 7, 8 and 9 "the" becomes an internal anaphora, and it is significant that the objects indicated are:

... the extra hands
... the crop
... the goat

If we are guided by the anaphoric structure, "... the extra hands" are equated with the crop and the goats, but in another sense the hands perform a function since they "... tend the crop" and "feed the goats." In this manner the labour power of hands produces sustenance of value and the hands of themselves have value. Brand has produced two levels of meaning of "hand," the first being a metaphoric understanding of the process of labour, the second being its implicit association with "mind." The grandmother's words imply that "mind" exists in opposition to "hands" and that the respective values attached to these two human attributes are mutually exclusive. There is also a third implicit notion that whereas "your mind won't rust", the hands might atrophy.

The infinitive in "to tend the crop" recalls the infinitive in "to work in the fields," and the two lines are almost identical in meaning. However, the infinitive in "to tend the crop" has its prolongation in the conjunction "and" at the beginning of the two succeeding lines. This repetition of "and" serves to underline the accumulation of duties of the young girl, to emphasize the usefulness of the hands and also to objectify the girl as "extra hands." But the progression of the personal pronouns also leads to the objectification of the subject. The "I" of line 1 is the same person referred to in the adjectives "my" then objectified in "your." The person thus designated is excluded from the "we" of line 7. The young girl is thus reduced to her labour potential and valued for her contribution to the opposing "we." But the "we" could also be inclusive of the initial "I" and the unnamed eleven-year-old girl becomes even further subsumed in a relentless process of integration into what one can only surmise is a cycle of poverty and frustrating labour. The essential loneliness expressed in this early poem is found much later on in a poem in which the content is different but the sentiments expressed are quite similar. In *Chronicles of the Hostile Sun* we read:

> I am not a refugee,
> I have my papers,
> I was born in the Caribbean,
> practically in the sea,
> fifteen degrees above the equator,
> I have a canadian passport,
> I have lived here all my adult life,
> I am stateless anyway.[11]

In "Eleven Years Old" we listen to the words of a young person,

THE OTHER WOMAN

we evaluate her situation and arrive at our conclusions. In "I am not a refugee" we are faced with the conclusions of an adult. The facts are irrefutable and there is not even the vain hope presented by the earlier poem. However, in both cases the future is equally pessimistic and closed to positive development unless one believes in miracles and indulges in hope.

"I am not a refugee" derives its poetic significance from a careful symmetry that is immediately obvious in the pattern of repetition of "I."

The first and the last lines both begin with "I am" but this identification of the being, of the Self is, in both cases, a negation. The first negation provokes the question about the identity of the "I" and this question is answered in the last line by the second negation. The second negation is emphasized by the adverb "anyway," which expresses a certain degree of resignation and despair. The poem is structured by a play on oppositions and contrasts. In this crisis of national identity there is no search for ancestral roots, there are no allusions to parents, there is no stable point of reference. It is in this context that we are to understand the following lines of "Old Pictures of the New World" in *Chronicles of the Hostile Sun*:

> now I am frightened
> to be alone,
> not because of strangers,
> not thieves or psychopaths
> but, the state.[12]

The metaphor of Babylon stands out in its stark barbarity. The "state" provokes fear because it assaults the individual psyche and dehumanises with great efficiency. The state as we have known it in our colonized and neo-colonized countries of origin has been the imposition of institutions in the form of unfeeling and meaningless structures to which entire peoples have been subject. For us the state has been the very source of alienation and acculturation. For colonized women, the state has been the instigator and guardian of the right to rape physically and psychologically and to delegitimize successive generations of mothers who have had to survive consistent debasement. The state as structured control has given concrete meaning to systemic racist sexism.

But this consciousness of Babylon as the epitome of contradictions, hypocrisy and sheer barbarism could lead to a dangerous pessimism. The US invasion of Grenada is one example of this type of barbarism, and a great degree of pessimism is revealed in Brand's treatment of this imperialistic enterprise.

The Ivoirian poet and essayist Zegoua Nokan has written in *Les petites rivières*:

> L'art doit être optimiste.
> Oublions le marécage, la boue.
> Chantons notre courage, nos victoires.[13]

For Dionne Brand, the experience of the rapid and sordid demise of the Grenada revolution is such that the words of Nokan strike no chord in *Chronicles of the Hostile Sun*. It is evident that at times the experience of Babylon is too bitter, too deeply humiliating for optimism, and the poet sets about expressing her individual perception and that of many others. However, the very act of producing this ideologically determined work is a continuation of the fight against the political and socio-economic constraints of Babylon. Despite the absence of optimism in *Chronicles of the Hostile Sun*, there is no despair since the unambiguous commitment to human dignity and justice remains.

But Brand's discourse is not merely anti-establishment in its sentiment. She has also produced a discourse that breaks through the canons of Eurocentric codes of theme and language. Published in 1990, *No Language is Neutral* is a significant aesthetic breakthrough in Canadian poetry. In "hard against the soul" Brand expresses her womanhood in the fullness of its sexuality. This is a sexuality that is appropriately contextualised in feeling and spirituality:

> this is you girl, this is the poem no woman
> ever write for a woman because she 'fraid to touch
> this river boiling like a woman in she sleep
> that smell of fresh thighs and warm sweat
> sheets of her like the mitan rolling into the atlantic.[14]

The anaphora "this is you girl," introduces each of the six stanzas and serves both as an introduction to what will follow and, in the case of the last five stanzas, as a conclusion of the preceding stanza. We do not know if the demonstrative "this" is addressed internally or externally or both. We do know that the demonstrative refers to a number of connected signs that produce a semiotic structure peculiar to this poem since the seme of "this" might be abstract or concrete. It seems sufficient to know "this is the poem no woman ever write for a woman because she 'fraid."

In "no language is neutral" Brand writes "No language is neutral seared in the spine's unravelling." She then shows how the bending and unbending of slave labour have secreted and produced a language that is articulated through the centuries of silence. Thus silence is a language where "talking was left for night and hush was idiom and hot core."

Silence is also an important semantic and semiotic element in the poetry of Philip, Espinet and Harris.

M. Nourbese Philip's most accomplished work is undoubtedly *Looking for Livingstone: An Odyssey of Silence*. In this work, which defies classification according to genre, Philip makes an in-depth poetic study of silence. The study also expresses a deep philosophical understanding of the complexity of temporality and space.

The variety, versatility and dynamic structural experimentation of *Looking for Livingstone* is an integral part of the ideological and aesthetic messages conveyed by this significant literary work. In many ways this is a philosophical and aesthetic crystallisation of all of Philip's earlier writing and a distinctive development in Canadian poetry. What Philip has contributed is a distinct and distinctive ontological perspective that has its parallel in the work of the Guadeloupean novelist Simone Schwarz-Bart. What is truly significant is that the ethos of Caribbean writing that she has produced has emanated from the Babylon in which we live.

In one sequence of *Looking for Livingstone* Philip writes:

in the beginning was
the ravage
      in
word inside time
         inside
History
     Silence seeks the balance
in revenge
the cut in precise
        cleaves to the ever in Word
seeking to silence
Silence[15]

And in a later sequence:

in the beginning was

                not

word

    but Silence
    and a future rampant
                with possibility

and Word[16]

In Philip's work silence has dimensions that are both spatial and temporal. In its spatial dimension it is as versatile as the anagrams to be derived from the seven letters of the word "silence," and in each case the space is inhabited by different social beings whose ontological realities are determined by distinctive temporal characteristics. This type of literary experimentation recalls the work of the Martiniquan, Edouard Glissant. In his novel *Malemort*, Glissant manipulates the names of individual characters who are ontologically transformed as their temporal and spatial realities evolve. Philip takes this even further, and the use of anagrams of "silence" is not merely a literary game but the exploitation of onomastics for very precise ontological reasons.

The experiment is highly successful because it is aesthetically functional in the quest for Livingstone. *Looking for Livingstone* is an intellectual challenge of the highest order and a certain number of clues to its unravelling are to be found in Philip's collection of essays *Frontiers*.

Livingstone is both himself and a symbol of all the conquering anthropologists, missionaries and other imperialists who have defined Africans and other colonized peoples. The word, through text, has usurped the expression of those who are silent. But the quality of silence in its specific context of space and temporality proves to be a multi-dimensional strength of the various peoples visited by the poet in her quest. The level of communication is more profound and more meaningful since it is social and psychic and no longer depends on codified semes which could be manipulated into ambiguity and deceit. The "dialogues" between poet and Livingstone reveal the superficiality of their communication, even though they are presented as interdependent beings.

Claire Harris' work also reveals a certain interest in silence and time. In *Translation into Fiction* she writes:

> In our dealings with You the knife and the whip in one form or another have been a constant   One day we woke stretching and shaking the sleep from our eyes to find ourselves chattel   You did not erupt the elemental God
>
> in Your silence
> we were ravaged[17]

There is an ambiguity in the text which could signify that the "You" is God or European slave masters. If we read this as an address to God, His silence aptly describes the paradoxical relationship between Africans of the Americas and their God. Since "the elemental God" has permitted us to be "ravaged" when He would only have had to utter a Word, of what interest or use could He be to us? If the oppressor has indeed been assimilated to God, then there is a conspiracy against us that makes revolt or even protest a futile exercise.

In a section of *Fables from the Women's Quarters,* the story of Rigoberta Menchú is told in italics at the bottom of each page. The concern with the condition of women wherever they may suffer is evident throughout Harris's work, and in *Translation into Fiction,* for example, there is sensitive treatment given to the mother of an Argentinian killed during the Falkland Islands absurdity. In the first pages of *Translation into Fiction,* we have examples of semiotic elements of African, Aboriginal and European spirituality. These expressions of psychic perceptions in poetic form have resulted in a complex but intellectually and visually stimulating poetic art that has given a distinctive voice to Western Canada.

But Harris's spiritualism is not to be confused with spiritualist mystification; it is an actualization of the historic realities and experience of those who have preceded us through a process that validates that past experience through present ontological reality.

In *Drawing Down a Daughter,* Harris writes an important prose sequence in which she recounts a tale of a Diablesse being told to some children. It is obvious that the tale has a precise didactic purpose: teaching the children of the superficiality and fickleness of men in their relationship with women. But the tale also teaches that womanhood as a force, as psychic energy, has its own means of exacting sanctions. The narration of this tale is a multi-layered texture that weaves together psychic reality, folktale and seemingly autobiographical details into a coherent whole. Within this narrative Harris writes: "But I have so little control over what is being written that I know the story is writing me."

This brief insight into her *ars poetica* should be appreciated in the context of Harris's consistent expression of forces and energy beyond her own. In this same collection Harris writes of a child born with the

courage
of enslaved ancestors in her eyes[18]

Harris invokes Obatala, asking the divinity to make her a daughter who is

A woman of our grandmothers and their wisdoms
And still a woman with the light of dawn on her
And grant her old age and grace[19]

The consciousness of the African, Indian and Aboriginal ancestors is one of the major characteristics of the poets under discussion. In Harris's work there is a diachronic reality to this energy and also a deep synchronic dimension to the experiences of womanhood, with evocations of other mothers facing childbirth, other women and their children, and specifically of the young Anthony Griffin shot by Montreal police, of a South African named Maria Thalo and her experience of searching among the unidentified bodies of the dead for a loved one.[20]

In "Spirit Lash" Ramabai Espinet expresses a similar communion of spirit. She writes:

But our dead are with us still.
They do not sleep, unstilled
Like yours whom you fear.[21]

The poet explains

You cannot provoke the ghosts of the collective ancestors of all our dark races forever, and receive no comeback. A lash is coming from beyond, and the spirits riding that lash (all the swarthy spirits) will show no mercy as you, the real spooks: colour of bone-ash and driftwood bleached for centuries in an aging sun, fall before their wrath. We call such force a spirit lash.[22]

The didactic purpose of Espinet's work is unambiguous. Her brief introductions also evoke her specific ancestral dead and their unidentified companions who lived

Behind the moon and God's back
Pain knowing no end
We lived alone, like
Shadow murdering shadow
The stars alone for safety
Tassas beating in the dark
Rum, stickfight, chulahs
Flights to nowhere[23]

In her work Espinet uses the psychic world of Trinidadian realities as a source of semiotic structure. In the poem "Mama Glo" — an evocation of *Maman de l'Eau* — it appears that Espinet is drawing her poetic energies from this powerful female divinity who transcends time and place.

In the name of all suffering mothers, Espinet also invokes Kali to deal with those the poet calls the "merchants of death" and in the poem of that name she defiantly writes:

I and I wage war
Trenchtown has never seen
I and I move
With unfettered revenge

> Against you
> I and I fight
> The doomsellers
> We claim our children[24]

The use of language patterns associated with Rastafari becomes a significant poetic device as the poet reiterates a consistent theme of non-conformity and the need to destroy Babylon.

Espinet reaches back into experiences of her ancestral and of her lived past and also reaches out into the contemporary experiences of other women. The poem "In Antigua" is dedicated to Arah Hector, murdered in 1989. In "For Patricia Deanna", Espinet expresses with deep feeling the death of "a young pregnant Caribbean woman, Patricia Deanna [who] fell to her death from a balcony as she tried to escape from immigration officials who had broken down the doors to the apartment where she was baby-sitting. She was in Canada, pregnant, illegal and utterly alone."[25]

The poetry of Brand, Philip, Harris and Espinet has to be fully appreciated within its own context, as the voice of thinking, feeling and conscious artists who bring significant aesthetic and philosophical density to their writing. Their breadth of linguistic diversity and the depth of allusions recall Edouard Glissant's words in *Un Champ d'îles*

> Toute parole est une terre
> Il est de fouiller son sous-sol
> Où un espace meuble est gardé
> Brûlant, pour ce que l'arbre dit[26]

This poetic definition of polysemy is most appropriate to the work of the poets I have discussed. It is interesting to note that, though their work is structurally varied and though they use a wide variety of linguistic and aesthetic devices, the semiotic strategies are very similar.

The conclusion I draw from the study of these poetic texts is that the only way to survive with dignity in Babylon is to proclaim fundamental values that are different. Dionne Brand, M. Nourbese Philip, Ramabai Espinet and Claire Harris proclaim their right to affirm their own difference. The knowledge of the self, consciousness, solidarity, affirmation of woman and of womanhood, and confidence in the vision of the world that these views engender are the themes of non-conformity that underline their works. Points of reference in Africa, India, the Caribbean and Canada bring together ancestors from a diversity of psychic realms, and these are the semiotic sources that structure the works studied.

But ultimately, in the turmoil, injustice and suffering of Babylon, the spirit lash appears to be the most efficient weapon.

Endotes

[1.] See for example "For Stuart" and "four hours on a bus ..." in *Chronicles of the Hostile Sun*. In these two poems Brand reveals some of the reactions to her and to her poetry. "For Stuart" concerns an incident still talked about in Sudbury.

[2.] See H. Nigel Thomas in "A Commentary on the Poetry of Dionne Brand" (*KOLA*, Vol. 1, No. 1, February 1987, pp. 51-61). Thomas's words on the social purpose of poetry recall the writings of the Ivoirian poet, essayist and dramatist Zegoua Nokan in his foreward to *Les malheurs de Tchakô* (Honfleur: P.J. Oswald, 1968): "L'écrivain, partie intégrante du peuple, doit exprimer les peines, les joies de ce dernier, son combat pour l'amelioration de sa condition ... La substance d'un poème ne réside pas dans la musique des mots et la profusion d'images. Il existe des situations poetiques. J'ai tenté, içi, d'en apprehénder quelques-uns."

[3.] For a discussion of the close interdependence of ideology and aesthetics, see F.I. Case, "Idéologie du discours esthétique césairien," in *Aimé Césaire ou l'athanor d'un alchimiste* (Paris: Eds. caribéennes/A.C.C.T., 1987, pp. 337-346).

4. See Nokan, note 2.

5. Despite the general tendencies of literary criticism, the notion of discourse analysis should not be limited to prose. In so far as there is human communication, there is discourse. Molino and Tamine have written: "Mais la poésie est aussi discours et, comme le discours, s'organise autour d'un axe, d'une progression qui constitue le fil du discours. Cet axe peut prendre deux formes: il y a d'un côté la progression narrative, qui est celle des événements d'une intrigue et de l'autre la progression d'un raisonnement plus ou moins cohérent" (Jean Molino and Joëlle Tamine in "La Construction du poème" in *Recherches sémiotiques/Semiotic Inquiry*, Vol. 1, No. 4, 1981. p. 360).

6. In referring to poetic structures I mean those elements — phonological, lexical, grammatical and graphological — that give coherence and consistency to the form and substance of the poem.

7. By aesthetic structure I mean the interrelation of elements given in the preceding note, with semantic and semiotic factors taking into account the explicit and implicit literary and social contexts.

8. In this work I define "hope" and "optimism" in the following manner: hope is a positive perception of the future based on ideological or socio-psychological mystification and often leads to resignation to the present context; optimism is a positive perception of the present and future based on the socio-economic realities and potentialities of the present context and precedes action to modify that context.

9. In so far as the poem is discourse there is narration.

10. Brand, Dionne. *Earth Magic* (Toronto: Kids Can Press, 1979), p. 42.

11. Brand, Dionne. *Chronicles of the Hostile Sun* (Toronto: Williams-Wallace, 1984), p. 70.

12. *Chronicles*, p. 63.

13. Nokan, Zegoua. *Les petites rivieres* (Abidjan: CEDA, 1983), pp. 98-99.

14. Brand, Dionne. *No Language Is Neutral* (Toronto: Coach House Press, 1990), p. 7.

[15] Philip, M. Norbese. *Looking for Livingstone: An Odyssey of Silence* (Stratford: The Mercury Press, 1991), p. 31.

[16] *Ibid.*, p. 40.

[17] Harris, Claire. *Translation into Fiction* (Fredericton: Fiddlehead, 1984), p. 25.

[18] Harris, Claire. *Drawing Down a Daughter* (Fredericton: Goose Lane, 1992), p. 18.

[19] *Ibid.*, 40.

[20] *Ibid.*, p. 91.

[21] Espinet, Ramabai. *Nuclear Seasons* (Toronto: Sister Vision Press, 1991), p. 79.

[22] *Ibid.*, p. 77.

[23] *Ibid.*, p. 10.

[24] *Ibid.*, p. 67.

[25] *Ibid.*, p. 45.

[26] Glissant, Edouard. "Un "Champ d'îles" in *Les Indes* (Paris: Seuil, 1965), p. 20

Bibliography

Brand, Dionne. *Earth Magic.* Toronto: Kids Can Press, 1979. Republished by Sister Vision Press, 1993.

'Fore day morning. Toronto: Khoisan, 1978.

Chronicles of a Hostile Sun. Toronto: Williams-Wallace,1984

No Language is Neutral. Toronto: Coach House, 1990.

Winter Epigrams and Epigrams to Ernesto Cardenal in Defense of Claudia. Toronto: Williams-Wallace, 1983.

Espinet, Ramabai. *Nuclear Seasons*, Toronto: Sister Vision Press, 1991.

Glissant, Edouard. "Un Champ d'îles" in *Les Indes*. Paris: Seuil, 1965.

Malemort. Paris: Seuil, 1987.

Harris, Claire. *The Conception of Winter*. Stratford: Williams-Wallace, 1989.

Drawing Down a Daughter. Fredericton: Goose Lane, 1992.

Fables from the Women's Quarters. Toronto: Williams-Wallace, 1984.

Translation into Fiction. Fredericton: Fiddlehead, 1984.

Nokan, Zegoua. *Les petites rivières*. Abidjan: CEDA, 1983.

Philip, M. Nourbese. *Frontiers: Essays and Writings on Racism and Culture*. Stratford: Mercury Press, 1992.

Looking for Livingstone: An Odyssey of Silence. Stratford: The Mercury Press, 1991.

Isabelle Knockwood

Leonard Pace

An interview with
ISABELLE KNOCKWOOD

I have to write whatever happened

SILVERA: I had a chance to read your book *Out of the Depths: The Experiences of Mi'kmaw Children at the Indian Residential School at Shubenacadie, Nova Scotia.* Your publisher kindly sent me a copy. When did you launch into your career as a writer? Decide that this was what you wanted to do?

KNOCKWOOD: *(laughter)* Consciously, I don't think I ever launched a career, I just started writing. I always liked to write, starting with when I first learned to speak English, which was when I was five years old. I was just fascinated with how words go onto the paper, then you can read them again. That mental process fascinated me, and then I began writing. Just words I started with, simple words, and then my name. When I got my first dictionary I used to look up words and try to write them down on a piece of paper, and I made a little book out of it. That is what sticks in my memory. That's not the only book I ever made — I still do that, I've stayed with that. *(laughter)*

SILVERA: And what was your family's response to all this reading activity when you were growing up?

KNOCKWOOD: Nothing. They just let us go and do what we wanted to do. Our parents used to make baskets. My father used to shave these big strips where the basket was made from, and there were little pieces on the end, pieces that they used to throw away. Well, we used to take those pieces, and we would make little animals out of them, like chickens, different kinds of birds. And people, we made little people out of those shavings. And we would like draw and write on those shavings. I think it was part of taking a pencil in your hand and letting it draw. I didn't, as a child, know the difference between writing and drawing. Mi'kmaw is my first language and I had to learn English. Somehow or another, for a long time I couldn't distinguish the difference between drawing and writing.

SILVERA: I want to talk about what it was like for you growing up as a Aboriginal girl in Canada in the 1930s.

KNOCKWOOD: Growing up to me begins as soon as you're born — is that what you mean?

SILVERA: I guess what I'm interested in is what life was like for you and your family in the 1930s, growing up in Shubenacadie, Nova Scotia.

KNOCKWOOD: We were living off the land, my father was a hunter. That was in Nova Scotia — I was born in Wolfville, Nova Scotia — and when I was a year old we moved to Shubenacadie, and we lived out in the bush, off the land. In the wintertime my father hunted and trapped and fished, and in the summertime they grew a garden and we picked berries and preserved them for the winter and everything. I was a part of that. When my father went on a hunting expedition the whole family went to that expedition, and we stayed home in the camp while he went out hunting. And the same way with fishing. It was a family thing.

SILVERA: How many children were in your family?

KNOCKWOOD: I have two older brothers and an older sister, and I'm the fourth in line. I also have a younger brother. So there are five of us. Growing up in those days was peaceful, and it was quiet, there was nobody shouting at us. We ate, we played. If something had to be done, we were just asked gently. My mother was a gentle woman, and she would ask us in a gentle way.

I don't even remember fighting with my brothers and sisters. I don't remember much of sibling rivalry, that sort of thing. I remember, though, that we were required to look after each other. We were responsible for each other's safety. Because we lived in the woods we had to make sure that none of the children wandered off, and the oldest one was in charge of all the children, and everybody was in charge of the one that was younger than them. That's instilled in you as soon as you can understand and talk. My younger brother was born when I was fifteen months old. I don't ever remember being told I was responsible for him. I already knew it. Maybe it was from watching the others older than I was. But I felt very responsible for my younger brother. Right up to when I was put in the school and we were separated and ...

SILVERA: How old were you when you started going to school?

KNOCKWOOD: I was five. That's the thing I remember most because I was supposed to watch him, and all of a sudden I had nothing to do. I had no responsibilities and it wasn't a nice feeling.
SILVERA: Can you go into it a bit more? About what it was like attending the residential school and what effect it had on you?

KNOCKWOOD: It was hard on me. Not so much physically because I wasn't beaten. If you read the book, I was only beaten once, when

I was fifteen. But it was very hard on me emotionally and psychologically because I was in a strange environment and I wasn't allowed to speak my language. That was the hardest part, the most difficult part: not being able to talk. If you can't speak the language, that means you can't talk. And if you can't talk, you can't communicate, you're isolated. Abusers, that's the first thing that they do to their victims: isolate them. But at that early age I didn't know about abuse and I didn't know I was being abused, so I followed the rules because my mother had told us to listen to the nuns because they represented God.

I didn't know I was being victimized. I thought I was being educated. And because she told me I was going to go to school and I was going to be educated and how exciting that would be, I wanted to go to school.

Then all of a sudden I can't talk. I can't speak my language and so then I became very observant. You notice every little movement, every little gesture, every little facial expression. You notice every smile, every laugh. You notice even when a chair is moved a little bit, and you wonder what that signifies when the teacher's chair is moved just a little bit. You know something is different. The thing is you're not talking, and you're hearing words you don't understand — and it's just all sounds and you're in the dark about what's going on in your environment. And then you have to also deal with a big building. We've lived in the woods and now we're in this big building.

SILVERA: So how far was the residential school from your home?

KNOCKWOOD: It was five miles. Not far, but when you're five years old distance is the least of your worry. It's just far and you are away from home, from your family.

SILVERA: How often did you go home? On weekends?

KNOCKWOOD: No, we didn't go home on weekends. Sometimes we went home at Christmas time. Maybe in the eleven years I was there, I think I went home maybe about five times. And then we went home for the summer vacation every year. From June till September we were home with our parents every year.

SILVERA: I was quite touched by the section in your book where you talked about your memories as a young girl meeting with the elders and the storytelling tradition and the Mi'kmaw language. Can you talk a bit about that?

KNOCKWOOD: The elders. Oh, they were so beautiful, they were so gentle. What I remember from them was their gentleness and that they had an aura around them, that they were so serene — it was like so rewarding when one of them looked your way. *(laughter)* Today we don't have elders like that. We have elders who are smart and well-dressed and well-fed and they talk a lot. They talk fast, they talk a lot, and they know everything.

SILVERA: And in those days there was a lot of listening, a lot of time and space?

KNOCKWOOD: Yeah, and the elders didn't try to know more than each other. They didn't interrupt each other. They were so patient. They talked in a different way altogether. Their persona was so spiritual — I can't think of another word. When the elders used to come and sit in a circle in my house I was responsible to look after them, bring them tea and hang their hats up if they wanted.

SILVERA: How old were you then?

KNOCKWOOD: I think maybe four. I started when I was four. Right away. I don't know how old. You keep asking, at what age we started helping, but it isn't like all of sudden you're four years old, all of a sudden you have to help the elders. It isn't like today. It's just something you start doing right away, soon as you can carry a cup of water *(laughter)* and give it to the elders. So we could be two, we could be three, we could be four, we could be five. Right away you start doing that. You were taught that and it was really nice. The elders would talk about stories they heard from their grandfathers and grandmothers. It's not like today. It was a different world, a different language, a different era — it exists only in the back of my mind. I've asked other people that are my age — like in their sixties — and they all say the same thing.

SILVERA: How old are you now?

KNOCKWOOD: I'm sixty-three and, unfortunately, I don't remember the stories that were said, just bits and pieces. Sometimes me and my sister try to remember and we can't. She's a year older than I am and it's way back in our memory.

SILVERA: Tell me about the role of the Talking Stick, about the Talking Stick ceremony. Was this a principle way of teaching little children the legends?

KNOCKWOOD: No. I would say it was mostly used by elders in meetings. I think the first time I saw it the elders would use canes — they would tap the cane on the ground or the floor. If they were sitting outside they would tap the ground, and when they tapped the floor that meant talk. And they talked until they were through and then another person would do the same thing. Another elder would tap his cane, and then they'd all listen to him. And if it were somebody else's turn they would do that, and then it started to be used in council for politicians to reach a consensus. It doesn't necessarily have to be a talking *stick* — it can be a feather, an eagle feather. Or it can be passing pipe. Who's going to talk takes the pipe and smokes it. Or it can be just a small little stick with carvings on it — just something symbolic to show that you're the speaker and you have the floor. And when everybody says whatever they have to say, then they talk until they reach consensus.

SILVERA: So how often did this happen? Was it once a week, once a month?

KNOCKWOOD: I don't know. Again, you're talking about another time, another era, when time is not measured in minutes, days, weeks. It's measured by the moons, so that question kind of doesn't comply.

SILVERA: It still happens?

Knockwood: Yes, we use it today, not in a political sense but in a healing sense, for therapy.

SILVERA: So then it was for a political sense?

KNOCKWOOD: Yeah.

SILVERA: I was actually quite interested in your decision to work in Mi'kmaw and keep the language alive. In the introduction to your book you talk about the importance of the Mi'kmaw language. You were in Boston studying and you wanted to search out stories about your mother, with the idea that you might write something about the lives of Native women.

KNOCKWOOD: I remember that.

SILVERA: And so you took this course in biography and autobiography by Gillian Thomas, and you started working on a lot of oral tradition and stories.

KNOCKWOOD: Okay. Well, let me explain. In 1972-1973 I was living in Boston and I had joined this women's group — it was like a self-help group. We would talk about our mothers and I realized I couldn't find anything in the libraries that was written about Native women. So I decided that I would go to my mother and ask her questions. So I went to visit her before she died and I was able to ask her some questions, though at that time, I didn't really know what I wanted to find out. All I knew was I didn't know anything and I was just interested in it, probably superficially. I didn't think it was gonna become a big thing in my life.

Anyway, I went to talk to her. In 1976 she died and in 1989 — that meant I was fifty-four, I was married twice and both my husbands had died, all of my children had gone and left home. That's when I decided to go back to school and I enroled at St. Mary's University.

In my third year I enroled in Gillian Thomas's class for biography and autobiography because by this time I had all those tapes and all those stories my mother had told me, but I didn't really know what to do with them. So I thought in her class I would find out what to do with them: how I would write them, put them in book form. She suggested that I take these tapes and write a book on them, put it in manuscript form. It was a class in women's studies, and it focused on oral traditions in women's studies.

I took that class and I took all these interviews I had done over the years and some of the stories my mother had told me, and we began to put it in book form. I was still a student — I wrote the book as a student, in my third year. I didn't know anything about writing a book, and I didn't know about the publishing business. I just brought in all these papers and she helped me to organise them. I also had a lot of photographs I had taken of the school. It was falling apart. I thought it was going to cave in, so I took my camera and I took a picture of every room in the school because I thought I would show them to the former students, and I would ask them what happened in this room, show them the pictures, and that's what I did. That's how I started to jog their memories.

I had this idea in the back of my mind that the school would talk to me, that the bricks would talk to me. I can't explain it — I just remember going back and staring at that school. I would wait for the school to talk to me. *(laughter)* I had to chuckle at that because I talked to several people after that, and they would say, "Yeah, I have a brick from that school and it reminds me of this and that, it talks to me." It's like a talking brick. Anyway, I took all these photographs and I would show them to former students and they would tell me what happened. I would tape their stories, and some of them didn't want their names used — I think I have twenty-nine students who would use their names, but I interviewed close to forty people.

A lot of people didn't want their names in it. They didn't want to be associated with the book. They said, "I'll tell you all this, but don't use my name." I'm really grateful to some of them — they put me on the right path and I was able to track down the stories that way.

SILVERA: You also talk quite a bit about being punished by Catholic nuns and priests for speaking the language in the residential school. What effect do you think that has had on you, or on other Mi'kmaw people in terms of their abilities to be writers?

KNOCKWOOD: It terrified me. The things that happened to you as a child don't leave you easily. I think that's why I write. I remember in 1976 when I came home from Boston to live on the reserve, I was with people who showed me their poems and stories and songs they had written, and they would tell me that nobody knew that these poems, songs and stories existed. We used to hide our creations. I'm pretty sure that this is happening today. People still write poems and they still sing songs, but they're not sharing them because they're victims of silence.

SILVERA: In your introduction you also talked about a lot of your memories, which seem to be mostly unhappy ones as a student, and then about your friend Betsy and both of you walking together and helping to heal each other.

KNOCKWOOD: That's a good memory. I can visualize us walking along and talking, trying to figure out what happened to this one and what happened to that one — we all felt like a family, we felt like sisters and brothers. And that vision of the two of us walking together for me is not unhappy — it's thoughtful and it's puzzling, and it's in the process of trying to figure out something, but it's a happy memory. We're very close now. We were friends before, but that has really bonded us.

SILVERA: How old were your children when you started to work on this book?

KNOCKWOOD: I think my youngest was born in 1969, so he was fourteen.

SILVERA: I was just wondering about your time during that period. Trying to work on the book, going to school, having children, what was it like for you? I know raising a family and doing all these different things is not an easy task.

KNOCKWOOD: Oh, I was writing long ago. Even before that I started writing on the book. I moved back to Canada in 1981, and in '81-'82 I decided that I was going to write at least ten articles for the *Mi'kmaw News*. I started in January and I think I wrote ten articles and I submitted some poems, mostly to have somebody correct my English. *(laughter)* I learned a lot through those articles because it was my punctuation that was a little bit crazy. But seeing your article in print really helps you to write. They make it look so nice *(laughter)*. The first time I saw my name in print I was so excited.

My children were actually younger when I started, and I brought up my granddaughter since she was seven. While they were in school all day I would sleep, and at night I would write. I was trying to sort out, not so much about the Native residential school but to sort out Native spirituality. I was trying to figure out why the Europeans would want to ban our ceremonies, why did they want us not to perform our rituals, and I couldn't understand what they meant, or why it was such a terrible thing to be a pagan. I thought: well, it must be powerful if they don't want us to do it. And it was like the language: they didn't want us to speak it. Why? I was so curious. And that was my first interest — Native spirituality — and I started writing on that.

I got this nickname. Behind my back, people used to ridicule me and call me Mother Earth. Because I used to go to the elders and ask them if we didn't have any churches, and they told me it was the Earth and that our ancestors regarded the Earth as our Mother. I put that in print a couple of times and people started to call me Mother Earth and now that's my spirit name. As I said, my first interest was Native spirituality and my second interest was Native women. I wanted to write a book about Native women.

But when I moved to Shubenacadie in 1985 the school was there; that was something concrete, something I could see and remember. I went back to university and, naturally, the first thing I did was that book. An interesting thing happened to me in 1989, after my husband died. My children had all been gone, and I was left in this big house all by myself. I had just come back from the funeral and I had his obituary in my head and I was saying, "In some cultures they throw in the wife". *(laughter)* I was saying, "Well, in another time, my life would have been just for him." And then I thought: what would they say if I died? What would they put in my obituary? And I wrote the obituary about what they would say about me if I had died then. Then I thought: no, this is not good enough. I don't want them to say just anything. I want to be myself. And I said, "This is what I want in my obituary." And that's when I said, "She is the author of four books." Then I listed them. *(laughter)*

SILVERA: What did you do with the obituary?

KNOCKWOOD: I must have just thrown it out.

SILVERA: You should have saved it. *(laughter)* Despite all the hardships of life, what are some of the positive aspects of being a Native woman and a writer and a mother?

KNOCKWOOD: What I value most in my life is my creativity. Starting with my children, having had six children, and the creative powers of being a grandmother. My family has grown into fourteen grandchildren and six children — that's twenty human beings that I've helped to create. Especially the six children and then the offshoot of grandchildren. It's the creativity of human beings that I value most in my life, and from that it's the craft people, artists, writers. And then I look on the reserve, and we have no resources. We are poor — we live below the poverty level — but we're highly creative and that's what I value. I have a lot of faith that we'll make it.

SILVERA: Do you write full-time?

KNOCKWOOD: Well, I'm going to have to now because I'm working on another book.

SILVERA: Before this, I gather, you didn't write full-time?

KNOCKWOOD: No. Well, I have six children.

SILVERA: So now?

KNOCKWOOD: I'm alone. I can think and talk a lot, but I need people. You need people to create energy. Which is where grandchildren and community come in.

SILVERA: Do you read other Native writers?

Knockwood: Not too much.

SILVERA: Of what you have read, do you have any you like?

KNOCKWOOD: When I was writing the book I didn't want to read what other people had to say about Indian residential schools. Apparently, there was a book out about ... It was called *Schooldays*. I didn't read it because I didn't want to be influenced. I wanted the story to come from the people, the former students themselves. I didn't want to fall in the trap of not telling the truth, of going back into my childhood when I was told not to talk of what happened there. I didn't want to be a child, I wanted to write like an adult. I wanted to say I was told not to talk about it, but I'm not a child any more. I'm an adult, and the nuns are not standing over me, and I can do what I want, and what I want is to expose them. That's what I wanted.

Silvera: How do you see your writing? As a political act or as a creative source or the two combined?

Knockwood: Very political. Because I was so angry at the way Native people were treated. I'm an activist in that way. I would have been at Oka in the flesh. I was there spiritually. But physically, I had to set my priorities and I decided I was going to finish my book and learn how to write and learn how the system works and what I had to do to be published. I knew I couldn't say everything I wanted because there are certain laws against defamation of character. I had to learn all those things and had to learn how to research, to be persistent, not to give up. Many nights I used to be so tired, but I would always tell myself I can sleep when the book comes out. *(laughter)* I can sleep all I want to. But I would have been honoured to go to Oka because I would have stood at the frontlines beside the warriors. I would have been proud to.

Politics is like policy, and if policies are oppressive and victimize you, you have to stand up and say no. You have to stand up against and for what you think is right. And if that means that you have to demonstrate, make noise, carry signs, put up a blockade and tell people they can't come in, they can't come near if they're not going to honour their word or treaties, tell them you can't come here, then you have to do that. No matter what the cost, I feel you're going to have to do that.

Silvera: For those writers that say they only write for themselves, or that they write but it's not political — what do you have to say?

KNOCKWOOD: I would say that's their calling. But many of us would not be satisfied just writing pretty words because our world is not pretty when you're a victim. If you see other people that are being oppressed you can't sit pretty and watch other people being oppressed. You have to say something for them too.

SILVERA: Tell me about publishing this book. Did you have much difficulty in finding a publisher?

KNOCKWOOD: The first publisher I went to was a man in Halifax. He publishes textbooks and I was told he has quite a reputation for having a good market — his books sell well, he has established a market, and if he would publish my book, I was told, it would be a best-seller. He kept the manuscript for a whole year and didn't call me.

SILVERA: So was he kind of a mainstream publisher?

KNOCKWOOD: Yeah. *(laughter)* And those are not my values. I'm not interested in a big market. It would be nice, but what turned me off was he wanted me to drop Gillian Thomas as an editor, and she had seen me through so much — she wasn't only my English professor, she was also my counsellor. There were times there when I couldn't write, it was so painful that I wanted to quit. She saw me through that and she saw me through to the completed project and that's hard to do. And I wasn't going to drop her for nothing. Even if the book didn't get published, I wouldn't have dropped her. She's still my friend today. After a year, we sat down and looked for another publisher. Roseway Press accepted the manuscript.

SILVERA: Was it a struggle to write in English about your experience?

Or did you feel that sometimes it was difficult to express what you felt?

KNOCKWOOD: No, by that time I was pretty good in English. I could speak and write the language, I was fine. Remember, I learnt it at five to six years of age.

SILVERA: How did the media respond to *Out of the Depths?*

KNOCKWOOD: Very well. They were very responsive. But I have to mention that in *The New Maritimes*, in the April 1994 issue, there was an article that came out by Marilyn Millwood and it was titled "Demons of Memory," and though it wasn't damaging, it was a pretty bad report. She was accusing me of not relating the stories accurately that were told to me. She's a white lady and I just *(laughter)* thought she wasn't there — how can she know what went on, or how it was to live as a Native? I think she was ego-tripping. And I think she kind of would have liked to have written the book.

SILVERA: So apart from her, the reviews were positive?

KNOCKWOOD: Yes, very positive, but I was surprised by her. I had previously showed her my work — she came to my house, I showed her my photographs, and she also helped me, she gave me information she had found. So I thought we were helping each other, but this article showed up in *New Maritimes* and I said, "Oh my God, she stabbed me in the back. Why would she want to do that?" I still can't fathom that.

SILVERA: Do you know if *Out of the Depths* is being used in schools and universities?

KNOCKWOOD: It's used right throughout Canada in various schools — in social studies, Native studies, anthropology and so on. I'm very pleased about that. But that's all I wanted, for the word to get out.

SILVERA: Is there anything that you want to say in this interview?

KNOCKWOOD: The people I interviewed — I feel really privileged and honoured that these people trusted me. Not one of them came out and said that I misrepresented their stories. And when I worked on the stories they all told me they would support me if I was taken to court. Every one of them said they'd stand behind me. I don't know if I'd be able to trust my story with somebody else. There's like forty former students out there. I don't know what they think of me. If it weren't for them, the book wouldn't be there, and the ones that didn't want their names used were the ones that kept me on the right track. There was this little old lady that lives in the town of Shubenacadie — she was a non-Native, she didn't want her name used — and she's the one that helped me with the last chapter about Father McKee. She's the one that put me on that trail. And I asked her so many times if I could use her name because I wanted her to get the recognition. But she said, "No, don't use my name, the book is written and that's a reward enough for me."

SILVERA: I noticed in your book you did an interview with Rita Joe. I'm curious. Was she in the same school?

KNOCKWOOD: Yeah. Rita told me, "You write about all the bad stuff and I'll write about all the good stuff." She said, "I don't want to remember the bad stuff." And I said, "Rita, I can't do that, I have to write whatever happened, good or bad."

ahdri zhina mandiela

Liz Kain

An interview with
AHDRI ZHINA MANDIELA

**the
true rhythm
of
the language**

SILVERA: Let's begin by asking about your place of birth — Jamaica, right? It seems like a good enough starting point. What influence has this had on your work?

MANDIELA: Jamaica has given me specific cultural references. Even today, it's well-steeped in African influences, cultural nuances. My Jamaican cultural nuances, I think, play out best in my writing, in how I over/under/stand language. I have always had a comfortable and supple grasp of my mother tongue, both written and oral ... as well as the English I heard and learnt from books and practised mainly in school settings.

I think being born anywhere else in the diaspora would have given me comparable access to other kinds of cultural content, like history, even style, but having been born there, I know Jamaican inside out. Very few people can read or write the language.

Its structure and symbol system are Old World conceptualizing, yet today, it's almost a techno tool in the way it adapts and reshapes vocabulary as desired by its users.

It's extremely complicated, though seemingly simple. I guess many hybrid languages are like that, yet I don't think I would have gotten this kind of Old and New World access being born in another place and, I dare say, even another time.

SILVERA: What role does mother tongue play in your work?

MANDIELA: Mother tongue, being Jamaican, gives me a definite perspective on language, both written and oral use. Even when I write in English, I think I conceptualize in Jamaican. It seems to yield more precise symbols, hence crisper, more descriptive images. It's like thinking, transforming, pictures into words — Jamaican in my mind, and English or Jamaican on paper. I think that makes good poetry.

SILVERA: Do you consider yourself a dub poet or the work you do dub poetry?

MANDIELA: At this point, I don't even care to define, label, the poetry I create. I'd rather talk on defining poetry. There's a lot of writing, ranting, raving, prating, prattling and debating masquerading as poetry, and certainly some under the guise of dub. In the arena of poetry in relation to musical elements, dub sits in the centre by definition — my own, mingled with others.

My work plays with one foot firmly placed in this centre, my arms and second leg reach out to harness the images in my head, just in the groove. We've known static poetry for centuries, and I think dub poetry has been in this danger zone for quite a few years now.

SILVERA: I ask both questions because of your first book, *speshal rikwes*, which was written for the most part in dub, or the

Jamaican language. Can you talk about that? Was it a conscious decision? And was the title also conscious?

MANDIELA: That book was my acknowledging where I play in this words-music arena. The title? A definitive choice linking that Jamaican musical phrase to poetry. The language? Some pieces Jamaican, some English, others a mix of both. The intent was to present the images with true form, content, style. A close to stream of consciousness, maybe? It certainly wasn't a flexing.

SILVERA: How important is the role of performance in poetry?

MANDIELA: Poetry meant strictly for paper has no need of a compelling, convincing oral or physical presence other than the reader's. But works meant to be heard need an inspiring presence.

The latter sometimes offers more than the words' images and makes for an impressive performer and performance, but either way, images without a voice, or voice without images, is tolerable at best — more often just disappointing.

SILVERA: What has been the response to dub poetry in the last five to ten years in Canada and the US?

MANDIELA: I think the response to dub poetry in the past while has been an indirect fascination. Dub poetry's form is not very different from some African American musical and lyrical styling, yet there is an in-the-pocket groove thing which dub poetry excels in more precisely than other forms. I think people recognize this, but they don't know exactly how it's achieved, hence the fascination — indirect because it's overshadowed by the "phenomenon" of reggae in the same manner with other perceived "things Jamaican."

SILVERA: What about its acceptance in the literary community and in academia?

MANDIELA: I think it was the militancy of dub poetry that was first accepted in literary and academic circles. It was an induction rather than an injection, less of innovation and new direction and more of a sign of the times. It was something to be dealt with because it was loudly demanding space. If not accepted, it would have wreaked havoc in these circles, havoc in the sense of their falling behind, not being abreast of the folk thing.

The phenomenon of "dancehall" music is perched in this similar place. "Art" and academic circles are having to view it, discuss it, decide what to do with it — induce or inject! — though dancehall has the edge right now. It has already been injected in the "art" circle, but the other has much catching up to do. In fact, I think a belated injection is in order, signed Dr. Dub.

SILVERA: Was a British-English presence prevalent on the island? And how did that influence your style of writing?

MANDIELA: There was definitely a British presence in Jamaica while I was growing. Even though I encountered it mostly — almost exclusively — in school and books, I realized it was disrespectful of these bounds so I had better learn it well enough to control its roving. And this I did. By grade one — junior one then — six, seven years old, I was a prolific reader.

Compositions, essays, were effortless and simply time-consuming. By the time I got to writing poetry, I knew I'd never have to read another English book to write well. In fact, I seldom did between 1980 and '90.

SILVERA: What were the first books you read when you were a child?

MANDIELA: First school texts? I recall the condescension of the early Nola readers, riddled with the non-insightful, uneventful times of Nola and family and friends and pets. Our readers then progressed into tales from around the world. By grade three, I recall clearly the Brave Little Boy and the Dike — one of the stony Dutch types — and oh yeah, King Midas and his precious marigold. Outside of school, two books stick out in memories of those early years: *The Reader's Digest* and *Lorna Doone*.

    I remember *Lorna Doone* because it was not a fairy tale or a fable — it reads more like a biography. That idea was shattered when I joined my high school compatriots in the seedy, day-dreamy world of Harlequin paperbacks and realized *Lorna Doone* was just a hardcover version of that world. I decided then that the now tame pornographic works offered more challenging escapades. They held my focus at ten through sixteen years old.

    The Reader's Digest brought my earliest and most picturesque images of Canada and the US. It was my Encyclopedia Canadiana collection. The stories were all about foreign, often set in snow. All the ads were edible — Kraft dinners, peanut butter, cream cheese, biscuits of all sorts — and even to this day, I will open a *Reader's Digest* just to do the Challenge Your Word Power section! My mother had a monthly subscription — seemed like a life insurance policy, or maybe she knew her destiny was with Canada?!

    These monthly instalments are the first books I remember in our house. Along with the dictionary — English — they were the only books I re-read. Gave up the *Digest* and Kraft cravings by nine years old. Still hanging with the dictionary, though.

SILVERA: How long have you been in Canada?

MANDIELA: Came to Toronto, Canada, in November 1973. Rain season. A little better than a winter arrival but not by much.

SILVERA: How do you think being away from home has affected your writing?

MANDIELA: The major and most damning yet liberating effect of being "away" from "home" has been in my struggle to reconcile relocating my entire being to a new place, the dark diaspora. Dub embodies this struggle and the totality of its effects and influence in style, content and form. The preponderance of English simply reflects the language most used in my home. I still think in Jamaican. I notice this most when I have to make decisions around which langauge I use and when speaking to my daughter, born in Canada.

SILVERA: In the introduction to *dark diaspora*, your second collection of poetry, you wrote that the dark diaspora spans some thirty years of events and emotions influencing the psychological make up of the Black psyche, as evidenced in a Black woman's journey in 1990s Canada. What makes these poems different from, say, a male dub poet's perspective?

MANDIELA: I think, would like to think, I imbued the character in *dark diaspora* with a uniquely woman-centred voice. She's not necessarily a politically conscious being, but she is a feeling, seeing, responsive woman. I spoke my own heart through her, though most of the work is outpourings from other women, entrusted to me in some direct and often oblique fashion. Men are not entrusted with the same info, definitely not with the same emotional content which charges the work from start to finish. We — men and women — speak on the same subjects from different places. For instance, the poems "for my sister," "lover," "on my way home," "in the canefields" — the pieces which wrench inside the character — would not be the same from a male dub poet's perspective.

SILVERA: Are you a feminist?

MANDIELA: I am as much a feminist as I am a dub poet.

SILVERA: Do you feel that feminism has influenced your work at all?

MANDIELA: Much of feminist theory fits with my ideals. I discovered this in university, where I read a lot of texts in and out of the school context. I started writing poetry in my first few years in university, so I have no doubt that feminism travelled with me, especially on much of my introspection and reevaluation journeys.

SILVERA: Do you ever experience a tension between feminism and dub poetry?

MANDIELA: Feminism and dub poetry have never produced tension within me. Poetry is what I do. Feminism simply and only partially influences how I do this.

SILVERA: When and how do you write? Early morning, at night?

MANDIELA: I simply record whatever flows as soon and as conveniently as I can. I've awakened from dreams to record poems then returned directly to sleep. I seldom do this any more as work tends to take precedence over sleep, so I hold on to the latter for as long as I possibly can these days. Yet most of my writing is done in the late night or early morning, preferably after a short or long nap. My body-mind functions best under the moon.

SILVERA: What role does your daughter play in your writing and in your creativity?

MANDIELA: My daughter, Jajube, my "sunshine-itinually," keeps my mind clear and precise. I bounce ideas, phrases, explanations, music off her continually. At other times she's a willing, though more often than not unconscious, prototype for young and old images.

SILVERA: Let's talk about dub. What is dub?

MANDIELA: Dub is a style of writing that reflects the true rhythm of the language in use, rhythm being recognised as a musical element. I guess you could have dub poetry, dub prose, dub storytelling. I dare say dub would venture successfully into other forms — dance, video ... But then where do we want to take dub?

SILVERA: In *dark diaspora* you say the aim was to expand the literary tradition of dub poetry. Can you expand on that?

MANDIELA: Like I said before, dub poetry has been for a while in a dangerous zone. I think the real danger is the widespread acceptance of the form, yet I will push, along with others, as hard as ever for this acceptance. But complacency lurks, especially on the literary front. Sure, people are exploring more musical elements, but there is no poetry without words. Where is the innovation, re-manipulation, regeneration with words happening in dub poetry? On very, very few fronts. *dark diaspora* was one of my attempts in this direction, and I'm noticing some younger people, mostly women, fronting stage scripts with poetry bases. Haven't seen much of this since a post-Shange flurry.

I think we must constantly challenge, even while accepting tradition.

SILVERA: ahdri, I would like to talk about some of the work in this book. In the poem "Who is your lover now?" is there a sub-text?

MANDIELA: The poem "lover" has a definite sub-text for many Black women. Our lives, or at least parts of our lives are never in any public light. The aim was never secrecy, yet the sentiment was "ain't nobody's business if I do" and "we all know where I've been ..." The poem simply says, if I can talk to you about *all* of me, or if you can talk to me about *all* of me, then I can fuck you, I could love you ... the references being more historical than political.

SILVERA: What about the poems "A snow white morning," "ice culture" and "Black ooman?"

MANDIELA: "Snow white morning" is unlike most of the other poems in *dark diaspora*. It's my story — this is actually how I ended a writing session which lasted till eight one morning. "Ice culture" is the chilling scream or silent plea we all make on realizing there's no milk and honey ah fahrin, especially when you're trapped there. "Black ooman" is a classic piece of dub in style, form and content. Its content is pure militance and resistance. Stylistically, the music grooves with or without musical instruments, and the linguistic form is raw chaw Jamaican. This is probably the only poem I can remember writing for a specific community. In 1985 I wanted to reaffirm the "budding" Black ooman community in Toronto. Outside of the one-track theatre-arts community which first acknowledged my talents, T.O.'s Black ooman dem were the first to embrace me and hold me in special places, sometimes as a showpiece, other times a work horse, but always precious.

SILVERA: What dub poets influenced your work?

THE OTHER WOMAN

MANDIELA: There are five poets of all the hundreds of works which I've read which I can concretely connect with influencing my work, either through style, form or content. Of the five, two are women: Miss Louise Bennett and Mari Evans. Miss Lou has been in my psyche since I was young. Her work in general has always affirmed for me the validity of reading, writing and the free use of Jamaican speech. One of the first works I wrote in Jamaican was in tribute to the conviction and stick-to-it-iveness which have made Miss Lou's work great.

There is one poem in Mari Evans's *Black Woman* which I will carry with me always: "I who would encompass millions." This piece revealed to me at eighteen years the importance of the artist being situated within a community, large or small. Since then, no more "single bed" for me.

The other three poets are male — two dub poets and Bob Dylan. In my late teens I gathered a sizeable collection of Dylan's recorded works, listened to them over and over and over again, realized his word-ramblings were very similar to the hidden stream of consciousness of his generational compatriots. Even grew to like his no-singing and simplistic lyrical styling.

My real dub poets' influence? Oku Onuora and Mikey Smith, and both less because of their work, more because of the personal artistic connection we shared. Mikey Smith was killed a few months after I met him in Jamaica in '83. At the time I was only becoming familiar with his rep. I had not read, seen, or even listened to any of his work then. In fact, I heard, read, nothing of his till after his death. The impressionist piece I wrote in November '83, which appeared in my first collection of poems, *speshal rikwes*, "mih feel it/wailin fih mikey," came after sensing a return of his spirit one night. I always felt he returned because he was supposed to visit me two days before his death. Anyway, "mih feel it" was my first impressionist piece and my first piece which lay bare for me the kind of emotional volcanic action in any piece of art. I cried almost uncontrollably when I premiered the piece in performance the following year in my first poetry performance with a Jamaican audience, March '84.

Living in Toronto, I had no exposure to dub outside of the local scene, which did not impress me. My initial friendship with Oku was like a crash course in dub, but even at that time I didn't label my work as dub though I recognised the similarities. It wasn't till I returned to Toronto late in '84 that people really started to embrace my work as dub, and there was much about dub which I had learnt to respect. I accepted and actually started to consciously write dub poems: "Black ooman" and "clean hands" and "miggle passige." "Black ooman" represented for me the best of what I had by then learnt and respected about dub. My friendship with Oku was most instrumental in this process.

SILVERA: What makes your poetry different from that of a male dub poet? Is there an obvious difference that's based on gender?

MANDIELA: Of all the male dub poets, Mikey Smith and Oku have impressed me most. Their approach has been very oral, and the variety of musical elements and stylings which riddle their work has always reminded me of my own focus.

I remember Jean Breeze and Anita Stewart (Anilia Soyinka) as the first female voices expounding dub in Jamaica, which I admired. Breeze was touting poems like "aids" and "slip." Anilia was hooked up with Poets in Unity. I never distinguished a distinct female voice within their work or my own till later. Female as a subject matter and protagonist not being sufficient, writing "Black ooman" and feeling its impact were a turning point for me. I think that's when I really got off my single bed, and my most immediate and identifiable community carries a Black female aesthetic. My voice is a tap to this community. I not so simply turn on the artistic flow, and like the poem "in the canefields" says, her mind has become my mouth.

SILVERA: What political or cultural statement is your work making?

MANDIELA: I think the form, style and content of my poetry is firmly rooted in what I would refer to as an African diasporic cultural environment, steeped in history and politics and specific social nuances, these being constant frames of reference for my work. Whenever I write poetry I always think where is the work situated, pushing the boundaries, yet there are no boundaries — at least not for me. Just being able to and choosing to write "professionally" has both political and cultural ramifications, as it has always had for Black women, people, in this Western art ethic.

SILVERA: Is dub poetry political?

MANDIELA: Dub poetry can be political in form and content. The form still challenges several literary norms as far as content goes. Whether it's with respect to subject matter, target audience, artistic motive, these elements existing singly or in combination. Content is most often political, but poetry needs to be artistic, period. I'd say that's where style resides.

SILVERA: What are you currently working on?

MANDIELA: I'm making a *step in poetry*, on cd-video and in performance. On the literary front, some children works and long-term will see several time-based art projects.

Ramabai Espinet

Elaine Savory

Ali Kazmi

RAMABAI ESPINET
talks to ELAINE SAVORY

A Sense of
Constant Dialogue
*Writing, Woman and
Indo-Caribbean Culture*

ESPINET IS CONCERNED about the relative absence of the Indo-Caribbean woman as writer in both the Caribbean and Canada. To bring this issue to the forefront is important. We decided that it is also important to construct our discussion as dialogue. Though dialogue is an important element in a number of Western thinkers from Socrates to Bakhtin to Gadamer, we are thinking here of dialogue as an essential part of the oral traditions of the Caribbean, especially for women. These traditions have shaped images of human learning through interchange and collective transformation. For both Espinet and me, this is part of a conversation with the world.

I particularly wanted to frame this piece as a dialogue because when Carole Boyce Davies and I co-edited *Out of the Kumbla: Caribbean Women and Literature* we were very conscious of the absence of Indo-Caribbean women writers in that book, except for a brief mention in the introductory essay.[1] At the time, there was just no material available. This did not mean that there were no women writing from within the Indo-Caribbean community, but none were visible enough to provoke essays on their work. The question is why?

In 1994 this question still needs to be asked by readers of Caribbean literature. As "insider" and "outsider" we use a dialogue to help us to shape the issues. What is most important is that there be an end to silence and a receptivity to what is said.

The beginning of a literary tradition is particularly exciting. Espinet conceives of the Indo-Caribbean woman taking part in a complex Indian experience, a journey across time and space, from India to the Caribbean to Canada and the United States. South Asian culture is complex: religiously, socially, historically. The history of the migration of South Asian peoples and the particular experience of women add substantially to this complexity.

Espinet has talked at length about some of the issues we raise here in "The Absent Voice: Unearthing the Female Epistemology of Cane" and, following the publication of *Nuclear Seasons*, in an interview with Lee Pui Ming. In "Absent Voice" she discusses Indo-Caribbean culture in general and the place of women in particular: "In societies where Indians are already marginalized, Indian women's expression is even further undermined."[2] In the interview she argues that Indian people in the Caribbean suffered the irony that a strong ethnic cultural identity, an advantage in many ways, worked against them as a Caribbean people. They lived apart from other ethnic groups and, as indentured people who came after slavery, were even permitted to retain their traditions and languages, but this often set them apart from the mainstream of the Afro-Caribbean struggle. This irony can be seen again in the story of Indo-Caribbean women, whose place within secure family structure and coherent religious culture may have looked to many to be an advantage, but whose self-determination was held back in comparison to that of Afro-Caribbean women. Thus their voices have been absent from the region's public artistic expression.

It is impossible to talk of the Indo-Caribbean community without speaking of the whole Caribbean, since this community has contributed much to the culture, including, as Espinet mentions, musical rhythms in Soca and various aspects of cuisine, perhaps most famously roti, the Caribbean version of a traditional Indian bread. Obviously, the Indo-Caribbean community itself is also influenced by other cultures which inform Caribbean society. To understand the present Indo-Caribbean experience it is necessary to know the history of the indentured labourers who first came from India to Guyana and then to other territories. Although Espinet is sometimes frustrated by the need to provide all this information, she is committed to lessening the ways in which the Indo-Caribbean community is ignored when Caribbean culture is discussed or imaged.

The call for dialogue, for knowledge, is particularly urgent because of the history of women. In every society women suffer layers of stereotyping; the specifics depend on how the particular society constructs the intersecting images of women's gender, race, ethnicity, class, nation and age. If one of the first jobs of the feminist critic is to undo the damage done by un-remarked sexism in influential male writing, then one of the first jobs of the female writer is to challenge the stereotypes by which she might have been silenced. Espinet lists the stereotypes that particularly afflict Indo-Caribbean women. The stereotypes suggest that Indian women are stupid or uneducated, good-looking and well-dressed but unable to speak well, easily seduced, submissive and willing to please a man, sensual and the best whores, overly thrifty.

One particularly effective way of defeating such slurs (lodged in common speech and myth in the Caribbean) is for the Indo-Caribbean woman writer to make new myths. Espinet considers possibilities: the Trickster figure (so far confined to a male persona), the Warrior-Queen (stories having this figure in the Caribbean are about African women), the Maaticore ceremony (an Indian ceremony held the night before a Hindu wedding and intended to impart sexual knowledge to the bride from her female circle), the stories of Indian women resisting rape by white overseers in the fields and also trying to protect themselves from beatings by drunken husbands.

Espinet's poetry shows her revising both Indian and African-Caribbean myths, refracting them through a female consciousness which as much resists co-option into stereotype as it retains a desire for community. In "Tamani: A Cane-Cutting Woman" the female protagonist overturns the myth of submission by killing the assaulting overseer and preparing as best she can to deflect a drunken husband's rage. The poem contrasts the image of rural solidity ("The bison plodding low on the red land") with the woman holding her cutlass "green with grass" after she has wiped it clean of the overseer's blood.[3] But such a woman was silent, and it falls to her descendants to tell her story and to recreate the image of the Indian woman. In "Crebo" and "Mama Glo" the female spirit is both myth and modern feminist consciousness. Mama Glo, a Trinidadian water spirit, finds "Rivers of words/ Not blocked by debris".[4] In "Crebo" her persona both gets out of and returns to her skin. She finds at the end of the poem that her "tongue grew long beyond words."[5]

The first step towards this wording of the Indo-Caribbean woman comes from an acceptance of inheritance, as "Hosay Night" indicates. This is the opening poem in Espinet's collection, and in it her persona remembers a collective past which brings together in her consciousness present and past lives, "I was a small boy on Flag Night/ A small girl on Ganges Street."[6] Without this " ... key turning/ In the rusty iron lock of memory,"[7] there can be no beginning of the journey. Similarly, modern feminist stereotypes must be avoided: "Orthodoxies" angrily insist, "Are you a Feminist?/ Or simply a Person Person?/ A Marxist Feminist?/ A Marxist-Leninist Feminist?"[8]

Espinet's short story "Barred: Trinidad 1987" begins with the perspective of a woman trying to cope with the loss of her keys and her fear of someone breaking into her house but moves back and forth in time, economically and feelingly sketching the Indian woman's different experiences of waiting and of threat at various moments in her life in the Caribbean. Her self-protection and resistance remove her from the internalized and dangerous anger that can lead to suicide, which, as Espinet notes in "Absent Voice," is amazingly high among young Indian women in Trinidad, Surinam and Guyana.[9] The story moves in and out of Creole, reiterating and then exploding the myths and prejudices which attempt to construct and contain even a contemporary Indo-Caribbean woman's life and the domestic violence the peasant woman eventually confronts:

> And, in between the waiting and his forced entry, I might die before the night is out of nerve-wracking loneliness and anguish ... I am Indian, plain and simple, not East nor West, just an Indian. I live in the West ... He on the bed and quick quick I chop him two, three times, me ain't know how hard ... We are lost here, have not found the words to utter our newness, our strangeness, our unfound being ... Indians ain't have no backbone, no stamina. You ain't see how at the slightest sign of stress they does run and drink Indian tonic? (Boy meets and loves girl but the arranged marriage gets in the way. Boy and girl drink GRAMAZONE and perish together — desire literally burning a hole through their bowels) ... I have lived through the long night.[10]

As Espinet points out, during the past fifteen years, Caribbean women writers have emerged as a significant group of contemporary writers. Indo-Caribbean women writers are emerging now and are part of the establishment of the collective women's voice which has quickly established itself as an essential part of the Caribbean literary canon. Clearly there are new voices emerging in the Caribbean and in Canada, many of them young. Espinet lists Mahadai Das (Guyana), Madeline Coopsammy (Canada), Radjandaye Ramkissoon-Chen, Niala Maharaj, Ruth Sawh, Debra Singh-Ramlochan, Rawwida Baksh-Soodeen (Trinidad), Sita Parsan, Asha Radjkoemar and Sandra Bihari (Surinam).[11]

As editor of *Creation Fire,* Espinet discovered new voices, among them women of Indo-Caribbean descent. But for the most part, their writing goes on amidst a life busy with other commitments. Ramkissoon-Chen, for example, is a consultant obstetrician and gynaecologist. In Canada there are more male than female Indo-Caribbean writers: Neil Bissoondath, who is fairly well known for *A Casual Brutality,* and Arnold Itwaru and Sasenarine Persaud. Among women writers, there are Shani Mootoo (*Out on Main Street*) and Michelle Mohabeer, a film-maker who accounted for her roots as a Guyanese woman in *Coconut, Cane and Cutlass.*

The question of the female cane-cutter's voice in literature is an important one and raises questions of the relation of class to aesthetics. The first women to write in any culture are understandably middle- and upper-class women with education, for they are the first women to have access to the literary tradition. If the cane-cutter spoke for herself, presumably she would choose the oral Creole tradition, which is particularly strong and various in the Caribbean. But the cane-cutter is also and for the moment only able to speak to the community as a whole through the voice given her by the new Indo-Caribbean women poets. We have to avoid, I think, the essentialist assumption that only the one who lives the experience entirely can make sense of it. In this sense we are all, as writers, insiders and outsiders simultaneously, if we are not to accept a dismal confinement into writing only about ourselves.

Much as we need to make sense of a collective literary movement, to speak of Caribbean women's writing, we also need to understand that each text owes much to the particular and complex issues surrounding the development of an individual writer. This is most important when we look at Caribbean texts because of the immense degree of plurality in the culture. Caribbean identity is not just a matter of ethnicity, or race, or gender, or class, or nationality or linguistic register, but of their shifting interactions.

Despite this, simplistic images of Indo-Caribbean culture have long been prevalent. It is often assumed that Indo-Caribbean culture is either Hindu or Muslim. But Espinet grew up in a Christian Indian household in Trinidad. Her family came to Trinidad in the 1870s and were also part of the larger movement of Indo-Caribbean families to Canada in the late '60s when times were hard in the Caribbean. Another important aspect of Espinet's work and life has been her participation in the growth of the vibrant Caribbean women's movement, especially in Trinidad.

There exists an especially productive tension in any writer's consciousness between the sense of unique experience and the sense of collective history, but this is heightened in the case of a woman writer who is pioneering expression of a whole group of women as well as pursuing her own insights. Espinet speaks of her struggle against reticence and centuries of self-censorship within the Indian community, particularly for women. Textuality which articulates an experience previously silenced challenges the community's assumptions. For the Indian woman who constructs that textuality, there is, as Espinet points out, the fear of making the private public knowledge, of interfering in matters which are habitually a male province, of violating a sense of modesty, of betraying a cultural expectation that women will participate in work and family life but not become bold public figures. Espinet's discussion of these issues clears space for all Indo-Caribbean women who write.

Caribbean female textuality inevitably complicates our sense of the world and our sense of language, expressing that which was never previously expressed. Euro-American theory — even when self-consciously radical and challenging of hegemonies, including the coherence of "master narratives" — often seems, unconsciously or consciously, to reaffirm Eurocentric assumptions of cultural universality. The Caribbean, with its experience of competing Eurocentric ideologies and an intellectual inheritance informed by its many cultures, is in a position to be sceptical of the extent of applicability of any theory. The dialogue between the general and the particular is especially strong in texts produced by Caribbean women. Whilst each text is grounded in a complex particularity, there is also the collective contribution which Caribbean women's writing makes to our apprehension of the world as a larger text inscribing immensely productive human difference. In the dialogue that follows, we explore some of the complex and inter-related issues which arise from becoming an Indo-Caribbean woman who writes in the early 1990s. — ELAINE SAVORY

SAVORY: Who is the Indo-Caribbean woman writer for you, Ramabai?

ESPINET: Her place, whether she lives there physically or not, is the Caribbean. Obviously, she is of Indian extraction, but having said that, there are all the immutable shadings of Caribbean reality to consider — is she a woman of Indian racial origin only? Or of mixed race, for example? I am interested in how a woman's particular placement within Caribbean society affects the way she constructs her sense of self and subsequently her writing.

It could be that a woman of mixed racial origin who is part Indian — unless the non-Indian parent is non-Caribbean, in which case there often is a difference — prefers not to affirm her Indian identity and instead defines herself from the locus of her other racial origins and heritage. I have observed this myself, and I can think of several explanations for this, the most obvious being that the Indian is still the newcomer to the Caribbean, the "last person to come to town." Thus that group forms the bulk of the peasant group in the two largest areas of concentration, Trinidad and Guyana.

The peasant Oriental still meets the urbanized Creole culture of the West Indies as a stranger. In spite of education and the rewards of thrift and entrepreneurship, social mobility for Indians took — and is still taking — a great deal of time. Where it occurs, it often means that the Indo-Caribbean must lose that which marks her as Indian, in order to "belong" to the urbanised Creole culture which still despises her un-creolised ways.

In Trinidad more than Guyana, I believe, and largely through the influence of the Canadian-based Presbyterian missionary effort, a Christian Indian middle-class developed in relative isolation from the surrounding Creole culture. This class's social norms, their cultural practices, their food, their entertainment, etcetera, were significantly different from those of Afro-Trinidadians and from their "unconverted" brethren and sistren. It is a peculiar and invisible group, small but influential, which consolidated itself in secrecy without challenging the larger field. It might have been a necessary passage, because while they were thus unnoticed they achieved a considerable degree of leverage in the society — educational opportunities for their children, a relative degree of wealth and so on. Consolidation in the Hindu community, the bulk of the population, as well as in the smaller Muslim community, took on different manifestations.

SAVORY: What you are doing here is to begin to unpack the levels of identity which contribute to a person naming herself or himself "Indo-Caribbean." Like all names which bring together a huge number of people, names which consolidate a communal identity, it must flatten individual differences. There are times when that communal name is essential, protective, reinforcing. But there are also many times when it is simply not enough.

ESPINET: There is a great difference in the ways in which Indians have made accommodation to life in the Caribbean. This is important to remember, as is the fact that "Indo-Caribbean" is far from being a term which signifies homogeneity. It is a portmanteau term which has immense internal contradictions. The common Indian origin is as far as one can get in terms of definitions. Add to that the differences in actual historical experiences between Guyana, Trinidad and, say, Jamaica, St. Kitts or Guadaloupe, and you can see what I mean.

The other thing I should add is that — partly because of our late arrival — our pride in things Indian was late in coming, not within the intimate circles of village or family but in terms of the dominant Afro-Creole mainstream. This is not unnatural, given the circumstances of any immigrant group and particularly one which existed at a level which was very close to slavery. In the alien land Indians clung to familiar things, but a consciousness of what this meant and a defiant and assertive pride in their heritage came relatively late. It probably began slowly in the late '50s and gained momentum among young people, in particular, in the '70s in Trinidad. It is a major force to contend with today, even though there is a deep divide between the Hindu fundamentalists and others of less garrisoned convictions.

SAVORY: It has to take considerable courage for the woman writer who begins to challenge assumptions about women in her culture because one of the constants in world culture has been the struggle of women to deal with patriarchies of various kinds. I think the most important image that comes to me from *Nuclear Seasons* and from your interview is that as a woman writer you are both insider and outsider at once, risking community and belonging. So often, the choice is one of silence among community or speaking outside it — a real Catch-22. If we don't speak, we aren't known fully by our communities and families. Yet if we do speak, we seem to risk the security of the close and intimate circle because we create ourselves in the world as someone different from the one the community thought it knew. Always, then, an outsider-insider. How do you respond to this? Does the tension between belonging and not belonging provide a crucial impetus for poetry writing? I suppose I see this to some extent in your poems and this is why I frame the question.

Espinet: This is a predicament faced by all writers, I should think. But no, the tension between belonging and not belonging does not provide a crucial impetus for me as a writer. I don't believe I've had any particular urge to be an insider. But I do think there is a contradiction between needing to speak and becoming known. Finding a voice is important, but one loses privacy and anonymity, which are still the ultimate freedoms.

These are the first steps, the first risks, maybe, but one takes them blindly. I think writing enables one to feel a sense of constant dialogue, but with whom I don't know. The state of our outsiderhood is a consistent part of the writing life, it seems, but in a way too it's a relatively comfortable place to be. I don't know that I risk community by writing any more than I do by ordinary living.

The Indo-Caribbean community in Trinidad — the one I know best — is extremely conservative. It has preserved itself by being such. There are all sorts of established codes — some very sophisticated in terms of teasing and irony, for example, which keep its members in check, especially its female members.

My own questioning of these rules occurred early, and I found both in my own case and that of others I observed, alternate strategies always placed one outside the community. So the risk of writing is that of becoming known and losing anonymity because words are keys to so much of one's self. The question is: do I want revelation? I don't think so. The other question is: what is the appropriate fictive construct and just how does it aid and abet the stratagem of anonymity?

Who has a place in this Caribbean sea? Who has a voice? Who has a loud voice? Who has a whispering little voice, passing wisdom down in secret, learning in secret? We survived by not disturbing the peace too much. We have paid a heavy price for that. The price of invisibility. And I don't see why we should continue to pay. We too need a share in literature, in life, in the bounty of these islands. We have already shared in its hardship.

If there is a "crucial impetus" it is rage at innumerable ills in what I consider to be my own domain. Not the least of these is what I feel to be a denial of the Indo-Caribbean presence in the Caribbean scheme of things and the threat of being obliterated entirely. We had an experience which is being erased from the official history as well as from our own minds as our old people die off. Their struggle, their heroism, their endurance, all that they gave us, count for nothing as we struggle to remove any tell-tale marks of India which still cling to our feet, like the mud from the cane fields. I am not romanticizing the past. It's just there, part of our present and part of the history of these islands. And I just don't feel like being erased.

SAVORY: How do we know what speaks to community and what speaks to the individual in a writer's text? This is important where a writer draws on several locales and experiences, for example, for you, Trinidad, Canada and being of Indo-Caribbean descent. If I'm your reader, and the Caribbean is my most familiar cultural experience of adult life, that does not make me an insider to your Caribbean. Actually, even if we were sisters from the same family, your Caribbean would differ from mine in some important ways because you have your own ways of seeing things — it's a matter of degree, of course, and of the extent of shared perception through shared living.

So though I can strongly experience your poetic and fictional world, I read it without the reverberations of memory and attachment which you have. So may many Canadians who do not know Trinidad, though your Canadian references will reverberate for them. Of course, there is a significant group of readers, women of Indo-Caribbean descent living in Canada, for whom your texts will map a very particular set of connections and places as well as being specifically your creation of them. But is there a real dilemma in always speaking from a place which is both home and not home? And where is home? On the one hand, you draw on a common inheritance and revise and reshape it according to your original vision. On the other hand, when you revise and reshape, you step outside the commonality of experience and memory. Thus certain contradictions become central and important to the work because they are the core of the movement back and forth between ancestry and international mobility. Do you agree?

Espinet: This is a very political issue. I'm well aware that there are reverberations of memory and attachment to which I refer that may be perceived by a general readership as insider knowledge. To some extent, I respond to this by providing glossaries for my writing where I find them to be necessary.

But I think that the experience of Indo-Caribbean people should not remain within their relatively isolated community. It is part of the general historical movement of peoples into this archipelago and as such belongs to all, impacts on all and should be known by all. That this experience is not part of our common intellectual heritage, when Indo-Caribbean people make up twenty percent of the region's population, is ample evidence of the way this ethnic community has been marginalized.

I can't see that it's my task as a writer to provide the kind of insider knowledge necessary to understand that experience. Historians, sociologists, linguists, psychiatrists — where are they? Where are the thinkers among us who would attempt to elucidate the Indo-Caribbean experience? To date, they have not emerged in a significant manner. The intellectual enterprise of the Caribbean has marginalized and ignored the Indo-Caribbean experience in much the same way that its practice of politics, culture, etcetera, has done.

This does not mean that there are not many Indo-Caribbean professionals. However they tend to be "banked" in what I call the "investment professions" — in law, medicine and engineering, for example, and these are not disciplines which investigate the self. Is this changing? I think that it's beginning to change and in about five years we might begin to see a difference. There are a few literary critics, historians, etcetera, but I still don't think there has been adequate examination of this experience in Caribbean intellectual life. The argument goes that if this intellectual knowledge is to be enlarged then Indians must begin to do it for themselves. Why? Is the Indo-Caribbean experience not part of our common ethnic heritage as Caribbean people?

In an ethnically diverse region like the Caribbean, it has begun to strike me forcibly just how people write out of their own essential experience as if they live in a homogeneous society. Well, maybe they do. The literature itself illustrates just how the "all-ah-we-is-one" slogan is false. And when some writing adventurously begins to cross ethnic boundaries, it is often quite interesting to note the degree to which we, living side by side, are strangers to each other. One telling example of this is Naipaul's attempt to construct the fictional character of Jimmy Ahmed in *Guerillas*.

Another recent example is Olive Senior's story "The Arrival of the Snake Woman" which tells the story of Miss Coolie. The story suggests a setting, initially, of the early years of Indian indentureship in Jamaica. I know, from conversations with her, that Olive was aware that she was venturing into unknown regions and opening up something unspoken of in Jamaican literature. The story is a child's eye-view of the arrival of the Indian outsider.

Yet "coolie" is an incredibly loaded racist epithet in the Caribbean for Indo-Caribbean people. It speaks of contempt and low-status. It is possible that the early indentures were described as "coolies," even in some non-derogatory way at first, and then later, even with respect in some cases, as "Miss Coolie" was. It is possible, but I have no knowledge of this. As far as I know, "coolie" has always been used as a pejorative term. As competition between both racial groups intensified, prejudice grew, of course. Both sides ended up looking down upon the other in a variety of ways.

But in the late '80s and '90s can we write a story about a character named Miss Coolie? "Coolie" is as offensive to Indians as "nigger" is to Afro-Caribbean people. Had the tables been turned and an Indo-Caribbean writer turned out a similar story about cultural confrontation featuring a character called "Miss Nigger" by Indians in a largely Indian community, there would have been instant recognition of the work as racially offensive. In the '60s the incidental character of Miss Blackie in *A House for Mr. Biswas* added fuel to the general disapproval of V.S. Naipaul. Yet Miss Coolie exists unchallenged. I use this example to show the degree of disdain that still exists in mainstream Caribbean society, on the whole, for its citizens of Indian descent.

SAVORY: I suppose that a sense of breaking new cultural ground must inform your sense of form as well as content. How do you see your use of form? Does it come out of a sense of international women's writing now or out of a combination of inherited forms from your particular cultural experience and modern, international influences? What are the major questions about form which arise out of your understanding of the Indo-Caribbean experience? Clearly, this is also a political matter because, as we understand in the Caribbean context, virtually nothing stands outside politics. All human activity is set within contexts of domination and subordination which the writer generally tries to recast or even simply to identify. Language itself is a conduit for political attitudes.

ESPINET: I feel no constraints regarding form. I feel free to take, or make, or break and to mix anything from anywhere if it's right. In a way, this is my sense of being Caribbean and essentially a hybrid. That is inevitable. We were thrown here into a flux of different cultures, forms, languages, etcetera, and somehow had to fashion a semblance of order just to go on living. All of us in the Caribbean experience this. And what we as Indians brought to this archipelago and threw into the pot helped to make it what it is. For me, there is no question that our contribution has been ignored or marginalized, and I don't like it — even the elements of Indian cuisine in Jamaican patties or curry goat are not acknowledged, obvious though they are.

There is no doubt, though, that some kind of renaissance in the Indian cultural sphere is happening in the Caribbean at present. It is an insurgent wave, driven by young people who are too habituated to modes of rebellion expressed elsewhere, as in popular culture, for example, to accept their second-class status. It also seems to be taking a fundamentalist direction. I don't know if this is inevitable, but there it is. What it will mean in the long run for literature and the arts in general, I don't know. But to the extent that it builds a sense of self-esteem and pride in young people so that they become more free to affirm their authentic nature, I think it's positive.

Going back to form — in the poem "Merchant of Death," I use Rasta talk and two lines of one of Bob Marley's songs: "If a fire make e' bun/ And if a blood make e' run." I have been pounded by some Indo-Caribbean friends for this. One in particular, a Guyanese poet, insists that it takes away from the "purity" of the Indian experience.

That is a matter for very far-reaching discussion, I think. A Brahminical sense of "purity" certainly operates in the Indian sphere at the level of the ideal — but not at the level of daily experience, and the experience in Guyana has been very different from that in Trinidad, although there is common ground. There is also within that concept of "purity" a fixedness which denies the evidence of creolisation. And there are other negative elements as well, such as racism against Afro-Caribbean people, a patriarchal sub-set which is destructive to women's development and the evocation of a nostalgia which conceives of India as a monolith, almost a relic.

Unfortunately, there is massive ignorance about India. We all suffer from it. It is true that we were allowed to keep what we came with, culturally, but for peasants with access to nothing — not even renewal of those original cultural roots — that proved to be very little. And initially that culture did not help us to live in the new environment. In a contradictory sort of way, those who came in the earlier period of indentureship jettisoned more, rapidly. At any rate, what remains in Trinidad and Guyana as "Hindu culture" is often very localized to particular villages in India. In time rituals became generalized and spread so that they are now accepted as the norm. This would provide fascinating anthropological data if it were investigated. There is a vigorous contemporary movement back to Indian roots, particularly in the religious sphere, and understanding of the religious texts has now been enhanced by more scholarly exploration, so there is also a greater connection to India in the area of religion. But at the level of daily life, customs, rituals, beliefs, etcetera, what is taken for granted as "Hindu" or "Indian" are still the relics of life in small villages in India. The "jhandi" prayer flags are a good example of this.

There is a danger of running aground in the shallows of ideology — shaping the art to fit the constraints of a particular political or other kind of thrust. That is frightening. That we must resist. Experience is layered in a very complex manner, and if we are open to it, surprising and wonderful juxtapositions can occur. The notion of a "pure" or "essential" expression militates against this kind of surprise, in art as well as life. I am too much of a Caribbean person to tolerate this.

There are so many possibilities. And yes, it angers me that in the Caribbean we deny or are afraid of our own plurality.

SAVORY: As I said before, we are centrally concerned here with political issues. Your poems have a lot of political content, and perhaps it would be good to understand how Canada as well as feminism and the Caribbean contribute to this. I find that my feminist political sense has become very complicated. Then there is the need to protect free spaces — here I empathize with your poem "Orthodoxies." But when we become people who refuse political correctness, we of course refuse another possibility of community or solidarity. That can be isolating. How can we be both politically useful and honourably aware of important contradictions in every ideology?

ESPINET: Well, I find that to be political is to be alive. There is no distance between the politics of everyday life, writing and actual living. They meet in an interlocking grid, and to deny that they do is to "drop asleep driving," to quote the calypsonian Chalkdust.

One never sits on the fence. One silently supports the status quo, or one engages in the process of change, and change is always a continuing process. I mean one never wants to arrive because that would mean stasis and death. To some extent one can never experience real despair or real triumph. So I think now, at any rate.

I don't know how to answer your specific question about how Canada as well as feminism and the Caribbean contribute to the political context in my poetry. Feminism — not narrowly defined by country or style of polemic but meaning the empowerment of women on all fronts — is always part of my writing. As for the two geographical areas in which I do most of my living, I cannot perceive them as autonomous units. They are so bound by the politics of the sphere of influence within which they fall that to see it otherwise is just folly. One cannot view political events these days except globally. The whole world has now woken up to the fact that the United States functions as the great world bully. Will the world allow this to continue? As citizens of the world we are in this together and must take collective responsibility for what happens.

But dreams are not bound by geopolitical realities. I believe in the Caribbean as a wonderful unique place. This is threatened by many things, not the least of which is the cultural imperialism of the United States, purveyed through processes as disparate as soap operas and religious fundamentalism. Will our Caribbean triumph over this cheap kind of frumpery? I think so. If I didn't, I would lie down and die.

SAVORY: Let me ask you how your most recent work responds to Canada, where you now live.

ESPINET: The city of Toronto, in which I live, is dramatically different from any place else in Canada and perhaps the United States at this moment. Toronto was proclaimed last year by the United Nations as the most racially and ethnically diverse city in the world. I live in an immigrant city. My job brings me into daily contact with immigrant groups.

But as part of the immigrant mass now putting its stamp on this city, I am intensely aware of my identity as an Indo-Caribbean person and my writing cannot help but respond to this. There is a large Caribbean population in this city and within that a large Indo-Caribbean population. This provides the ground for a kind of dialogue which simultaneously is rooted in notions of home and exile and which does not happen at "home." For example, I write a regular bi-weekly column in a community newspaper, *Indo-Caribbean World*, mostly on women's issues as they relate to this community, but often on other socio-political or literary issues. I find it interesting to note how much of a dialogue is beginning to develop here concerning identity, place, origins, cultural retention, accommodation, with a vigour that I have not seen in the Caribbean. There is a sense of space here within which this dialogue is occurring, and this may be because there are parallel communities also doing the same kind of investigation.

At any rate, people are provoked to react and they do, often with strong statements of disapproval which stem, in my view, more from the fact that a silence is being broken than from the issues being raised. This is a very serious concern and one which is too complex for discussion here. The silence of the Indo-Caribbean woman needs much fuller investigation. But of the fact that there is a "silencing" that occurs, I have no doubt.

In Toronto there is also a strong network of women who talk to each other, who are organising around issues such as violence against women and who work to build solidarity with women's groups such as South Asian and other Caribbean groups. A literary journal, *Diva*, is also produced regularly and includes contributions by women of colour as well as South Asians, including Indo-Caribbean women. Other publications include *Rungh* magazine from Vancouver and *The Toronto Review of Contemporary Writing Abroad*.

On another note, I have found a great deal of support here among the community of artists, activists and organizations which are investigating the complex social and cultural issues surrounding South Asian migration. Desh Pardesh — Home/Out of Home — is an organization which focuses upon South Asian art, culture and politics in the West. I worked recently with a Sri Lankan dancer, Sudharshan Durraiyappan, an exponent of Bharatanatyam who is working in the innovative style of Chandralekha. We worked together to create a performance piece out of a long poem I wrote called "Indian Robber Talk." "Robber Talk" is, of course, a part of the Carnival traditions of Trinidad and Tobago. This production had its premiere on the opening night of Desh Pardesh's annual festival in 1993. There is a lot happening in Toronto — too much, I sometimes think. But it is a vital and stimulating place to live and work.

Endnotes

[1] Boyce Davies, Carole, and Elaine Savory Fido, eds. *Out of the Kumbla: Caribbean Women and Literature* (Trenton, New Jersey: Africa World Press, 1990).

[2] Espinet, Ramabai. "The Absent Voice: Unearthing the Female Epistemology of Cane," N.p., p. 1.

[3] Espinet, Ramabai. *Nuclear Seasons* (Toronto: Sister Vision, 1991), p. 11.

[4] *Ibid.*, p. 28.

[5] *Ibid.*, p. 30.

[6] *Ibid.*, p. 9.

[7] *Ibid.*, p. 9.

[8] *Ibid.*, p. 33.

[9] "Absent Voice," p. 2.

[10] Espinet, Ramabai, in "Barred: Trinidad 1987" in *Green Cane and Juicy Flotsam: Short Stories by Caribbean Women,* Carmen C. Esteves and Lizabeth Paravisini-Gebert, eds. (New Brunswick, New Jersey: Rutgers University Press, 1991), pp. 81-85.

[11] "Absent Voice," p. 8.

Bibliography

Boyce Davies, Carole, and Elaine Savory Fido, eds. *Out of the Kumbla: Caribbean Women and Literature.* Trenton, New Jersey: Africa World Press, 1990.

Espinet, Ramabai, "The Absent Voice: Unearthing the Female Epistemology of Cane." Np, nd.

    ed. *Creation Fire: A CAFRA Anthology of Caribbean Women's Poetry.* Toronto: Sister Vision, 1990.

    Nuclear Seasons. Toronto: Sister Vision, 1991.

Esteves, Carmen C. and Lizabeth Paravisini-Gebert, eds. *Green Cane and Juicy Flotsam: Short Stories by Caribbean Women.* New Brunswick, New Jersey: Rutgers University Press, 1991.

Lee Pui Ming, "Interview with Ramabai Espinet," CKLN Radio, Toronto, February 1992.

Rita Wong

Rita Wong

Jumping on hyphens
A bricolage receiving "genealogy/gap," "goods," "east asian canadian," "translation" & "laughter"

---

*This sprawl of a "paper" to Kwong Lee **tai tai**,
the first chinese woman to come to Canada.
Spring, 1860 — according to the Colonist, no less.*

(pre)face:

WHAT ARE SOME of the contradictions i negotiate as a chinese canadian woman writing about east asian canadian writing?

On the one hand, i don't want to embrace my ethnicity and hold it up as a badge of suffering. "Don't want to go on moanin' the old 'yellow peril' blues for the rest of my days" (Kiyooka 16). Evelyn Lau speaks of being "relieved that I wasn't being slotted into yet another panel of women writers or multicultural writers struggling to say something about their multiculturalism when for some of them it made little impact on their work" ("Getting Heard" 88).

On the other hand, i cannot shut my ears and eyes to the fact that every day most of us *are* influenced by our "multiculturalism," whether we choose to be aware of it or not. However we come to terms with it, whether we verbally acknowledge it, or ignore it, we are visibly different. It colours our perceptions. As Joy Kogawa writes, "By now we know that, however much we may wish to flee, our ethnicity will thud after us" (*Itsuka* 265).

In this essay i would like to explore how various east asian canadian women writers deal with our "difference,"[1] by focusing on the "immigrant" as she is constructed generation after generation.

There is a selfish[2] desire driving this paper; i'm hungry, hungry, hungry to read other asian canadian women's words, always looking voraciously, one eye out in the bookstore, the library, for a sister who can put into words how i'm feeling, who can help me see with a different slant or place something in perspective.

(body) stuck between theories & practices

I've created a fake sense of community.
(Paul Wong, quoted by Gagnon, on the Yellow Peril exhibition 48)

If you treat an indirect structure directly, it escapes, it empties out, or on the contrary, it freezes, essentializes. (Barthes, quoted by Minh-ha 41).

In attempting to structure a discussion around east asian canadian women writers, i am already making a space in which it would be all too easy and all too dangerous to freeze the writers into a limited construction, focusing on their identity as (in)visible women and forgetting that each writer has her own approaches, her own tendencies, and that each piece of writing has its own aesthetics, rhythms, quirks. I see an incredible variety between, for example, Joy

Kogawa's tight poetic style in *Obasan*, Sky Lee's (melo)dramatic *Disappearing Moon Cafe*, Jam. Ismail's humorous, experimental *Scared Texts* and Evelyn Lau's bluntly autobiographical *Runaway*— a huge variety of traditions, attitudes, priorities, cultures interacting ... To link these writers and their texts may be dangerously to ghettoize ourselves once again, yet i am pushed by a necessity to sketch out some of the tenuous links between these women's writings in my own search for an identity, no matter how brief and historical, no matter how unfinished; a moment of building an imagined community, a base for support, for action, since identity exists within a context, a group of women who say to me, yes, i know that feeling, yes, you're not alone. Thus, a self-consciously strategic essentialism underlies this essay, based on the need for a "community-generated critical context" (Fung 17).

> Sometimes your voice escapes you
> nervously, fearful of its own
> bony fins
> (Lai "Trap II")

Working towards a collectivity with permeable boundaries, just enough for a sense of definition but not so much as to confine. Continually manoeuvring in and out.

Keeping in mind that asians are often seen as a "model minority," successful economically and in education (University of British Columbia having been called the university of a billion chinese by some), and at the same time that "they" are somehow exotic (safely distanced into being "other"), we need to, as Mitsuye Yamada says, "raise our voices a little more, even as they say to us 'this is so uncharacteristic of you' " ("Invisibility" 40).

Reading and writing are processes of self-construction and affirmation, though certainly they need to be partnered with action in other spheres, as the literary collides with the political, the social. Autobiography, visual art, rear their beautiful heads, broadening that category of "literary" into the interdisciplinary, crossing borders between asian canadian and asian american because our american cousins have so much to offer, reading novels such as Lee's *Disappearing Moon Cafe* and Kogawa's *Obasan* with an eye to history, herstory, our stories. Both texts construct foremothers within the structure of the novel, using an established form to shape the telling, saying it *is* possible to speak and be heard. The more we read and write, the more words, ways, we can manoeuvre.

> form and content
> foment discontent *(who said this?)*

writing as an act that is never finished, that engenders more writing, thought, action:

receptivity? a context

In viewing reading as a process, it is helpful to consider how some asian canadian writing has been publicly received. Writing does not exist in a vacuum; by looking at reviews, publishers, prizes, one may get a sense of how our society places some of this writing and how this in turn influences our own readings.

Kogawa's novel, *Obasan*, is taught in many universities and has won many awards; it is likely to come to mind first when a reader tries to think of an asian canadian book. Her sequel, in contrast, has so far met with mixed reviews. Part of its reception seems based on comparisons and the high expectations of some readers. Carol Redl states that *Itsuka* "is likely to both thrill and disappoint those who loved *Obasan*" (*Edmonton Journal*, March 1, 1992, D7), while Stan Persky writes, "*Itsuka* pales in *Obasan*'s shadow" (*Globe and Mail*, March 28, 1992, C8). Both Persky and Redl seem to find the political aspect (which existed in *Obasan* but was placed more in the past) of *Itsuka* unpalatable or heavy-handed.

Redl says:

> The beauty of *Itsuka*'s poignant love story is offset — some might say defaced — by accounts of the jockeying for power of individuals and organizations such as the National Japanese Canadian League and the Japanese Canadians for Democratic Discussions. The Japanese-Canadian community's internal wranglings are, at times, downright vindictive. Kogawa herself seems to launch a personal vendetta against one member of the community who, given the nature of books, is rendered basically defenceless against the attack. Surely, considering the fact that the collective goal of redress occurred, members of the community should forget their past animosities. (*Edmonton Journal* D7)

This reminds me of the "unspoken chinese edict" that Sky Lee deliberately breaks; although there is a desire to tell "only happy mentionables for the family record," Lee's protagonist in *Disappearing Moon Cafe* reiterates that our stories need to be more than wish-fulfilment — they need to tell the unpalatable, the painful side as well (Lee 180). Similarly, Kogawa is risking the image of happiness, of united community, to reveal the ruptures within. She is telling us about those parts we may not want to hear but perhaps need to. The politics in *Itsuka* are more contemporary, are closer — we cannot read the novel with the same sense of historical distance that we might read *Obasan*.

In Persky's review we come up against the concept of literary quality, of what is "good": "The rhetoric of Community Studies 101 is laid on with a trowel ... *Itsuka* offers some interest as anecdotal sociology; as literature, almost none" (Persky C8).

It is very possible that the criteria for judging "good" literature are based on traditional, male-centred assumptions and that this emphasis on Literature distracts one from reading the text on its own terms. If readers put aside restrictive categories and just try hard to listen, to suspend or postpone judgement, what will they hear, what will they open themselves up to? The question of evaluating "good" literature is one which i will return to since it is a problem i have with my own response to many of the texts i discuss.

Ironically enough, Evelyn Lau's autobiography met with the reverse of Persky's attitude; her writing was judged more on its sociological and less on its literary aspects. Lau states:

> *Runaway* was published to a great deal of attention, but that was because I wasn't seen by the majority of the media as a writer. I was the young prostitute, the street kid or the would-be social worker ... Nobody wanted to know that I had been publishing in literary magazines since I was twelve or thirteen ... Some reviewers bypassed the writing in the book completely, only to jump up and down as is fashionable and applaud my courage and the courage of my publishers.
>
> I would have rather that reviewers slammed the book as a terrible piece of self-indulgent adolescent writing than to say how marvellous it was because here was a little street kid getting heard ("Getting Heard" in *Prairie Fire*, 1991, 90).

On the one hand, a literary damning with faint (or no) praise; on the other hand, a literary bypass. A critical catch-22. The perils of publishing don't stop us from writing, but do give us food for thought. As Midi Onodera puts it, "Criticism by well-informed, well-intentioned white critics tells us mainstream beliefs but does not tell us what we mean. We must begin this process of comprehension ourselves" (Onodera 31).

receptivity? a personal response

While Evelyn Lau is aware that her colour sometimes shapes people's reactions to her — stating in *Runaway*, "He fantasizes often about Oriental women and that was why he picked me up" (*Runaway* 199) — she does not foreground or privilege this aspect of her identity, choosing instead to place the emphasis on herself as writer, as human being. I refuse to be condescending about her youth (her books were published while she was a teenager); her writing does not always conform to what i have learned to consider "good," but as Aruna Srivastava states:

> I recall a question about the literary quality of "ethnic" poetry [substitute writing in general]: what do we do with the fact that we perceive some poems to be, simply, "better" than others? I answer, predictably, by pointing out that notions of literary quality are inevitably ideological, that we are as readers and critics resolutely historically situated ... (Srivastava 31).

I find Lau's writing is sometimes over-emotional, sometimes trite, as well as having moments of powerful honesty and clarity; i was uncomfortable with her writing and with my standards for judging it. These standards i have been taught (and i have been *such* a good student[3]) — emotional is okay, but not too much, don't go overboard — don't hold up when i consider that british Romantic poets ("I fall upon the thorns of life"), writers every bit as "over-emotional" as Lau, are judged as "good" and are included in the canon, given literary respectability, where Lau's diary, so far, has not been. (It has sold well, but i have yet to see it taught anywhere.)

Lau's poetry in *You Are Not Who You Claim* is concerned with who and what she experiences today — "Lawyers," "Writers," "What We Do in the Name of Money" ... The poems fit into a humanist mode and do not explicitly mention race. The "i"s, "he"s, "she"s and "you"s in her poetry could be white, yellow, brown, black; the voice's emotions and descriptions seem to be what are significant. While this is not a way i would choose, i respect Lau's decision to write in an "accessible" style. She has set her own standards for writing; her aesthetic is one with a wider appeal. Whether or not this internalizes white standards, it seems to be empowering for Lau as an individual. Sneja Gunew has suggested:

> Both women and migrants internalize the process whereby the culture constructs them, and it requires a great deal of self-conscious analysis before they are able to step (and only ever in part) outside these constructs (Gunew 168).

In her own way Lau is working both in and out of these imposed constructs; rejecting the roles of obedient chinese daughter, reformed street waif, she seems determined to be a writer worthy of respect.

Text and reader both need to be questioned. Amy Ling, in a discussion of asian american women writers, points out:

If I find that these women have written what traditional department colleagues would not consider "fine literature," then I must, like Jane Tompkins, redefine "literature" to be broader than the "stylistic intricacy, psychological subtlety, [and] epistemological complexity" that is the current measure of a "good" book, and examine instead "how and why it worked for its readers, in its time." In other words, I do not categorize a writer or her book as "good" or "bad" in the abstract but try to answer the questions: Good for what? For whom? Under what kind of circumstances? And I maintain that I am still studying literature, the written voice of a specific group of people at a specific time (Ling 151-160).

The judging of "good," the setting of critical rules, i defer until there is more asian canadian writing to pick and choose from, until i can figure out a way of evaluating that is more than the internalization and perpetualization of my liberal education. As it stands now, i examine what i have access to, what circumstances allow me, and this leads me to Sky Lee's *Disappearing Moon Cafe*, which i also had some problems with, much as i admire the book on the whole. As Denise Chong has noted, despite the cleverness and intricacy of the plot, the novel is marked by a "cutesy sort of melodrama" that "sometimes tends to excess" (Chong 23). At times this exaggerated mode may subvert readerly expectations (of the quiet, controlled oriental), but it is sometimes off-putting and could also play into a different stereotype — that of the loud, exotic chinese, whose families are dramatically incestuous and dynastic. A risk but one i'm glad Lee took; i read in an uneasy dual motion between subversion and stereotype, giving Lee the benefit of the doubt when i can.

At times Lee's excess and exaggeration *do* work; for example, it reminds the reader of "the manner of traditional chinese storytelling and popular theatre" as the book's dustjacket states. Cultures clash; the result isn't always poetic and nice — why should we try to prettify it? In the following passage, for instance, the women's emotions run rampant as the mother-in-law asserts a destructive power:

> "Go back home to your own family! You have more than enough gold here to pawn for a passage." Mui Lan sneered, knowing full well that a spurned daughter-in-law would rather commit suicide than go back to her parents' home, for all the ten generations of everlasting shame that she would cost her family, in fact her whole village.
> "No!" Fong Mei gasped as if strangling, and broke down into uncontrolled heaving and sobbing. (*Disappearing Moon Cafe* 59)

The sneering, heaving, sobbing is uncomfortable and reminds me of a soap opera, but it demands release. The telling, painful and awkward as it may be, is necessary; as the narrator points out, we cannot state only what we want to hear and remember:

> Like my mother, I will speak of other times only if they were happy ones. Yes, yes, Hermia agreed wholeheartedly with me, only happy mentionables for the family record; another unspoken chinese edict among so many.
> I wonder. Maybe this is a chinese-in-canada trait, a part of the great wall of silence and invisibility we have built around us. I have a misgiving that the telling of our history is forbidden. I have violated a secret code. There is power

in silence, as this is the way we have always maintained strict control against the more disturbing aspects in our human nature. But what about speaking out for a change, despite its unpredictable impact!
(*Disappearing Moon Cafe* 180).

Speaking out is not easy; the least we can do is to open our minds to hear one another's voices. My criticism of Lee's novel is meant to be constructive and should not keep us from remembering that the book plays an important role in confirming the process of building a chinese canadian presence.

Unlike Lau, Lee deliberately focuses on our identity and history as chinese in canada. The novel's exploration of a fictional family's four generations in canada, weaving actual history and fiction together, is exciting and fresh for someone who has not read any other novels dealing with chinese canadian women.[4]

mind you: not-an-immigrant?

We carry
our spices
each time
we enter
new spaces
the feel
of newness
is ginger
between teeth
(Gill, *Immigrant Always* 33)

In the back of the Granville bus
a man touches my hair
asks what country
I have been refugeed
again
I crack my gum
and say
the USA
(Lai, *Glory*)

"Where do you come from?" he asked, as we sat down at a small table in a corner. That's the one sure-fire question I always get from strangers. People assume when they meet me that I'm a foreigner.
"How do you mean?"
"How long have you been in this country?"
"I was born here."
"Oh," he said, and grinned. "And your parents?"
(Kogawa, Obasan 7)

As the above quotes make clear, in our daily lives we are reminded that no matter how banana we are (white on the inside, yellow on the outside), we "look" like immigrants, like "others."[5] Whether we get angry, frustrated, resigned, or just used to this, i think it is useful to set aside the sometimes distracting question of what constitutes Good Literature in order to work out some ways of responding to this perpetual-immigrant syndrome. For example, artists such as Jin-me Yoon engage with this continual misconstruction playfully; Yoon, poker-faced in a send-up of the inscrutable oriental, places herself, a canadian, in cheesy tourist snapshots, inviting viewers to examine their own assumptions. She turns a common annoyance into a site of productive humour.

While i may have run the risk of falling into the "immigrantness" that is sometimes imposed on me, i had wanted to write an essay about narratives of immigration. Ironically enough, however, when i looked at the body of work (all in english) that i have access to, i realized that most of it is by writers who were born in canada — some, like Lydia Kwa, Laiwan and Jam. Ismail, were born abroad but are fluent in english — and much of it deals more with the after-effects, the transitional ripples through generations that result from immigration, rather than the actual act of immigration itself. Early immigrants were often illiterate in english; getting access to their stories from them (as opposed to getting access to them through their children and grand-children) depends more on oral than on written transmission. For this reason the Chinese Canadian National Council has put together a "Voices of Chinese Canadian Women" oral history book project[6] called *Jin Guo*.

The first generation's voices need to be heard too; their absence in this essay is conspicuous. The access we have to their stories is through their descendants' writings, through someone else's representation, and in another language, english. For example, in Sky Lee's short story "Broken Teeth," it is through the daughter that we hear her mother's story.[7] Limited by my english-language education, i focus on writers who are fluent in english — not with any intent to privilege them but with an awareness that their writings should be balanced with other earlier perspectives and that my very use of english re-inscribes societal hierarchies of language.

Instead of looking at immigration per se, i shift towards the generation gap, intensified by cultural and linguistic differences, as it operates in Evelyn Lau's diary *Runaway*, Lee's *Disappearing Moon Cafe* and "Broken Teeth," Kogawa's *Obasan* and *Itsuka*, and Anne Jew's short story "Everyone Talked Loudly in Chinatown" so we may get a sense of the varieties of ways in which the gap has been represented, of how we often read the "immigrant" through their descendants' eyes.

Outright rebellion was Lau's response to her immigrant parents. Running away from home at the age of fourteen and living on the streets for two years, she states:

> My parents were strict, overprotective and suspicious of the unknown society around them. By kindergarten, I was already expected to excel in class, as the first step, in my pre-planned career as a doctor or lawyer (*Runaway* 1).

The unbearable restrictiveness that Lau perceives in her parents is a theme that runs through both life and fiction; Lau's rebellion is on the extreme, but it is on a continuum with, for example, the mother in Anne Jew's story, who screams, "How can you be so fearless! Going out with a white boy!" and the father who slaps her (Jew 27). Immigrants who are wary of the outside culture, who ignore their children's desire to fit in, yet place heavy expectations ("doctor," "lawyer") on them are often viewed through a filter of resentment (tempered with love and respect, depending on the writer's circumstances).

To escape the psychological pressure of being a model obedient chinese girl, Lau immerses herself in the streets, in what could be termed "canadian" experience, and in what Lau at one point describes as "that little girl's fantasy ... her idea of freedom" (*Runaway* 312). For Lau, this is an act of survival and relative honesty, in contrast to:

> My mother in her kitchen, a thin woman rushing back and forth to clean cupboards, sweep floors, make meals, wash dishes — it was never-ending. There was always something that needed to be done! None of this is pleasant to bring up. She kept everything in order while each of us disintegrated (*Runaway* 151).

Part of the order is the keeping of traditions; at one point, Lau's father phones her, expecting her to come home for chinese new year:

> Every Chinese person, he said, attended this dinner no matter how busy they were. He expected me to come home and help make the meal ...
> They expected that I would transform back into the dutiful daughter for the occasion. As Dr. Hightower said, if I went

back they would think that "God had dinged you on the head and made you their compliant little girl again" (*Runaway* 159).

Lau refuses to go back, knowing her parents will lecture her about her "lack of schooling, lack of a job, lack of everything but bumming off people" (*Runaway* 159). The generation gap is aggravated by cultural conflicts. Dr. Hightower acts in some ways as an ironic counterpoint (Lau names him Hightower), a white male authority's acceptance or condoning of Lau's choice to be independent. She needs support wherever she can get it; this does not mean she must buy into everything that authority represents. Lau's desire to be a writer, to be accepted by many people, demands this separation from her family. The break between generations in this case is sharp and drastic, although Lau oscillates between love and hate throughout the book. She posits writing as a substitute for her family but comes to reject that equation:

> One of my biggest shocks for me was to realize that when I wanted to be a successful writer, I wanted the love and acceptance that presumably went along with it. For a long time I thought that when I got a book published, it would be like acquiring a new family, one I wanted. This reasoning bears a remarkable resemblance to why I went on the street — to feel accepted, to find a home. Both ideas are illusions (*Runaway* 340).

The search for a community, for acceptance, is unresolved; it is still in process after *Runaway* ends. It will be interesting to see how or if Lau resolves this in the years to come; currently, the role of her immigrant parents seems to be more a force to rebel against than one to integrate into her writing. While i have been foregrounding the cultural aspect of Lau's autobiography, i must add that within the context of her book, she writes of many other experiences — for example, drug addiction, prostitution, and writing are given as much, possibly more, emphasis as her family.[8] Currently working as a freelance writer and publishing in many literary journals, Lau is still independent; she is finding her own space near the "mainstream."

Sky Lee deals with the generation gap in a more diverse way, presenting the strengths and weaknesses in women's bonds as they progress over generations. The character of Mui Lan, an early immigrant, reveals the effects of her harsh life. Uprooted from a village in china composed mainly of women (the men were working overseas) and dumped into a chinese canadian community that was predominantly male,

> She arrived and found only silence. A stone silence that tripped her up when she tried to reach out. Gold Mountain men were like stone. She looked around for women to tell her what was happening, but there were none. By herself, she lacked the means to know what to do next. Without her society of women, Mui Lan lost substance. Over the years, she became bodiless, or was it soulless, and the only way she could come back was by being noisy and demanding — because if nothing else, she was still the boss's wife, wasn't she? (*Disappearing Moon Cafe* 26).

"To be shrill and demanding in the face of silence; to be denied harmony and have only cacophony as your weapon; this manifests itself in the way the story is told." (R. Wong 136) Lee's writing and Lau's can be read as attempts to "manipulate the recognized dominating discourses so as to begin to free ourselves *through* rather than beyond them." For example, Gail Scott cites a feminist film critic who "recommends a return to melodrama, which she calls narrative at its most hysterical" (Scott 88) — unashamedly female, yet also critically approached (Scott 80).

Lee starts by tracing "the mother-in-law vs. daughter-in-law battle [which] cripples following generations" (R. Wong 135). The enmity between Mui Lan and Fong Mei is a traditional chinese tension transplanted to canadian soil. However, a cross-cultural tension that rises between generations emerges soon enough between Fong Mei and Beatrice:

> One generation between mother and daughter, and already how far apart their goals and sentiments. They shared a common experience, but while Fong Mei hated this country, which had done nothing except disqualify her, Beatrice had grown up thoroughly small-town Canadian (*Disappearing Moon Cafe* 164).

The women of each generation are represented through a sympathetic narrator-descendant who is nonetheless aware of the flaws and limits of her ancestors. Kae states:

> Funny how I can still get protective of the women in my family, how I can give them all sorts of excuses for their littering. In the telling of their stories, I get sucked into criticizing their actions [sound familiar?], but how can I allow my grandmother and great-grandmother to stay maligned? Perhaps, as Hermia suggested, they were ungrounded women, living with displaced chinamen, and everyone trapped by circumstances. I prefer to romanticize them as a lineage of women with passion and fierceness in their veins.

> In each of their woman-hating worlds, each did what she could. If there is a simple truth beneath their survival stories, then it must be that women's lives, being what they are, are linked together. Mother to daughter, sister to sister. Sooner or later we get lost or separated from each other; then we have a bigger chance of falling into the same holes over and over again. Then again, we may find each other, and together, we may be able to form a bridge over the abyss (*Disappearing Moon Cafe* 145-146).

The strength of women's bonds, of bridges between generations once the myth of male lineage has been deconstructed, is the nugget of hope that gives Lee's novel a positive resolution. Able to place herself into a context, Kae gets a slightly inflated but comic sense of her own importance:

> Don't you see?" I gesticulate emphatically. "I'm the fourth generation. My actual life, and what I do in it, is the real resolution to this story. The onus is entirely on me. Yipes, what do I do now?" (*Disappearing Moon Cafe* 210).

Kae's understanding of her mother, aunt, grandmother, great-grandmother enables her to avoid their mistakes and to make decisions based on her own desires instead of what the system dictates as correct. Telling becomes action. Kae is a reminder that "we have agency and are not simply victims of oppression" (Fung 18).

Lydia Kwa's poem "Travelling Time" also alludes to this constructive use of history:

space
like dough
worked through by a woman's fingers
ball stretched to a length, until the middle gaps
with air:

hole in time, through which we might
enter another's history
nothing will be the same again

Kwa's image of the dough captures a common traditional female experience and transforms it into a link between generations; this link allows us to learn, gives us the hope that "nothing will be the same again."

The necessity of learning our foremothers' stories is also a significant topos in Joy Kogawa's *Obasan*, which "traces the daughter's reconstruction of [the] absent racial/maternal figure" (Lim 301). Alternatively, Manina Jones phrases it as follows: "*Obasan's* narrative act may be seen as motivated by the desire for a kind of reunion, as a way of relating mother to daughter, of returning home" (Jones 224).

Kogawa has suggested "There are cultures that are more silent ... that perhaps rely on intuition" (Redekop 17); i read the mother's quiet calmness in *Obasan* initially as such an accepting, comforting silence that depends on a high-context "commonly shared cultural identity and world view" (B. Lee 3) which allows assumptions to remain unsaid. However, as Mason Harris has pointed out:

> To function, loving silence requires a community where everyone is perfectly known and from which no one feels alienated. A world where response is "simultaneous" and

thus does not require words cannot deal with a drastic breach in continuity with the past. Without community, the loving silence of Naomi's childhood becomes [a] negative silence ... an inner "retreat" from which there is no return (Harris 46).[9]

Once Naomi's mother has left, the silence that was loving becomes one of uncertainty, of loss; it is only when she hears her mother's letter (to Grandpa Kato, via Nakayama-sensei who, unlike Naomi, is literate in japanese) that Naomi can begin to put her to rest: "The song of mourning is not a lifelong song" (*Obasan* 246).

In some ways Aunt Emily, Obasan and Naomi's mother form a trinity of foremothers for Naomi; each one has something valuable to give or teach her. In *Itsuka*, Emily, "a militant nisei, a second-generation made-in-Canada woman of Japanese ancestry" (*Obasan* 3), drags the reluctant sansei Naomi into the politics of the redress movement, initializing a participation that eventually flowers into "Reconciliation. Liberation. Belongingness. Home" (*Obasan* 286). Emily stresses the importance of community: "The dispersed are the disappeared, unless they're connected ... If you aren't joined to those you love, your heart shrivels up and blows away in the dust" (*Obasan* 3).

Witness to Obasan's decline, Naomi discovers her own capacity for rage (*Itsuka* 69):

Her last act of service was to wait for Stephen in order to praise him. An extreme and extravagant gesture. In the end, he did not hear. Obasan, who devoted all her days to our remnant family and especially to Stephen, did not deserve that long last loneliness (*Obasan* 82).

The rage is for Stephen, the understanding for Obasan, who as one of the issei, is sacrificed. Naomi states: "I remember Nakayama-sensei saying that issei immigrants were the people of sacrifice. They came to the new land to perish in the culture clash. They offered their lives for the young" (*Obasan* 249).

Naomi recognizes the legacy of the issei: "They endured for the sake of the long-term good, for the well-being of the whole. They endured for a future that only the children will know" (*Obasan* 250). Embodied in Obasan is the issei's position — one which Naomi respects and Stephen rejects: "[Stephen] was always irritated at me for being 'too young' and he scorned the issei, the immigrant generation, for being 'too dumb' because they didn't understand English" (*Obasan* 11).

Third-generation Naomi is linked more closely to the second-generation (Emily) and first-generation (Obasan) than Stephen, although Emily and Obasan do not signal much appreciation of her commitment. Naomi's love finds a third significant outlet in her mother, whom she continues to put to rest in *Itsuka*:

> It occurs to me ... that the dream was the final signpost in my steadfast journey towards Mother. All my waiting life I kept my heart turned towards her and away from the tiny choices of love offered in the inch-high rooms of possibilities. I sought her and only her, tumbling downstream, back and back till I reached her grave and I sought her in dream beyond the grave, in the stream that circles for ever and in the song that does not vanish (*Itsuka* 95).

Kogawa and Lee both posit the writer as a bridge between generations and between cultures. As Kogawa states,

> the Asian Canadian person bears the bridge [between east and west] within. As writers who are also Asian Canadians, it is our task to ferret out the stuff of our lives, the preconscious and silent matter that resides in our limbs ("Random" 325).

Being on the bridge, on the hyphen between asian and canadian, without privileging either side (Mathur 5), strikes me as a place i'd like to be. Yet i will not end on this note (no happy ending just yet) but circle back to the conflicts that demand attention.

Anne Jew's story "They Talked Loudly in Chinatown" uses an adolescent girl's point of view to present cultural and generational conflicts in a humorously callous yet touching way. At one point the narrator says calmly, "As I enter the house, I pass my grandmother's room to go upstairs. She is lying in there dying. I throw my bag into my room and head into the kitchen. I take out a bag of chips from the cupboard and pour a glass of orange juice and join my brother in the living room where he is watching a rerun of "The Brady Bunch" (Jew 22-23).

The mother-in-law versus daughter-in-law struggle is something that Jew, like Lee, makes note of:

> My mother can't wait for my grandmother to die. She is always telling my brother and me how she was treated like a slave by Grandmother when she first married my father.
> "Why didn't you stand up for yourself?" I ask.
> "Oh, you don't know what it was like then" (Jew 24).

This brief exchange signals the differences between the narrator and her (grand)parents, a difference that grows wider with age:

As I started to grow up, I stopped going to Chinatown with her [grandmother], and then I stopped spending time with her altogether. I started to play with friends who weren't loud and who weren't Chinese. This upset my mother. She was suspicious of all other cultures" (Jew 25).

Implicit in the narrative is a resentment or embarrassment towards her parents, a motif we've seen in Stephen in Kogawa's novels and in Lau's diary. Another response is guilt for not fulfilling one's duties, as Sky Lee shows in her story "Broken Teeth": "Suddenly she accused,

Your grandfather died last week."
... I had never met my grandfather — her father. He lived in Hong Kong. And I was born here. So why accuse me, mother? Yet, her guilt-ridden blow struck with the desired effect" (S. Lee 20).

In Taien Ng's story "Shun-Wai" the narrator is from Hong Kong, but this does not nullify the generational-cultural conflicts or the guilt:

When she [the mother] came to Canada with my father, she didn't have an inkling of the English language. Then my father left her. Now she's got an accounting business, and a house with a garden, and Jesus. And me, of course, which is probably why she turned to Jesus.
My mother and I aren't often on speaking terms any more. She says I'm like a gwua-mui — a white girl — never listen to the parents (Ng 122).

THE OTHER WOMAN

If the narrator acts as a bridge between generations in the story, it's a bridge that doesn't get crossed:

> "Tell your mother not to yell at me," Poh Poh [grandmother] said to me sadly.
> "Mom," I said. "Stop yelling at your mother."
> My mother ignored me and continued talking loudly for a while. Poh Poh just went into the kitchen (Ng 124).

Even bridges have their points of stress, points that carry greater or less tension according to the weight put on them. Having covered some of these tensions, i would like to examine language hybrids[10] a little more closely since language barriers often play a significant role in the generation gap.

To end this section, i'd like to refer to Jam. Ismail, who releases generational tension through light humour. Here is space to play, even between generations:

> your grandchildren are better behaved this year,
> laurel said, they're less rambunctious.
> no, holly demurred, they have their own beds
> (Scared Texts 125).

tongue a strategy: when/if you can translate?

Some writers, not so comfortable with the implications of english dominance, and aware of a sense of loss, experiment with other languages to disrupt the english. Laiwan is one such writer:

> English, with its history of imperialism and colonization of minds, is a syntactical problem. Its writing reinforces its

history because it was the only language accepted in its colonies. At this point, I know how to speak Cantonese at the simple level of a child. I get my writing translated into Chinese to decolonize the english and to throw in a spanner to make it work. I am dependent on english to deflate that which itself has created. I am dependent because it has become the *native* tongue that most of the reading world knows or wants to know. It is the audacious syntax that generates its own meanings and expectations within contexts it knows nothing about (Laiwan, *Yellow Peril Reconsidered* 40).

One choice is to operate on the premise "to speak another language is to enter another consciousness" (Philip 15); in so doing, translation and language-contamination become a space of possibility, particularly if one is trying to construct a genealogy of mothers and foremothers, a community and a grounding context from which to grow. For some women, there seems to be a need to know where we're coming from before we can work out where we want to go. However, there are also many barriers.

This is demonstrated in *Obasan* when Naomi finally hears her mother's voice through the letter read by Nakayama-sensei. "Many of the Japanese words sound strange and the language is formal" (*Obasan* 233). Naomi is separated from her mother not only by historical events but also by a cultural and linguistic barrier. With the help of others, the barrier is bridged and Naomi is gently directed towards a path of healing.

Language barriers between generations often come up in asian canadian writing, for example, in Ana Chang's untitled poem addressed to her mother:

Since coming to Vancouver, we've been moving apart, so/ slowly, not apparent to our eyes. Until one day we looked into/ each other's eyes and did not recognise and the sounds out of our/ mouths sounding strangely familiar, we did not understand (Chang 67).

And in Jean Yoon's story "The Conversation of Birds," the guilt trip this can entail is made clear:

"You are very bad not to speak Korean." Mr. Im crossed his arms across his chest...
"Well, yeah. I guess."
"You must come to school. I have a special class for older students too." Thanks but no thanks, I thought. I'd be in the dummy class again. Mom would be poking me to see if I'd done my homework and Mr. Im would be pointedly correct. That was the last thing I needed (Yoon 60).

Some women are in the position of Taien Ng's narrator:

I understand Chinese well enough, but if you asked me to say anything in it, I'd probably stare at you dumbfounded. It's not that I don't know my own background. I know damn well I'm Chinese. My mother keeps reminding me of the fact. As if I would ever forget" (Ng 124).

As Adrienne Clarkson has pointed out in an interview, one can function just fine in canada without speaking or knowing chinese (Goh 94) or some other ancestral tongue; for Clarkson, french was a more practical option. While I support the choice to be unilingual (or to not speak a [fore]mother's tongue, knowing that for some learning another language is a burden), i am also interested in the limited efforts that have been made towards bridging, for example, chinese and english.

Unlike the voices in Ng's, Yoon's and Chang's writing, Sky Lee's narrator, Kae, having studied chinese, has more language to manoeuvre with, but is still limited, needing Hermia's help to translate her grandmother's letters (*Disappearing Moon Cafe* 41). She is sensitive to the fringe-interference of chinese with english: "I wonder too, about the volatile lunacy that wasn't my great-grandmother's alone, but lurks in our peasant backgrounds, in our rustic language" (Kae 63).

Throughout the book, Lee's translation of chinese phrases into english — for example, "they guzzle vinegar," "turnip head," "tiger heat," "go die," "ten-parts" — serve to root the story, give it a distinctly chinese grounding. (R. Wong) Sometimes a clumsy clash, sometimes a productive mingle, the chinese and english enact a side-step, shuffle, hop and dance.

At times translation can be used to excite a sense of knowing yet not knowing, feeling "an unknown home" as May Yee phrases it:

'Ngen' — Grandmother. Her name sounds almost the same as the Chinese word for 'people.' How appropriate, because she embodied for me the people of China, so unknown to me, yet evoking a feeling captured in the word 'home,' an unknown home (Yee 63).

Given:

language is first of all for us a body of sound. Leaving the water of the mother's womb with its one dominant sound, we are born into this other body whose multiple sounds bathe our ears from the moment of our arrival. we learn the sounds before we learn what they say: a child will speak babytalk in pitch patterns that accurately imitate the sense patterns of her mothertongue. an adult who cannot read or write will speak his mothertongue without being able to say what a particular morpheme or even word means (Marlatt 171).

A schism between mothertongue and meaning leading to "an unknown home," distance from the mothertongue. Those who "return" to china, though we've never been there before.

mouthing off: translation spilling into laughter

There are some wonderful moments of a humorous, clunky, punning mode of translation-formation; for example, we see some of this in Joy Kogawa's *Obasan*:

> 'Sakana fish,' Stephen mutters as he steps on the brakes. Aunt Emily looks startled. 'What did you say?' Some of the ripe pidgin English phrases we pick up are three-part inventions — part English, part Japanese, part Sasquatch. 'Sonuva bitch' becomes 'sakana fish,' 'sakana' meaning 'fish' in Japanese. On occasion the phrase is 'golden sakana fish' (*Obasan* 218).

Emily herself continues this vein in *Itsuka*, with her benjo (japanese slang for toilet) songs: *O Susannah/ Cry all you want for me,/ For I come from British Columbia with/ a benjo on my knee* (*Itsuka* 18).

Humour also marks the writings of Jam. Ismail; her playful, quirky oscillation of identities in the following passage reminds us how limited our labels are:

> young ban yet had been thought italian in kathmandu,
> filipina in hong kong, eurasian in kyoto, japanese in anchorage, dismal in london england, hindu in edmonton, generic oriental in calgary, western canadian in ottawa, anglophone in montreal, metis in jasper, eskimo in hudson's bay department store, vietnamese in chinatown, tibetan in vancouver, commie at the u.s. border.
> on the whole very asian (Scared Texts 128).

In Ismail's writing we can see fragments of what i have discussed earlier — for instance, the language barrier is taken up and shades of language-competence thrown together:

> hibiscus mentioned that mushrooms are good for cholesterol
> jaggery scoffed: what d'you mean, good for!
> chestnut dehisced: she means good against, good against cholesterol.
> flame-o'-the-forest said to jaggery: we know you speak better english and that you know what we mean
> (Scared Texts 124).

Ismail often enacts language with a twist, deliberately avoiding correct English usage, as in this quote: "wat's sauce for the goose, is source for the gender. so it was out of this primordant a cord with the mother that i developed skills then considered male (Ismail, "Essay on Gender and Writing" in *Sexions*).

"A cord" plays off umbilical cord and accord, while the old saying "what's good for the goose" gets a new gander.

Ismail experiments with sound to disrupt english: "people who romanticize androgyny often talk thru ther hads. it is not so symbol!" ("Evidens of Natural Selection" *in Sexions*) and, like Laiwan, with chinese characters as in this excerpt:

> well   .of loneliness   .its good.
> 4.ix. feeling lonely   &liking it.
> oh the drag of a task   befor (one gets to) the freedom
> with in.   attitude to word servants.
> bum sits by window
> fingers reach for , rose.
> some roses wont depetal into hips.
>
> hand ꝫ writing | upon a ⊓ surface
> It forms
>
> 聿 A pencil, pen forthwith, and then
>
> 肂 To dig a grave.
>
> 肆 To practise toil, pain, sprouts
>
> 肅 Circumspection, respect
>
> 肄 O expend to expose our excessive reckless now
>
> 肇 begin, to range

this avid barter, switch on the sens of timing ("Diction Air" in Contemporary Verse 2 40)

In "deconstructing that Great Book, the dictionary" (Srivastava 31), Ismail is also making space for other languages, other ways of seeing.

tired hand waves good-bye:

This essay has been a scrapbook, a collection of "some speculative fieldnotes on that intermittent time, and interstitial space, that emerges as a structure of undecidablility at the frontiers of cultural hybridity" (Bhabha 312).

   very much still a project-in-process:

   show me the legend for
   weaving colours into dark spaces
   (Kwa "Locating the Legend" 40)

Appendix: Excess

   on immigration:

No wilderness self, is shards, shards, shards,
shards of raw glass, a debris of people you pick your way
through returning to your worse self, you the thin
mixture of just come and don't exist. (Brand 29)

After a while her mother took her to bed and tucked her in, and sat in the kitchen with the fearful vision of her daughter always outside of the window of the blond family, never the centre of her own life, always rejecting herself, and her life transformed into a gigantic peep show (Bannerji "The Other Family" 144).

   on collectivity:

Hermia asks Kae: "Do you mean that individuals must gather their identity from all the generations that touch them — past and future, no matter how slightly? Do you mean that an individual is not an individual at all, but a series of individuals — some of whom come before her, some after her? (*Disappearing Moon Cafe* 189)

The more ears I am able to hear with, the farther I see the plurality of meaning and the less I lend myself to the illusion of a single message (Minh-ha 30).

Endnotes

1. " 'What's the difference?' as if I cared? Or yes, I mean it, help me see?" (Minh-ha 84).

2. Selfish in the sense that my self needs this, needs to flesh out some of the (self —) absences in my canadian education/training.

3. "As Paulo Freire shows so well in *The Pedagogy of the Oppressed*, the true focus of revolutionary change is never merely the oppressive situations which we seek to escape, but that piece of the oppressor which is planted deep within each of us and which knows only the oppressor's tactics, the oppressor's relationships" (Lorde 123). Just how much have i internalized?

4. There is more action south of the border; as early as 1945, one can find Jade Snow Wong's book *Fifth Chinese Daughter*. Amy Ling's book *Between Worlds: Women Writers of Chinese Ancestry* is very informative about historical chinese american texts. Contemporary anthologies of asian american women's writing include *Forbidden Stitch, Home to Stay, Making Waves* and *Ikon 9*.

5. Read that statement in a matter-of-fact tone; earlier, i might have said that as a complaint; after so much repetition, it just becomes a given.

6. I have not yet been able to get a hold of the book.

7. Amy Tan's *Kitchen God's Wife* and Maxine Hong Kingston's *Woman Warrior* are other examples of this.

8. "On the one hand, I play into the Saviour's hands by concentrating on authenticity, for my attention is numbed by it and diverted from other,

important issues; on the other hand, I do feel the necessity to return to my so-called roots, since they are the fount of my strength, the guiding arrow to which i constantly refer before heading for a new direction" (Minh-ha 89). Lau avoids both; she does not state that her "roots" are a fount of strength but neither does she get diverted from those other important issues.

[9.] I omit Harris's association of *Obasan* with negative silences because i think her silences are much more complex than that. See Lim's article, page 303.

[10.] "Hybridity is never simply a question of the admixture of pre-given identities or essences. Hybridity is the perplexity of the living as it interrupts the representation of the fullness of life; it is an instance of iteration, in the minority discourse, of the time of the arbitrary sign — 'the minus of the origin' — through which all forms of cultural meaning are open to translation because their enunciation resists totalization" (Bhabha 314).

Bibliography

Asian Women United, eds. *Ikon 9: Without Ceremony*, 2nd Series, No. 9, 1988.

Asian Women United of California, eds. *Making Waves*. Boston: Beacon Press, 1989.

Bannerji, Himani. "The Other Family." *Other Solitudes*. Linda Hutcheon and Marion Richmond, eds. Toronto: Oxford University Press, 1990, pp. 141-152.

Bhabha, Homi. "DissemiNation." in *Nation and Narration*. Homi Bhabha, ed. New York: Routledge, 1990, pp. 291-322.

Brand, Dionne. *No Language is Neutral*. Toronto: Coach House Press, 1990.

Chan, Anthony. *Gold Mountain*. Vancouver: New Star Books, 1983.
Chang, Ana. "Untitled." *Capilano Review*, 2nd Series, 1991, pp. 66-67.

Chong, Denise. "The Concubine's Children" in *Many-Mouthed Birds*, Bennett Lee and Jim Wong-Chu, eds. Vancouver: Douglas & McIntyre, 1991, pp. 59-78.

Chong, Denise. Review of *Disappearing Moon Cafe* in *Quill & Quire*, No. 56, May 1990, p. 23.

Fung, Richard. "Multiculturalism Reconsidered" in *Yellow Peril Reconsidered*, Paul Wong, ed. Vancouver: On Edge On the Cutting Edge Productions Society, 1990, pp. 17-19.

"Seeing Yellow" in *Fuse*, Winter 1991, pp. 18-21.

Gagnon, Monika, ed. "Panel Discussion" in *Fuse*, Fall 1991, pp. 48-49.

Gill, Lakshmi. "Immigrant Always" in *Shakti's Words*, Diane McGifford and Judith Kearns, eds. Toronto: TSAR, 1990, p. 33.

Goh, Maggie. "I'm Just Me: Adrienne Clarkson" in *Between Worlds*, Maggie Goh and Craig Stephenson, eds. Oakville: Rubicon, 1989, pp. 91-100.

Gunew, Sneja. "Migrant Women Writers: Who's on Whose Margins?" in *Gender, Politics and Fiction: 20th Century Australian Women's Novels*, Carole Ferrier, ed. St. Lucia, Queensland: University of Queensland, 1985, pp. 163-178.

Harris, Mason. "Broken Generations in *Obasan*" in *Canadian Literature*, No. 127, 1990, pp. 41-57.

Ismail, Jam. *Diction Air*. *Contemporary Verse 2*, 11.2-3, 1988, pp. 37-42.

from *Scared Texts*. Bennett Lee and Jim Wong-Chu, eds., *Many-Mouthed Birds*, Vancouver: Douglas & McIntyre, 1991, pp. 124-135.

Ismail, Jam. *Sexions*. Kitsilano: np, 1984.

Ito, Sally. "Foreigners" in *Dandelion*, No. 16, 1989, pp. 60-62.

Jew, Anne. "Everyone Talked Loudly in Chinatown" in Bennet Lee and Jim Wong- Chu, eds. *Many-Mouthed Birds*, Vancouver: Douglas & McIntyre, 1991, pp. 22-27.

Jones, Manina. "The Avenues of Speech and Silence: Telling Difference in Joy Kogawa's *Obasan*" in *Theory Between the Disciplines*, Martin Kreiswirth and Mark Cheetham, eds. Ann Arbor: University of Michigan Press, 1990, pp. 213-229.

Kiyooka, Roy. "We Asian North Americanos" in *West Coast Review: The Asian-Canadian and the Arts*, No. 16, 1981, pp. 15-17.

Kogawa, Joy. *Itsuka.* Toronto: Viking, 1992.

> *Obasan.* Markham: Penguin, 1981.

> "Some Random Thoughts From a Novel in Progress" in *Visible Minorities and Multiculturalism: Asians in Canada,* Victor Ujimoto and Gordon Hirabayashi, eds. Toronto: Butterworths, 1980, pp. 323-328.

Kwa, Lydia. "Locating the Legend" in *Matrix,* No. 30, 1990, pp. 40.

> "Travelling Time" in *Contemporary Verse 2,* 12.4, 1990, pp. 34-37.

Lai, Larissa. "Glory" in *Capilano Review,* 2nd Series, 1991, p. 17.

> "Trap II" in *Contemporary Verse 2,* 14.2, 1991, p. 29.

Laiwan. "Savage" in *Capilano Review,* 2nd Series, 1991, pp. 112-119.

> "Ubiquitous China" in Paul Wong, *op. cit.,* pp. 40-41.

Lau, Evelyn. "Getting Heard" in *Prairie Fire,* No. 12, 1991, pp. 88-92.

> *Runaway.* Toronto: Harper Collins, 1989.

> "A Transient Ascension" in *This Magazine,* 24.1, 1990, pp. 36-39.

> *You Are Not Who You Claim.* Victoria: Press Porcepic, 1990.

Lee, Bennett and Jim Wong-chu, eds. *Many-Mouthed Birds.* Vancouver: Douglas & McIntyre, 1991.

Lee, Sky. "Broken Teeth" in *West Coast Review: The Asian-Canadian and the Arts,* No. 16, 1981, pp. 15-17.

> *Disappearing Moon Cafe.* Vancouver: Douglas & McIntyre, 1990.

Lim, Shirley Geok-lin, Mayumi Tsutakawa and Margarita Donnelly, eds. *The Forbidden Stitch.* Corvallis, Oregon: Calyx Books, 1989.

Lim, Shirley Geok-lin. "Japanese American Women's Life Stories: Maternality in Monica Sone's *Nisei Daughter* and Joy Kogawa's *Obasan*" in *Feminist Studies,* No. 16, 1990, pp. 288-312.

Ling, Amy. *Between Worlds: Women Writers of Chinese Ancestry*. New York: Pergamon Press, 1990.

"I'm Here: An Asian American Woman's Response" in *New Literary History*, No. 19, 1987, pp. 151-160.

Lorde, Audre. "Age, Race, Class and Sex: Women Redefining Difference" in *Sister Outsider*. Trumansburg, New York: Crossing Press, 1984.

Marlatt, Daphne. "musing with mothertongue" *in the feminine*, Ann Dybikowski *et al*, eds. Edmonton: Longspoon Press, 1985, pp. 171-174.

Martindale, Kathleen. "Power, Ethics, and Polyvocal Feminist Theory" in *Contemporary Verse 2*, 11.2-3, 1988, pp. 54-65.

Mathur, Ashok. "The Hyphenation of Identity" in *NACOI Forum*, August 1989, p. 5.

Minh-ha, Trinh. "The Plural Void: Barthes and Asia" in *Sub-stance,* No. 36, 1982, pp. 41-50.

Woman Native Other. Bloomington: Indiana University Press, 1989.

Morrison, Sheila. "Author Evelyn Lau: One Step at a Time" in *Newest Review*, June-July 1990, pp. 37-39.

Ng, Taien. "Shun-Wai." in *Out of Place*, Ven Begamudre and Judith Krause, eds. Regina: Coteau Books, 1991.

Ng, Winnie. "Immigrant Women: the Silent Partners of the Women's Movement" in *Still Ain't Satisfied*, M. Fitzgerald, C. Guberman, M. Wolf, eds. Toronto: Women's Press, 1982.

Onodera, Midi. "A Displaced View" in Paul Wong, *op. cit.*, pp. 28-31.

Persky, Stan. "*Itsuka* Pales in *Obasan*'s Shadow" in The *Globe and Mail*, March 28, 1992, p. C8.

Philip, Marlene Nourbese. *She Tries Her Tongue her silence softly breaks*. Charlottetown: Ragweed Press, 1989.

Redekop, Magdalene. "The Literary Politics of the Victim" in *Canadian Forum*, No. 68, 1989, pp. 14-17.

Redl, Carol. "Tender Love Story Burdened by Political Wrangling" in the *Edmonton Journal*, March 1, 1992, p. D7.

Scott, Gail. *Spaces Like Stairs*. Toronto: Women's Press, 1989.

Srivastava, Aruna. "Imag(in)ing Racism: South Asian Canadian Women Writers" in *Fuse*, Fall 1991, pp. 26-34.

Tompkins "Sentimental Power" in *The New Feminist Criticism*, Elaine Showalter, ed., pp. 156-157

Watanabe, Sylvia and Carol Bruchac, eds. *Home To Stay*. Greenfield Center, New York: Greenfield Review Press, 1990.

Wilson, David. Review of *Runaway* in *Quill & Quire*, No. 55, December 1989, p. 28.

Wong, Nellie. "Asian American Women, Feminism and Creativity" in *Conditions: Seven 3*, 1981, pp. 177-185.

Wong, Paul, ed. *Yellow Peril Reconsidered*. Vancouver: On Edge On the Cutting Edge Productions Society, 1990.

Wong, Rita. Review of *Disappearing Moon Cafe* in *West Coast Line*, No. 24, 1990, pp. 135-137.

Yamada, Mitsuye. "Invisibility is an Unnatural Disaster: Reflections of an Asian American Woman" in *This Bridge Called My Back*, Cherrie Moraga and Gloria Anzaldua, eds. Watertown: Persephone Press, 1981.

Yee, May. "Nei um lung, ma? (Aren't you cold?)" in *Fireweed*, No. 30, 1990, pp. 62-64.

"Out of the Silence: 'Voices of Chinese Canadian Women' " in *Resources for Feminist Research*, No. 16.1, 1987, pp. 15-16.

Yoon, Jean. "The Conversation of Birds" in *Fireweed*, No. 30, 1990, pp. 58-61.

Yoon, Jin-me. "(Inter)reference Part I, (Im)permanent (Re)collection" in Paul Wong, *op cit.*, p. 49.

Carol Talbot

An interview with CAROL TALBOT

It's important to write from your soul

SILVERA: I want to talk about growing up here in Canada. First, where were you born?

TALBOT: I was born in 1940 in Windsor, Ontario, and I lived there until I finished high school at eighteen.

SILVERA: So what was it like growing up in the '40s and '50s as a young Black child?

TALBOT: I think you know you are Black as early as you can remember because you've been labelled in the society, especially when you start going to school, and kids call you "nigger" and there's nothing you can do about it. I grew up sort of on the edge of the Black community. The Baptist church was the one our family went to, and then a few blocks away was the British Methodist Episcopal and the African Methodist Episcopal Church. The community was centred around the church, so a lot of the Black kids went to similar schools.

THE OTHER WOMAN

Now the school I went to, as I said, it was on the outside, so there were Black kids in the school but not a lot.

SILVERA: What does that mean "the outside"?

TALBOT: Well, there were streets where there were a lot of Black people and ours wasn't — it was maybe a couple of blocks from that. We'd walk to church — and the church was where the Black community lived — but the school I went to was going in the other direction from downtown. It was very multicultural, a lot of European immigrants. I remember there were a lot of Italians and Jewish kids in my school. A lot of our social life had to do with church. We went every Sunday to Sunday school. It was a three-hour ordeal.

SILVERA: So basically the church played a very central role in your life?

TALBOT: It was very important because it was the community. Those were the role models that I saw: the church people, good people, but very few were educated. When I was growing up all I remember is that there was one doctor that we went to — like all the Black people went to the Black doctor, *(laughter)* and there was a Black dentist. These were accomplishments that we revered in the community. They'd be like folk heroes, on the one hand, breaking the ground sort of thing. You could count them on one hand, the Black professionals. I don't think there was a lawyer. But we respected the people like the deacons in the church and so on. It didn't matter what they did as work — you knew the work-world didn't reflect people's status as human beings. There was one police officer in the church and he had high standing.

SILVERA: Did you come from a large family?

TALBOT: Not my immediate family. The natural children are just myself and my children. My brother, who is actually a cousin, was adopted in our family. He was my mother's sister's son. Later, my parents adopted three other girls, but that was after I left home.

SILVERA: So who were these kids? Where did they come from?

TALBOT: From Children's Aid. To this day I have this ingrained thing: family takes care of family. And I'm distressed because a lot of the forces around us now work against that — your friends even, or my own daughter, she doesn't have my attitude. What did I do wrong? *(laughter)*

The old people, they weren't in homes. My grandfather had a stroke and my grandmother took care of him. Then my grandmother lived with one of her daughters. Black people lived in the extended family sort of thing, taking care of people. In our family part of the Sunday ritual was old people. We would go visit my great-grandmother, my grandparents and other old people, like great-uncles. I don't really know what relation they were, we called them uncles or aunts. So it's sort of instilled in me. Anyway, I have a real respect for how my parents cared about old people, instead of expecting the system to take care of our problems rather than the family taking care of our problems. I remember my mother going down the street with soup for somebody who was sick and that sort of stuff.

The church meant a lot to me because it was a connection to the roots even though it's a distorted connection. But the spirit wasn't distorted, and there were certain rich things, like when you sing in a Black church and the people are all in harmony. *(laughter)* And they don't read music, but they sing, and it's joyful to hear that kind of music. That kind of music still speaks to me.

SILVERA: What do you mean by this "distorted connection"?

TALBOT: Well, my view has changed. I don't go to a church. I think Black people adopted the Christian, patriarchal perspective without thinking it through first.

SILVERA: Tell me about the role of books, storytelling and reading in your family.

TALBOT: My mother had about a grade eleven education. My father had completed high school and did very well, but because of racism in society he couldn't get employed in a factory when he finished school. My mother worked as housekeeper in white families, but she told us stories and all the nursery rhymes and fairy tales.

I always loved reading, I grew up with the love of books. My dad read more intellectual sort of stuff and religious stuff. My mother always encouraged us to read. She used to have to make rules, like we couldn't read before breakfast, *(laughter)* and the worst punishment she could do was deprive me of reading for a few hours.

SILVERA: What kind of books were around? Was the Bible very prevalent and were there other books?

TALBOT: There were other books too. There were a lot of paperbacks that we weren't supposed to read. In those days paperbacks weren't what they are today. That's where you could get spicy stuff, nothing like what you read now. When parents were away, we'd sneak and read these books. *(laughter)* But mostly it was books from the library.

SILVERA: When did you publish your first book?

TALBOT: My first book was published in 1977.

SILVERA: And that was?

TALBOT: It was called *Anne-Marie Weems: Fugitive Girl of Fifteen*. I co-wrote it with Georgia Boyd. It is the story of a young girl who was born in Maryland in 1853. Her family had been sold into slavery. One story tells of her journey to Canada and her determination to be free! The book was done in comic strip form, to attract young readers.

SILVERA: What inspired you to do that? I thought it was an important book, particularly at that time. As I recall, there wasn't a lot of literature available about Black Canadian children.

TALBOT: Well, that's what inspired me because there wasn't anything. When I was growing up in the '70s there was very, very little, and when I was going through my period of Black identity I realized there was nothing for young people. I had just moved to Parry Sound during the Martin Luther King era, and I was reading a lot of stuff which rapidly raised my consciousness and self-pride.

SILVERA: Why were you living in Parry Sound?

TALBOT: That's where I moved to when I got married. *(laughter)*

SILVERA: How old were you?

TALBOT: Let's see, from about the age of twenty-three to thirty-one. That was a significant time in my life because of the separation too. Then in 1972, at thirty-two, I started working in the Human Rights Commission. This was a time when a lot of Black people were coming into Canada, Toronto was changing its face, and that was when somebody convinced me Egypt was Black, and I started to read. I started to educate myself in Black history, and I went through a period where I didn't want to look at white people — it bothered me just seeing them. *(laughter)* It wasn't a really good time to get angry, not when you're working in the Human Rights Commission. I had a few adventures there. *(laughter)* That didn't go over too well. *(laughter)* But it was important to me. I started to write poetry, recapture myself, and got some affirmation from people about my writing.

SILVERA: When did you know you wanted to be a writer?

TALBOT: I didn't think of myself as a writer. I went to university, and I went into sciences, and in my second year went into English, but even then I didn't think of myself as a writer.

SILVERA: So it wasn't something that you knew or felt?

TALBOT: It was something I wanted to be and do, but I had been convinced for a long time that I wasn't a creative person.

SILVERA: By who? Teachers or ...?

TALBOT: I don't know. By the system, I think.

SILVERA: But somewhere you were convinced? *(laughter)*

TALBOT: Yeah, then I finally discovered that I'm really an off-the-wall person *(laughter)* and wildly creative. As a very young child, I remember wanting to be like the son. I wanted to be the person who was going to be outstanding in the family. I was going to be an achiever, and I think, you know, when I got separated it was sort of zoom! — the elastic went back and I had to start finding who I was, not who I'd been programmed to be.

SILVERA: Were you separated at the time you wrote your second book, *Growing Up Black in Canada?*

TALBOT: Yes, and the book is sort of autobiographical.

SILVERA: Talk to me about that. What inspired you to write that book?

TALBOT: At that time I had been writing poetry, a lot of poetry, and I had a lot of stuff in my drawer. *(laughter)*

SILVERA: Don't we all ...

TALBOT: I went through a period when I had quit the Human Rights Commission. I was unemployed for a while, and I wrote a lot, a lot of different things. My daughter was going to visit her dad and I didn't know what to do with myself. I then said to myself: I'm going to write, I'm going to make a studio. I remember doing this. I fixed up this room that I never ever did write in. *(laughter)* I wrote on the kitchen table and I went for walks and I gathered wildflowers and I decided I had to get rid of the anger. The things about racism and stuff, eh? I didn't want to make that my life-work, writing about that, so I decided I would write a letter to my father. At that time he was with the Federal Human Rights Commission and I thought he would understand. So that's how the book started. It was going to be a letter.

SILVERA: Ah, I see. It certainly did change.

TALBOT: And then I was sharing it with a friend, and reading parts of it to her, and she said, "This is a book, why don't you write a book?" And so I kept going, kept writing. It wasn't a letter my dad really appreciated, you know. *(laughter)* When I gave him parts of it to read I got a poem back about my European ancestors that I shouldn't forget. *(laughter)*

SILVERA: How did the publishing happen? Did you have a difficult time finding a publisher?

TALBOT: No, it just happened! I just happened to be in the Underground Railroad one day, and I picked up a *Contrast* newspaper and saw a Williams-Wallace book launching. I didn't even know whose it was. I thought: oh, here's a publisher. I sent her a query letter, a little sample of the book, and that's how that happened. She called me and said come on down.

SILVERA: Great.

TALBOT: I had to rewrite it, though. You know that whole process. *(laughter)*

SILVERA: In *Growing Up Black* you talk a lot about going through school in Windsor. For example, in the book you talk about the "nigger call." What do you mean by that?

TALBOT: Well, in those days we were called coloured, eh? And you didn't want to be coloured because it was a derogatory term. Then, of course, in school we weren't taught any of our own history, or if we got any history it was about the Underground Railroad, and there wasn't much of that, so it was about being slaves, eh? So as a child you didn't want to be associated with coloured. Not that I wanted to be white. I think my mother was trying to be white and trying to get us as close as they could because it was painful being Black, you didn't get anywhere. I remember not wanting to be associated with the negative connotations, and so I didn't want to look poor. So, for example, I didn't even want to take brown bread to school. I wanted Wonderbread and it had to be wrapped in wax paper not in bread wrapper, which the poor kids had their sandwiches wrapped in. I remembered in school we didn't have any literature at all except *Black Sambo.* I remember that in public school.

SILVERA: How was that for you as a Black child?

TALBOT: I liked the book, but I didn't want anybody to know I liked it because of the pancakes. *(laughter)* It was in the back of my kindergarten room.

SILVERA: Why didn't you want anyone to know you liked it?

TALBOT: I didn't want anybody to associate me with Sambo. We didn't want to be called Sambo, I didn't want anybody to think I identified myself with Sambo. I was six years old at the time.

SILVERA: I can clearly understand. What is your feeling about those kinds of books within institutions today? Do you think books like *Black Sambo,* like *Huckleberry Finn,* should they be on library shelves or banned?

TALBOT: No, I don't believe in banning them. What I believe in is amplifying the shelves with balance. If you're going to have these books, then we need to have authors like Alice Walker, James

Baldwin and Black Canadian authors. That balances it. And if you're going to teach *Oliver Twist* or Charles Dickens, for example, teach Oliver Twist the same time as you're teaching the treatment of Blacks because they treated the whites badly too. In other words, it's not censorship we need, it's full education. My perspective is: if you mis-educated me, if you're mis-educating Black children, you're mis-educating your own children and a whole society.

SILVERA: What role would you say your father had in your upbringing? What influence?

TALBOT: He had a really strong role in the community. He was a community activist. I remember him going to sit-ins. He was on something they called the interracial council in Windsor, and so he had these white friends and Black people too — a group of interracial people who were trying to make changes in society. I remember my mother being upset because she didn't like him to be standing out. To her, it was unwelcome publicity. She always took public opinion polls, you know what I mean? *(laughter)*

SILVERA: Are both your parents second-, third-generation Canadians?

TALBOT: Yeah. I think it was my father's grandparents that came from the States. I know my great-grandmother was born in Canada. On my mother's mother's side, there's a fair amount of Native Indian in our family. My great-great-grandfather arrived at the Detroit-Windsor border in 1841.

SILVERA: And they settled in Windsor?

TALBOT: No, actually my dad came from Dresden. My mother came from Amherstburg. You know where Dresden is? Dresden is west of the Chatham area, the Buxton area.

SILVERA: Yes, all of those were originally Black communities ...

TALBOT: Yeah, and Dresden is where *Uncle Tom's Cabin* is supposed to be. Amherstburg is just south of Windsor. There are a lot of Black people around there in Harrow and Shrewsbury. Those are really old communities.

SILVERA: Are those communities still there?

TALBOT: Oh yeah.

SILVERA: I just love the chapter "Only Your Hairdresser Knows for Sure." It's quite humorous and yet bitter sweet, there is so much herstory there.

TALBOT: Yeah, we could still be writing it, eh? *(laughter)*

SILVERA: Tell me about writing that piece.

TALBOT: Hair is, well ... it was more of a problem than skin colour for me. You could have light skin, but your hair could give you away, eh? *(laughter)* When I went away to university my roommates didn't know that I was Black. Cause I had my hair straightened. But hair was — when I was growing up I remembered my mother always complaining about hair. She was always trying to control it. She didn't want us to look like Topsy. Do you know who Topsy is?

SILVERA: A little girl?

TALBOT: Yeah, in *Uncle Tom's Cabin* there's Topsy. In those days little girls that had really kinky hair, their mothers would put it in braids, eh? My mother didn't like being really Black, so she'd put it in two braids or four braids, and we have very tough scalps, *(laughter)* and I got pulled a lot, eh? Pulled so it could look neat and look straight because it's all pulled in. When we got to be eleven or so then she started to straighten our hair with the hot comb, eh? And that was not fun.

SILVERA: Yeah, I know. I was there many times.

TALBOT: You've been through that too, eh? *(laughter)* You know white people are really naïve. They don't know that. I remember in Windsor all the high schools had swimming pools — you had to take swimming. Then you'd have to be in school all day with your hair in its natural state. I could have been a really good swimmer in high school, but I didn't want to get my hair wet. *(laughter)* It was like a demon that would ambush you.

SILVERA: I felt at home reading that section. I remembered my own swimming classes. I never learned to swim in high school because of hair! I didn't want to jump into that pool, you know, and come out looking like a totally different person, to be forced to explain the texture of my hair, the sudden change in length. *(laughter)*

What other effects do you think that a Black Canadian upbringing has had on your writing?

TALBOT: It seems to me that a lot of us go through stages in our writing, and for me the early stage was that angry stage where you're dealing with the racism in various forms. Then there's the response to social issues related to racism because that comes out in your writing too. South Africa ...

And I think too the spirituality side of it — I'm still a very spiritual person although my parents don't recognize it. *(laughter)* I know that the spirituality, the sense of spirit they have in the Black church, I still have it. Maybe I'll call it by different names now, and I'll transfer it differently, but it's very much a part of me, although it's getting very feminist now. It's getting more feminist as I read more and I'm beginning to get angry again. I feel the patriarchal system has been detrimental to women. That is really scary. In that way my thinking has sort of shifted. So I'm still very much interested in spirituality, but it's moving in a different direction now. I'm also concerned about the kind of trip that our ancestors have been on with regard to religion.

SILVERA: You mean in terms of Christianity?

TALBOT: Yeah, and all messed up with the sexism and patriarchy and stuff.

SILVERA: In *Growing Up Black in Canada* I also found the food section most interesting. It seemed that through food, the Afro-Caribbean connection, the African-Canadian connection and the African from the motherland solidified. Did you go through a lot changes with food and its cultural meaning?

TALBOT: Well yes, but I went through this transition from the marriage to a white man, into the white society. My cooking changed. I learned not to put garlic in the meat, not to season the meat — like just have plain, bare-naked, roast beef. *(laughter)* You know, so not so much spices. And then when I came back out of Parry Sound into Toronto, where all the West Indians were seasoning food, the food tasted like home. And meeting different men and cooking the English way wasn't going down too good either. I didn't know of West Indian recipes so I had to learn ... So I've been through changes with the food.

SILVERA: At the end of your book, there's a section on diaspora where you state that Canadians have a long-term identity crisis. What were you referring to? Is it white Canadian versus U.S. identity? Or Black Canadian, First Nations, other non-white people born here who have this identity crisis? Then you go on to ask about do we as Blacks have this cultural confusion also ... So tell me about it.

TALBOT: I wrote a play about that. I call it "Canada Who?" It's all a spoof on not knowing who we are. And I have Canada on trial for its attitudes. In this play Canada is personified as a white male with a wife and a boy and a girl, eh? *(laughter)* I had a lot of fun in that play. I brought in Abe Lincoln and they won't let him testify cause he's American. I have John Brown coming in. But we're really okay.

How can I explain it? I went through a period of questioning identity when I was in my thirties — I felt like I didn't belong anywhere: I didn't feel Canadian because I was Black and we hadn't been acknowledged, I wasn't West Indian, but I tried to be adopted. The conclusion I came to at that time is that spiritually, I'm African. People are looking at me, and they don't see me as an African, but I know in my soul I'm African, eh? Then moving along in time, now I feel this country is my land, like the metaphors, the images of this country I'm familiar with, you know what I mean? I'm more in tune with the imagery that the Aboriginal people would use, perhaps African in Africa, because I know the plant life here, I know the animals, the weather. I believe there needs to be more dialogue with the Native people.

I was so happy to see the Commonwealth Games opening.

Did you see the opening of the Olympics in Norway? In the Norway one they used the Laplanders, who are the ancient peoples of that land. They were acknowledged. It was a major tribute. This 1994 Commonwealth Games, on the west coast, used the story of creation, a west coast Native story, so what they were saying is that this is our imagery in Canada. When I saw it I just said out loud: it's about time. Acknowledge where the soul of this country really comes from. That's where our salvation will be.

SILVERA: About the identity and soul, you talked about Native people. What about that Black Canadian identity that gets so lost?

TALBOT: It's really been lost and it's still lost. Like Black Canadians are still lost, a lot of us. It's almost like we got flooded by West Indians, and I just recently talked to ...

SILVERA: What does that mean that Black Canadians have been flooded by West Indians?

TALBOT: Well, the Black Canadian community, in a lot of ways it's still struggling to get education, to believe people can get education, to believe in themselves. They're still trying to be white, trying to get whiter. Do you know what I mean? In the Canadian Black community it's getting better, but there was resentment against the West Indians years ago because a lot of them came in with more education and could get better jobs, more recognition, that way. Black Canadians still don't know their history.

SILVERA: But why is that resentment against West Indians-Caribbean people rather than against the white Canadian establishment?

TALBOT: Because they have been well-conditioned. There is an old saying: you don't take on the masses. It's easier to point fingers and criticize your own people. You don't want to upset the white folks, you know!

SILVERA: In colonial history we've been taught that we're all so different: the Black Canadians are different from the Caribbean people, and the Caribbean people are so different from the ones born in Africa, so different from the Blacks born in the United States, Britain, Europe ...

TALBOT: Caribbean people, you see, and the Africans from the continent have come in with a very powerful culture, with their own music that has evolved over generations and their own foods. And ours is so diluted, you know. What little we had is in the church, and the church is not being looked on kindly. The food is not as distinctive. So it's sort of like being jealous of the better cousins, you know what I mean?

SILVERA: Well, I hope you're going to be writing about these things in future works. *(laughter)* But tell me, do you continue to work full-time?

TALBOT: Yes, as teacher. I teach English in high school and I do some work with the Ontario Arts Council Writers' Program, which I enjoy.

SILVERA: You also still have a growing family?

TALBOT: My youngest daughter has just finished university.

SILVERA: Do you have a special time now that you use to write?

TALBOT: No. I write when the spirit attacks me. This past year I haven't done a lot of writing. I do a lot of journal writing. I wrote a piece for an anthology and I've sent some pieces out to journals.

SILVERA: Are you aware of your books being used in any educational institution?

TALBOT: Not that I know of. People hear about it, people tell me that they've heard about it, or recommended it, so I don't really know where it has been. *(laughter)* Being in London, you're sort of off the beaten track here. Also, a Black librarian told me a few months ago that we didn't have a large enough Black population that would support my book or other Black writers. I made the point that it had nothing to do with how many Black children you have in school. It's important to have diverse literature.

SILVERA: So it's not being used at all?

TALBOT: One teacher who knew me wanted to use it, so she did.

SILVERA: But is it up to the individual teachers?

TALBOT: No. Mostly you use prescribed books.

SILVERA: I mean, do you use it at all?

TALBOT: Not as a textbook.

SILVERA: So where does that come from, when you use it as a text? How would that work in the high school system?

TALBOT: If you wanted to use it you'd have to get an agreement with the head of your department that it would be acceptable for whatever purposes.

SILVERA: Have you tried that? I think it's an important book about Black Canadian life that should be in the system.

TALBOT: I don't like to push myself that way, you know what I mean? So, no, I haven't. But kids use it as a resource a lot. They do independent studies or research. I know in our library it's hardly ever in.

SILVERA: And they have what, one copy? *(laughter)*

TALBOT: One or two. I don't know if it's even in all the schools. People are strange, you know. White people are funny. You know, even the school I was at, I don't know if either of the two male heads that I was under ever read my book.

SILVERA: But they know you have written?

TALBOT: Yeah, we had a book launching at the school and no comments, you know.

SILVERA: Do you remember any book reviews?

TALBOT: My publisher told me about one. It was mostly positive.

SILVERA: Do you have any connection to the feminist movement in Canada? What do you think of such a movement?

TALBOT: Well, I don't know overall about what it's doing in Canada.

SILVERA: Do you have any connection to the feminist movement?

TALBOT: *(laughter)* Yeah. A lot, in direct and indirect ways. I have served on the Status of Women Committee with the teachers on and off for a number of years. I've been going to the Michigan Women's Music Festival for the past four years.

SILVERA: Has that music festival changed you or helped you in any way in terms of your relationship to feminism?

TALBOT: Yeah. I'm really on a personal study of women's spirituality. Coming from the church and being a church person and then moving away from that is not easy — you can't just wipe out the symbols you have to replace them, and then I thought: well, that's interesting. Now it's sort of like re-educating in that whole area, like learning about the history of the goddess and the role that plays in Black thinking. In our history I think that we need to know it, and it's a whole area we're not being taught.

SILVERA: I just lost my thought. I was going to ask you something else about the feminist movement. Are you a feminist?

TALBOT: Yes.

SILVERA: Okay, fine. Go on from there, define what your feminism is...

TALBOT: I believe that the feminine energy is on the rise in the world and that it must rise. We have to counteract a lot of evils, and the only way is through feminist thinking, to bring balance. We're way over balance in patriarchy. It's destroying our world and killing our children. And I don't know if it's too late, but I like to be an optimist. I believe that the war is a really interesting one — it's not in the way that men understand because it's not guns, it's not maybe even on the conscious level. And I've come to believe, from the work I've done and the reading I've done, that what I do on the inner-level is really significant. I tell my students who want to be writers that theirs is a sacred task, and I try to explain it doesn't matter if you've published or not. Most of you will never be published, but the fact that you're doing this is very important because you're struggling with inner stuff, eh?

SILVERA: Did I ask you if you had a special time and a place to write?

TALBOT: I do have a special place. I'm not a programmed person that does stuff at specific times.

SILVERA: Earlier you said you were not a disciplined writer ...

TALBOT: I could sit down and I could write ...

SILVERA: Do you love writing?

TALBOT: I get captivated by it.

SILVERA: So you do love it?

TALBOT: I do. It's very important.

SILVERA: So what keeps you then from carving out a space, to say this is what I'm doing and I'm doing it now?

TALBOT: Well, if you're really busy with other stuff, you get crowded, eh?

SILVERA: Well, what's the other stuff?

TALBOT: Like school work. Also, I do a lot of knitting.

SILVERA: Are those things really important to you?

TALBOT: Yeah, they are important.

SILVERA: In what way? What do they do to you? Is this a creative process?

TALBOT: They're really important — like I'm sitting here looking at this wall hanging that is just about finished.

SILVERA: Well, tell me about that. You know this reminds me of Alice Walker's essay "In Search of Our Mother's Garden," where she speaks of the unsung creativity of our grandmothers and great-grandmothers, creativity such as painting, writing, which was never fully realized because they were always worrying for the "man" and at times under extreme conditions. In her essay she goes on to say that, despite the odds, their creativity did come out in sewing, canning vegetables and fruits, making quilts.

TALBOT: It is important, it's like poetry to me. It's off-loom weaving where you just start with threads. You hang them, you might have a rough idea of what structure it's going to be — like this started with two rods and a circle — but you don't know how it will end. The yarn's passing through your hands and the colours — just as you're creating it, it evolves right in front of you. You don't know what you're going to do next until you do it. And then you say: okay this little section, or I'm gonna do this, and you just keep doing it, and you look back and you did it. I've been working on this one for over a year. It's called my prayer shawl, it's therapeutic, it grounds me to do it sometimes. I went out and I bought some hand-spun yarn to make a wall-hanging — it's still hanging down there — then I went to South Carolina and I picked up some shells on the beach, right? And my plan is someday it'll be in a wall-hanging because I'm going to unite the east and the west and the north and the south.

Then this summer I got captivated into a lot of reading about quilting, and it's really exciting. I had started to read this book of essays by bell hooks. Have you read her essay about quilting? Well, what happened was I started to read her, but I thought: I don't know if I want to read this bell hooks, she's pretty heavy. Then I thought: this is an important writer, and I'd like to read some of her stuff, but I put it down. Then I was looking through it one day, and there's this wonderful essay about quilting and the Black culture.

Weaving to me is women. I use weaving imagery in my writing. In the "Crystal Cave" she weaves light. And our history is woven as strands of time, so there's something with the yarn and the colours. I like hand-spun especially, and I like earth colours. You know, sometimes you're in touch with something and you don't know what it is, but you hang on to it cause you know it's important. The yarns fulfil a creative part of me. If I were going to high school now, I'd probably major in art and music and writing too, but back then they didn't have the courses they have now and the encouragement.

Silvera: This is all so true. Tell me what you're working on at this point.

Talbot: I'm working on a collection of poetry that deals with feminine imagery and the need to have the rise of a feminine consciousness because our children are being killed around the world in the name of religion. Some of my poems are about the state of our minds. It's about the mutilation of the Earth, hurting the Earth. So that's what I'm working on. But the work of getting published is different from the work of writing, eh?

SILVERA: What do you mean?

TALBOT: Well, it's natural to do the writing, but to market the material is not natural.

SILVERA: What do you mean by that? Do you mean you write either to market or give away as gifts?

TALBOT: Yes, and I write to give as gifts.

SILVERA: I just wonder, is there a distinction when you sit down to write?

TALBOT: If I sit down to write to market it sort of fizzles. It's like I'm trying to write something so somebody will publish it, but what I really feel is more important for me is to write whenever I'm compelled to write, and so I try to listen for that. I often write at night. That's when it's quiet and it hits me.

SILVERA: Who do you write for? Do you write for a particular audience? Do you write for yourself?

TALBOT: *Growing Up Black in Canada*, like I said earlier, was first an expression for my father. When I was actually shaping it and revising it I knew I was writing for a community, a Black community, with ordinary common people who wanted a book that was not scholarly or sociological. I wanted to write something that was readable. Presently when I write I don't think about audience. I just write and I think about who it's for after I write it. I believe it's important to write from your soul, and that's one of the reasons I'm happy to be teaching and not writing for a living.

I think that we might need to change our construct around what's valid as writing. If we're writing in the community, we're speaking for people that don't write. It's sort of the white, patriarchal syndrome to say you have to get it published and receive critical acclaim. For me, a community is important. Often I'm invited to read in a community setting and it feels good because you're interacting with people, community, and they hear your words — it means something there. The work is valid as printed material, but it is also valid orally. It would be nice to have a musician or someone to work with, to read with music or drums — that's the way poetry should be heard.

Bibliography

Walker, Alice. *In Search of Our Mothers' Gardens*. New York: Harcourt Brace Jovanovich Publishers, 1983.

Himani Bannerji

HIMANI BANNERJI
talks with
MAKEDA SILVERA
and DIONNE BRAND

Writing was not a decision

SILVERA: When you were working on your collection of poetry, *Doing Time*, what was going through your consciousness? I don't mean generally, I mean specifically, while working on the book.

BANNERJI: What was I thinking? Well, I was thinking what I'm still thinking ... it was 1982. But I never thought of it as a book — I just wrote. Makeda took the poems and brought them into print. And I wrote a poem as an introduction. She actually typed them up, and if she hadn't taken them away from me, I wouldn't have done it. The proof of the pudding is in the eating. It's twelve years today, I still haven't put together another poetry book.

Makeda, in answer to your question, what was going through my consciousness then is still going through today: the same feeling of being imprisoned somewhere, somehow. You haven't seen my other writing, but there's a long poem that came out in *Borderlines*, on Iraq, and it isn't that different from *doing time*.

BRAND: Unless I'm reading too much into the title of the book, *doing time*, you say it's a prison and much more than a prison. Is it the same now?

BANNERJI: Horrible experience. *(laughter)* Yes, of course. Obviously, what you write about is what you're living through. Anyway, it was about being in a prison, where I don't feel in touch with people — well, I do in a very brutal way. In this case, the personal is the brutal *(laughter)*, and I think the personal is the brutal continues in this new professionalization that I'm experiencing. It is now bloodless, in a much more regulated form because, as you say, it's bureaucracy. But the bureaucracy is manned. It is not like a machine by itself. People doing these things, in my case, are white male sociologists and their sociology is essentially saying to us, "Get out of the university. If you come in, it's going to be impossible for you. If you shut up, you can stay ... " in other words, if you're silent.

BRAND: What does that do to the work, like poetry, your writing?

BANNERJI: You can write, and I do write, I don't publish them, but I do write, what you write is, you know ...

BRAND: What kinds of things?

BANNERJI: About bloodletting *(laughter)* and violence, really. It is about violence. I don't know if you saw a piece I did in *Resources for Feminist Research — Returning the Gaze*. It is about violence and disassociation, which in part actually produces fantastic personality disorders or physiological-emotional disorders. You feel like you could kill, quite frequently, and you feel often that you are being killed.

SILVERA: Actually, that's quite interesting, isn't it? This rage, it's not different from the way ordinary working-class folks or street people feel, is it? I mean even with the M.A. and Ph.D. you actually feel imprisoned like the poor or the disenfranchised?

BANNERJI: But this is where I think that one can say that there is no safe place. This is where the notion that the social is bigger than little segments of places comes in, right? This is where you are in the street, in that sense where street goes right through and out, where this street of violence is not just street violence. If it were only street violence, you'd be safer. What it is really, Makeda, is a continual living with violence. You must feel it. I don't even think I'm speaking of only my experience.

SILVERA: Oh, definitely.

BANNERJI: It has taken the best of my Marxist self at times not to feel like really doing things that maybe in the long run wouldn't fetch me much but in the short run *(laughter)* would fetch me satisfaction.

BRAND: What are you writing now?

BANNERJI: I'm writing poems at times. I'm not writing as a project. I just write at times, about violence.

SILVERA: So they're immediate.

BANNERJI: They're immediate and they're historical. They're also about India, in the sense that I am not able to separate out violence from colonialism. For example, if I'm going to talk about racism in Canada and what we're going through, how can I not talk about it as a white settler colony? How can I not talk about what the so-called psyche of this nation is, without talking about the bedrock of blood on which it has been created and the bloodletting that doesn't stop from Oka to everything else?

To explain my life here, your life, or anybody's life writing or poetry or prose for that matter, how can we not speak to this sort of rarefied relations of violence that are the microcosm of the macrocosm, in each local space? Like in philosophy, they used to say a piece of gold is always gold. Well, the piece of violence has the same relations here as in other places. So, for example, my real interest in Palestine and what has happened to the Palestinian people can't be just cut off from what I feel about what is happening to us here. Nor can I cut off my experience and feeling of violence about India. For example, what is happening with hindu and muslim fundamentalism: thousands of people have been killed in the last few years, in the name of God, in the name of religion, mobilized by major political parties, welded to IMF-World Bank politics. That is also my violence, that is also my world. I can't say India is a better place. I can't say India is a safer place. I can't say that India is not working out in its own particular configuration the relations of international-national forms of violence of state, class, gender — international relations of violence that are happening everywhere.

Makeda, you had asked me earlier about how it is that one functions as an artist in this environment ...

SILVERA: Yes, as a writer, a critic and a teacher.

BANNERJI: The only thing I can say is that I cannot see that if I quit my job and went away, I would become an artist separately out there in the world somewhere. I have not been able to — but I'd like to if I could — find the world that is so safe that I can engage in my artistic occupation as classical artists do. Since I write about some muck and I live about muck and in muck too, that muck is not going to end. It hasn't ended in India, it hasn't ended here. It's never going to end if I get a job somewhere else, or I hustle for National Film Board, or I hustle for the state, or I hustle for shelter. And if I have to live in a money commodity market, I have to make a living. So I make a living in this very strange place, the university.

To some extent, it is my stubborn decision that our kids, and also good, white, working-class kids who are trying hard to sort of understand the world somehow, need help to do so. I want to help to make it happen even if grades mean nothing in the scheme of world affairs. I try and put forward what I can, from the margin. I don't ever want to be the centre because I don't really think I would be me. I'm physiologically incapable of being that anyway, and psychologically I could never do it. And I don't see the place where I would go and do my writing in an unencumbered fashion because the world is with me everywhere. I am in the world and this is what the world is. It's not a nice world anywhere. It's not a nice world in any organization, from the family to the university, to the street, to the workplace to everything else we do. It's riven with these violences.

SILVERA: So does this mean that it stops you from doing creative work, or the kind of creative work that you would like to do?

BANNERJI: No, because creative work — unfortunately, the context in which I learned to do it is in the context of my life. Even if you gave me a beautiful mansion somewhere on a island, I'm sure I would carry on being me and my preoccupations would be the same or my preoccupation would follow me there just the same as here. So I don't really see that I can run away.

SILVERA: Do you see the kind of work that we do or that you do as a South Asian woman different from, say, a white, middle-class writer who is not really politically active on a day-to-day basis — a person who can go off somewhere, to that 'place', to write fantasy and write about flowers?

BANNERJI: I love flowers. I wouldn't mind periodically having fantasies and writing about trees and flowers and so on ... but I can't do it and I don't want to. It's not just that I cannot do it: I see it as a deprivation. I just cannot do it.

SILVERA: And why is this?

BANNERJI: I think it is because my personal is indelibly political, and I don't know a time in my life when it wasn't so. I grew up in a family of lots of violence, and so in some sense politics was in my life, in the shape of family violence. Bigger and bigger forms of violences have entered my life, and I have made it my priority to fight that. So, yes, I do love flowers — it has not prevented me from loving flowers, trees, animals and children *(laughter)* — but I don't decide to write about things. This is where probably I'm different from you and other people: I don't decide to write about what I write, I write about what I feel drawn to write about. Now, if you did a retrospective of what I have written about, you'd find that it has to do with memory, history ...

SILVERA: I think that a lot of people from marginalized backgrounds write about memory, history. And about family ...

BANNERJI: And even with a middle-class background, I still write about memory and history because I'm also talking about the violence that

I saw at home. Nowhere have I seen a world where there were not relations of power, one way or another, manifested in the most grotesque ways — from the old age of my mother and the treatment that she was meted out, to my own upbringing, to my sister's upbringing, to everything else. There was money to eat, there were so-called good homes, but inside the good homes the lies that happened — which is why even now I cannot go with these people and talk about South Asian culture as being so wonderful. I can't romanticize the reality of that life. Perhaps middle-class white women here, and maybe non-white middle-class women in India, can get away and find a place where they feel they are really left at peace to write about whatever it is that they write about. I admire that they have found that place. Frankly, I haven't looked for it.

BRAND: In your introduction to *Returning the Gaze: Essays on Racism, Feminism and Politics,* I think you privilege what you call "critical writing" over creative writing. It seems to me you were talking about it in a particular context but generalized it. I can feel this — particularly being in the university with feminist professors who use the creative works of women of colour in their teaching in a particular way — in a way which short-changes that work by reading it as sociology or anthropology. However, that is the narrowest of contexts. Creative writing is critical writing as much as academic writing. Do you know what I mean?

BANNERJI: I do. And I think this is a very, very good issue you raised. Partly, the introduction was marked by the fact that I was in a struggle with this Toronto publishing company, which made me turn to Makeda at Sister Vision Press. After they solicited the manuscript, they sent me back a letter saying none of these people knew how to write. Really insulting terms in this letter. And basically what they were saying is: you guys don't know how to write, how to do intellectual, critical work. All you know how to do is emotional stuff, stick to experience. Talk about experience and then it's fine, we'll take that. But don't ever dare to submit theoretical and political work because you don't have the training.

BRAND: But they publish bell hooks.

BANNERJI: But that's how it is. We talked earlier about commoditizing and marketing. Some of her essays don't present very substantial problems to deal with, particularly in terms of serious analytical writing. Her first two books, I would say, were attempts to do so, but the essays that she has done since then have been occasional, and in some sense white people are quite happy to say, "Sorry we did such bad things to you," right? But to say more than that, to say that you are a very important critical analytical thinker, that's where the boundaries are drawn. So I think that, initially, my response was marked by my rage at being sort of told off by this publisher — and not on my behalf because it wasn't only me. I had only one piece in there. So in a way it was that anger that kind of brought that privileging of critical writing in.

I think that the other thing that I didn't talk about should be fleshed out, and that is that I have also seen a fair amount of anti-intellectualism developing within the popular movements, where analytical work is called "academic" work. This is the thing: everything in Canada is institutionalized, so intellectual work is not called intellectual work, it's called academic work, as though the university, the academe, is the only place where it has validity or where it can be done or thought through.

Most writers that we teach in Marxism, at least — until the Second World War period never had anything to do with the university. It takes years even now for people to annotate Gramsci, who wrote the *Prison Notebooks* without a library, sitting in a prison. But that didn't prevent Gramsci from using from Plato to Machiavelli to Marx and everything else to make sense of what happened in Italy. This kind of fit that used to exist between intellectuals and popular movements or communist movements — movements in those days were organized in a different way — seems to have undergone a severance in our time. Where there is not a rejoicing in the intellectuals of our movements ...

BRAND: But hasn't what you describe as happening in the university — the kind of professionalizing of teaching — hasn't that also happened to Marxism? It's not anti-intellectualism, but I think it's a view that Marxism in a sense has been bureaucratized.

BANNERJI: It has been bourgeoisized ...

BRAND: If you look at, for example, the Communist Party here — for many years, that was the whip that it held over other progressive movements. Academics too. That they knew best because they knew Marx. *(laughter)* So some of that shit is coming from somewhere ...

BANNERJI: I think that what I said — I'm trying to write about it, it needs to be fleshed out, and it is sort of like a pull-and-push situation — but it has come to a danger that we actually are saying that there is a cut-off between doing work at a theoretical level and an emotional-experiential level. I also think — since what we have discussed so far are the venues or sites of struggle — that I want to say that universities are not places cut off. The realms of theory writing are not realms cut off. The fact that some people get privileged in this kind of Cartesian form and some people get privileged as "the people of the body" and, of late, as "the people of emotion" ...

Feminism, in its own way has done a number on it too in the peculiar way it has used the notion of experience. Feminism has actually reduced experience to the immediacy of feelings and expressiveness rather than talking about experience as an attempt, as a way of consciously organizing, thinking through, what happened to you. There's a difference between, say, an impact on you and something you describe as your experience.

BRAND: Why it happened, how it happened.

BANNERJI: And even to name it. For a woman to say "a man beat me up" is different from her saying "I am suffering from patriarchy." If she names her experiences as patriarchal experience, she's already done a lot of thinking and processing of this daily life in a kind of organized, analytical fashion. As a teacher, I imagine that people who are anti-racists, Marxists, feminists — people at that site — would be able to use, what I'm saying. Maybe I will use what they are saying to develop my theorization. But then there is writing also to be done about the same matter in other ways in other places. So the boundaries are not so clearly defined, as if this is the only site. But it does bother me, and I think it is also a reaction on my part to being always, always typed "people of emotion."

It also bothers me to see, for example, younger people saying "I don't want to read this. I won't read *Capital* because it is too abstract and produced at a level that is not accessible." Well, if *Capital* isn't accessible, then I'll have to make myself accessible to *Capital*. *Capital* was not written in and for a university. It was written for working-class people. There were attempts in schools, classes, teachings, etcetera, within the context of the Communist movement to get people to read it. Even now in India, for example, in trade union schools they teach text out of Stalin. Now people don't like Stalin here and in many places, but in terms of people having to read, to stretch, to think, to rework, to do vocabularies, etcetera ... this is part of literacy training.

BRAND: Well, you see, that's so heavy because part of literacy training in America is television. It's synthesized to the narrowest, most shallow kind of expression, that is the culture. Part of it is also the visceral anti-communist response that one is taught living in Canada or the US, it is contained in that homogenizing, shallow-making training you receive from television, radio, advertising, etcetera. It's all about being able to synthesize very quickly what you must buy. Right? *(laughter)*

BANNERJI: I agree with you, and I personally think that that's why it has to be thought through more carefully. You've put your hand on it. But part of what I'm saying is — this is where part of my response came from because I do feel that these things are produced in the context of a movement, whether at the level of, let's say, reading Bernstein and Lenin or at the level of reading *Prison Notebooks* or reading the *Prison Letters* of George Jackson — ideas, politics, books, have to become people's things again.

What is lacking right now, I think, is a kind of general movement, a place for people to come together. This is something that I've really suffered from. If you ask what I've suffered from in the last many years, it is not the university per se. It is that fracturing of people's work. It damages our thinking. This is what begins to define my work here as theory. And then when I write a poem I am a poet. But really, what is it that I wrote in the introduction to *doing Time* that I didn't write in the introduction to *Returning the Gaze?*

That same anger, that same problem is mediated in a different kind of language, which brings you to prose or poetry. As someone who teaches at the university, I could never stop responding to things in other ways, where equal criticality can be brought to poetry, to short stories, without which theory has no body. This is why I have been unable to teach what they call "traditional" sociology. Because I can't do it without using poetry. I can't do without using novels.

SILVERA: I want to go back to *doing time* and this construct of the prison. Can you talk about that and whether in 1994-1995 you still see that construct in the same way?

BANNERJI: What I was saying about the construct of the prison relates to the state and other institutions and regulations, the fact that there is very little place to go in terms of organized politics, and there's huge organization from the top which basically tells you what to do. Whatever it is I thought was the prison has not disappeared. It has become, I think, in the present crisis, extremely visible. It's going to get harder from the street to the university, which ties up with my saying that there's a fantastic change in the last ten years. For example, in five years of my teaching time sociology has been pushed back, away from teaching courses like "race" and racism, to teaching stuff on crime and delinquency.

I'll tell you the new focus that is coming to sociology. This is the new focus: crime, delinquency, social order is one focus, and urban sociology — again meaning poverty management — reminiscent of the '50s, and then, last but not least, the family. So these three — the great triad of old sociology — have come back again. Even in this day and age, when they do a new program they still have something called "deviance."

BRAND: I think what's going on here, is that the university is synthesizing the social upheaval outside into crime and that would make sense, given that it is the function of the university to define these things to assist state management.

BANNERJI: In these few years what I have discovered is that I have become the insider to this institution, maybe a marginal one, but I'm still a part of it. I'm having to go to meetings on committees, seeing the inner workings, where professionalization has now extended its antennae towards me. All this literary writing or critical writing that I produce, is it sociology. I do good work as a teacher, even if it was always marginalized and unremun-erated. You know, the very first time I applied for a job was at the end of 1988, and the very first time I applied I did get a job because they had tremendous necessity for hiring people in certain areas, and I got hired to teach about Third World women and feminist theories about gender, race and class.

I began to realize more clearly — which I always knew, but know experientially, physically — the effect of the institution. I have to tell you I find that extremely debilitating and humiliating, rage-provoking. This cannot even be expressed through any proper channels. So I've gotten involved in something that is the inner politics of the university now. And, obviously, I have not fallen in with the élite. I have fallen in on the other side, and the other side is very disempowered.

In the last five, six years — in the name of academic freedom and freedom of speech and in this diatribe against so-called political correctness — there has developed an onslaught on teaching even feminist courses. In my department, for example, feminist theories do not count as method.

BRAND: So you can't take a feminist course?

BANNERJI: If you do, it counts only as theory, if that. It doesn't count as a methods course for doing social research. Even important feminist theorists and their students have to get special papers to show how their courses can qualify as a methods courses. They cannot take this course and automatically call it training in social research. So there has been a real onslaught against whatever little gains we have made. Brecht said theatre is in the world. The university is also very much in the world.

The university is very much in the world and the world is in the university. We have about 48,000 students. A large number of the undergraduate students are non-white. Less than probably one percent of the graduate students in liberal arts are non-white. Where do they go? Why are they not there? What pushes them out? They are not all terrible students.

BRAND: The university in America or England or wherever is part of that whole empire-making world, state-making mechanism. It makes a class. It makes people who go out and govern, manage and so on. That's where you get your basic training to manage. So in that context you can see the moves they make in what you call "the onslaught on the feminist theory," etcetera.

BANNERJI: But the other interesting thing is that I have been asked why I am asking students to stay in school if schools produce this ruling apparatus. This is a very peculiar, complex problem. On the one hand, there is this vague rumour about equal opportunity and mobility. Everyone else's children are supposed to be mobile, except ours. Everyone else's children are supposed to be educated and self-reflective, except ours. So in the mini-context of our university there is an interior sort of contradiction to deal with, like why shouldn't there be Black students in graduate school?

Why shouldn't there be? Schools and universities do produce something in spite of themselves. They do produce students who read not only what is prescribed in a course but who do other things. They open up other fields. What I would like to know is why our students, our children, cannot be in this course, why there has to be this concerted move to weed them out? Experientially, I mean. Nobody tells them to leave directly. The mandate of liberal democracy is not to go out and tell them but to organize situations and disincentives and experiences which then actually make students so angry and so powerless, so unhappy that they have to go.

Why is it that courses around "race" and racism, for example, are seen as marginal courses, even though they are seen as so necessary for the university's management, so to speak? So they're managing courses in some sense, they're signals of management, but they mustn't be allowed to be developed further than ...

BRAND: They're for white students. In some sense there's the whole society which brings this pressure to bear on the university to do that, to do the courses on racism, etcetera, because of some shit flying outside. There's the need for people not to be running up and down Yonge Street breaking up things, so they need to appease that element in a certain way, but they also need to teach their future managers how to handle things. I don't think those courses are for us, even though the impetus for them comes from us, from outside. But potentially what they get in the university are, I think, courses on how to manage it in some way. Or courses giving future white ruling classes the methods and vocabulary to manage it.

BANNERJI: And the state's legitimation apparatus in this country is very developed — not the least of which is multiculturalism. To make a ministry, to create these so-called ethnic identities, to fund people on the grounds of that, on the one hand, and then saying these people are ethnicizing everything. It is on those grounds that they're going to fund people and also create managers of communities. If within that there are dissenting voices, those are not the voices that are heard as voices of multiculturalism.

BRAND: The funny thing is multiculturalism, I think, is not recent. Think about the making of the Department of Indian Affairs — of the whole mechanism, of the way the Canadian nation-making state functions in making these kind of marginalities. It makes the Department of Indian Affairs. Then it proceeded to make, to talk about, Two Founding Nations, so it made a French entity and an English entity.

It's always been making multiculturalism. So too, the press from other people who came here and didn't see themselves represented in what the face of that state looked like, which was white Anglo or Franco, but which was tenuous and which changed once in a while or coalesced with someone like Pierre Trudeau. Then, of course, the basis on which the society is shaped, with racism as a characteristic of it, made those of us who entered, question and push against that whole structure or demand certain kinds of things. When we asked for no racism they gave us something else — a new version. You know what I mean?

SILVERA: Multiculturalism, right? *(laughter)* What's your sense of the women's movement here in Toronto? How do you relate to it? Where do you locate yourself at this point?

BANNERJI: I hear there is a movement, *(laughter)* but I don't know where to go and look for it. I don't know if you've found it. Give me an address and a phone number and I'll call it. Seriously, what I did find when I came here were interesting books about patriarchy and women teaching courses or just beginning to — not in the university but outside, places like Women's Place — about women's experiences and about literature as you enter it through a woman's experience. So, for example, I began to like Sylvia Plath. Eventually I found Adrienne Rich, who I liked a lot too. Then I began to read writers like Audre Lorde who really helped me make sense of some of my experiences in a way that, let's say, I did not find in Sylvia Plath.

But I did learn a lot from these people who were writing about, defining, something particular called women's experience, and it resonated with what I knew to be true in my life and other people's. So I'm indebted to that movement, whatever that movement is. I knew a lot of people, but I didn't really become too close to anyone. And the issues that they were raising around violence towards women and then the issues we have subsequently been thinking through — women and political economy, women's work — were very important.

Again, I must say that Makeda's work has been very important to me. That book *Silenced* concretized for me a lot of what I always thought people talked about in theorizing gender, race, class. But the way the interviews were done, put together, what they said, how you profiled them or projected them — to me, this is concrete, something to hold in my hand as to how gender, race, class work together, what a reflexive analysis is when it is concretely done, when it is on the ground. And to this day I have not actually seen a book that has done it the way *Silenced* did it. We continue to use it, partly as a lens to read other theorization through.

Very early it became apparent to me that what was called the "feminism of Germaine Greer," for example, or the "feminism of Kate Millet," or even Marxists like Juliet Mitchell, did not address this. I began to read less well-known people, other writers, namely Black women writers coming from the States — Barbara Smith and people like that. Somehow, for me, that became a very important thing. So, if you talk about my relationship with the women's movement, that is the women's movement, even though these women were not in my immediate environment. Angela Davis' book *Women, Race and Class* was overwhelmingly powerful for me, and so was reading bell hooks' first book, *Ain't I a Women*, then *Feminist Theory from Margin to Centre*. If you think about these people today — others may have done more work than they have done — but they really put this whole issue on the map as not being peripheral to the whole question of how to understand society.

The wonderful thing about them was that they showed there wasn't the cut-off between our lives as we live them and thinking through intellectual matters. It enraged me that some would say that Black women doing this work were not feminist. We had this controversy at OISE: white women were feminist, but we were not. We were concerned with race, so we were anti-racists, but they were feminist. So my relationship with the so-called women's movement is and was really quite complex. I did benefit, initially, from understanding just a general gender analysis, a kind of an inter/intra-sexual analysis of patriarchy. It is reading Black women's writing that I began to fully understand the huge outreach of this something called "patriarchy" as socially-structured, state-organized organization of people's lives. If people say I am a theorist, then that's where my theorization comes from. I hadn't read people like Stuart Hall. My reading of race-gender issues didn't come from reading Shivanandan in *Race and Class*, or Hall, or Gilroy and so on. It came from reading women's work and about banal things like domestic workers, working-class Black women, or immigrant women in Toronto. None of these people would ever be considered, let's say, as the greats among the theorists.

SILVERA: In your essay in *Unsettling Relations: The University as a Site of Struggle,* you talk about this universality of culture and their bourgeois belief — that there is or was such a thing as the universality of culture. Do you remember that and is there really such a thing?

BANNERJI: I was thinking of the canon of great literature or great theory — of people who are very comfortable. I won't go into the long history of what the Enlightenment did or didn't do. People who are very comfortable have taken a lease on the notion of universality, and they have spoken very particularly to their own concerns and, in the language of universality, of transcending particularities and boundaries. Actually, what has been smuggled in has been the work and life and history of one group of people who are in a position to decide what is history, what is theory, what is the universal. The universal has become the personal property of a group of people.

It is not true that cultures are universal. Not only are they not universal internationally, they are not universal within a country. Classes and groups of people in every society have produced completely different ways of self-expression, thinking about the world, politics. This has challenged deeply the whole notion of universality. So that's what I had in mind: the fit between the bourgeois social location and bourgeois theorization — "theorizing abstractly," which is what they claim they are doing. Actually, what they're doing is theorizing from within where they are. These things fit with the life they have, so when they discredit our saying that our lives can produce theory too, they say: that is particular, that is women of colour theorization, that's Black feminist thought. They have an adjective that fits beside it, so it's not just feminist thought, it's *Black* feminist thought and very particular. And we participate in it too. So Sandra Harding can produce feminist thought, but Patricia Hill Collins calls her work *Black Feminist Thought.* Many discredit our claim that experience and life can become productive of theory and analysis.

SILVERA: That really is disturbing and it happens repeatedly. In this culture we are forcefully reminded of "otherness" and "outsider," and it's enough to make you want to commit violent acts and engage in madness. Frankly, I don't mind being called a Black writer, a lesbian, etcetera, because those parts make up my identity, speak to a particular reality. What I resent is their arrogance and the monopoly on the universality of culture. They are the writers, the teachers, the painters, without a hyphen.

Let's talk about you, Himani, about your family background and where you grew up.

BANNERJI: I come from a family that could be called "landed gentry" — not very big but not very small. There are quite a few lawyers in my background. My father was a district judge and then a high court judge. I was born in 1942 in Dhaka, part of pre-partition India at that time.

India became independent in 1947 and the country underwent partition, so two countries were created, Pakistan and India. Pakistan was divided in two parts, West Pakistan and East, with a lot of India in between West Pakistan and East Pakistan. I grew up in East Pakistan from '47 to '59 and that is where I finished my school. Part of my father's family — I don't say my family, I wasn't too close to them — lived in a village where they had land. My father lived in Dhaka, which was the capital of East Pakistan then. This region has become Bangladesh. It's an independent country. It had a war with West Pakistan and it separated and now it's a new country — Dhaka was then the capital of East Pakistan and is now capital of Bangladesh. I grew up there. I grew up with my parents, my two younger brothers. My older three brothers and sister lived in Calcutta in India.

Most of my growing up, my father was a high court judge. We lived in very secluded, separated space from the city. Probably this part was once meant for British administrators. In this part of town, where the officials lived, there were hospitals, courthouses, offices and all that. Then the other side would be the other city, where the so-called masses — the people lived. So I grew up on this side of this border where we lived in these very secluded homes — not owned by our families but government bungalows — with lots of isolation, lot of land around them and trees. There were lots of servants, lots of government orderlies and not much interaction with people except to go to school.

My father, as far as I can understand, was a very difficult man with very, very strong fits of temper. My mother seemed very submissive and she had a very hard time. Interestingly enough, I didn't identify with my father, I identified with my mother. I mostly spent a lot of time reading. I liked school, unlike a lot of children whose homes were more fun, who hated school. My schools were more fun because I met kids my age. At home, we weren't allowed very much freedom to go anywhere, to be with people, and not too many people visited us. It could also be a function — I'm not sure — of my father being the only hindu high court judge — it was mostly a muslim bureaucracy on top.

There wasn't very much social interchange between my family and the other families that lived near us. Basically, I think of my childhood as having a lot of isolation in it, loneliness too and a lot of books. There was a lot of fear when my father would get mad. Things would become awful around the house at that time. Very early on, I think, I became very protective of my mother, and I guess I learned about power directly through that.

SILVERA: So is your father the violence you were speaking about when you said earlier that you grew up with a lot of violence?

BANNERJI: Yes, it is my father that I speak of.

SILVERA: What was this violence? Was is physical, psychological? And what form did power take in this relationship?

BANNERJI: He didn't beat my mother, but he was a very, very violent tempered man, so I saw a lot of night-long quarrels and uglinesses of all kinds towards my brothers, who he did beat quite severely. He didn't beat me because he believed, like a lot of men did in his time and of his class, you don't beat women and girls. So I was spared that. But if you watch a lot of violence, you can't just be not a part of it. In my case because of my family violence, my mother's history and so on, I never quite saw the beauty or seduction of power, and I saw power everywhere. And there was a big nationalist movement and the romance of it, the figures, images, maybe produced a rupture in me ...

I liked games. Unlike a lot of girls, l was very fond of sports. I guess I didn't create much trouble, so I never experienced much repression in schools. Where I did experience it was at home, in terms of being isolated from people, growing up in a very feudal kind of family, where staying out after sundown or going anywhere by myself was forbidden. If I did go and visit a classmate, I'd be driven there, brought back. I found it all very, very hard. We didn't go to India almost at all. We didn't know India.

SILVERA: What year did you eventually go back to India?

BANNERJI: I finished my high school in East Pakistan and went to India in my first year in college, to visit Calcutta. My father and mother wanted to say goodbye to my brother who was going to the United States. My father fell ill. They went to India for three weeks, it was in 1959. We never went back.

SILVERA: Never went back to East Pakistan?

BANNERJI: No, my father fell ill and died in 1963. He was very ill for all those years and then he was dead. My brothers would come to East Pakistan from Calcutta and my sister to visit us for the summer holidays, and they would bring books and art and ideas that were very new and very important and very interesting to me. I learnt a lot about the Soviet Union and communism. In a way, my brothers brought in some fresh air into my world. And I liked them a lot.

My brothers were communists, and my father was very anti-communist. I obviously chose my side very early. Then, when I went to Calcutta, because of partition and this lack of relationship between the two countries, my father's pension and everything else were frozen. We moved suddenly from a lot of prosperity to a lot of poverty. Before he died, some of his money was released by the government of Pakistan, but by then the little money we had was spent on his treatment. My two brothers by that time were in the States, and they sent some money, so we lived with that. I, however, was very happy. Suddenly I had no surveillance. We lived with a lot of people.

Calcutta was a fantastic discovery for me. The city was then maybe three or four million people. Now it's grown to fifteen. It was such an amazing thing. I made friends. I could visit my friends, they could visit me. My father was too ill to exert any control. It was very good. My mother had no formal education. She could read and write Bengali some but not very much, enough to read novels and write letters. But English education? She didn't have any.

SILVERA: What are some of your happier memories of childhood or growing up? Did you have a good relationship with your mother?

BANNERJI: I liked my mother, and as I grew up I began to like her more and more, even though my world was more of a boy's world. The one good thing in my upbringing is it was not expected that I would not study, that I would not have a profession, or that I would immediately get married. That sort of thing wasn't there. Nor was forcing of religion. My mother was just too busy and had too many kids and never had the temperament to force herself on anybody. So I didn't grow up with a mother who was very judgemental. I also began to see that she resisted a lot of things of my father's world, which was actually high bureaucracy. She somehow stayed very rural right through her life. She never ever wanted to urbanize herself or do anything that was modern and fashionable. I began to think that takes a lot of integrity because it was her form of resistance.

SILVERA: When did you begin to teach?

BANNERJI: I finished my M.A., and within a very short time, I started to teach at the university in 1965. I was twenty-two or twenty-three years old.

SILVERA: What university was that?

BANNERJI: It was in Calcutta, a university called Jadavpur where I still go to do work. I taught there, I studied there. I read quite a lot of literature and also political material. Then I got married in 1965, married very poor, married on my own. I liked my in-laws. I lived in a joint family until I left and was good friends with my mother-in-law. She was a very extraordinary woman who managed this household with very little money, like magic. I was her second-in-command. My husband and I were the only earning members, and we ate well in the beginning of the month, then we didn't towards the end. I don't think people here can even imagine how poorly college and university teachers live in India.

My daughter was born in 1967. We had married kind of experimentally. You couldn't live with people then without marrying and all that. And having married, we both found it difficult, but we did not have much guts to separate there. I got this assistantship and admission for a Ph.D program in the English department of the University of Toronto. Our university in India used to — and still does — give three years off to beginning faculty, to improve themselves, to do a Ph.D., because they hire people with an M.A. as junior lecturers. I came here with a teaching assistantship at the University of Toronto, on leave from my job at Jadavpur University.

After I came here — after six, seven months — I earned enough to sponsor my husband and bring my daughter to join me. We couldn't work out things and we parted in 1973. He went back to India soon after that, to his position at the university. I didn't go back because I had never seen a divorced woman from my own society, not until I got divorced. We figured out it would be very hard, not just on us but on our daughter because people were very negative and judgemental about these things.

BRAND: When did writing poetry happen? Writing poetry, writing fiction, how did that fit into that whole ...?

BANNERJI: It takes me back to how I was before I came here. I wasn't a kid. I was already teaching for five years ... It never dawned on me that to write and to teach were separate things. I don't even remember when I didn't know about writers. Russian literature, for example, was very real to us by age eight or nine on. Tolstoy was read. People read all of that. Look at our vernacular literatures done by very political people. Again, to be a critical reporter and a writer-teacher were not so separate either, so writing was never a special thing for me to take up, as it were. I worked. I worked in India and I didn't give much thought to writing as a self-conscious vocation. I published quite a lot of literary criticism as a matter of course.

In Canada I wrote all kinds of things which I never published. It wasn't until 1981 or 1982 that a friend took some hand-written things and produced *Separate Sky*. And that's the time when I met you, Dionne, and Krishantha and people who were beginning to write. We didn't have a place to write, but we did write. With regard to the movements that were taking place, we always read with those people, so we got ten minutes, fifteen minutes at the end of something. There was a flow of politics happening here. When I came the Vietnam war going on, and then what happened in Chile in '73. More and more steam gathered, and there was a feeling of the relevance of one's political concern, which wasn't really to do with the Canadian writing scene but with our kind of writing. So writing was not a decision, but it did need a milieu, which I found in people like Dionne, like Makeda, like Krishantha, and other men and women who are writing.

Even when you're not sure if you're publishing, you write. It becomes a part of being you. Things happen, you go home, you think and something happens and then you write. You keep writing because you're interested in making sense of what you saw, what you heard, what is happening around you politically and socially and ...

BRAND: But that's not true of a lot of people.

BANNERJI: No it isn't true of a lot of people, but I'm talking about people like me. It's part of how I know to make sense. Different people use different mediums to think things through. At times, you only let your gaze go towards your enemy, and in some sense your agenda then is made over by that enemy. Even though we're saying we have to look horizontally, between or among ourselves, this intervenor is always in our lives: you make a film through National Film Board, I meet your film through them. I will not be able to totally undercut the fact that we have met because of them. So our gazes are very often directed at that. I think if you talk of deformation, that's where a lot of deformation happens to us and it's not really even a matter of making a decision to rise above it. You are always already roped in, in that kind of a situation, and it's a devil's job to not look at that and to look at the formations among ourselves.

BRAND: I think we're all in an insane situation and trying to make sanity.

BANNERJI: It's very depleting, but it is also what we write about. It's a very peculiar thing that this muck is also out of which my writing came. I don't know about others who are more fortunate, who had other things and safe places to write from. I never did. We were talking earlier about this: of course, I love flowers and trees. Why is it I don't write about them? Why do I always find myself, without making a decision, writing about certain things? And those things are not random, they seem to kind of fall in a pattern. I take it by now that those are my major preoccupations. My unconscious is more reactive to those things. We can't run away from history and I can't pretend to be who I'm not.

Carmen Rodríguez

Agnes Huang

Carmen Rodríguez

I live in a language that's not mine

Part I
Living and Writing in a Hyphen

Mi amor, reconozco a mi madre en el hueco largo, oscuro de tu espalda. Déjame descansar, rodeada de piel, metida en tu mampara. No me dejes salir. El mundo es tan grande, hace tanto frío. Llévame metida en tu casa de huesos y rumores, la única que tengo. Mi país existió hace tantos años con sus paredes de agua azul y nieves altas. Lluvia del sur, Macul en otoño, río Valdivia pujando vida hacia Niebla, Mancera.

Mi amor, hace tanto tiempo que te quiero, que te busco, y tú sin saberlo. Ahora estoy aquí, en ti. No me dejes salir.

My love, I recognise my mother in the long, dark hollow of your back. Let me wrap myself in the quiet of your skin and rest. The world is so big. It's so cold out there. Carry me inside your house of murmurs and bones, the only one I have. My country existed such a long time ago; the blue of the ocean, the height of the snow, so far away. Southern rain, Macul in the fall, Valdivia river pushing life towards Niebla, Mancera.

My love, I have wanted you for so long, searched for you for so long. Now I'm here, in you. Don't let me leave.[1]

THIS EXCERPT comes from one of my short stories. Like most of my stories, it was written in a place called Exile. I was forced to leave Chile by the September 11, 1973 military coup, and I have lived most of the last twenty-one years of my life in Canada. I have become a Chilean-Canadian. Chilean dash Canadian. Chilean hyphen Canadian.

Chile: Valdivia, where I was born. Blue, wide, calm river. Rain, green forests. Cerro Bellavista, Valparaíso, age seven, playing with Soledad and Luisa on the street, singing the national anthem on Monday mornings at school, in our starched uniforms, freshly polished black shoes. Chile: speaking Spanish, but not just any Spanish; no. Chilean Spanish; Spanish from Chile: *ya pu pelotúa no seái tonta, pu, tírame la pelota, soi retarda u qué*... Chile: *empanadas* on Sundays, my mother's home-made buns, my mother's hands, my mother's lap. Chile: Carmencita and Alejandra, perfect little women, dark and soft, big, curious eyes. Santiago, Chile: 1970, one million people on the street, celebrating our triumph over colonialism, over imperialism. For the first time in history, a country had freely elected a marxist government. Chile: three years of intense work, shanty towns, universities, factories, Mapuche communities, women's groups. The Chilean upper class, the political right, the fascists, the American companies, ITT, the CIA, *los milicos*, the military. Chile: 1973: military coup. The bright spotlights of an interrogation room, my little girls against the wall, guns on their backs. 1973: 30,000 dead, 2,000 *desaparecidos*, erased from the map; one million exiled. Exiled. Remember that word.

Canada: for the first few years I didn't really live here. I lived here, but I was Chilean. I lived in function of my quick return. I lived so that I could tell people here about what had happened there. I lived making sure that my daughters would not forget Chile, would not forget their mother tongue.

But one day, sitting at the kitchen table with a blank sheet of paper in my old beat-up typewriter, this is what came out:

>Machine sobbing
>voices
>outside
>in the world
>
>I chew over a certain pain
>
>Old fantasies
>already born
>already aborted
>strain upwards
>between my legs
>like flesh
>with filthy fingernails
>
>I chew over a certain pain
>
>Filthy nails
>black
>shiny nails
>red

> I bleed ephemeral images
> death rattle in chorus
>
> My tongue
> swollen to the nth degree
> bursts
> a thick fluid
> drowns the supreme attempt
> to articulate
> ar-ti-cu-late
> a meaning
>
> I have forgotten all
>
> *My weapon is dead
> the future does not exist.*[2]

I titled that poem "Original Language." The day I wrote it, I had been finally hit by the fact that I would not be going back to Chile for many years. The dictatorship had put me on the black list that banned me from entering the country legally. The revolution we had begun to make in the early '70s would not be ours for a long, long time. Most probably, not in our lifetime. What was there left to live for? What kind of world would I be able to offer to my kids?

I stayed in Canada, and for the last twenty-one years, the struggle to build a better world has taken many different forms. Also, in the last ten years I have been moving from being Chilean, to being Chilean dash Canadian. I live here, I work here, I struggle here, I write here. My space is here and now. But I cannot forget where I came from. My heart lives here too, but is always facing south. So I have come to the conclusion that I live in a hyphen. Let me explain to you how this feels:

Sometimes it feels like a bridge; it's nice. You just walk back and forth. When it feels like that I even tend to believe the cliché of the Canadian Cultural Mosaic. Other times, it feels like a slide. You are at one end of the hyphen and — swoosh! there you go, sliding back to the other end, without being able to hold on to anything. This produces a little anxiety, but it's fun, after all. But, most times, living in a hyphen feels like a see-saw: Chilean (up) — Canadian (down): See-saw. The most painful part, though, is that once in a while, when one side of the see-saw hits the ground too hard or lands too fast, you get ejected, just like that, and again you land in that country called Exile; you feel like you don't really have a home, like the woman in my story at the beginning of this piece, the one that finds refuge, a temporary home, in her lover's skin.

For me, living and writing in a hyphen implies translation. I write in Spanish, my mother tongue, and then re-work my pieces in English, my second tongue. My Chilean side speaks Spanish. My Canadian side translates. In a creative essay I wrote for *Colour. An Issue*, a special edition of *West Coast Line* published recently, I said, "I carry two tongues inside my mouth, or maybe it is just one, with two tips ..."[3] I move easily between the two tips, even though the younger one is highly influenced by her older sister. You see, you hear ... I speak English with an accent. But who doesn't? I don't write with an accent, though, because I write in my mother tongue. However, I translate with an accent. Most often, friends and colleagues, native speakers of English, help me get rid of the "accented" translations. How does this sound? Do you really say it like that in English?

But translation is hardly about words. How do you translate a posture, the movement of the hands implicit in the speech of a Chilean working class woman ... How do you translate the cadence, the rhythm of the words ...

"Yo no sé qué se imagina, que una es bestia de carga, que no se cansa, los lomos ya no me dan más de tanto trabajar y el lindo de terno y corbata rescándose las entretelas en la oficina ...."

But it is important to translate. It is important to use the hyphen of my bilingualism, my biculturalism, the hyphen of my double identity, as a bridge, so at least I can invite other Canadians to read my work. I *want* other Canadians to read my work. I have so much to tell!

My first collection of poetry, *Guerra Prolongada/Protracted War*, was published by Women's Press in a bilingual edition. I'm very proud of this book because it recognizes my hyphenated identity and it validates my mother tongue. I am also very proud to be part of the collective that publishes *Revista Aquelarre*, a bilingual Spanish-English quarterly of Latin American women in Canada. These bilingual efforts are one way of telling Canada that we Latin Americans are here to stay, that we belong here, and that we have a mother tongue, even though it is not one of the official languages of Canada.

Living and working in a hyphen is not easy. Translation is hard work. You write, you translate. You rewrite, you translate again. But the fact is that as immigrants we have got used to working double to be recognized and then paid for half. In this country I have been a janitor, a cook, a teacher ... I have worked with brooms, mops, pots, pans. The struggle is the same. Only these days I am working mainly with words: powerful tools. Or are they weapons? La lucha continúa. Gracias.

Part II
Going Home: Reflections on Issues of Colour, Culture, Gender and Exile[4]

Destiny

time measured
in baggage
photographs
pounds

time to probe
turn the corner
of dreams

danger

What Does Not Exist

who'll pay for
the injury and the loss
roots in the air
and all crushed up

my job is to walk
walk briskly
as if I knew where I was going

Lights

my child face
my young face
watch me
from the wrinkled and silver
mirror

Naked Out There

southern home
little girl
eyes knees
silky tail
sulky girl
whistling girl

northern home
woman
bushy legs
a fiend's mouth
eyes kept
behind glass
cynical woman
sweet woman
hidden in the trappings
of tits and ass

I'm going home[5]

These poems were written in a country called Exile. They were written in Spanish, my mother tongue, and then reworked in English, my second tongue. I carry two tongues inside my mouth, or maybe it is just one, with two tips. I lost my first home in 1973; if I hadn't left Chile then, maybe death would have become my second home and for sure my tongue would have never grown another tip. But I came to Canada instead, and I learned how to live and speak again. Chile is the home of my childhood and youth. Canada is the home of my wrinkles and grey hair. Canada is the home of the here and now. Chile is the home of my history and memory.

When I was growing up in Chile women were assigned one of two roles: the mother or the whore. Whores spoke loudly, wore tight skirts (with no girdle underneath ...) and skimpy lace underwear; they also painted their face, smoked and wiggled their ass when they walked down the street at the rhythm of men's sexual remarks and suggestive whistling. Of course, you didn't want to become a whore. Oh no!

Mothers were ladies. They wore a girdle, which meant that they didn't go around teetering all that "loose flesh" and opening men's "natural" appetites. Mothers spoke softly and had the attributes of a virgin. Obviously, they did not have a sexual life before marriage, and once they were allowed to have one, they only "endured" it; they did not enjoy it. Orgasms had been invented for whores, not for mothers.

If you had been brought up in a "decent" home, you wished to become a mother. I was brought up in a decent home, but ... horror of horrors! ... I did not wish to become a mother, especially when I was the daily witness of my own mother's life. My mother was a *dueña de casa* ("owner of the home"), a housewife who worked like a horse, scrubbing, washing and cooking. Besides, I never knew what kind of suffering she had to go through at night when she got in the bedroom with my dad! But did the fact that I didn't want to become a mother mean that I wanted to become a whore? Well, at least the whores seemed to have a better time than the mothers ...

At age twelve, my mother gave me my first girdle. That's when the struggle began. I refused to wear it, and with the girdle in the drawer, I began my life as an exile. By refusing to conform, by challenging my assigned position in society, I began a long journey in search of a home, a centre. Obviously, I didn't know that then, and it has only been after many years of territorial displacement and a great deal of thinking, talking and writing that I have begun to understand the complexity of my exile as a Latin American woman at this time in history.

I live on the margins of the margins. Having chosen to move away from a place of acceptance and comfort, from a role with a clear script, having been pushed away from the place of my birth, I have lived most of my life in a country called Uncertainty, in a place of loss. Unable to be the mother and not quite having become the whore, "stuck" in a country that I didn't choose to live in, I am still looking for my country, for my home. Sometimes I think I have found a home in words such as "revolutionary": "I am a revolutionary," I say. "Writer": "I am a writer," I say. "Mom": "I am Carmencita's mom; I am Alejandra's mom; I am Ted's mom," I say. For brief instants I have found my home, but then I find myself looking again.

The mirror is a good place for looking. I hated myself when I was a kid. All I could see were the big teeth and the glasses. After all these years, I am more gentle with myself, and sometimes I even like what I see. Again, brief instances of centredness, contentment. But the interesting thing is that since living in Canada I have been forced to see something that I had never seen before: colour. In Chile I didn't have a colour. I was like everybody else. Colour was not an issue. Here, I have been forced to see myself as a dark woman, "a woman of colour."

Do I like this term? Can I live with it? Sometimes I can, sometimes I can't. I can live with it when it brings me close to other women who may have gone through experiences similar to mine, women who live in the margins of this society because of the colour of their skin. Then I like it. I cannot live with it when I realize that it is a term largely determined by the fact that there is a dominant colour and culture that not only I am not a part of, but that looks down on me and others like me.

But if society wants to define me, "put me in my place," by pointing to the colour of my skin and my accent, there is little I can do about it. Call me what you wish. What I do know is that I am a lot more complex than what you see or hear. I have several cards up my sleeve, and I may choose not to show them to you. I am a traveller, a wanderer. I live in a language that's not mine, in a country that's not mine. But who doesn't? Perhaps "home" is only a search interrupted by brief moments of contentedness. Perhaps home is nothing but my own dark skin, reflected in the Canadian mirror of my here and now. Perhaps.

Endnotes

[1] From a work in progress.

[2] Carmen Rodríguez in "Original Language" in *Guerra Prolongada/ Protracted War*. (Toronto: Women's Press, 1992), pp. 49-50.

[3] Carmen Rodríguez in "Going Home: Reflections on Issues of Colour, Culture, Gender and Exile," in *Colour. An Issue*, Special Double Issue, *West Coast Line*, Nos. 13-14, Spring-Fall 1994.

[4] Part II was first published as "Going Home: Reflections on Issues of Colour, Culture, Gender and Exile," in *Colour. An Issue*, Special Double Issue, *West Coast Line*, No. 13-14, Spring-Fall 1994. It appears here in a slightly different form.

[5] "Destiny," "What Does Not Exist," "Lights," and "Naked Out There" are from *Guerra Prolongada/Protracted War*.

Lenore Keeshig-Tobias

An interview with
LENORE KEESHIG-TOBIAS

Keepers
of the Culture

SILVERA: Let's talk a bit about you as a writer. How and when did you begin to write?

KEESHIG-TOBIAS: Maybe I fell in love with the idea of writing when I was in grade three. That's when I started experimenting with language and what happens when you change words around a bit. I remember even before I learned to read, being at my grandma's house, sitting off in a corner by myself. She had this wonderful book cabinet, little claws for legs and nice glass doors. I would sit there and pore through her books. Gradually, I was able to read, and I spent a lot of time there. As I got older, I used to wonder why there weren't any stories about Indians. I could see stories going on, on the reserve, and these stories were just as beautiful as the stories on the bookshelf.

SILVERA: What were the stories on the bookshelf? Can you remember the books?

KEESHIG-TOBIAS: Mostly Dickens. I read a lot and my parents often read to us — they came from a literate family, particularly my mother. When my father was away working she would do a lot of reading to us. My father too. I remember one story called "The Lion." It was a very sad story about a young girl growing up in one of Africa's parks. Her father was a game warden, and they took in an orphaned lion club and grew it up. Because we like animals we could identify with that. There would be times when my mom would be sitting on the edge of the couch and my dad would be in the armchair. We would be sitting on the floor all around them. They would come to an episode in this story that was so sad, my mother would start to cry, and then she would give the book to my father, and he'd read until he started to cry and give it back to her. She read until she could read no more and she gave it back to him. Meanwhile, we were sitting on the floor at their feet sobbing our hearts out. *(laughter)* My mother also read poetry to us — "The Highwayman" and "The Lady of Shalott" and "The Raven." She also read to us from the Bible.

SILVERA: What kinds of stories?

KEESHIG-TOBIAS: Oh, stories of the Trickster, Nanabush — that is why I'm so attached to Nanabush — and, of course, there were other stories, from grandparents and aunties and uncles. We are an oral culture, so it is always there. Everyone has their story that they tell very well — hunting stories, anecdotes, what happened on the way to the store, whatever. When I was at boarding school, that's when I started writing fictional pieces. I used to keep a journal then. I wrote two pieces: one was about my brother's death; he was seven days old when he died of spinal meningitis. He was born in Wiarton near the reserve but was sent to Sick Children's Hospital, a little baby all by himself. The other piece was a long poem called "The Valley of the Blue Grass Trees." It was all in metaphors — about growing up in a boarding school, being a prisoner and just escaping through fantasies and moonbeams. It was about dreams and love — you know, adolescents falling in love and all the wonderful images they make up.

SILVERA: Were you born in Wiarton?

KEESHIG-TOBIAS: Yes. I was born in a small town, Wiarton, which is about fourteen kilometres from the Chippewa's Nawash reserve. It's on the Bruce Peninsula, about forty kilometres or so north-west of Owen Sound. It's a beautiful part of the Niagara Escarpment. I'm the oldest of ten children; there are five girls and five boys. I have cousins upon cousins. I don't know how many aunties and uncles I have. My grandparents lived just up the road from us, a five-minute walk. We lived in a rather isolated section of the reserve and we never went visiting much. Everything we had was right there. If we needed help, there was my grandmother. We played in the bush and by the lake.

Later, I came to Toronto where I met my children's father. We married and moved about, and then nine years after that — the year we separated — I came back to Toronto to attend York University as a mature student, with a writing portfolio. So my three kids and I moved to the city. I had so much energy at that time. It was incredible. In fact, putting an application into York was a matter of survival for me. I was living on the reserve, stagnating. I wanted to learn, and I started to use the mailbox library. I just sent a list of books that I wanted to the regional library and they would send me back a bag of books. I was so hungry for knowledge. I did Fine Arts, with an emphasis on creative writing. I did theatre and music and music appreciation and visual arts. Those were the things I wanted to do, and I've done them — I fulfilled those promises I made to myself when I was a kid. And they were good years for my kids. They basically grew up on the campus.

SILVERA: And when did you start to write professionally?

KEESHIG-TOBIAS: I started off working for a magazine called *Ontario Indian*. I was there as a summer student and then went on to be a full-time writer and then an assistant editor.

SILVERA: Tell me about your time with *Sweetgrass*. How was that formed and what did that come out of?

KEESHIG-TOBIAS: That came out of the *Ontario Indian*, which started out as an in-house newsletter for the Union of Ontario Indians, and it evolved into a first-rate international magazine, a wonderful forty-eight-page magazine, four-colour, on glossy stock. It was incredible. Unfortunately, the Union did not seem to realize what a wonderful public relations tool it had. Even though we weren't dealing with Union issues, in a very subtle way we were putting out cultural information, giving readers a context in which to place the events of the day. The magazine died.

Those of us who had worked on the magazine went on to found *Sweetgrass*, the magazine of Canada's Native Peoples. We were going to be a little more political and call it the magazine of Canada's First Nations, but then we thought of our funding and our advertisers and stuck with Native Peoples. I worked on it from 1982 to 1985. Basically, we started from scratch. My responsibility at that time was research, development and implementation of the editorial policy. That was what I concentrated on; I didn't get into advertising or fund-raising or public relations.

There were five founding members. A lot of us were taking

part-time or short-term contracts to feed ourselves. My time with *Sweetgrass* was voluntary, so I worked four years without a salary. At the outset I thought that I would give two years of my time to the magazine; by that time it should be on its own, and I could go back to my poetry and my children's stories. Unfortunately, it didn't turn out that way. By the time I quit in 1985, I was completely burnt out. After that I spent a year crying and licking my wounds and putting myself together.

Part of the difficulty with the magazine was convincing advertiszers that Native People are consumers. We were battling that negative stereotype: welfare recipients and alcoholics. We still hadn't convinced them that Native People eat at McDonalds, smoke cigarettes, drive cars, trucks, wear jeans, Cougars, they like Duncan Hines. The other difficulty was getting Native organizations to advertize with the magazine. They had the attitude that because they were a Native organization and we were a Native organization they should get a discount. We had problems making deadlines, the infrastructure was new, we were just learning to work with each other and learning to work as a collective. That was hard. There was also a certain faction on the board that did not want to work that way. They wanted to work in a hierarchical set-up, where you climb up the ladder, and if someone is in your way, you grab their foot and pull them down.

In terms of funding, we did approach the federal government, but we didn't meet their mandate! We weren't a regional publication, we were a national publication, and that was not within their mandate. It was ridiculous, that old divide-and-rule tactic.

SILVERA: Did the board try to do any fund-raising?

KEESHIG-TOBIAS: Yes. Although I think we could have had more input from the board, we had some really good people there.

SILVERA: What did you do after your time with *Sweetgrass?*

KEESHIG-TOBIAS: I was writing a lot of poetry and children's stories. When my two daughters were small there was very little culturally relevant material and no contemporary stories — the stories dated back to years and years ago — so I decided to write children's literature.

SILVERA: As a Native writer, did you encounter problems getting those kinds of works published?

KEESHIG-TOBIAS: I did when I tried to go into the mainstream. They always wanted me to restructure my stuff, and in some cases people didn't like what I was writing, they thought it was too political.

SILVERA: So that often came up?

KEESHIG-TOBIAS: Yeah, it did. But when I stuck to Native presses there was little or no problem.

SILVERA: That seems to happen quite frequently with a lot of writers. It seems writers of colour, once they enter mainstream or try to, their work is often re-written to the max, hardly recognizable. The voice is lost. It seems they always take one or two of us and then ...

KEESHIG-TOBIAS: And tokenize.

SILVERA: Yes, definitely. Let's talk about your children's book *Birdtalk*. How did that story come about?

KEESHIG-TOBIAS: I was a university student and my older children were young. My daughter Polly at that time must have been six years old and in her first year in public school. We were in a very diverse, multicultural neighbourhood, the Jane-Finch area. I wanted to be there because I liked that aspect of that area. I wanted my children exposed to other cultures. Anyhow, there was an incident one afternoon when her classmates wanted to play cowboys and Indians. She didn't want to and she found it very hard to try to explain to them why it wasn't a good game to play. What immediately happened was that they questioned her identity. The story evolved out of that and out of how I tried to handle the situation — not turning it into a confrontation but talking with Polly and trying to empower her with an understanding of where we come from and what our culture and our history is and by going to the teacher and talking with the teacher about the situation.

SILVERA: And how was that?

KEESHIG-TOBIAS: That was okay. I always made it a point of going to talk with the teacher if there were things that I didn't like, for example, a certain perspective, Native People in a negative or inaccurate position.

SILVERA: I want to talk about a bit of your own growing up. Years ago, when I first interviewed you, you talked about going to segregated schools on the reserve, missionary teachers and other aspects of school and what you experienced as a child.

KEESHIG-TOBIAS: I went to school on the reserve up to grade eight. It was a mission school, and there were certain aspects of that which I didn't like. But I guess we all have a hunger for learning and exploring new things, and that's what I liked best about school.

SILVERA: What didn't you like?

KEESHIG-TOBIAS: The attitudes of the missionary teachers. I remember one of those beautiful autumn days with apples strewn under the trees. We were out at recess, all of us, running around and making a great commotion. One of the nuns came out and yelled at us, scolded us for acting like "wild Indians." And we stopped and started talking. I remember the older kids, they went over and broke into the nuns' pigeon house — they had those pigeons with the great big breasts, fantails I think they're called. The kids grabbed some feathers out of them, gave feathers to all of us. Then we all found sticks about a foot long and stuck them into the apples, and we started running around the school, whooping like wild Indians. They called us wild Indians and we were going to be wild Indians!

For us, school was the first place we learned who and what Indians were, and that wasn't nice. When we were at home we didn't have to know who we were; we just were. We were aware that things were rough, but the "heathen savage" part of it came from school. You have to remember, this was a Roman Catholic missionary school. It was the Iroquois tribe that massacred or martyred the Jesuit fathers and we're Ojibway. At that time, the Ojibway were enemies of the Iroquois. So we were "saved" by that plus the fact that we were born into a Christian community. Or most were because when the missionaries went through they really went through. In fact, on our reserve at one time there were the Roman Catholics, the Methodists and the Orange Lodge, and at that time there were only about 500 people on the reserve.

Back to school. In my time it was a fairly large community. There were a number of villages on the reserve, about three main villages. Each had a school. All we had to do was walk up the hill, and I remember I loved that experience. However, some time after that, the clergy pushed to segregate the schools. That was when they introduced bussing on the reserve. There was one bus and two separate schools, and I remember the fights on the bus between Protestant and Catholic kids.

SILVERA: So you went to segregated schools on your reserve until ...?

KEESHIG-TOBIAS: Up to grade eight. Then the kids were bussed to the local outlying communities for high school. If the facilities were not available in that area, some of them boarded in London or Toronto. I was sent to a boarding school, the Loretto Academy, in Niagara Falls, partly because my father was working there in Niagara Falls, New York, at the time. Two years of grade nine and then grade ten. I had to repeat grade nine. I know now, years later, why. Coming into such a totally different environment, I went into culture shock. I couldn't study. I was always worried about my family and I was lonely. I didn't know how to handle those feelings. I wanted to be there, but I found it really hard. We used to have a study hall, but I had always studied on a stool, my books on a chair, with my sisters and brothers running all around. I'd never sat there for two hours at a stretch to study before. Everything was so rigid. My marks went down. I was scared and shy. In French class, I remember, one day the teacher who was the prefect — she threw the blackboard brush at me. I'd never taken French before. I didn't know "oui" from "si" and I kept confusing the two. I remember being called into the prefect's office, and she condemned me for "wasting taxpayers' money."

SILVERA: So when you left there where did you go?

KEESHIG-TOBIAS: We went home and into a local high school off the reserve. That was grade eleven. By that time, I had pretty well lost all ambition for school. I wanted to be an artist, a dancer, a writer, a painter. I wanted to do mathematics. There were just no role models — at that time you could be a teacher, a nurse, a secretary, or a hairdresser. And you could always, of course, be a mother. Some choice. So I quit and came to Toronto and lived at Rochdale when I was eighteen.

SILVERA: Tell me more about the Trickster. I find him a fascinating character.

KEESHIG-TOBIAS: This is where I go into my "rhetoric." *(laughter)* The Trickster is the best-loved personality coming out of these stories — maybe I should say "teachings" — because that is what they are. I hate to say "legend" or "folklore" or "mythology" because it gives the wrong connotation. The Trickster is the son of a mortal woman and the West Spirit, usually raised by his grandmother — that's where the matriarchy comes in. The Trickster is usually a man, and is known by many names throughout the continent: Nanabush, Nanaboosho, Wanaboosho, Raven, Hare, Coyote. It is through the Trickster that we learn our place in the family, in the community and in society, how we sit in the universe. We learn what to do and what not to do. More often than not we learn not to do what the Trickster has done. When I was growing up I heard the Trickster disappeared when the Europeans came. It seems to me that they tried to replace the Trickster with Jesus Christ. There was a problem there: Jesus Christ was so perfect. Not only that, he was white — actually he wasn't white, was he?

SILVERA: Well, we're taught that he was white.

KEESHIG-TOBIAS: Right. *(laughter)* My poems are around that. As well, I've had a Christian upbringing and I've grown up in this white society. I also have my Native culture. In my poetry I deal with both types of symbols, Christian and Native, and how those two juxtapose each other. For example, I have a series of Bear poems. In Christianity, Bear is understood as the devil: the Bear Cub then signifies the change from the heathen pagan ways. But the Bear, for us, is a very powerful symbol. The Bear is a healer. So it is a matter of balancing them out. My dreams are often vivid, so vivid I cannot help but write them down. Then later on I go back and see the symbolism there. I realise where it comes from — from my childhood roots.

SILVERA: At some point in your writing did you look for role models and find none? Did you look for other Native writers?

KEESHIG-TOBIAS: Other Native artists? I knew there were some contemporary writers, and I wasn't satisfied with their material. I thought there were too many clichés and rhyming couplets — basically imitations of white models. Writing is a new tool for us, but we've always had the spoken word, we've always had our own types of poetry. When the Europeans came they came with their years and years of a written literary legacy — and, of course, culture and everything great and wonderful — we kind of got sucked into that.

In learning anything new, you learn by imitation first. I guess our early writers worked along those lines and imitated the 18th century poets, with the rhyming and the metre and the metaphor. People have finally learned how to use this tool adequately. They're still copying, imitating, but Indians are now superior — our culture is superior to your white culture. Some of the poems in that era are okay; it's a step that needs to be there.

After that, Native writers start reviving the Native metaphor, but again it's the rhyme and metre. I wasn't satisfied with that. After that, comes Native humour. Then Native writing comes in on its own and gone are the rhyme and the metre and the metaphor. What comes in is the Native rhythm, the Native metaphor, the ability to laugh at ourselves. We can do that because laughter is healing, and this is where we are now.

SILVERA: How did your childhood inform your writing? Has it given you strength or ... ?

KEESHIG-TOBIAS: I think what it has done is to give me something to write about *(laughter)* and to try and look at the hypocrisy in the way our community was responding to Christianity.

SILVERA: What was it like then? Has it changed any?

KEESHIG-TOBIAS: Things have changed now. We don't have segregated schools, but still within our community — we've been colonized and we're still under the *Indian Act* —.there's still that mentality there within some of our people. Actually, I think we've had a great heavy dose of cultural self-hate. Right now on the reserve we have a very right-wing Council. They're also Christian. *(laughter)* They've got practical experience and practical wisdom, but in terms of understanding human rights and understanding what self-government and self-determination are about, there's a real struggle between a new wave of people and a new wave of thought made up of people of my age. In that group, I suppose, we're liberals or left-wingers. *(laughter)* What they call us up here is the Pony-Tail Group *(laughter)* — some kind of hippies, I guess. But what it is, is well-educated people who want to take a chance at self-government and self-determination and actively work toward that.

SILVERA: So in that way things are changing?

KEESHIG-TOBIAS: Things are changing, but we still have to deal with the cultural self-hate. Last week, there was a rumour that our school board, which is now locally controlled, was going to favour the language and wasn't going to allow any Native culture into the schools. That notion is being pushed by a group of fundamentalists up here, fundamentalist Christians. They don't want to have anything to do with the culture, but they want to learn the language — to me, that's like learning road signs. *(laughter)*

SILVERA: They want to learn the language but not the culture?

KEESHIG-TOBIAS: Not the culture. They don't even want the culture used to teach the language. On the outside, when I lived in Toronto, it was easy to go out and fight for stories. I never thought that the same kind of thing would happen here in my own community and that we'd get opposition from our own people. So it's that cultural self-hate we still have to reckon with and heal.

SILVERA: And also the struggle to keep language and culture together.

KEESHIG-TOBIAS: Exactly. I think again because of the residential school syndrome and Christianity up here, people are really questioning and they scrutinize very severely the people who would be teaching, say, Native culture. They really do. To me, that's the pot calling the kettle black. The same thing happened in our daycare. They wouldn't allow the drum in there. Members on the daycare committee said that some of the people who play the drum, or who were part of the drum, were not respectful enough. *(laughter)*. It's so frustrating sometimes. So despite everything, the decision was made that no religion whatsoever would be taught in the school and there would be no Christmas, no Easter, no anything and that if they did do anything, they would just do the basic which translates to just emphasizing the commercials. *(laughter)* It's moments like those I just want to pull out my hair. I'd rather my kids not learn anything than just spend money on Easter eggs or Christmas stuff and get sucked into that whole system — that's how frustrating it is out here.

SILVERA: When do you find time to write? You obviously don't write full-time.

KEESHIG-TOBIAS: No, not any more, although I'd like to now that Emma and Adam are at school. Emma's just got into grade one, so she's at school all day, and Adam is at school half a day. Were it not for my two grandchildren being here with me for a while, I'd be sitting down to write pretty regularly.

SILVERA: That's what I wanted to ask you. How has writing changed over the years? Now your children are growing up, but you ...

KEESHIG-TOBIAS: But then I have this new set of children now, my grandchildren. And I have to have responsibility for my grandchildren.

SILVERA: So that puts away your writing full-time.

KEESHIG-TOBIAS: It does, but also I've turned to doing more storytelling and Native awareness workshops and talks up in this area.

SILVERA: So you're doing a lot of internal and much-needed work in your community?

KEESHIG-TOBIAS: Yes. And, of course, there are my political commitments. Last week, for example, I was on the phone all morning with the Rights and Freedoms Committee of the Writer's Union. The committee was planning to have a protest, September 20, 1994, at a school up in Collingwood in my area. This particular school board had taken W.P. Kinsella's Indian books off the shelf. They didn't take them off the shelf, they censured them. There's a difference there — it's not *censored*, it's *censured* — so those books could only be used under the guidance or tutelage of a teacher.

SILVERA: What happened with you and the Writer's Union?

KEESHIG-TOBIAS: There were some frantic phone calls I made to get the information I needed to understand what exactly the situation was. I eventually got a hold of Clayton Ruby, the chair for that committee. We talked about it, and I told him that I'd read all of Kinsella's Indian books and that I agree with other Aboriginal peoples that the books are maliciously racist and I would never recommend these books to any young person, unless that young person was going to be guided through the book by a teacher or someone who is knowledgeable and respectful of Aboriginal people and trained in anti-racist education to help the child or young person understand the difference between irony and mockery.

SILVERA: What was the response?

KEESHIG-TOBIAS: Clayton still felt it was censorship. I felt there was a better way to handle the situation — to make a compromise, to let the books go to the reference shelf, so they are used in a really pro-active, educational way rather than trying to set up a confrontation. I suggested, too, to make a compromise with the particular Native group and the board by offering to buy books to increase the Native collection in the library. I'm sure it can be substantiated that the reason groups like this particular Native group wanted to ban

Kinsella's books was because there's such a lack of really good Native books authored by Native people and a lack of books by respectable and reputable non-Native authors.

If there was a balance there, then there'd be no question about Kinsella's stuff being left on the shelves — people could see how disrespectful his stuff is compared to other works. Clayton wanted members of PEN and members of the Union to be part of that protest and to go up there and hand these books to the students as they went to classes in the morning. I suggested that people who would be part of this protest be the ones to contribute to enhancing the schools Native book selection. Otherwise, if they're going up there to hand out Kinsella books, it's like handing out Ernst Zundel's material. And then where would it all end? I really had to stress that there's a difference between *censure* and *censor*. Censure is harsh criticism. On the other hand, if they were trying to ban something like Rudy Weibe's stuff or M.T. Kelly, then I'd have no problem with a protest, but W.P. Kinsella?

SILVERA: I know you're also involved in the racial minority group within the Writer's Union. How did that come about?

KEESHIG-TOBIAS: The group was formed right after I joined the Writer's Union. I joined the union right about the time the split happened at the Women's Press over that anthology — what was the name of it?

SILVERA: That was *Imagining Women: Short Fiction,* edited by the Second Second *(sic)* Story Collective, Women's Press, 1988.

KEESHIG-TOBIAS: I paid really close attention to that because I knew how the women of colour felt. We had experienced the same kind of thing — people assuming they could somehow tell a story the way a Native woman would, that they could teach Native children something about Native culture that Native people couldn't themselves teach. I've run across that kind of condescension, be it conscious or unconscious. I was keenly aware of it and really followed it in the media because I was thinking about how I would respond to things like that. Maybe in a subconscious way, I was looking for a way to get involved and to add my voice to the issue. I joined the Union primarily to see what it had to offer Aboriginal writers — if I felt it was worth it, then I would encourage other Aboriginal people to join. The Union has done things on contracts, reproduction, grievances and copyright, so they've done a lot of leg work. I joined and right away certain members in the Union wanted to know if there was racism in writing and publishing. At the following AGM they were going to have a panel discussion on "is there racism in writing and publishing?" The only visible minority writer they knew of was Dan Moses. He said, Oh, I don't think I'd be able to do that, but why don't you give Lenore Keeshig a call ... *(laughter)* I was on that panel and it was a very, very hard panel. The other panellists included two men, a South Asian man and a white publisher. After a while, there were no questions being directed to them, questions were all directed at me. I was really under attack. It was volley after volley of questions, accusing me of reverse racism, and how dare I take away somebody's "magical forest."

SILVERA: So was that about appropriation?

KEESHIG-TOBIAS: That was part of it. What they did not want to look at was is there racism in writing and publishing? All I could respond was, of course, there is, otherwise you wouldn't have the South Asian Press, you wouldn't have a Sister Vision Press. You wouldn't have these presses and magazines.

SILVERA: So did this lead to the committee?

KEESHIG-TOBIAS: In a roundabout way. I wasn't able to stay for the plenary of that AGM, but a couple of people got up and tried to put forth a resolution that they form a committee to investigate racism in writing and publishing. That was voted down. It was such an attack on me and what I stood for. Nothing was done for at least a month or so and I was at loose ends. So I called a number of people who were very supportive of me before and after that panel and asked if we could have a meeting because I wanted a debriefing. I wanted to know what went on.

It was there that we formed the Ad Hoc Committee on Writing and Publishing. Some of the members were from the Writer's Union, some were from the community at large. I think only two men attended any of those meetings. One was Daniel Moses and the other was David McLaren. Out of those meetings, we created a questionnaire which we circulated. As soon as the Union found out that we had formed an ad hoc committee, immediately it came forward to offer assistance with photocopying and with postage and stuff like that, which then led to the questionnaires slowly dribbling in and a whole year of lobbying of members within the Union.

During that time I worked with Clayton Ruby because I wanted to bring this through the Rights and Freedoms Committee. To me, it was an issue of rights and freedoms. It didn't have to do with other business, it didn't have to do with censorship. Then the committee requested we take a proposal to the National Council, a proposal to have a planning session that would bring together maybe eighty racial minority writers for three or four days to talk about concerns, set up priorities and make recommendations. That was done and we were still lobbying to have a closed meeting, much like the Writing Thru Race Conference that took place in Vancouver in June 1994.

The issue of Native voice also came up. A symposium on Native voice was held in one of the great big lecture halls — I believe this was at Queens University in Kingston — and Daniel Moses and I were sitting *(laughter)* up in the audience, watching. Finally, I couldn't take it any more and I stood up and said, If you're talking about Native voice then I think Daniel Moses and I should be right up there. And I grabbed Dan by elbow and said, Let's go. We got up and marched right down and took the floor. Meanwhile, there was a lot of commotion from the facilitator, who was trying to get the whole group to vote on whether or not it should allow us to speak. We got to stand at the podium and express our concerns.

Later on during that meeting there was a resolution — we were trying to get a committee established and there was a lot of lobbying around the word racism. I wanted to keep it in and some people said, well, you're not going to get anywhere if you keep it in, so take it out. And so we acquiesced and it turned out to be something like "issues of concern to racial minority writers." It was some time after that resolution was accepted that the racism word was put back in. Then there was another resolution passed that I be appointed to set up a committee for racial minority writers and that this committee would then plan the planning session. I tried to recruit members from the Union, but there were very few. Finally, we went out into the community at large to find people to sit on the committee. A couple of years later, in 1994, we had the Writing Thru Race Conference.

SILVERA: What was the conference like for you? Being in Vancouver, with so many writers of colour, particularly after all the controversy that took place?

KEESHIG-TOBIAS: It was most refreshing and I was so pleased. I have so much admiration for Roy Miki because he was under intense pressure, especially the last few months before the conference. It was really so important for me to see that and be part of it. I wish it were longer and I wish there was more chance for the Aboriginal writers to get together. Many of us had never really had an opportunity to meet as a group.

SILVERA: What Aboriginal writing panel did you participate in?

KEESHIG-TOBIAS: Only one, writing for children. I brought the bibliographies I had worked on and curriculum materials I had worked on and independent publications, to show what could be done for children and what could be done in the schools. I also talked about how difficult it was for me to get *Bird Talk* published — until I presented it to Sister Vision who just scooped it up.

SILVERA: I want to come back to *Bird Talk*, but let me just tell you this: I was reading *Books in Canada* and saw this article called "Writers and Politics." It was a piece on the Writer's Union of Canada. Michael Corrin was saying he had problems with writers who become overtly political and that that's one of the reasons why he would never join the Writer's Union of Canada. It seems to me there is this whole school of thought that if you are a "good" writer, then you cannot or should not be political.

KEESHIG-TOBIAS: As if the status quo was neutral.

SILVERA: Well, exactly. He ended the piece by saying he had more respect for writers who spent the weekend behind a dusty desk reading dusty books in a library than he did for someone speaking about politics. Funny, isn't it, that he thinks that this is a neutral position and is apolitical?

KEESHIG-TOBIAS: And that stories are little innocuous things. Stories have power, books have power. They either break you, destroy you, or they empower you. They can make you laugh and forget about your worries for awhile, or they can give you new insight into something. I think it was Maria Campbell who told me that a storyteller cannot separate her art from her spirituality from her politics. I believe that. That's the way I operate.

SILVERA: Do you think that in your writing, in your storytelling, you struggle also against a patriarchal language?

KEESHIG-TOBIAS: I've never really been aware of that. Let's put it this way: I guess I've been aware of that subconsciously. *(laughter)* All my children's stories are about young girls, Aboriginal girls. And the poetry I write about ...

SILVERA: Was that conscious?

KEESHIG-TOBIAS: It was conscious, come to think of it. Most of the stories and stuff about Aboriginal people were about brave little Indian boys — very little about girls, except for Pocahontas. I wrote about my daughters because I wanted them to understand that there were certain aspects, certain events, in their lives that we share, that are teachings — a respected Indian elder, I think his name was Lame Elk or Lame Deer, he said, "I wasn't put on this Earth for nothing." *(laughter)* That's what our traditional people teach: you're put on this Earth to learn. We learn through our experiences. I'm a woman writer. There's no other way I can write except through my woman's eyes, my Aboriginal woman's eyes. That's how I see the world.

SILVERA: What does it mean to you to be an Aboriginal woman writer writing in Canada today?

KEESHIG-TOBIAS: It's reclaiming and recreating the woman's role as keeper of the culture, as first teacher, as first storyteller. What I try to do is reflect in the work I do our connection to the Earth and how our stories are connected to the Earth.

SILVERA: What impact does the feminist movement have on your writing? Or does it?

KEESHIG-TOBIAS: I think it has had a great impact. Particularly in my early days when I was a young mother and university student, I needed that kind of liberation, and I found it in the books and magazines. When the issue of racism within the women's movement surfaced I could look in that and I could see parallels. I could hear the voices of women of colour and Aboriginal women in that movement and how they needed to speak for themselves, how they needed to be heard, and how white women had to face their own racism.

SILVERA: For us as Aboriginal women, Black women, other women of colour, do you see that there's still an invisibility in mainstream Canadian women's literature?

KEESHIG-TOBIAS: Yes, I think there is.

SILVERA: How can we change that? How can we become more visible within this so-called Canadian literature?

KEESHIG-TOBIAS: Well, through people coming to understand how important politics is in writing. The reason people like me are discounted is because I'm so political.

SILVERA: Exactly.

KEESHIG-TOBIAS: And so I'm censured for that. *(laughter)*

SILVERA: Exactly. I don't see how any writer of colour can claim not to be political, though I do know quite a few who have stated this.

KEESHIG-TOBIAS: That's right. One thing I found through the years is that a lot of us don't write for the market, we don't write for the sheer enjoyment or luxury of writing. We write for our communities, we write to empower our communities. We use a language which at one time was used as a weapon to oppress us. Now we take that weapon and we're turning it around. We're not using it as a weapon, we're using it as a tool to empower ourselves, our communities, our daughters, our people.

SILVERA: Yep, that's very true. How has this issue of appropriation manifested itself in Canadian literature?

KEESHIG-TOBIAS: W.P. Kinsella. You can also see it in television and in the film industry. I think what it has done is to deny Aboriginal people's distinctiveness. Status quo writers think that they have the country and so they think the stories go along with that. This is probably the last frontier and I'll fight it to death. That's how important our stories are to us. There's no way that I want them confused and lost and appropriated and turned around and fed to our children.

SILVERA: What about this notion of the imagination? The one that keeps coming up in every mainstream literary discussion, that anyone should be able to write from the imagination?

KEESHIG-TOBIAS: They can write whatever they want — it's fine with me. But they got to be strong enough to stand up and take the criticism. So far they're not, they're all whimpering about that. As if middle-class, white writers can transcend Rosedale and plop themselves down on a reserve in Northern Ontario for six weeks or six months — what's the difference? *(laughter)* — and come up with a story that is truly evocative of the people who have lived in that place, that land, for generation upon generation. It can't be done. People's imaginations are limited by what they know and don't know, by what they think they know. What they're doing is rehashing their own myths. It doesn't work. People like me, from within the culture, can see through that. It's not authentic at all, it's just a jelly-mould or something.

SILVERA: So you do think that the writer has a responsibility?

KEESHIG-TOBIAS: Oh, most definitely. The writer, the storyteller, the artist, has a responsibility.

SILVERA: And who is that responsibility to?

KEESHIG-TOBIAS: That responsibility is to the readers or the listeners. But there is also a responsibility to the people one is writing about. Is the information accurate? Is it derogatory in any way? Is it perpetuating offensive stereotypes? And then, of course, there's the responsibility to the profession.

SILVERA: Do you get the sense that your work and that of other Native women writers is making some kind of difference in Canadian literature and in the education of First Nations people?

KEESHIG-TOBIAS: I think so. First it was Native women, Aboriginal women, who started writing, and they were the first people to get published. However, it's the men that have achieved the notoriety and *(laughter)* ...

SILVERA: Yeah, it's supposed to be that way *(laughter)* ... It happens in all our communities. Yep ...

KEESHIG-TOBIAS: Yes, there are so many parallels we share. Women are the grounding of the literature, of the stories, the keepers of the culture. We make the way safe and we ensure that the integrity of the stories is kept. On the other hand, the recognition that the male writers get — and I'm not saying all of them — some of it is just plain tokenism because they purport to be non-political. But as non-political as they purport to be, they're the ones who get recognition.

SILVERA: I was also thinking of that question. Not just male writers but also the few women writers the mainstream takes off with — suddenly, they represent everything that's Aboriginal or everything that's African or Black or Asian. For example, Terry MacMillan, the media has just taken off with her and suddenly she has become the voice of contemporary, heterosexual Black women. And then, Amy Tan. Maxine Hong Kingston has been around for many years and has written really good stuff, but she has somehow not gained the same stature.

KEESHIG-TOBIAS: I can't think of any Aboriginal women writers who have been taken off with. It's the men. To me, that's just a reflection of the patriarchal society that Canada is, a reflection that has repeated itself so many times through the 500 years since Contact — to ignore the women, even though the women are the real culture bearers, the culture brokers, even. All the credit is given to the men and the men become the chiefs. Paula Gunn Allen in *Sacred Hoop* wrote about that.

SILVERA: Can you recall the first novel you read by an Aboriginal woman?

KEESHIG-TOBIAS: Maria Campbell's *Half Breed*.

SILVERA: How did you respond to that book?

KEESHIG-TOBIAS: It was really hard because she told the story truthfully. For anyone to grow and understand as well as to heal, you have to confront the negative aspects of your culture. And that's alcoholism and other kinds of abuses. She did that, but she did it in a very powerful and uplifting way. We had to deal with that, we had to feel that depth and despair so we could go on and do other things. The first Aboriginal woman writer that really influenced me was E. Pauline Johnson, Canada's Indian poetess. *(laughter)*

SILVERA: How did you find out about her?

KEESHIG-TOBIAS: My mother read her to us when we were children. Her stuff is so wonderful to read out loud. It really is.

SILVERA: So your mother read a lot to the family?

KEESHIG-TOBIAS: My mother read a lot to us. The same with my father, but then he was more of the storyteller.

SILVERA: What were your parents like? Are they still on the reserve?

KEESHIG-TOBIAS: My parents are both still on the reserve. My father is an industrial painter and my mother is a student and social counsellor. My mother is high-school educated; my father had a grade eight education. My mother spent a number of years at summer school and now has a certificate in guidance counselling, so basically she is everybody's mom. She makes sure that all the kids go to school and have an allowance for books, money for clothing, and a boarding place. If they have a problem, she's there to counsel them. She's also the truant officer, and she's there to mediate between the parents and the teachers, the parents and the kids.

SILVERA: What do you see as your future political and literary work in your community?

KEESHIG-TOBIAS: I'd like to in the near future get a Native writers' retreat up here. The priority would be Native writers. And maybe once we get that established, I'd like to open it up to other writers. Do it in a very small scale and hopefully it will grow. Beautiful as Banff is ... *(laughter)* it's a chore to get out there! *(laughter)* Why does inspiration have to happen in the mountains? It doesn't have to. *(laughter)*

SILVERA: Speaking of that, what advice would you pass on to young Aboriginal women who want to write?

KEESHIG-TOBIAS: I would tell them to come to understand storytelling and understand the stories. Get to know the symbolism. If there are butterflies in a legend, what does it mean? The lightening doesn't strike birch trees. Why? And then all those things can be woven into the present-day reality of Aboriginal people. And, of course, read as much as one can about Aboriginal people — not just fiction, poetry and drama but also history and criticism — and then I'd go on to a multicultural literature.

SILVERA: Do you think that a lot of so-called established Aboriginal writers have stuck to that in their work? Do you think they have been true to the symbolism and meanings? Have they used it effectively in their craft?

KEESHIG-TOBIAS: No, I don't think they do. I think we're still calling out from colonialism, so the emphasis has been English literature. A lot of people have an English literature reference. I stayed away from that consciously. I'd rather go through bumbling around and making mistakes than have that kind of background. And I'd rather get it from Aboriginal writers whom I respect. They've already done the work of ciphering through it, *(laughter)* sifting through it.

SILVERA: What place do these writers write from?

KEESHIG-TOBIAS: From within the scope of things that they know and understand — from their experience.

SILVERA: Their experience and where they live? You mean whether it's in the urban area? Or the amount of contact they've had with their community? Do you think that has an impact?

KEESHIG-TOBIAS: It has an impact, but I think some things are in your genes, inherited memory. They still come through somehow. Maybe they're disguised in some way or form, but if you read this stuff carefully, you can identify people who identify themselves as being Aboriginal. It shows in their work. It doesn't matter if they come from the reserve or from the city. It shows. Then there are people who claim to be Aboriginal but don't acknowledge their Aboriginal culture. There are a couple of writers like that. You read their stuff, and you can't tell if they're Native or not — they've never identified. You'd never see them hanging around the Native Centre, you'd never see them at Native conferences. They may use things superficially and you can tell.

SILVERA: Who are the Aboriginal writers you respect? The ones whose work you really like?

KEESHIG-TOBIAS: Down in the United States there's an Aboriginal woman writer, Leslie Marmon Silko. And then there's Paula Gunn Allen and Simon Orcheez and Gary Hobson — there's so many down there. In Canada my very favourite is Dan Moses. And Bernella Wheeler and Rita Joe and Beatrice Culleton and others ...

SILVERA: I want to go back to your children's book *Bird Talk*. We talked earlier about publishers' unwillingness to accept the manuscript. The more I think about it, the more bizarre it seems. *Bird Talk* is such a wonderful story. As you know, we've done quite well with it. It has certainly been one of the Sister Vision Press success stories.

KEESHIG-TOBIAS: I was so happy when Sister Vision also suggested including an Ojibway translation.

SILVERA: The book also received the prestigious Martin Luther King Award in New York City, right?

KEESHIG-TOBIAS: Yes, for that whole weekend, I was on the verge of tears — even right now, while thinking about it — because I really have a lot of admiration for Martin Luther King and his work. To me, it was like getting an Eagle Feather. That's why I do my work, for the things that he dreamed about.

SILVERA: How was the book chosen?

KEESHIG-TOBIAS: The book was chosen by students at a number of public schools in New York City. I believe they went through about seventy books. The award was given to me and my daughter Polly, who did the illustrations and whom the story is based on. We received a cash prize and airfare to fly to New York City to receive the award. Polly went to receive it — it really began with her experience — and she had a wonderful time. The children there loved her. They could really identify with her and that story.

SILVERA: We were really ecstatic when we heard. It is quite an honour as publisher to receive such praise for that wonderful book.

KEESHIG-TOBIAS: It certainly is. I remember driving somewhere after I heard the news. I had to just pull over on the side of the road and cry. It's kind of a shame that it didn't happen here in Canada. Oh well ... *(laughter)* just a reflection of culture in Canada. *(laughter)* You got to go elsewhere for recognition. *(laughter)*

SILVERA: So what's your next project?

KEESHIG-TOBIAS: I want to do this Ojibway alphabet book in English — another children's book, an alphabet book, very simple. A is for Administration building. *(laughter)* Or A is for Anishnawbe, the name we call ourselves. C is for Chief and Council and my dad says Chief and Council talk a lot about nothing — you know, in a child's voice. That way I can touch on some very common understandings and try to get into some deeper understandings like the importance of aunties in Aboriginal society. And I can also touch on land claims and all the sort of things that people are so freaked out about. I will be so politically correct people will shit bricks. *(laughter)*

SILVERA: And where do you see your political work with the Union going?

KEESHIG-TOBIAS: If the next couple of years don't become easier for me and for others as racial minority writers — I've given it my best shot, I've done what I can do and I'll just bow out. It's been tough being there — people making snide remarks within ear distance, saying things behind my back, people getting up and interrupting my talks to ask how many books I've published, questioning my credibility as a writer.

SILVERA: Very interesting. Who are these people?

KEESHIG-TOBIAS: Members of the Union, so they're people who have published. So what's make a writer? Is it the quality of your book or the quantity of your books? Native people recognise me as an author, they also recognise me as a traditional storyteller and they give me tobacco when I storytell or when I go to speak. I have recognition within my own community and that's really all I need.

I don't want to start another organization. Because books are so important to me, I'd like to see this happen from within the Union. I mean, these people claim to be Canadian. Do they understand where the word Canadian comes from? Do they really understand that? Or is it just some cute relic? We're all put here for a reason and that is what I tried to express when we were at the Writing Thru Race Conference. I believe we're a living breathing part of the prophecy that says that Turtle Island will be the place where the four colours of people will come together as one. I want to make that happen, that's my motivation, I want Canada to be a part of that. Whatever Canada thinks and feels has a direct impact on Aboriginal people. I mean, they're living on our land, they're treading over the bones of our ancestors. We have no other place to go. We don't come from somewhere else.

Lillian Allen

Patrick Nichols

Lillian Allen

Poems are not meant to lay still[1]

BECAUSE WORDS don't (always) need pages, I have published extensively through readings, performances and recordings. I have been reluctant to commit my poetry to the page over the years because, for the most part, these poems are not meant to lay still.

As I prepared poems for this collection, I had to "finalize" pieces I had never imagined as final. Like a jazz musician with the word as her instrument, reading and performing these poems is an extension of creating the work. In some ways, I had to reverse this process to ready these poems for print, to find their written essence. Pages do need words.

These poems breathe, they are alive. Sit quietly with them, read them aloud, or shout them in public places.

And remember: always a poem, once a book.

Enjoy.

By the time I was formally introduced to literature in high school, I was amazed and dazzled by the sheer festivity of the Jamaican language. To my delight, I found I was also excited with the sensuality and power of the written word — its ability to transport me to new worlds, to describe emotions. Writers who wrote passionately out of their own situations engaged me the most.

Growing up in Spanish Town, Jamaica, in a British-style school system, I was conscious of the tension between how we expressed ourselves in a natural, joyous and feisty way outside school and how we were supposed to express ourselves at school. It was assumed that if we wanted to make something of ourselves and get ahead, we had to leave our culture and "bad talk" behind. Very early I knew this was not an attack on "bad" culture or "bad" language. Such an orchestrated strategy to "keep these people in their place" and to stigmatize something so fundamental to a people's identity and sense of self was a deliberate attempt to degrade and destroy the very essence of who we are. It was my first recognition that racism and discrimination are also based on social and economic realities.

Jamaica is known as the dynamic little country that gave the world reggae music. A predecessor of dub poetry, reggae emerged from the grassroots. Its birth was an undeclared act of subversion — no invitation was issued and no permission granted. An authentic people's voice with a rhythm of resistance and hope, it carries a universally felt heartbeat and a message of defiance and resistance. Reggae was associated with ignorance and lack of sophistication and was much frowned on by the arbiters of Jamaican taste and culture. It subverted the complex and subtle structure of censorship under capitalism, a structure maintained by the imposition of class-based and racially-based standards for expression. These "standards" conspire to negate, exclude and limit the possibilities for expression.

It is precisely because of reggae's success and the nature of that success that dub poetry developed. Reggae was rooted in the lives and concerns of ordinary people. Its stance was dignified and demanding, its messengers sincere. Without reggae, dub poetry could never have existed. And without two remarkable figures of the

20th century, Louise Bennett (who is now living in Toronto) and Bob Marley (at rest), there would be no dub poetry.

Louise Bennett — Miss Lou, as she is affectionately known — emerged in the '40s which was a time of shifting political consciousness in the region. In the '30s there had been massive strikes throughout the Caribbean and massive migration to Britain. Now, along with the mobilization of various sections of the labour force, came an awakening of national identity and to the potential of nationhood.

Louise Bennett developed a persona that fit in with the African tradition of the artist as preacher, teacher, politician, storyteller and comedienne. Because she lived in a society that relied heavily on spoken communication, she wrote in the language that most Jamaicans speak most of the time. And she did it long before it was acceptable. She wrote of their triumphs and pain, their follies and foolishness, but most of all, she gave them a mirror of who they are and gave them permission to be proud of themselves and to fight back.

>   Ef wi kean sing "Linstead Market"
>   An wata come a me y'eye,
>   Yuh wi haffi, tap sing "Auld Lang Syne"
>   An "Coming thru de rye."[2]

Miss Lou presented "problems of classification and description" for the literary establishment. Although she had been publishing since 1942, she was not acknowledged as a writer. Despite exclusion, Louise Bennett took her words — through performance — directly to the Jamaican people. Today her books, stories and poems form a *major* document of Jamaican social history and culture. She is a stunning example of resistance, self-sufficiency, freedom and self-determination.

With the social and political movements of succeeding decades, art and culture took on a new and significant role for Jamaicans. The '60s brought the Black Power Movement in the United States and its poets of resistance — Jane Cortez, Sonja Sanchez, Nikki Giovanni, Gil Scott-Heron, Amiri Baraka, The Last Poets and others. The liberation from British colonial powers fanned post-independence aspirations, and the rise of the Rastafarian movement — emphasizing Black people's role in history and a return to African roots — brought a spiritual dimension to political determination.

Bob Marley appeared on the heels of Louise Bennett. Like many of the artists of the '60s and '70s, Marley looked to Miss Lou for inspiration and used the body of her work as a reference point. He built on her work and got on, in a more direct manner, with the business of calling the system to account.

In the early '70s, in the dance halls of Jamaica, competing sound systems with highly skilled DJs and refrigerator-size speakers vied for the biggest crowds. This was the indigenous pop culture of the people, and this music did not find acceptance on the island's radio stations until much later on. Star DJs — The Mighty U-Roy, Big Youth and I Roy — chanted messages over instrumental versions on the flip sides of popular songs. DJs were so marginalized from the mainstream of official Jamaican culture that no subject matter and no individual, no matter how powerful, was sacred. These DJs talked about anything and everything, from the private and personal to social and political taboos.

The mixers of the music, the studio engineers, became conscious of the way live DJs worked with the music and the interactive dynamics of their performances in the dance halls. The engineers and studio mixers attuned their techniques to create re-mixed versions of the instrumentals. The mixers' techniques of echoing, repeats, fades, the dropping in and out of instruments to create internal rhythms, ignited the imagination of a generation of young poets: Oku Onuora, Mutabaruka, Jean Binta Breeze, Mikey Smith, Nabby Natural, Malachi Smith, Poets in Unity, among others. These groups of word practitioners, all born in the early '50s, echoed the rhythms, the excitement and the concerns of the period.

It was in this period — the late '70s — that Oku Onuora, describing his poetic creations and the poetic ventures of some of his fellow poets in Kingston, Jamaica, first pressed the term dub poetry into circulation. By giving it a name, Onuora inadvertently precipitated the crystallization of a new and distinct poetic form. It was not just a matter of liberating poetry from the constraints of academia. Onuora expressed the deep resolve of his contemporaries:

> I am no poet
> no poet
>
> I am just a voice
> I echo the peoples
> thought
> laughter
> cry
> sigh
> I am no poet
> no poet
> I am just a voice.

Dub poetry is not just an art form; it is a declaration that the voice of a people, once unmuzzled, will not submit to censorship of form.

Dub poetry developed simultaneously in and outside Jamaica. It surfaced in the major metropolitan areas where West Indians migrated, especially in London, England, and Toronto, Canada. In London, Martin Glen, Benjamin Zephariah and Linton Kwesi Johnson engaged their communities with their activist poetry. In Brixton's embattled Black community, Linton Kwesi Johnson set his political poems to a menacing reggae bass line:

night number one was in BRIXTON
SOPRANO B, sound system
was beating out a rhythm with a fire
coming down his reggae-reggae wire[3]

The working-class Johnson emigrated to England from Jamaica in 1963. He is best known for his militant poetic contribution to the political struggles of Blacks in England, in particular, and of the working class, in general.

Those of us working in Toronto — Clifton Joseph, Devon Haughton, Ahdri Zhina Mandiela, Ishaka, Afua Cooper — although thousands of miles from the source, discovered that our artistic responses were similar. Instinctively, we set out to shape this new expression, to work with a form whose aim was to increase the dynamism of poetry, to strengthen its impact and immediacy, a poetic form that could incorporate many aspects of performance, drama, fiction, theatre, music, opera, scat, a cappella, comedy, video, storytelling and even electronics. It was poetic ammunition, an artistic call to arms.

When I first started to write I wrote plays and short stories. Because it was impossible to get an encouraging word from publishers at the time — "there wasn't a market for such works," it was said — or to get a play produced, I switched to poetry. It was, to put it simply, more portable. It was art-to-go. Take-out art. Me, my poetry and the public. No middleman.

It wasn't always easy at those community meetings in the '70s though I found a captive audience for my poetry. For a long time, I was scheduled to perform during the break, when everyone was reaching for coffee, or at the very end, after six speeches, five-and-a-half of which were unnecessary. It was: "Thank you folks for coming ... *la luta continua* ... we'll pass the bucket for donations (big speech on importance of donating here) ... and now Sister Lillian will read some of her poetry."

It wasn't easy wrestling prime time from the political heavyweights, but the audience came to love and expect the poetry and demanded it when it was not there. Even today, political events in Toronto's Black community include poetry and other cultural offerings as an integral part of articulating issues, forging collective energy and making essential connections.

From the mid-'70s, dub poets were activists working in Toronto's Black community on many issues: racism, police brutality, the racially-biased streaming of Black children in the school system, the plight of single mothers in public housing, racist immigration laws and practices. We worked for the upliftment and liberation of African peoples. We worked to organize Black parents, for African liberation support committees and in solidarity across racial and cultural lines. We worked in white organizations and created possibilities for others. We wrote, performed the works of other poets and experimented. We believed in possibilities.

That art is political — that the cause of our art, like the cause of art that maintains the status quo — must be declared openly. Art in itself is symbolic. Though it can play a major role in people's lives and in social and political movements, it cannot change the structure of social relations. Our work as poets extends beyond mere creation: we take our poetry and our convictions into the community. We organize, we network, we participate, we protest, we celebrate, we build community.

But the limitations of a Black nationalism that has macho tendencies, that defined political, social and personal problems solely along racial lines, coupled with the patriarchy of the male-dominated white left, made it imperative for women to challenge women's oppression. A woman and Black at every moment in my life, I felt the need for a new vision, one that included not only Black people's and working people's rights but also the full and equal participation of women, so it was imperative that the fight be carried on, on this front also. As well, I began to see a clear link between the specificity of people's lives and the power structures. I made specific connections between oppression of women and imperialism, creating new awareness. Where most art reflects or carries consciousness, my poetry began to create consciousness:

> *ITT ALCAN KAISER*
> *Canadian Imperial Bank of Commerce*
> *privilege names in my country*
> *but I am illegal here*
>
> *I came to Canada and found*
> *the doors of opportunity well guarded*[1]

My work became so eclectic that I was invited to read at many different events by many different groups: labour unions, schools, cultural and community events, universities, art groups, women's conferences, folk festivals, new music festivals and women's festivals, literary groups, Black heritage classes, libraries, weddings, nightclubs, benefits, rallies and political demonstrations. Sometimes my poetry would be the keynote speech at an event.

Publishing was another story. *Rhythm & Hardtimes* was the first book published in Canada to include dub poetry. It was self-published and self-distributed, and this demystified publishing for many who had never before considered publishing. Seven self-published books immediately followed. Several more have been published since. Some of these books have sold in the thousands. *Rhythm & Hardtimes* itself sold over 8,000 copies.

The marriage of dub and music was not always an easy or happy one because dub poets worked primarily with the word in a form that was already complete by the time we began to collaborate with musicians. Years of experimentation with music and musicians were rewarded in 1985 when I brought together a fine group of grassroots musicians, along with members of Canada's new top pop group, the Parachute Club, to produce *Revolutionary Tea Party*, an album that won Canada's 1986 Juno Award for best reggae/calypso album. My second album, *Conditions Critical*, released in 1988, also won a Juno. The albums propelled dub poetry beyond the bounds of the literary or the arts communities and into pop culture.

The accessibility of dub poetry is one reason for its cross-appeal. The political subject matter is relevant to most of the world's population. Dub poetry validates the lives and aspirations of those ignored and excluded from the dominant culture; it articulates a just vision of the future; it carries a spirit of defiance, celebration and empowerment. There is a spiritual connection because it asserts revolutionary possibilities, most importantly for those who must struggle for freedom and transformation.

The first generation of dub poets wrote of police brutality, of immigrants' dashed dreams, of hard work and little pay, of the oppression of Black women at the hands of Black men, of the need to nurture and to fight back. We made art part and parcel of political work.

In May 1993 in Toronto the first International Dub Poetry Festival brought together over one hundred dub poets from over twenty countries, including practitioners from Canada's First Nations, Ethiopia, South Africa, the US, France and Germany, to reveal that though dub poetry has only just begun it is already a growing international phenomenon.

Because dub poetry is not strictly page-bound and because institutions in our society do not account for our existence, we have gone directly to the public: recording, performing and self-publishing. We side-stepped the all-powerful middle-man who serves as the arbiter of culture. Dub poets — with our activism and solidarity work, our network of readings and poetry across the country and our political stance and media profile — have emerged as a major national Black cultural presence in Canada. Dub poets have galvanized Black culture, Black writers and a progressive culture of resistance in Canada and have set a standard for political art unparalleled in this country.

Endnotes

[1] This piece appeared in a slightly different form as the Preface and Introduction to *Women Do This Everyday: Selected Poems* by Lillian Allen (Toronto: Women's Press, 1993).

[2] Louise Bennett in "Bans O' Killing" from *Jamaica Labrish*.

[3] Linton Kwesi Johnson in "Five Nights of Bleeding".

[4] Lillian Allen in "I Fight Back".

Maria Campbell

Thomas King/Books in Canada

Maria Campbell talks to Beth Cuthand

It's the job of the Storyteller to create chaos

storytellers are the thunders ...
the thunders shake the ground ...

CUTHAND: I want to talk to you about the idea of marginalization. It's a hot topic, and a lot of folks of colour and Aboriginal people have been marginalized from the mainstream publishing industry and the Canadian literary canon. Do you feel marginalized?

CAMPBELL: No, I don't feel marginalized, at least not these past few years. But I work mostly in oral traditions — you know, oral histories and storytelling, so I'm writing for my community. But for sure, there was a time when I first started to write that I felt completely alone. The majority of writers were white. Just never saw brown faces, Aboriginal or other. I'd go to conferences, gatherings, and they were friendly, but I was different and people didn't really know what to do with me. They included me or tried to, but I was patronized most of the time and I didn't like the feeling. When I tried to articulate how I felt they were hurt or accused me of acting the victim, so I just dropped out. What was the point? I dropped out of the Writers' Union and out of the other organizations. I'd joined them because I was looking for a "writing community" and I'd thought that could make a difference for new Aboriginal writers.

CUTHAND: But why did you drop out? Was it because you felt misunderstood?

CAMPBELL: Yeah, I felt misunderstood, but then what the hell? We're always misunderstood when we go into their world, marginalized, we know that. I knew that when I joined them. I guess I dropped out because I couldn't deal with the patronizing. It was making me crazy. I just don't make a very good pet Indian or halfbreed, Beth, and in a way that's unfair because there were some really great people, but they understood and remained friends, and I found better uses of my energy, in my own community where it was needed and appreciated.

CUTHAND: I guess I don't feel marginalized. I think it's for the same reason you are talking about that I have a community of people for whom I write. I don't write for white, mainstream Canadians. If they understand my work, that's fine, but if they don't, it doesn't matter.

CAMPBELL: Yeah, that's true. Really, I'm writing for my community. I sometimes get really frightened when I'm publishing something — not of mainstream but frightened that my own people will be upset, reject me or whatever. But even if they are upset or reject me, I can understand the place they come from. I might be lonely, but it is lonely, and that I understand, and no one will patronize me. Patronizing is so damned ugly and insidious.

THE OTHER WOMAN

CUTHAND: Do you think it's that way now?

CAMPBELL: Not in our community, but it is in the larger community — even more so because now they are aware, and that's due to our discussions on the appropriation issue. So now they are either damned mad or they are so "politically correct" that it's impossible to make a conversation because of their fears. We need to keep talking, but we need to talk as equals. There's nothing wrong with disagreeing — that's how we teach each other and understand each other. You can't discuss things if someone is being careful or guarded. Really, they still don't understand what the issue is.

CUTHAND: Well, obviously you've chosen to put your energy into writing for your community. Who is your community?

CAMPBELL: My community is primarily Aboriginal people because they have a good sense of who they are and where they come from and anybody else who has the same sense. I know my place and I'm tired of explaining it to people who don't honour their own place and their own history. You don't have to be Native to know what I'm saying. I can tell when I'm reading to a room of people that they know because they honour the things they have. That knowing is an unspoken thing.

CUTHAND: I had an experience in Colorado and I concentrated on performing the story there. A couple of people walked out and there were others in the audience who were uncomfortable with that form of storytelling. Somehow it wasn't legitimate in the mainstream. And afterward there were some Native American women who stayed and waited and talked to me. This Chicana writer from Boulder said that was the way it was in the mainstream — the fashion of reading was to read almost in monotone. Your words will work for you, you don't have to put in any extra reflection, no effort or performance.

CAMPBELL: I know what you mean. I've had people come up and tell me, "Well, that was a performance." In our tradition it is more than the words, it is the energy behind them, within and in front of the story. When I tried to explain that they didn't understand.

CUTHAND: The form of delivery for poetry in the United States and maybe some places in Canada is to deliver words like an incantation ...

CAMPBELL: I always wondered about that. For a long time I thought I couldn't write poetry because I couldn't get that kind of rhythm going. When I started to go to our old people for mentoring, the first thing they told me was to get that notion out of my head. Did I want to tell a white man's story or did I want to tell ours? When I said ours they said, then listen. In our tradition when you are invited to come and share a story you are not just reading words, you are sharing the energy that came to you with the story, and when you do that the community feels it and they become a part of it. And it's not always the words that they become a part of — sometimes it's the sound, the movement, sometimes you won't hear the words, or you don't remember the words until after many tellings. When the storyteller, writer, poet tells or reads in this way that is *magiwin,* the giveaway. That is the ultimate ceremony.

CUTHAND: So the real test of our writing comes at that moment when we give it away and they give it back.

CAMPBELL: Yes, I believe that. In ceremony people understand all the cues and respond accordingly. Now I don't understand why that should be such a problem: we all have cues, it's just that different cultures have different cues.

CUTHAND: Sixteen, seventeen years ago we talked a lot about the healing power of the word and the importance of telling stories. That was then, this is now, and I think we've both moved away from that point. We've come to that place where we don't have to write to heal ourselves. But why are we writing now? What drives us now that didn't drive us fifteen years ago?

CAMPBELL: I think that seventeen years ago — has it been that long? — we were the chosen storytellers. I don't know who chose us — yes, I do — Grandmother did. As those chosen storytellers, we were in pain and we needed to heal ourselves and we did. Today, we are making medicine with the community in the stories we share. It's not just pain any more. The important thing is not the book, the film, the play. The important thing is the ceremony the stories come from.

An example is En'owkin Centre, our school, a place for writers to come together to make their medicine. There is no star, only an energy built from all the people and the places they come from, giving all their opinions, their wisdoms and their truths and being excited by the work.

CUTHAND: Yeah. This is just what happened to me. There's an understanding and an identification with the work that gives me the energy to keep on going.

CAMPBELL: That's why I don't feel marginalized. I get energy to do the work. Why is it so hard for people to understand that's where I want to be? This way of working, writing, is ours, and it needs to be respected. If it were, there would be no problem. We could then really share, discuss, and exchange different methods and approaches. Maybe if we were on this ground, there would be no need to have discussions about appropriation. We could get on with the job of telling the stories our country needs to hear. The stories that come from place and from people — all peoples and all places — not just "mainstream's" interpretation of those people and places.

CUTHAND: Does it matter to you that you are reviewed by scholars who write literary articles about your work?

CAMPBELL: Yes, it does bother me because they don't understand my place or my history, and they are using standards of measurement that are foreign to the place I come from. Someday, I'd like to be reviewed by our own critics and scholars. We do have them — how we are going to convince mainstream of that will be the problem. Outside critics need to recognize that we already have our own literary styles, forms, genres, and that what we are doing is developing those in this time. That is our liberation.

CUTHAND: You know, to make revolution, and we're talking about revolution within our own community. We have to be tremendously brave to push against the boundaries that our own people have created for themselves.

CAMPBELL: That's the job of the storyteller. It's the job of the storyteller to create chaos. All you need to do is look at nature and that's part of our circle. Why do we have electrical storms and all those kinds of things? We might think they're bad because personally they are affecting us, but sometimes we need that. Things don't grow in the spring if thunder doesn't shake up everything. So sometimes — well, nearly all of the time — we have to speak with a strong voice, so the circle will stay strong. Because if we don't do that, then the link to our past and our ancestors is going to break. That almost happened to us. Colonization almost did that to us. Our circle was so changed, but somehow there were people who just kept making medicine and pretty soon we came along, and other people of our generation came along and this is now our place. We have to speak from here. That's what self government is, that's true sovereignty and that's the real revolution, and that's why we have to make ceremony, and that's why we have to be damned brave and shake things up like the thunders.

CUTHAND: It means we have to be sovereign human beings who carry on from our ancestors.

CAMPBELL: We can make the trail like our ancestors did for us. Make medicine, put the stories forward along with the energy so another generation can carry them into our future. To hell with feeling marginalized.

Saloni Mathur

bell hooks
Called me a "Woman of Colour"

I PROPOSE this essay as a map, a map of spatial and temporal scenery that attempts to locate a specific terrain. But a map, by definition, involves the setting of boundaries, so I would like to propose a different kind of map: a sight-seeing one, tracking movement through a variety of sites, a map of coming and going, of moving in and across, a scenic map and somewhat crumpled. The terrain of this map is the complex set of shifting relationships that constitute the category "women of colour."

More concretely, I address some of my own ambivalence towards being a "woman of colour" in today's academy, an ambivalence I am deliberately sustaining. I intend to explore the term "woman of colour," its place and function in feminist discourse and its development over the last dozen years from an active self-claiming on a radical margin to an almost hyper-visible construct in feminist discussions. I also address how the increasing fixity of this term raises several important political issues. By narrating a number of scenes in my map, I will explore the many complex ways that a category like "women of colour" gets inscribed in feminist discourse which, in turn, transcribes its subject. Finally, I will distinguish very broadly between the Canadian and American contexts for this term, both to emphasize my own shifting locations and to explore how national frameworks can inform the narratives through which a subject formation takes place. At the end of the essay, I pose some questions and offer a re-framing of my original ambivalence.

Scene 1

It is my first year in graduate school, and I am sitting in the living room of a professor's home in a small southwestern Ontario city. There are about thirty other women present. We have gathered for a dinner reception to honour bell hooks, who gave a guest lecture earlier that day while visiting our university on a speaking tour. I remember she spoke passionately and with conviction of her experiences as a Black female writer and cultural critic, about the interlocking nature of oppression and about the struggles we must wage in solidarity against racism, sexism, classism and cultural imperialism. Now we were sitting on the floor; a group of white students and I are seated in front of her, listening and nodding and eating our dinners from the plates we have balanced on our laps. She is sympathizing with the problems of students and reflecting on how her own life has been constituted by struggle. Then directing her gaze to me alone (and here my memory shifts into slow motion), she says across her dinner plate, "And, furthermore, We, as Women of Colour, should ... " I can't remember the rest of her sentence. The memory of the moment ends with her looking at me across her dinner plate and me fixated on those three words.

In Canada at that time I had never been referred to as a "woman of colour" before, nor had I any understanding of the term. I was sure that bell hooks had made a mistake. I even glanced around the room, thinking that I had caught a comment, or a gaze, directed at somebody else, perhaps a real woman of colour, maybe at a Black woman who was sitting behind me and eating her dinner. But there was no such "other" in my shadow. Indeed, bell hooks had been speaking to me, excluding the other students, white Canadian women. What kind of category was this "women of colour?" I asked myself. And what did it mean to be identified that way? How had I become a part of this We constructed by an African-American feminist scholar?

That was the day, I often tell people, that bell hooks called me a woman of colour.

Since that encounter with bell hooks, I have *become* a woman of colour. What I mean by that is that I have become increasingly engaged in a discourse that continues to situate me as such. As a middle-class woman of South Asian origin, born in India and raised in Canada, my entry into this culture is a product of a complex set of historical trajectories. I am accustomed to naming, labels and categories. My experiences have been variously contained, both willingly and reluctantly on my behalf, as those of an immigrant woman, a visible minority, an Indo-Canadian, an East Indian, of South Asian origin, as second generation (or is it first? I'm no longer sure), etc. But to add to the list, I now find myself entering the '90s as a woman, or person, or feminist, of colour. The act of claiming a position is itself empowering, but having it assigned to you (yet again) is cause, I think, for some reflection.

The difficulty, of course, in addressing this label is that it cannot be separated from the complex political relations that produced it. The term "women of colour" has both generated and been generated out of a central confrontation within feminist theory over the need for identifying difference and diversity among women as being the most crucial foundation for feminist practice. bell hooks herself has been at the forefront of radical critiques that point out how gender has tended to be privileged by white, middle-class, Euro-Western feminists over all other forms of difference, while race, class, and sexuality, which may equally transform women's experiences of oppression, have been either subsumed by gender or ignored entirely (hooks, 1981, 1984 and 1990). Such critiques have insisted that feminist theory and practice must understand the simultaneous and interlocking nature of systems of oppression and their multiple axes along various forms of difference. In the face of this challenge, the term "women of colour" has become increasingly employed by non-white women as a basis for a new model of political identity, one that forges a theoretical voice privileging otherness, difference and specificity, while remaining rooted in an alliance or coalition (see Sandoval in Haraway, 1991: 55-56). Thus "women of colour" has been a central concept in the dismantling of a particular convergence of racism and the women's movement and has its origins in the urgent need for discovering more inclusive strategies for building theory.

While the term is in one sense about the urgent need to recognize difference in women's lives, it also evinces movement towards the construction of a subjectivity that speaks this experience. The volume edited by Cherrie Moraga and Gloria Anzaldua, *This Bridge Called My Back: Writings by Radical Women of Colour*, represents one of the earliest efforts towards a radical self-claiming of identity and experience by non-white women in the United States. The term "women of colour" was embraced as an emancipatory strategy and a theoretical site in which to locate the struggle for self-representation. When it is linked to the power of the speaking subject to appropriate her experience, language, sexuality and history, the term has been praised as "one of the most novel ideas" that has arisen in the Anglo-European imperialist context (Alarcon, 1989: 37). Since then, the term seems to have been adopted by feminists in Britain, Canada and elsewhere, not simply as a racial or colour identification but as an active claiming of a "common context for struggle" (Mohanty, 1991: 7). It has become increasingly interchangeable with the term "Third World women," to the extent that both terms attempt to name a political coalition organized around specific sets of exploitative structures and their relationships. The term emerged as a strategic political and theoretical construct, one that transcended the simple terms of race and was actively claimed by non-white women. In short, the term and the tensions it engages are at the political forefront of feminist theory and practice. As such, it has adopted its own complex currency.

Scene 2

It is a little over a year ago, the first year of my doctoral studies, and I am doing some reading in my apartment in Montreal. The phone rings and I answer it. It is a white Canadian woman, in one of my seminars, who also works for an art magazine, and she is telling me about a large-scale conference, in the planning stages, to be held in Montreal. The conference is international in scope, bilingually committed (to French and English), and the theme is Feminism and the Arts. I was duly impressed. With substantial funding from a wealthy institute, the organizers had assembled twelve women to be on the planning committee, a list, she recited, of prominent (to me even famous) feminist theorists, artists, activists, directors of research centres, etc. In short, a group of very powerful women in Montreal's feminist community. It sounds very exciting, I tell her.

"We had our first organizational meeting last night," she continues.

"Uh huh," I say.

"And I don't quite know how to say this ... the project looks very exciting, really ... "

"Mm-huh," I agreed.

" ... and I don't want you to take this the wrong way ... a number of things were discussed last night, the funding, the research required, the kinds of issues and panels we might like to see ... "

"Yes," I say.

"So please, I hope you'll understand ... it was only our first meeting, but we became a little concerned that our entire planning committee was made up of white French and English women only."

"Oh, I see."

"And," she apologizes (cringing, in fact), "no women of colour are really being represented."

"Oh," I say, anticipating her next question.

"Would you be interested, perhaps, in serving on our committee?"

We both laugh a little nervously. She, because it had been awkward to ask, and me, at the obviousness of my single qualification for being included among such a prestigious group of feminist intellectuals. I, a student impressed by the project and able to recognize a good career opportunity when I see one, of course say yes and agree to attend the next meeting.

Identity, I have learned, is a series of trade-offs, a strategic business of selecting the role that might serve best one's provisional ends.

There is no doubt that the term "women of colour" has received substantial political popularity. Since 1980, that is, for the last fourteen years, the term "women of colour" has solidified from an active self-claiming on the radical margin to a recognizable entity within the realm of mainstream public and official discourse. Now we are all using the term. "Colour," in this sense, has served as a symbol of visibility.

Initially implicit in the term "women (or people) of colour" was an attempt to gain visibility in the blanched universe of a dominant Euro-Western society. But it has become a hyper-visible term, made into a commodity and slightly over-determined. One of the effects within feminism has been the creation of a dubious dichotomy that posits the category of "white women" in opposition to those who are presumably "of colour" (see Martin and Mohanty, 1986: 193). Often it has been used to identify otherness in a way that lumps it together, in a familiar inventory of "other," with terms such as "gay," "lesbian," "working-class women." Even more often it is posited as a singular opposition: white feminists versus women of colour. As a category, then, "women of colour" has become increasingly constructed as the "other" to feminism, replacing earlier formulations in which the "other" was Men (Strathern, 1987).

The following question thus arises for me: what is being served by this sort of formulation? How is this otherness being inscribed and reproduced, and whose interests does it ultimately serve? As Chela Sandoval has asked provocatively, are women of colour being "othered," separated, segregated in feminism for the safety of white women? (Sandoval, 1990: 60).

The increasing fixity of the white-versus-colour dichotomy raises a number of important political questions and objections. As an analytic strategy such terms tend to collapse economic specificity into chromatic relations. "Privilege" becomes virtually interchangeable with "white," subsuming the important context of class background under an assumption of racial marginality. Such a dichotomy also tends to equate the notion of "colour" with race, implying that white women somehow have no race, are non-racial, or are racially neutral, with no history of racial privilege to consider. Ruth Frankenberg and Hazel Carby (1990) have both argued for the need to recognize that "white people are raced" in the same way that men are gendered and that the category of "whiteness" is socially constructed and not a neutral or normative state of existence.

Further, there is the difficulty of defining who does and doesn't have colour. The use of the term "colour" as an empirical category has left many non-white (for example, First Nations) or racially mixed women feeling marginal to a discourse that is ostensibly about them. In "Are Asian-Americans Being Conned?" in a recent issue of *New York Asian News*, the author writes, "Just as I was getting accustomed to 'PC' standing for 'politically correct,' not 'personal computer' (or, I might add, 'postcolonial'), I discovered that it might also stand for 'people of colour'... Do Asian Americans qualify as 'people of colour'? ... What kind of classification is this 'people of colour'?" (Peters, 1991: 11). The reluctance of many to "become" people of colour is part of a fear that one's individual history and one's experience of being on the cultural periphery will become erased under the rhetoric of chromatic solidarity. Above all, this poses the problem of coalition and the difficulty of organizing around racial signifiers.

Scene 3

Two moments come to mind. They are different, but, for me, they resonate together. The first occurred earlier this year after I sent an article to a Canadian journal by women of colour. I called the editor a short while later to see what she thought of it. "It's wonder-

ful," she exclaimed on the phone. "We really liked it, and we'll publish it in its present form."

"Really?" I said. Hearing these words from an editor was a little like a Catholic being blessed personally by the Pope.

"Yes, yes," she said. "Voices like yours are important to us. We'd love to receive some more of your work — in fact, send us anything and we'll be pleased to publish it."

"Anything?" I asked meekly.

"Yes. Anything!"

Oh gee, thanks, I thought, and hung up the phone, sure that even the Pope would be a little more discriminating.

The second moment, both related and not, was a conversation I had with a white fellow student. She had heard that I was writing on the subject of women of colour and was dealing with similar questions in a paper of her own. "How do you feel about the category?" she asked me flatly.

"Well, I'm not sure yet," I answered. "I have some ambivalences, but I'm trying to think through them a little more clearly."

"That's very interesting," she told me. She had some similar concerns. Did I mind if she cited me in her own paper?

"Well, sure you can cite me, but there's not much to cite. I haven't finished the paper yet. I don't know how I'm going to develop it. Maybe we could meet and discuss it."

She interrupted me. "Well, you see, my paper's due tomorrow. Could you give me three or four lines summarizing where you stand on the subject? Three or four lines, as a woman of colour?"

Sometimes, I have learned, the politics of location are more like the politics of being locked in an empty room.

The assumption that women of colour suffer oppression in more than one way has led to a tendency in identity politics to stack oppressed identities, to rank women along hierarchies of oppression and to be overly concerned with who is more oppressed (Parmar, 1989). Pratibha Parmar suggests that, in Britain, this has led to a dangerously fixed configuration that paradoxically undermines the importance of understanding how simultaneous systems affect different women's lives (1989). In the United States, the phrase "women of colour," in the sense in which it means little more than "women *with* colour," has functioned in a similar way. Race has simply been added to the framework of a hierarchy of oppressions, while a unitary understanding of the Western woman remains fixed at the centre of such configurations. Norma Alarcon has suggested that, in spite of the radical nature of certain critiques, the result in Anglo-American feminism has been a particular closure, one that denies the theoretical possibility of non-unified subjectivities in favour of a fully closed narrative of identity and self (Alarcon, 1990). The simple privileging of a racialized subject, in many instances, has not been enough to carry out the much-needed unconditional overhaul of Western feminism.

And yet in some feminist texts a familiar account has emerged that hinges on "the critique by women of colour" to tell the story of progress in feminist thinking (Hurtado, 1989; Nicholson and Fraser, 1988; Moore, 1988). Such narratives tend to posit the work by women of colour as a singular, monolithic inquiry into difference and also to construct a now-familiar entity, "white feminist research," representing all the negligent assumptions of early feminist writers. The tensions born out of the meeting between these two homogeneous sets of women constitutes an almost Hegelian narrative of development in feminism. One off-shoot of this phenomenon in the United States is Third Wave Feminism, which presumably splashes upon the shores soaked by the Second Wave of the 1960s women's movement, wetting new ground or travelling a little further, as waves do, than its predecessor did (di Leonardo, 1991). This is not to deny the enormous significance or the centrality of an anti-racist challenge to American feminism. Nor is it to ignore that some women of colour in the United States have actively constructed this Third Wave. It does mean asking: what gets contained by such a narrative of wave-like progress? How is it articulated? Whose interests does it serve? How does thinking about feminist knowledge as waves obscure or wash away some of the tensions that produce it? And, finally, what are the boundaries that delimit and define the contours of such American shores?

Scene 4

My family and I are close to the border.

In this case, it is the actual, physical border between Canada and the US. The 49th Parallel, it's called, because it is inscribed on the 49th line of latitude, though I have often wondered parallel for whom? Today we are crossing it on a winter afternoon, travelling south in my mother's old Volvo, which no longer has heating. I am driving with my coat and gloves on, my sister is next to me in her black leather jacket, and my mom is in the back seat with a pair of new warm socks, a shawl wrapped around the shoulders of her sari.

As we approach the border crossing, we are met by the customs officials. I roll down the window for the official and the car fills with cold air. The official asks me the routine questions: Are you a citizen of Canada? Are you bringing any goods? Where are you going? And where are you from? I answer them all, like a good little Canadian, respectful of authority and of the very border itself. I also add, because of the sheer excitement of crossing the border, that I am going on a trip with my mom and my sister. The customs official seems uninterested and ejects the same line of questioning at the passenger's seat. My sister obliges him with the same set of answers. Finally, he turns to the back seat of the car and looks at my mom who has been sitting there patiently. Turning back to me at the wheel, he asks, "Is your mother a Canadian citizen?" as if she isn't there, as if she is an object I'm smuggling across the border. Yes, she is Canadian. The customs official looks suspicious, but then again, that is his job, to be suspicious, as my mom attempted to assure me later.

"Does she speak English?" the official asks me next.

I stare at him in silence.

"Do you mean, as opposed to French?" I want to say, but only because I know he doesn't mean that. "Or do you mean is she, like, capable of language," I wish I could say, to point out the basic requirements for English. Nor do I say, "Why are you asking me and not her? Is that standard practice for mothers in back seats?" I also do not say, "And why in the third person, as if she were somewhere outside the car?" And finally, I do not say, "Why do you expect so little from us?" feeling tired by the thought of the long history of state practices denying South Asians movement across borders. All of this I do not say. Instead, I break the silence by answering his question. Yes, she speaks English, I reply. The customs official waves us on, and we continue down the highway in our old Volvo.

Some things, I have learned, do not change when one is located on the border.[1]

Though I live and study in New York City, my "home," in the sense that Mary John (1989) has spoken of it as a "site of enunciation," remains firmly within Canada. For that reason, I want to distinguish broadly between the American and Canadian contexts for feminism, a distinction that obviously will be inadequate but one I want to make momentarily for the purposes of considering my shifting location.

Canada and the United States are similar and different. With respect to the larger global context of the international division of labour, the historical field of the development of late capitalism and the internal dynamic of neo-colonialism, both countries occupy the most privileged ranks. There is no striking difference between their feminist traditions, whereas one might characterize French feminism as different from American feminism. But a more nuanced difference between Canada and the US emerges when one attends to the two very different narratives of subject formation within each country.

To be a woman of colour in the American academy means, among other things, to be a part of an American coalition of women who have radically seized this political identity, to become part of an emergent "multicultural" formation (which is regarded by the Left as terribly exciting) and to be suspicious of its expression in the increasing dominance of academic sites, such as Cultural Studies. In Canada, on the other hand, to be a woman of colour is to finally stop being a "visible minority," the preferred identity of our multicultural hegemony as an "official federal policy" (that is, multiculturalism as bureaucracy). In Canada it means to swallow the tension produced by accepting the call to action from the South and resisting the ongoing dominance of American intellectual knowledge production. Finally, to be a woman of colour in Canada means to participate in coalition with American women while remaining at "home" within the ideology of a mosaic.

In short, to be a woman of colour in today's academy in either country is to participate in a complex arrangement of relationships. For me, it has sometimes meant being a native informant for white intellectuals, an authority on issues of racial difference, a privileged item on panels at conferences, a carrier of the weight and the burden of self-representation. Finally, to be a woman of colour today means to be always unable to escape racism, be it on this or that side of a national border or an experience born out of the border itself.

Epilogue

When bell hooks called me a "woman of colour," she was, as an African-American feminist writer, incorporating me into her collective We. In doing so (albeit in the interest of coalition), she inscribed me as a "subject" of her discourse. Similarly, when my fellow students or the journal editor located me "as a woman of colour," they effectively cast me as the same unitary subject. The moment of entry into their categories signals a moment of occupying an essentialized identity. This was the "fit" that was uncomfortable for me. Part of the difficulty, I suggest, lies in how to negotiate these essentialist moments, how to navigate through a shifting terrain that frequently collapses individual specificity. While "women of colour" is used to privilege difference and multiplicity, it does this through provisional contexts, by marking an essential conceptual unity. It is this particular reliance on essentialist definitions that was (and still is) the source of my discomfort.

In *Essentially Speaking* (1989), Diane Fuss explores how "essentialism" circulates in a variety of contemporary critical debates. By highlighting the very complex relations between feminism and essentialism (through the work of Irigaray, Wittig and other poststructuralists), Fuss identifies the essentialist/anti-essentialist polemic as one of the structuring debates of feminist theory. One of her aims is to "weaken the hold" that polemic has had on feminist thinking. To this end, she distinguishes between "falling into" or "lapsing into" the use of essential categories and "deploying" or "activating" essentialism as a strategic move, an intervention. For Fuss, essentialism in and of itself is neither good nor bad, progressive nor reactionary, beneficial nor dangerous (1989: xi). Instead, "the radicality or conservatism of essentialism depends, to a significant degree, on *who* is utilizing it, *how* it is deployed, and *where* its effects are concentrated" (1989: 20). Thus the manner in which an essential category is inscribed in discourse is ultimately dependent on a subject's complex positioning in a particular political or social field.

The intellectual practice of Gayatari Spivak seems to embrace this fact in all its radicalness. Positioning herself within the academy as sometimes Marxist, sometimes feminist, sometimes deconstructionist, sometimes postcolonial, she deftly shuttles between various "identities." Not only does she do this textually, she has also spoken in interviews to the political implications of this theme. Recognizing a historical reliance on essentialism within feminism and the irreducibility of this moment in any given discourse, she states:

> Since the moment of essentializing, universalizing, saying yes to the onto-phenomenological question, is irreducible, let us at least situate it at the moment, let us become vigilant about our own practice and use it as much as we can rather than make the totally counter-productive gesture of repudiating it ... I think we have to choose it strategically ... I am an essentialist from time to time (1990: 11).

Both Fuss and Spivak present an argument for the strategic use of essentialist claims. In Spivak's terms, since one "*cannot not* be an essentialist," then why not seize this for political ends? (1990: 45). "Women" or "women of colour" can occupy these categories within a specific social field, remembering that the context defines its political effectiveness. Further, the strategic potential of self-positioning must be played with an awareness of the limits of positionality itself. Spivak offers no single solution: what she offers instead is a disciplined 'vigilance' (McRobbie, 1985).

In another sense, the question of essentialist identities marks one of the many contours of the political landscape of the Anglo-Western conjuncture between feminism and postmodernism. While there are diverse positions which characterize both feminism and post-modernism and while there is little consensus among feminist theorists on the value of postmodernism for feminist practice (for example, see the volume edited by Linda Nicholson, 1990), the site where these discourses intersect helps to situate the politics of women of colour. Postmodern discourses provide a basis for feminists to avoid the tendency towards constructing theory out of the unitary experiences of white, Western, middle-class women. By displacing subjectivity across multiple discourses — feminist, racial, lesbian, national, socioeconomic — the stakes in a postmodern politics lie precisely in a reconfiguration of the traditional unitary subject of feminism (that is, woman). The narratives offered by women of colour offer a grounded political sense of identity, at once multiple, competing, fragmented, contradictory.

When I began this essay, I must admit, I was concerned with the limitations of the concept "women of colour," with the way it fixes a white versus colour dichotomy in feminism, with the way it inscribes my own location and with the sense that all of this sets a particular horizon of limitations on the speaking position of its subjects. But writing, mapping the scenery, has led me to frame the problem very differently. It is no longer, for me, a problem of being fixed into an essentialized location but one of how to articulate oneself in shifting relationships.

How does one negotiate the multiple locations, the provisional identities of a postmodern feminist landscape? And what does it mean to theorize a practice on the basis of movement through this flux? These are the questions that now concern me and have helped me to situate my earlier ambivalence. My difficulty with the label "woman of colour," I have realized, is not the fixity it seems to imply but the very fluidity of its strategic practice.

There is, of course, no single answer to such questions, just as maps, more generally, have no fixed destinations. The term "woman of colour" has (among other things) been formulated as part of a chromatic dichotomy, used to collapse women's economic specificity, fixed in a particular hierarchy of oppression and hegemonically deployed as an empirical order. Moreover, it is articulated differently in different national (or ideological) frameworks. Given that one is constantly moving along or across all kinds of borders, the term is always radically contingent. One of the challenges to feminist politics is to delineate a practice that shuttles between the necessary use of certain labels and categories, while simultaneously bracketing them for critical interrogation. Finally, I would like to re-emphasize that the tensions within the concept "woman of colour" do not call for its dismissal. On the contrary, the many ambiguous meanings it can have demonstrates that, at the very least, it is an important site for a strategic politics. It is on these terms that "women of colour" continually need to interrogate their place and function in feminist discourse, need to look at the political implications of "naming" their experience and need to persistently expose the social and ideological contexts within which their names, labels and categories of identity are produced.

Endnotes

[1] A paper presented by Ana Dopico inspired me to think about "border crossings" as metaphors for marginality. Her paper, "Latin American Culture and the U.S. Academy: Towards an International Practice of

Cultural Studies," was presented at the conference on Americanist Visions of Cultural Studies at Columbia University, March 6, 1992.

Bibliography

Adams, Mary Louise. "There's No Place Like Home: On the Place of Identity in Feminist Politics" in *Feminist Review*, No. 31, Spring 1989.

Alarcon, Norma. "The Theoretical Subject(s) of *This Bridge Called My Back* and Anglo-American Feminism" in *Making Face, Making Soul*, Gloria Anzaldua, ed., San Francisco: Aunt Lute Foundation Books, 1990.

"Traddutora, Traditora: A Paradigmatic Figure in Chicana Feminism" in *Cultural Critique*, No. 13, 1989.

Anzaldua, Gloria. *Borderlands: La Frontera*. San Francisco: Spinster's Press, 1987.

Making Face, Making Soul: Creative and Critical Perspectives by Women of Colour. San Francisco: Aunt Lute Foundation Books, 1990.

Carby, Hazel. "The Politics of Difference" in *Ms. Magazine*. September-October 1990, pp. 84-85.

Christian, Barbara. "The Race for Theory" in *Making Face, Making Soul*. Gloria Anzaldua, ed., San Francisco: Aunt Lute Foundation Books, 1990.

di Leonardo, Micaela. *Gender at the Crossroads of Knowledge: Feminist Anthropology in the Postmodern Era*. Berkley: University of California Press, 1991.

Dopica, Ana. "Latin American Culture and the U.S. Academy: Towards an International Practice of Cultural Studies." Paper presented at Americanist Visions of Cultural Studies: A Working Conference, New York City, Columbia University, March 6, 1992.

Frankenberg, Ruth. "White Women, Race Matters: The Social Construction of Whiteness" in *The Third Wave: Feminist Perspectives on Racism*, Norma Alarcon *et al.*, eds., New York: Kitchen Table Women of Colour Press, 1991.

Fuss, Diane. *Essentially Speaking: Feminism, Nature and Difference.* New York & London: Routledge, 1989.

Gilroy, P. "It Ain't Where You're From, It's Where You're At ... The Dialectics of Diasporic Identification" in *Third Text*, No. 13, 1991, pp. 3-16.

Grewal, S. *et al.*, eds. *Charting the Journey: Writings by Black and Third World Women.* London: Sheba Feminist Publishers, 1988.

Haraway, Donna. *Simians, Cyborgs, and Women: The Reinvention of Nature.* New York: Routledge, 1991, pp. 149-181.

"Situated Knowledges: The Science Question in Feminism and the Privilege of Partial Perspective" in *Feminist Studies*, No. 14 (3), pp. 575-599.

hooks, bell. *Ain't I A Woman: black women and feminism.* Boston: South End Press, 1981.

Feminist Theory: From Margin to Center. Boston: South End Press, 1984.

Yearning: Race, Gender, and Cultural Politics. Boston: South End Press, 1990.

Hurtado, Aida. "Relating to Privilege: Seduction and Rejection in the Subordination of White Women and Women of Colour" in *Signs*, Vol. 4, No. 14, 1989.

John, Mary. "Postcolonial Feminists in the First World's Intellectual Field: Anthropologists and Native Informants" in *Inscriptions*, Vol. 5-6, 1990.

Lorde, Audre. *Sister Outsider: Essays and Speeches.* California: The Crossing Press, 1984.

Lowe, Lisa. "Contradiction and Hybridity: The Identity of the Subject." Paper presented at the Americanist Visions of Cultural Studies: A Working Conference, Columbia University, March 7, 1992.

Mani, Lata. "Feminist Scholarship in the Age of Multi-national Reception." *Inscriptions*, Vol. 5-6, 1990.

Mani, Lata and Ruth Frankenberg. "Crosscurrents, Crosstalk: Race, 'Post-coloniality' and the Politics of Location." Paper presented at the AAA Meetings, November, 1991.

Martin, B. and Mohanty, Chandra. "What's Home Got to do With It?" in *Feminist Studies/Critical Studies*, Teresa de Lauretis, ed., Bloomington: Indiana University Press, 1986, pp. 191-212.

Minh-ha, Trinh. *When the Moon Waxes Red: Representation, Gender, and Cultural Politics.* New York and London: Routledge, 1991.

Woman, Native, Other: Writing Postcoloniality and Feminism. Bloomington: Indiana University Press, 1989.

Mohanty, Chandra. "Feminist Encounters: Locating the Politics of Experience" in *Copyright 1*, 1987.

et al., eds. *Third World Women and the Politics of Feminism.* Bloomington: Indiana University Press, 1991.

Moore, Henrietta. *Feminism and Anthropology.* Great Britain: Polity Press, 1988.

Moraga, Cherrie and Anzaldua, Gloria, eds., *This Bridge Called My Back: Writings by Radical Women of Colour.* New York: Kitchen Table Women of Colour Press, 1983.

Parmar, Pratibha. "Other Kinds of Dreams" in *Feminist Review*, No. 31, Spring 1989.

Peters, Ari. "Are Asian Americans Being Conned?" in *New York Asian News*, September 1991.

Sandoval, Chela. "U.S. Third World Feminism: The Theory and Method of Oppositional Consciousness" in *Genders,* No. 10, 1991, pp. 1-24.

"Feminism and Racism: A Report on the 1981 National Women's Studies Association Conference" in *Making Face, Making Soul.* Gloria Anzaldua, ed., San Francisco: Aunt Lute Foundation Books, 1990.

Spelman, Elizabeth. *Inessential Woman: Problems of Exclusion in Feminist Thought.* Boston: Beacon Press Books, 1988.

Spivak, Gayatri. "Can the Subaltern Speak?" in *Marxism and the Interpretation of Cultures.* Cary Nelson and Lawrence Greenberg, eds., Chicago: University of Illinois Press, 1988.

In Other Worlds: Essays in Cultural Politics. New York and London: Routledge, 1988.

The Post-Colonial Critic: Interviews, Strategies, Dialogues. New York and London: Routledge, 1990.

Strathern, Marilyn. "An Awkward Relationship: The Case of Feminism and Anthropology" in *Signs,* No. 12, 1987, pp. 276-292.

Afua Cooper

J.L. Hodgins

An interview with
AFUA COOPER

If you're
true to your voice

SILVERA: Where were you born and how has that place influenced your poetry?

COOPER: I was born in Westmoreland, Jamaica, in a rural district. Our district was in a valley and we had no electricity at the time, so basically our main forms of social interaction and entertainment were the church and listening to stories. The people were poor people, working-class people — most were farmers who combined farming with other activities. My family leased land and did farming, though my father was by training a mechanic and he worked for the West Indies Sugar Company. Westmoreland is a sugar parish and so there was a whole hierarchy. Today the sugar industry doesn't dominate the parish anymore. The tourist industry has taken over, though sugar is still strong and is a big employer of farmers. It is a parish with a lot of history, a lot of pain — you may recall it was in Westmoreland that the whole Frome Sugar Factory Strike demonstration occurred in 1938 and the riots which led to the formation of trade unions and political parties in Jamaica. I lived there until I was eight years old and after that I moved to Kingston.

Silvera: What kind of work did your mother do?

Cooper: Well, my mother was what we call a housewife. She combined that with selling cakes, other sweets, and cooked food at a local school.

And it's now that I realize the impact and influence those early years had on my life, on my art, on my poetry. I mentioned earlier that one form of entertainment was storytelling because we didn't have much. By the time six o'clock come, darkness come, you wash up, you eat up your dinner, and you either go to your bed or you listen to somebody telling a story.

Silvera: So did you have books in your household or would you say that your main entertainment and your love for poetry came from that oral tradition?

Cooper: Both. We had books in our household. I had older siblings who were obviously going to school. My father read to us. We had books like encyclopedias, some textbooks, and, of course, the Bible. But perhaps the whole oral aspect was stronger because we were very close to both our grandmothers but especially to our father's mother. She was a storyteller.

I remember the geography of the place, villages being sandwiched between. The lushness of the place, the very dark nights. The peeni wallees — those are little fireflies. So with the dark nights and the fear of a child you started to think of duppies because duppies were very much a part of our oral culture, even though we couldn't see them. I had the experience of seeing one, actually being attacked by one.

SILVERA: By a duppy?

COOPER: Yeah. *(laughter)* It's true ...

SILVERA: By a duppy? Well, tell us about that. Is this for real? Or do you think it's really connected to the fear of the night and ...

COOPER: It's an interesting question because I was coming from church that night, but it wasn't ...

SILVERA: What kind of church? A traditional church where there's an organ, piano, a sit-down church, or a clap-hand church?

COOPER: It was a clap-hand church and people get into spirit and that kind of thing. I myself was very religious. When we had altar call I remember being six years old. I would probably be the only child who would answer the pastoral call and walk to the altar to be saved. I would pray intensely, I remember that. So anyway, we were all coming from church — it probably was around Christmas time — and my brother and sister were involved in a church concert. And I went with them to the church to practice.

It was very dark, we were the only people travelling in that direction. Then we saw this woman in front of us, wearing a pink dress, a light-skinned woman. And so we said, oh, there's a woman, let's try and catch up with her. We raced after this woman, and when we thought we were close to her she would jump further in the distance. But we didn't think it was funny until, after one more attempt, she turned around and she chased us — this was an older woman, about sixty. She chased us up the hill, and I was just terrified, by then I was screaming to the night. And then we saw the strangest thing — this is no fiction — the woman turned and she jumped down into a gully and disappeared.

SILVERA: So what did the woman look like? Could you see her face? Did she have a face?

COOPER: Yeah, she had a face. She was wearing a pink dress. Anyway, I couldn't speak for the night, I was dumbstruck and they had to rub me down with bay rum and smelling salts. The next day they identified her. It was a woman who had died and she had been buried near the gully where she had jumped.

SILVERA: I'm sure this added in later years to your vivid imagination and to your creativity as a writer ...

COOPER: You sound like you don't believe it, but anyway, the point that I'm trying to make is that that's the kind of environment in which I lived. The supernatural was real. But I haven't really explored that in my writing — the whole aspect of fantasy and the supernatural — though I do believe there is another dimension beyond this. I'm sure of that.

SILVERA: Let's talk about the use of language in your work. The role of mother tongue and how that plays out in your work. I'm particularly interested by your use of Patois in *Memories Have Tongue*.

COOPER: That's a crucial point because I came from a very rooted place. Slavery. Sugar. Yeah, I came from a place of very strong roots, Christianity, obeah. And strong Africanism. Westmoreland is, along with Hanover, the farthest point from Kingston in Jamaica. So we didn't have that urban influence. The geography comes out in my poetry — I always had that sense of the land, of the mountains and of the plains, of the sky and of the rain falling everyday. Westmoreland is a Garden of Eden.

About mother tongue? I guess if you're being true to your voice, and as you start to connect more and more to your voices, from that deep place you speak in multiple voices. One of dem is, of course, Patois, Jamaican speech as we call it. That's the one that predominates. If you are working-class, you don't learn, you don't speak, Received Standard English until you're in school. When you're at home, when you're with your friends in the schoolyard, when you go to the market, you speak Patois. But because of colonialism and of being part of the larger English-speaking world, you must claim the English language and I claim it as my own.

SILVERA: What inspired you to write "Memories Have Tongue" — I'm talking about the poem — about your grandmother and her bad memory. Can you say a bit about that history? I see there's quite a lot of history in this book because again you talk about the 1938 Frome Riot.

COOPER: We were very close to our paternal grandmother, and I think I came into this world with a strong sense of loss. You know sometimes people pass on their feelings, negative and positive, their hurts and their joys, to their descendants. And one of the stories that I knew probably even before I could speak was that my grandfather died when he was a young man — that's my father's father. And my grandmother who was a young woman with children had a tremendous responsibility of looking after them without assistance, without a husband. So she passed on these stories to us. I suppose she wanted us never to forget him, even though we didn't know him because he died when my dad was three or four years old. She would tell us all the time about her husband and her early life and then the riots at Frome and eventually how my father himself went to work at Frome. So I feel that I have a lot of connection with Frome, West

Indies Sugar Company. So, as you rightly said, there's a lot of that history woven into my poetry and that was one of the reasons I decided to pursue academic work in history.
Continuing with the feeling of using the mother tongue and with the role of the older woman and of the grandmother within Caribbean poetry and within my poetry ...

SILVERA: There's such a strong sense of history in *Memories Have Tongue*. I'm referring to the teachings on Christopher Columbus and your experience as a young girl in school. Can you talk about that, about the kind of education that one got in a colonial country and your impressions and reactions to Christopher Columbus.

COOPER: Fortunately, by the time I hit high school Christopher Columbus had fallen from his pedestal and was on the way out. I didn't learn British history or British literature in school. In my older sister's generation they did.

When I went to high school Michael Manley's government came into power and a new consciousness was ushered in. I also went to school in Raetown, Kingston and *(laughter)* Raetown is a notorious place. I was going to school where the big prisons were — the general penitentiary was right this side of our school. Raetown is a very working-class neighbourhood and the consciousness of the people was tremendously high. I remember once when Walter Rodney was expelled from Jamaica people were very upset.

And you got a different opinion on the street than you got from the radio. People thought the prime minister at that time was a real — well, the term we use now is Oreo cookie — sell-out. So that's the environment I grew up in. And there was a tremendous amount of Rasta influence. So there was that education we were getting from the street. In school what we would get was "talk properly," "learn to spell," and so on, but it was not a terribly colonized or colonial education.

Class was more or less prominent in school — not colour so much because you could be very dark-skinned — but if your father was inspector of police, you'd be elevated and the teacher would like you. And if you were brown and you were poor, then you'd still be nothing. So class, in my neighbourhood, was more important than colour. Maybe if I'd lived in St. Andrew and gone to Holy Childhood School or a similar school, it might have been different. I don't think I had a terribly colonial education. We didn't like the Queen and when she came to Jamaica we would boo her.

SILVERA: What year was this?

COOPER: This was 1972, so I was out of primary school. But what I was trying to say was that in that transitional generation — because the people before me definitely had a colonial education — we were the ones who came into a new consciousness. Rastafari was prominent in Jamaica, and reggae music and Black history and Black power and Walter Rodney and so on. So it was a strong and vibrant period.

SILVERA: What urged you to write "I Don't Care if your Nanny was Black"?

COOPER: We're making a big geographical leap now.

SILVERA: Yeah.

COOPER: That poem came out of the Canadian and American context and the racism that Black people suffer here and in the United States.

It's just constant, whether it's being shot and killed by the cops or a youth like Yusef Hawkins walking into a white neighbourhood and being killed by white youths who got off because they're white. It's just racism in every form whether its institutionalized or the daily, everyday kind of thing. "I Don't Care if Your Nanny Was Black" comes out of that. One of the commonest reactions white people have when Black people start to talk about their pain and grief is that they start to feel guilty, and they'll say things like, "I didn't do that, maybe my ancestors did that, but I personally didn't do that." Or they'll say, "Well, I'm not like that because I eat Jamaican patties and I listen to reggae music," or "My nanny was Black, so I understand." Which is total bullshit because everyone is responsible.

SILVERA: Yeah. I want to move on to another poem which is also another leap: "For Christine and I-Selena". In this poem it seems to me that you're making a connection to the womanish or to feminism. Can you talk about that? Or have I misinterpreted this poem?

COOPER: No, you haven't. Someone has described *Memories Have Tongue* — the book — as a feminist chant. I sort of stood up when the person said that, but it is true. I would say that's a true assessment, even though it's other things too. But it's connecting with Canadian realities, with some of the realities of life for poor working-class women in Canada. And there's a school of thought — right-wing thought — that if you have an affair, you shouldn't have children, or you should be sterilized, or the government should totally regulate your life. So it's a reaction to that anti-life and anti-human ideology.

SILVERA: Would you describe yourself as a dub poet?

COOPER: Yes, most definitely.

SILVERA: What does that mean? You write some of your poems in dub and others in Jamaican Standard English? Is there any difference? What is this difference between dub poetry — if there's one — and ...

COOPER: For me, describing myself as a dub poet and writing dub poems comes out of a larger consciousness, out of roots of history, out of the evolution of Caribbean or Jamaican orality. So for me, I don't have to consign it, and say, well, I have this poem and it has to fit into a particular musical or rhythmic pattern or I have to have reggae music in the background.

SILVERA: Do you think that a Canadian and American audience or a Canadian and American literary community neglects dub poetry in academia or in the high schools?

COOPER: Yeah, I would say so, even though more and more it's gaining more acceptance. Dub poetry comes out of orality, and for a long time orality has been marginalized and has been seen as something that poor people, working people, or Rasta people will engage in. And so it was not a part of "mainstream culture". Well, to call it "mainstream" is bullshit. It perpetuates colonialism, it perpetuates the use of a language that is alien to many people, and so the people were alienated from that language by how it gets used.

You go to certain, let's say poetry, readings and you just want to fall asleep. And when you look at the kind of people who are there — I want poetry to be accessible to everybody. Poetry is like food, and like food, everybody should have it and be nourished. This whole idea of art as something that's up there, that only some people can understand, is total bullshit. Art comes out of people, it comes out of a community. That's why dub poetry is so popular in Jamaica and the Caribbean. It reaches everybody and it perhaps reaches the people who have been alienated from the English language and its forms and manifestations, and these are poor, working-class people.

Silvera: What do you think of feminism? Would you consider yourself a feminist?

Cooper: I consider myself a feminist. I see feminism as a liberating tool, to liberate all humanity, but more specifically our focus is on the most vulnerable in society, and in this category of people are women and children. I don't want to go into that and elaborate on why I am feminist or the purpose of feminism because I think we have passed that. We have passed that stage of explaining or justifying ourselves as feminist. We are beyond that right now. Right now we're just out to get along with the program.

Silvera: What role do you believe your work can play in Canadian feminist literature?

Cooper: Like I said, I see poetry as food, to nourish. And feminism in my interpretation has a nourishing role, it has a liberating role, and my poetry is that: nourishing and liberating. I hope every time I go in front of an audience I can give something, I can give some nourishment, I can give ideas of how we can all free ourselves, I can give a healing gift. Those are the things I want to do, so it fits in that program of liberation and joy and healing.

Silvera: I also asked that question because one of your poems is about Marie Joseph Angelique, a Black Canadian woman. It's sad that a lot of students and professors in academia don't really know about that Canadian history, but you seem to be doing quite a lot of work around it, so that is why I also ask about what role you see your work playing in Canadian feminist literature and in academia, both in terms of *Memories Have Tongue* and your work on the history of Black women in Canada.

You're now a Ph. D. candidate at the University of Toronto. You're studying the history of Black women in Canada. What led you to this kind of research?

COOPER: When I came to Canada my first interest was in African continental history. And I actually did my major research in African history. Then it dawned on me that I'm here. I live here. I'm part of a long, African presence in Canada, and therefore perhaps my immediate interest should be with the African presence in Canada. I saw an exhibition on Black history in Canada that was put on by the Ontario Black History Society. That stimulated my interest in Black history here. Black people and other people of colour have been missing from the pages of Canadian history for a long time. You go in a class and you look in the books and you ask a teacher: you're teaching Canadian history, but where are the other people? The Canadian obsession with the Two Solitudes — the French and the English, and their conflicts and their love-hate relationship — it's gotten ridiculous. The country has changed so much. The Two Solitudes business should be out the window because we're now a mosaic and have been for quite a while. We have many races and cultures here. Interestingly, Canadian historiography has been obsessed with the Two Solitudes, and Native peoples have been totally neglected in Canadian history and all the history texts.

SILVERA: And what about the history of African Canadian and Black Caribbean people here?

COOPER: Well, one shouldn't be surprised that Black people are not included in the history texts in spite of our 400 years here in Canada. And so that has lead me on a mission of recovery and discovery because I wanted to — along with others, like Daniel Hill — write about the Black presence here in Canada. I want to add, to make a contribution, I want to make sure that we are recognized, acknowledged, and given space within the scheme of things.

My particular interest, of course, is in women. And I've looked at particular Black women. Marie Joseph Angelique is one. As you know, she was a slave who set fire to her mistress's house in 18th-century Montreal and eventually the city burnt down. She was caught, tried and hanged, her body burned and the ashes scattered. But when you look in most Canadian texts, this fact, this important piece of history, is missing.

At that time Montreal was the most important city in what is now Canada. At least half of it was burnt down and a lot of important buildings were burnt down. Yet this is not recorded in history at all. Why? I can only come up with a feeling that Canadians — Canadian history writers, those who support the mainstream and the establishment — schemed to hide the fact of slavery in Canada. Canada must keep its image as the haven for escaped slaves from the U.S. who had travelled here along the Underground Railroad. That was a later period. Slavery in Canada has been Canada's best-kept secret. So I think that's the reason this major incident is not included in history texts. As we know, there was slavery in Canada. In French and English Canada, Black people were slaves, Native people were slaves, Marie Joseph Angelique was a slave.

Apart from trying to recover and discover our history, I have a genuine love for history. I guess it comes out of my early background, out of being told these public and private histories. I guess it's also something you are born with, and I have a strong impulse to discover more and more about women's history and to put women's history at the centre of other histories.

SILVERA: So do you think the history of Blacks in Canada has been neglected? Or is it acknowledged and taught in university courses?

COOPER: Look at Toronto, which has large Black and so-called ethnic populations. Look at the history courses being taught in the institutions. It's still white British-oriented or white American or white Canadian. When you raise the issue of inclusion, you either face being stonewalled or you meet a wall of silence and hostility. We face a lot of obstacles within the universities. The racism we mentioned earlier, it appears on every front. It appears in subtle ways, it appears in overt ways, but it's there. The Canadian history profession and the university are two of the last bastions of white supremacy. But I believe they too will crumble. I believe we have a mission. I certainly believe I have a mission. At the same time, I don't see myself rushing out to the forefront with a sword or with a banner. I'm doing what I have to do with as much integrity as I have: to speak my truth without fear and to continue this work because it must be done and it can be done.

In my department I'm the only Black woman right now. We're not encouraged, and a lot of people expect you to drop out. When you think of what some of our ancestors went through with fewer resources than we have, you realize that this is nothing. I mentioned earlier that I feel a strong sense of history within myself and a strong sense of place, and I suppose I articulate this sense in my poetry and in my historical research. I feel very fortunate that both strands come together the way they have. A lot of my poems come out of my research and I think that's fabulous.

SILVERA: What place does your inspiration come from? In your introduction you speak about mythology and the feminine. Can you elaborate on that?

COOPER: My inspiration comes from everywhere — from just the very act of living. Sometimes I'm gazing into a candle's flame and I see a poem. A poem erupts from the flame and I write it — just like that. Or I may be walking, or I may be standing in front of a library looking at the tulips in May, and I write a poem from seeing the tulips swaying in the wind. Or I hear on the news that city council has vetoed a bill which would open up the fire department to women and minorities. So my inspiration comes from everywhere and everything.

I'm also very interested in my personal mythology because we live our lives as one grand myth. Sometimes the sad thing is that we don't know that we're living mythological lives. We all have personal myths or family stories and myths we absorb from television and other media without realizing it. When I speak of myth, when I say I get my inspiration from mythologies, I mean world mythologies — like the Adam and Eve story, or Shango being chased out of town and hanging himself and being found by his mother who laments over him — myths from different religions and cultures but particularly the African and Caribbean myths because those are the mythologies from which I spring and with which I'm most familiar. Caribbean mythologies would include the stories and the histories of the Amerindian people — the Arawak Indians, in the case of Jamaica.

SILVERA: I know you've talked about the land as a geographic space. I was deeply touched by your concept of land as more than a geographic landscape, as a psychic space, can you talk about that?

COOPER: We're so influenced by the unconscious. I am influenced by the great visionary Carl Jung and his approach to the unconscious, which is mainly through dreams. I'm an avid dreamer. I've been keeping a dream journal for the past twelve years. I respect my dreams, I value them, and they've been great teachers in my life. So when I think of my unconscious I think of a psychic landscape where dramas of all kinds take place. A lot of my poems come out of this psychic space because I think one reason we are here on earth is to get to know ourselves as much as possible. Someone once said, "Know thyself." It's a simple statement, but it's also very profound. It's up to each one of us to know ourselves as much as possible.

We can know this self by working closely with the conscious and the unconscious — the unconscious plays such a great role within our lives, sometimes it's directing our lives, and we are not even aware of it. A lot of things have come together for me as I tried to know myself: my work with dreams, my work in history and my work in poetry.

Let me give you an example: when I was doing some research I wanted to come to grips with land, with the land that I came from, Jamaica, and the physical and psychic suffering of the African people in that land. And, of course, if you're dealing with that you have to deal with the first people who inhabited that land, the Arawak people. You don't learn much about the Arawak people in school, so I started to find out as much as I could about these people, and there was very little written in history and anthropology.

Anyway, I found something, and as I tried to grapple with the destruction these people endured, the genocide, the slaughter, one night I had this wonderful dream of this woman, an Arawak woman, giving me a child. And it was such a wonderful gift. When I woke up I felt elated. I was doing research at that time on Atabeyra, the female Arawak deity, and I'm sure it was she who came into my dreams. So we have all these characters living in the psychic space and we don't even know until we make efforts to contact them. A lot of history as we know it is really mythology.

SILVERA: My next question is how and where do you write? Do you have a special time? A special place? What role do your children, partner, husband play? How do you negotiate your time with all of that?

COOPER: "Negotiating time" is an appropriate phrase. Sometimes I feel I'm in an impossible situation. Sometimes I go for weeks and not write a word and I feel like I'm going crazy. My first reaction is to say, well, I have children, I have all this work, I have to clean the house — but then I realize that's only partially true. Even if I were single I could say I don't have any time. So I think it boils down to disciplining yourself and working out a schedule and sticking to that schedule. I find that what works for me is getting up early at, say, four or five in the morning. It helps to go to bed early the night before! If I get up by four I start working and can work until, say, eight or nine when the baby wakes up. I'd say it's more challenging when you have children because you work as if you were under siege. The kids get up at eight, they go off to school or daycare by nine or ten, and they come back by five. So whatever you have to do, you have to do between those times or get up early and work. It takes a tremendous amount of discipline. Having a spouse or partner can also be problematic because sometimes it can be a quiet time, and you want to do some writing, but they may feel they're being neglected, or they might not understand why you have to be doing what you're doing when you're doing it. So, of course, in that case communication is the key. You need to talk and to have a dialogue.

SILVERA: How do you negotiate time between your creative writing and your work on your thesis, which is in some sense very different from a creative piece? Do you set out a certain time for each? How does that work in the face of everything you've said about children and partners?

COOPER: All this summer I did my creative work. I worked on my short stories and I worked on my manuscript of poetry. I didn't look at a single history book. I think that's the most effective way to work. I find it hard to switch between a creative piece and a factual piece, even though a factual piece is also creative and needs a certain amount of creative vision. I was working on a manuscript of poetry for children while I was studying for my exams. At times one helps the other. But come September, I'm going to be researching and teaching history. That's all I will do. I like to do thorough work and I want to work well and I want to give my best to whatever I'm doing at a particular moment. At the same time, that doesn't mean that between September and December I won't write a poem — a poet walks around with a notebook all the time and is forever receiving inspiration.

Beatrice Culleton

Stephanie Martin

An interview with
BEATRICE CULLETON

**I decided
to go with reality**

SILVERA: I first read *In Search of April Raintree* in 1984. Then I re-read it a few weeks ago before this interview, and my response remains the same in 1994. You know, I laughed and cried in the same places but even more this time. I was taken by the starkness, the painful honesty, in the telling of the story and the extraordinary love between April and Cheryl. Was the novel autobiographical?

CULLETON: In a general way. I grew up in foster homes. My family were alcoholics, there were suicides in my family, I was raped, and, of course, I had the thing with the identity.

SILVERA: What was it that inspired you, that pulled you, to write this novel?

CULLETON: The second suicide. I had two older sisters and both of them committed suicide, one when I was fourteen and she was in her early twenties, and then the other sister when I was about thirty-one and she was forty-two — that was in October 1980 and I decided then to write a book.

SILVERA: They committed suicide and you decided to write the book to ...

CULLETON: Try to figure out why all that stuff happened to my family.

SILVERA: In the book we meet Cheryl and April, but the other sister is not there, right?

CULLETON: I didn't write about my own sisters because they had family, and I didn't want to write about and intrude on the privacy of other people. So, of course, that's why I wrote fiction. I didn't write about my own family at all.

SILVERA: How long did it take you to complete that novel and how did you do it? Did you stop for a while? Did you reflect several times before the completion? I'm asking because it seems from re-reading the book that there was much pain in the telling of the story, though the ending is one of resolve.

CULLETON: It took me about a month to write the first draft, but it was really different from what I eventually turned out. I took it to Pemmican Publications, and they liked it and told me to re-write it, so I did. I started off in the third person and it sounded really like a Harlequin — not a romance, but it had that quality to it. Actually, I first went looking for a professional writer because I hadn't done any writing before. I thought the story was good, but the style, or whatever, was really awkward, so I thought I'd try and find a professional Native writer to work on it with me. Then I found out about Pemmican and they told me to try it myself. We went through different editors and one suggested I try and write in the first person. When I re-wrote it in the first person I pretty well had April and

Cheryl's characters pretty much figured out. The other thing I didn't do in the beginning was write about childhood. Because of the foster homes I'd been in I didn't want people touching my foster homes based on what was in the book.

SILVERA: The story is told by a young Métis girl. How old is she?

CULLETON: At the end of the book she is twenty-four. She is four or five when she starts to tell the story. It's been a long time. *(laughter)* I changed this and that to suit different things — I get nit-picky about details, so I went back and forth changing things.

SILVERA: Where did the title, *April Raintree*, come from?

CULLETON: The name first came to me when I started, so it was always there, and when I re-wrote I decided to call it *In Search of April Raintree*.

SILVERA: Does it have any particular significance?

CULLETON: April, for me, was springtime, the beginning of new things, that was why I picked April. And Raintree I'd never heard of being used for a Métis or Indian person in Manitoba, so I picked it because I didn't want to use anybody's real name. And *in search of...* gives you the idea of searching for identity. Rejection happens with a lot of us kids, it happened to a lot of us who had been through foster homes, but it happened to other kids as well.

SILVERA: What was the response in the Aboriginal community when the book first came out?

CULLETON: It was really good. I was really worried about it because I wrote the truth as I saw it, and it was why I was where I was at when I was young. I had to tell it the way I thought. I was nervous before it came out, but the response was really good. I first thought the readership would be adult women, but when it first came out young people were starting to read it and really get into it. I thought my readership would be women, there's parts in it that if I'd known young kids would read it I would have written it maybe differently. I was reluctant to swear in it, even writing for adult women. I was reluctant to use the words the rapist uses and Cheryl uses to describe the rape in detail. That was something I had to stop and think about, and I decided to go with reality. Then, when young kids did start reading it I was asked to edit *In Search of April Raintree*, so it could be used in schools.

SILVERA: Was this in the first printing? Or was this after the second printing?

CULLETON: *In Search of April Raintree* came out in April 1983, and I was asked in 1984 to do the re-write.

SILVERA: So you were asked that by the publisher to change the ...

CULLETON: No. By then I was working at Pemmican, and I was asked by the Native Education Branch in Manitoba.

SILVERA: The changes went into the second printing?

CULLETON: No, into a new book. *In Search of April Raintree* is just a little paperback. *April Raintree* is larger, and it's sold to the textbook bureau and educational institutions.

SILVERA: Really. When you started to work on the book you didn't think of an audience, did you? You didn't say, I'm writing for such and such ... ?

CULLETON: Not really. I just thought as I was working along that it would be adults, it would be women, who would be reading it. The other thing that surprised me was that a lot of men have read it.

SILVERA: And what has been their response to it?

CULLETON: The majority of the responses that I've heard have been very positive. Then once in a while I'll get hearsay stuff that somebody was not pleased about something, but nobody's said it to my face. *(laughter)*

SILVERA: April grew up in a Catholic household. I gather that she didn't like Mass ...

CULLETON: Hated it. *(laughter)*

SILVERA: Was her growing up in a Catholic household and going to Mass and all that similar to the experience of a lot of Native kids in foster homes?

CULLETON: Yeah, there's usually some religion. I don't know what it's like now, but if our parents had baptised us Catholic, then the Children's Aid would try to put us into Catholic homes or whatever we were baptised as. My own parents baptised me Catholic, they were Catholic.

SILVERA: Were they practising Catholics?

CULLETON: Pretty well, I guess. They're in their eighties now. I guess they believed in it — it's wearing off, I think. My mom went through the residential school, even though she was Métis. Residential schools were mainly for Indian children.

SILVERA: And where did Métis children go to?

CULLETON: I think they went to public schools unless they were orphans. Both my parents were.

SILVERA: Is that why your mom ended up in a residential school?

CULLETON: Yeah.

SILVERA: I liked April's character very much and the contrast between her first white foster parents who were very kind and caring and then the second foster parents who were quite disgusting, mean and racist, taunting her with names like "squaw", "half-breed", "dirty", etcetera. What did that do to April while she was growing up? What effect did that have on her?

CULLETON: That made her ashamed of being part-Indian, of being Métis. Also, in those days what we learned in the history books was very negative: the "good Indians" were the ones who helped the white man survive here, like Joseph Brant. In April's case there were a lot of negative, personal things that made her the way she was. Because she was going to be like that and maybe not very likeable as an adult, I had tried to build in her potential for being really good, likeable, as a child, and hoped readers would remember what she was like as a kid and stay with her, even though she was mixed up in her older years.

SILVERA: Particularly in April's high school years — her wanting to pass for white. Sadly, it seems to run so deep in the heart of almost every single kid who is non-white and grows up in this culture, where whites have taken or have assumed power — this desire to be white, the feeling of rejection, the non-validation of the self. I was interested in how April felt this and how her sister differed from her. It seems to me her sister, in the earlier years, really wanted to accept her Indian identity and that April didn't.

CULLETON: I used myself for both characters. Until I was about ten years old I was really proud of being part-Indian, even though I saw movies of cowboys and Indians and settlers and all that. It was always pro-white, of course, but I always rooted for the Indian anyways. My brother was raised in a foster home, too, and he grew up being very proud of being who he was. I never understood why — why was there that difference between us — so with Cheryl's character I explained it by having her raised with a Métis woman who has acquired some books, although there weren't that many that showed Native people in a positive way. That's what Cheryl had to contend with. She didn't have reality to fall back on either. I didn't know why one of my brothers turned out the way he did and why I was the way I was.

SILVERA: What effect did the cowboy-and-Indian movies have on you? Seeing those false images played out? Those myths ...

CULLETON: I always felt apologetic about it, and because it was the movies and what we learned in history, I thought it was the truth, the way it really was. If the Indians weren't attacking a bandwagon, if they weren't doing that, then they were being pitied, like in "Bonanza", the poor Indian — look at him, pity him. That kind of attitude was just as bad. I don't think I liked thinking of myself to be pitied or to be feared.

SILVERA: Why was April afraid to find her identity? Why did she give up on the search, unlike Cheryl, to find her parents?

CULLETON: Because she didn't really want to know the truth. She wanted a nice white picket-fenced yard and all that. She wanted to make it for herself, and that meant giving up stuff that was Native, and that included her parents. She didn't really want anything to do with her parents — she did try to find them, but it was a token search.

SILVERA: By the end of the novel do you feel that April had learned anything positive from her mother? Despite the alcoholism and the subsequent suicide?

CULLETON: I think her character was formed very young when she was living with her parents. I've seen a lot of and heard about a lot of Native people who go through what I went through and returned to being Native and not having to feel like they have to apologise about it. Once you've been to the other side, and you see it's not for you, you come back. The years she did spend with her own family helped to form her character, so in spite of the Dions and the Derocees, she was who she was already.

SILVERA: Can you recall the first novel you read by an Aboriginal woman writer?

CULLETON: When I was on my own I used to go to the library a lot and I remember reading a book about a young girl who went to a residential school in Ontario. Also, I read Heather Robertson's *Reservations are for Indians* after I started writing and, of course,

Halfbreed. When I wrote my book I didn't think it would get published because it was about Métis people and the market wouldn't be very wide.

SILVERA: Did you have any problems finding a publisher?

CULLETON: No. Pemmican had just formed in 1980 or '81, and I phoned the Manitoba Métis Federation, which recommended Pemmican Publications. I went there and took my manuscript — it was all pasted together because I did it on a typewriter, and that was the first rough draft I took to them. They liked it and were interested, so I was pretty sure it would be published.

SILVERA: Do you think that Cheryl's upbringing — despite her white, middle-class, liberal upbringing and the kindness she obviously received from her foster parents — played a role in her suicide? Her early years were so different from April's — to have lived in a white, middle-class, false environment and this somewhat false illusion of who she was as a Native woman. Her world seemed to change once she was on her own, on the streets living and making her way.

CULLETON: She didn't have it rough enough as a kid.

SILVERA: Yeah, it seems to me that she didn't have a concrete reference because all she had read — which was also very important — were these wonderful books about Native people, these near-perfect stories, and then when she hit the streets and worked at the Friendship Centre it was reality time.

CULLETON: She thought that it would be kind of easy to work to help put Native people back together again, and it was a rude awakening.

That despair can be really frustrating and disappointing and, for her, it was easier to become an alcoholic and later commit suicide, as a way of dealing with the twist her life took.

SILVERA: Do you also think her reconnection with her father and the search for her mother broke her? What happened there? She seemed so strong and powerful.

CULLETON: She had what I thought was a false strength. She didn't want to accept the things she'd have to accept — and part of it was her own alcoholism, which was a real weakness, almost a death certificate.

SILVERA: But it seems to me, reading, that she had a lot of real strength, and it doesn't seem to me that she was destined to be alcoholic — it was because of the kind of spirit she had, this searching and wanting the truth, then her disillusionment upon finding all this despair and no way out — then she turned to alcohol. But it didn't seem to me she started off being an alcoholic or that it was inherited.

CULLETON: What precipitated that was finding her father and finding out the way he was. That really had a disgusting effect, a betrayal, a real big betrayal because April had protected her in a lot of ways. April was like the mother. Without intending to, that's the role April more or less played for her sister — she was always looking out for her, protecting her. For Cheryl, finding her father — his alcoholism — and finding out that her mother had committed suicide was more than she could handle.

SILVERA: This book has been reprinted about ten times. What does that feel like? *(laughter)*

CULLETON: I don't know. Sometimes I wish I hadn't had to write it.

SILVERA: In what way?

CULLETON: I guess I'd rather my sisters were alive.

SILVERA: Do you feel that the book anyway is contributing to some understanding and that other Métis kids, or young people, can read it and it can help change their lives in some way?

CULLETON: In that way, yeah. I've been told by people it's almost like a Bible in their family, and that really makes me feel sad.

SILVERA: Is it used in schools and universities?

CULLETON: Yes. I've been to universities in Canada and in the United States. Last year I went to Germany and spoke at four universities there. I go to a lot of schools in the north, where people don't have a lot of opportunity to see real live authors.

SILVERA: And what kind of response do you get there?

CULLETON: Because I grew up in foster homes and a lot these kids are home with their own families, I'm surprised that a lot of times we have the same problems, or we go through the same things, like racism. Because of that I want to write more books for a younger readership. That's the plan, but I don't think about what I am going to write — I just go with whatever story comes out, and if some people think it's too rough, well, the kids will know what it's like for them or not.

SILVERA: What are you working on at this point?

CULLETON: Right now, I'm starting to work on a book called *Shadow Lake*. It's about a Métis writer who goes up north with her white husband — I write what I know about. I've been brought up in white foster homes all my life. I've never married or gone out with a Native man. I guess because of the way we were brought up I always feel Native men are more like brothers ... This woman who moves up north, is originally from Winnipeg, of course, *(laughter)* has been raised in foster homes, and she was molested when she was three years old, in a foster home and then by a priest, but she's an adult now, and she's gotten into writing books for children, young children, and she moves up north. I haven't quite figured it all out yet. Her husband and son die in a car crash, so she's left up there by herself either to move back to the city or stay up there, and she decides she can't go on without her family, so she decides to commit suicide. The novel is also about wolves. I really tell a story awkwardly *(laughter)* — that's why I hate it when people say what's *April Raintree* about? *(laughter)*

SILVERA: This sounds quite fascinating, but tell me more about the wolves.

CULLETON: I want to remind people that animals and the environment are so important, and so I want a close-up look at the wolves because I want this wolf to give my character Christine the power to go on with life and to do what's right.

SILVERA: Does she like wolves?

CULLETON: Oh yeah, *(laughter)* especially after she encounters this one. It's really complicated and hard to make it sound interesting — I'm not one of those storytellers. Indians are supposed to be good storytellers, I'm not. I've got to write it down. *(laughter)*

SILVERA: Why does Christine get suicidal? There's suicide in the first book, and now you are ...

CULLETON: Getting suicidal again.

SILVERA: Again in this new book. So why this theme?

CULLETON: I've been up north visiting these schools, and they told me that in the last year there'd been eleven suicides among young kids. It's still a real problem, so I want to write about it this time from the character's point of view, from her talking about it and telling what it's like and why she would do it. I'm not sure if it reads true, or if it will, because that's another thing I've never thought about. But it was one of the reasons why writing in the first person with *April Raintree* worked so well. April had no idea about being an alcoholic and neither did I — I only had to write more or less what April thought.

SILVERA: You grew up in Winnipeg, right? What was that like for you as a Métis woman, a young girl, after you left the foster homes?

CULLETON: Oh, I ran away to Toronto. *(laughter)* I was seventeen and didn't actually run away — I saw my social worker and told her I was coming to Toronto, but that was before I was officially released as a foster kid. The reason I came to Toronto was this is where both my sisters came, so I followed them.

SILVERA: So you're working on this novel. Has this been your primary focus?

CULLETON: I'm not always busy writing. *(laughter)* I watch television, read, and I have a wood-working business with my husband, Raintree Wood Designs. I do the bookkeeping and part-time work in the office. Sounds like I'm not too busy, but seems to me, I'm always busy.

SILVERA: Do you sometimes feel that you're still living *April Raintree* the book? It has been reprinted ten times.

CULLETON: I still get really emotional about it, especially sometimes when I least expect it—the issues are still valid and, like I said before, I really feel sad when I think of other people going through pain. I don't feel like I've had such a rough life, but when I think of the characters, for instance, I feel really sad for what they went through, or I think of myself as that little girl. I guess that's why we do the work we do. Because we do care.

SILVERA: What kind of advice would you pass on to young Native women who want to write?

CULLETON: Come to our workshops. *(laughter)*

SILVERA: Do you do workshops?

CULLETON: I've done workshops, but I was thinking more in terms of what Marrie Mumford at ANDPVA[1] was talking about. I think that kind of work is really important. It's important to get anybody writing because it can be very therapeutic.

SILVERA: When you say "that kind of work" what do you mean?

CULLETON: Running workshops for writers. If they've never tried it, they might not think about doing it, so organizing the workshops, that kind of thing, is important for the community. A lot of kids drop out before graduating, as I did, and spend a long time looking for themselves, or not looking for themselves, not bothering. I wish I'd known a lot of things a long time ago, rather than when I was in my thirties. But it's never too late — there is support in the community.

SILVERA: And you've been involved in some of these workshops, the writing workshops?

CULLETON: They've been mostly organized by schools for young school kids. I've been involved in that kind of writing workshop or in conferences, giving an hour or two here and there, but not in intensive or ongoing workshops. Talking to people in prison, I've done that — I haven't done it in Toronto, but in Manitoba and Saskatchewan I've been to prisons talking to inmates about *April Raintree*.

SILVERA: How has that been? Do you speak to women?

CULLETON: I've been to Stony Mountain and Heddinglee Jail in Manitoba and the Portage Institute and the Pinegrove Institute for Women in Prince Albert, Saskatchewan.

SILVERA: How was the response to your work?

CULLETON: It's very good. I remember when I first went there I was nervous about going to Stony Mountain because of what I wrote in

THE OTHER WOMAN

the book about the rape and the bitterness that April felt, but they were very receptive. Another thing, when I go to schools there's very few Native people — the majority of kids are non-Native, they're white, but they're very open and receptive, willing to learn, and that's encouraging. I'm always nervous because of my own experience in school. To me, school was a traumatic experience.

SILVERA: What kind of work have you been doing with ANDPVA? What is your involvement with it?

CULLETON: I just started working on *Into the Moon*. This is an anthology of writing put together by women who started this project, like Beth Brant and Lenore Keeshig-Tobias who have been involved in the running of these workshops.

SILVERA: So they were writing workshops?

CULLETON: Yeah.

SILVERA: How did you get involved?

CULLETON: I was asked if I would edit some of the work. A committee was formed and I am involved.

SILVERA: When did you come to Toronto?

CULLETON: I came in 1987.

SILVERA: What have you done since then?

CULLETON: I like to keep to myself. I hate it when I talk. *(laughter)*

SILVERA: What do you think of all the controversy around writers having political opinions or fighting to make changes in the literary community? Do you think if you're a good writer, you shouldn't be involved in politics? Or if you're involved in politics, it means you're not a good writer?

CULLETON: I haven't heard much on that topic, but I would say that's rubbish. Every writer I know is political in some way. You have to be. Part of why I write is hoping to change things. People will read my work and think about what I'm writing. First of all, I write to entertain — I don't write for anything else but that because I like to read to be entertained. That's the way I write, that's my first priority.

SILVERA: But surely not *April Raintree?* (laughter)

CULLETON: It was to entertain primarily. If I wanted to write the politics of the book, it would be really boring. It would be. I felt there were too many social-worker books and kids weren't reading them. I want people to read because it's enjoyable to read, but there's a lot of pain in it too.

SILVERA: What kind of relationship do you have with your family now that you're a writer?

CULLETON: Like I said, I was in my thirties before the book was published. My children were already in their teens, more or less. Now they're on their own, so it's not a big deal now.

SILVERA: Talk about your kids. How did they feel about having a famous mother?

CULLETON: It kind of invaded our privacy I feel.

SILVERA: In what way?

CULLETON: People were aware who we were, of the Culleton name. I just feel that I gave up some privacy. I'm not that famous or anything, but it's just that people, especially in Winnipeg because it's a smaller place — here I'm not known at all — I just felt I didn't want my family exposed to people knowing that I wrote *April Raintree*.

SILVERA: How did they take it? Was it difficult for them?

CULLETON: I don't think it was difficult for my son. Maybe for my daughter.

SILVERA: How old was he?

CULLETON: When it came out he was fourteen and my daughter was nine. I think it was more difficult for my daughter because of having somebody that people know about. Maybe people thinking that the story was for real. A lot of kids do think it's for real, and they would ask her all kinds of questions she couldn't answer. It was just an unnecessary thing that kids shouldn't have to go through. And yet they're proud of me, of course. The attention isn't totally negative or anything. It's just that I feel our life could be more private.

SILVERA: Do you think you paid some price for that? Are you all still quite close now?

CULLETON: Oh, I'm very close to my family.

SILVERA: Did it cause a rift or anything at that point?

CULLETON: Oh no, we just ignored it, more or less. We didn't really talk about it too much. If my daughter said anything, I'd just fluff it off, like it wasn't a big deal. It wasn't a real hardship, it didn't cause any trouble. It's just my penchant for being private and for my kids to have a private life. We're not like O.J. Simpson or anything. *(laughter)* But I feel I should have written it in my maiden name, which is what I use now, instead of Culleton.

SILVERA: Culleton is your ex-married name. And your maiden name?

CULLETON: Is Mosionier.

SILVERA: Why do you think you should have used your maiden name?

CULLETON: I left my first husband, so I'm not Culleton any more. And Mosionier is something I think my parents would have liked. My dad, he's eighty-five and my mom is eighty-one, so I wish I'd written under Mosionier just for them.

SILVERA: Your next book will be under that surname?

CULLETON: Yes.

(In deference to the writer stating that she now writes under her birth name Mosionier, the rest of the interview will be conducted using Mosionier.)

SILVERA: Do you think that the women's movement had any influence on you when you wrote *April Raintree?*

MOSIONIER: No, it's been Native persons that had the impact. When I write, of course, I write from a woman's point of view, but I was close to my brother, and I have a son, so I think that generally I try to think of people as a family unit in a traditional way. I'm old-fashioned, maybe, so when I think of a community I think of men, women, children — not in that order, of course. Women are really important to me because of my sisters. I don't consider myself an activist or anything in the women's movement, but I feel very strongly that this real paternalistic government has done a lot of harm. So, of course, part of justice is equality to me, and I feel women have to be empowered in that respect. I don't think we should have to put up with any paternalistic attitudes on the part of the Church and the government. So I feel that really strong, and I'd work hard to see things that way, but I don't want to ever become anti-men because of it.

SILVERA: Do you feel that's what feminism is?

MOSIONIER: Feminism? I can't even say it. *(laughter)* A lot of the feminist things I've heard sound anti-men or anti-male, and I don't like that division. I don't like it because to me the community is everyone, and equality has to be for everybody. The tendency is to get unbalanced — you know, when you're pushing for something, you push so hard on one side that suddenly it becomes unbalanced.

SILVERA: So you think that's what women who call themselves feminist do? Push for one side?

MOSIONIER: From my experience, from what I've seen, from what women have said to me. I've thought about it a lot, and it's partly why I don't identify myself as a feminist. I could be wrong.

SILVERA: So what do you identify as?

MOSIONIER: Just a Native, grassroots person. Just an ordinary, common ...

SILVERA: Grassroots person or a Native grassroots woman. Isn't that a separation between the person and the woman?

MOSIONIER: Well, now I use person *(laughter)* because somehow, somewhere, along the way I just started thinking of people as persons.

SILVERA: Do you feel Native women and Native men are treated the same, in terms of your community?

MOSIONIER: I think that the women have definitely had it harder than the men because of the European way of thinking, like women were "squaws" for such a long time, and that meant they were nothing in the eyes of the rest of society, but men were just barely above us — if they could have gotten rid of Indian people they would have. So there's that paternalistic treatment that spread to Indian communities as well, where all the chiefs were appointed and were all men — they would never even think of appointing a woman as a chief. It's carried on like that for a long time. If you look at the political groups, it's men that lead. There's still that problem. Which is another story. *(laughter)*

Endnote

[1] ANDPVA — The Association for Native Development in the Performing and Visual Arts.

Lien Chao

LIEN CHAO

Constituting Minority Canadian Women and our Sub-Cultures:
Female Characters in Selected Chinese Canadian Literature

ON JULY 12, 1992, the *Toronto Star* published a report on Toronto's Chinese community, one of a seven-part series on the city's minority communities.[1] The report begins with a description of a Chinese immigrant woman, a garment worker who sews lined skirts in her cold basement home for $1.10 a skirt, making an average of $4.64 an hour. "Speaking through an interpreter," the article says, "she doesn't want her name used. She worries about trouble with the company. She needs the work. Her husband is unemployed. They have two small children." Later on she is given a pseudonym, Tianmei Zhang. Her interpreter also tells the reporter, "She never gets out. She doesn't have any friends. She just takes care of her children and sews." Beside the article is a photograph taken in Tianmei Zhang's basement home; her two small children are playing behind her, while her head bends over the industrial sewing machine and her hands are busy with the garment pieces.[2]

According to Lois Sweet, the reporter who wrote the article, there are about 2,000 woman homeworkers scattered throughout the city who sew piecework in their homes. They work full-time and over-time, but they are paid far below Ontario's minimum hourly wage; their employers contribute nothing on their behalf to unemployment insurance or Canada Pension. Among them, seventy percent are Chinese-speaking immigrant women who, like Tianmei Zhang, do not speak enough English to communicate outside the ethnic ghetto or who are tied down to small children at home.

Tianmei Zhang's case typifies the experience of Chinese women in Canada — of Chinese immigrant women especially. Underlining their specific isolation and invisibility in Canadian society are the language barriers and cultural differences that all immigrants have to confront, but Chinese Canadian women also have to inhabit a distinctive ethnic community that was discriminated against in Canada for almost one hundred years and which had a local history of a married-bachelor culture.

Earlier, the Chinese immigration pattern was different from those of most other ethnic groups; instead of family immigration, most Chinese immigrants to North America were male labourers. Around the 1850s, about 25,000 Chinese men emigrated from the south and southeast regions of China to work along the Sacramento River in California, which was named Gold Mountain by Chinese immigrants in the US and Canada. In 1858, when the second Gold Mountain was discovered at the Fraser River Valley in British Columbia, many of the gold miners in California came to Canada. Later, approximately 17,000 Chinese males were recruited from Hong Kong and southern China as cheap labourers for the Canadian Pacific Railway, British Columbia section, and other construction projects in Canada.[3]

Due to labour market competition, anti-Chinese racism became the dominant ideology in British Columbia and other parts of Canada in the following years. Ottawa sent three Royal Commissions to investigate.[4] As a result, instead of educating Canadians to tolerate each other's differences, the Canadian government passed several discriminatory laws against Chinese immigration. The government imposed increasing "head taxes," from fifty dollars in 1886, to one hundred dollars in 1900, and five hundred dollars in 1903, for every Chinese, to be paid upon landing in Canada. The 1923 *Chinese Exclusion Act* prevented many Chinese from entering Canada, including the family members of immigrants who had hoped for reunion in Canada. As a result, the Chinese labourers' initial separation from their families was institutionally prolonged and hence instigated the formation of the Chinatown ghetto as a kind of replacement for the family.

A racist trope, "Chinaman," widely used from the 19th century up to the mid-twentieth century, seemed to suggest that Chinese males were a different species. Stemming from the labour-intensive work they were expected to do in Canada initially, the dehumanizing term, "Chinaman," defined the Chinese immigrant-labourer as man-machine. It also denied the existence of Chinese women, albeit for decades the female Chinese population did not equal that of the Chinese male.

The sex ratio imbalance among the Chinese in Canada remained a long-time problem. In the 1880s the sex ratio imbalance was 1.2 percent female to 98.8 percent male.[5] In 1924 the sex ratio was six percent female out of a total Chinese population of 40,000 in Canada (about one female to sixteen males).[6] In addition to the sex ratio imbalance, the general anti-Chinese racism in society made it impossible for Chinese men to meet women of other races. The few Chinese women in Chinatown during the 19th century had been made sexual commodities by the male-oriented culture in the local Chinatown. According to the 1885 Royal Commission, there were 160 Chinese females in British Columbia, of whom seventy were listed as "prostitutes." There were also fifty-five married women and thirty-five girls listed in the 1885 Royal Commission (393). But most Chinese wives and their children were separated from their husbands and fathers who were living in Canada for almost a lifetime. Not until after World War II when the *Chinese Exclusion Act* was repealed were family members of the Chinese bachelor labourers finally allowed to come to Canada for reunion.

Today the limited historical data on Chinese Canadian women in the Canadian Archives provide a researcher with minimal accounts of their lives in a racist and misogynist society during the last one hundred years. The *Toronto Star*'s recent report on the Chinese community, based on telephone interviews, offers no more insight than the number of yeses or noes to specific questions. The garment worker who did not want her real name printed is indicative of the collective invisibility of Chinese immigrant women in Canadian society today. The sub-culture of Chinese Canadian women has yet to be defined and differentiated in Canadian social and cultural discourses.

The absence of Chinese Canadian women from Canadian cultural records and academic disciplines results in her apparent absence in Canadian culture. As a Chinese immigrant woman, I am continually being struck by the lack of representation of minority Canadian women in most of the mainstream Canadian literature and modern drama that I have studied and taught. As a non-white reader, I have experienced a rejection of my subject position and felt pressured to adopt the position of the white mainstream reader. The texts that I have read and taught consistently alienate me and deny me and women like me a legitimate and respectable cultural identity within most existing Canadian literature.

In the last ten years the Canadian population has undergone a major change with increasing immigration from the Third World countries. As the non-white Canadian population increases, it is time for ethnic minority communities, women of colour and immigrant women to speak out in society and in cultural fields. It is significant that the Chinese garment worker was visited by a reporter instead of being called for a telephone interview. Had she been approached on the phone, she would probably not have been able to impart as much as she did in this article about her life.

I think that the historical silence of Chinese women in Canada can be broken by breaking through the silent archival documents and rewriting the existing history. Breaking through the silence means constituting minority women as agents. To illustrate this hypothesis I will examine some female characters in Winston Christopher Kam's drama *Bachelor-Man* and Sky Lee's novel *Disappearing Moon Cafe*. These two literary works constitute Chinese Canadian women as agents and help begin their socio-historical construction.

English Canadian literature is taught as beginning with British immigrant writer Susanna Moodie's autobiography *Roughing It in the Bush* (1852). Migration, one of the predominant experiences of modernity, is an established theme in Canadian literature. Nevertheless, non-white immigrant writings have not been absorbed into the Canadian literary canon. Since mainstream Canadian writers with European backgrounds dominate the canon, European immigrants' experiences have been read as universal. It is not uncommon for a white, bourgeois, heterosexual female character to be depicted as the heroine. But Susanna Moodie cannot speak for all immigrants, especially not for immigrant women like the Chinese garment worker known as Tianmei Zhang, who did not even dare to give her name in her account of her life. Many university students reading *Roughing It in the Bush* today as part of a survey course in Canadian literature feel offended by Moodie's racist bias against less educated people, against women with European origins other than English or French, against women from a lower class or speaking a local accent. The offensiveness these readers experience may stem from their being denied a subject position within the text. It indicates that Moodie's class and racial bias of the 1850s is, to a large extent, no longer an acceptable social practice today.

What is silenced by Moodie in this canonical Canadian text are immigrant women's experiences, experiences that have yet to be acknowledged in Canadian discourses. Canadian literary texts featuring Chinese characters are scarce. In the few that do depict Chinese characters, such as the widely-taught novel *Badlands*(1975) by Robert Kroetsch, the Chinese character is stereotyped into little more than an alienated caricature. Kroetsch uses the handy racist term "Chinaman" for the Chinese character in his novel centred around a white male geologist's journey to prove his manhood. The narrator, sharing the perspective of the other white male characters, "would not bother to learn" the name of the Chinaman.[7] For convenience, Kroetsch nicknames the Chinaman "Grizzly," after his encounter with a bear. Chinaman Grizzly is given the job of cooking on the white geologist's field trip. His behaviour is portrayed as eccentric in comparison to the white characters. His way of cooking, serving a meal, making love to the Native woman and his genuine muteness are carefully delineated to associate him with a bear, connoting that he represents untamed nature in contrast to the civilized and educated white men on the team. By making him a caricature throughout the novel, the narrator and the white characters have justified their excluding the Chinese character from expressing himself.

Any Canadian reader with a Chinese background or with racial sensitivity likely feels denied a subject position when reading about Grizzly, unless she or he adopts the perspective of the white characters and accepts the writer's caricature of the Chinese character. Although Chinese in Canada and the US had long been called Chinamen collectively, or Chinaman individually, using this term without laying bare the historical discriminatory context is exactly how racism operates in contemporary cultural fields. The creation of Grizzly in *Badlands* repeats and reconfirms a racial stereotype. This canonical Canadian text denies the Chinese character agency by depriving him of his Chinese name and proper behaviour. It silences the Chinese man by not allowing him to speak a recognizable language. Overall, *Badlands* undermines the Chinese character's experience by denying him a legitimate Canadian perspective and making him instead a constant, unchanging alien throughout the novel.

Kroetsch has a well-quoted dictum about the relationship between a cultural identity and literary products about such an identity. He says, "We haven't got an identity until somebody tells our stories."[8] As a mainstream writer depicting a racial minority character, Kroetsch's Grizzly clearly does not provide Chinese Canadians an acceptable identity. That Kroetsch is an established writer and literary critic and that *Badlands* is a widely-read novel makes it even more important for a Chinese Canadian reader or readers of other ethnic backgrounds to contest this racial and cultural appropriation. At the same time, it is necessary for non-white minority Canadians to realize that a community needs to have its own writers tell its history in order to create a collective cultural identity. This realization does not suggest that writings from cross-cultural boundaries are politically incorrect and should be forbidden or avoided. Rather, what is needed is an implicit respect for any other culture that a writer intends to represent. Minority writers, especially, minority women writers, urgently need to speak out to break through the historical silence of their communities in Canada and the US.

Breaking through the silence in systems of discourse and knowledge means going back through the silent data of the archives and rewriting the existing history. Chinese Canadian writer Winston Christopher Kam's drama *Bachelor-Man* is a good example of deciphering silent historical documents.[9] In the play Kam dramatizes ghetto life in Toronto's Chinatown in 1923. A Chinese woman, Queenie, works as a prostitute for married-bachelor labourers who had given up hoping for their wives to come to Canada because of the new *Chinese Exclusion Act*. Kam compares Queenie's situation to that of a married Chinese wife, Mrs. Wu, whose husband rents her out at night to make money. The play ends with the news of Mrs. Wu's suicide while Queenie is leading a funeral ritual among half a dozen bachelor labourers in a local tea-house she frequents for business. In *Bachelor-Man* Kam succeeds in making the silent archives speak about the Chinese Canadian sex imbalance of sixteen males to one female in the 1920s. The play contextualizes the lives of Chinese women living in a racist and misogynist society. It is from their perspective that the historical data have been made to speak. The racist and misogynist culture is exposed as an antagonistic environment in which Chinese Canadian women are confined.

Since facts and historical data cannot speak for themselves, historians and writers must refashion them with integrity. It is up to the historian and the writer to make minority women characters speak, to make a group of marginalized people agents. By making them speaking subjects, the writer empowers them. Further, by empowering minority women and their discourse, by giving otherwise marginalized or caricatured figures a voice and agency, the writer reconfigures the existing mainstream discourse.

Joan E. Hartman and Ellen Messer-Davidow define agents and perspective in the introduction to *(En)Gendering Knowledge: Feminists in Academe*:

> Agents act and monitor their actions. *What makes them agents is their capacity (not their intention) to act and, moreover, to act otherwise, to intervene in the world, to have an effect.* Knowers exercise their agency not only when they devise facts and theories, but also when they attempt to transform the disciplines or even when they choose a different voice.

Perspective has been defined visually as the function of positioning a person and a scene. The viewer's location and the configuration seen elicit the angle of vision, and, conversely, the viewer's location and the angle of vision determine the configuration seen. [Emphasis added.][10]

Hartman and Messer-Davidow point out that agents are those speaking subjects whose voices can make a difference to the existing mainstream institutions and knowledge systems. Minority women view the dominant system quite differently from traditional white male agents and differently from white, middle-class, heterosexual feminist agents. Only when enough women of colour and women from other marginalized categories become agents and voice their perspectives will the system undergo a thorough change.

The applications of this investigation on agents and systems are limitless. In all social and cultural fields where knowledge is created and exchanged, agents and systems are always mutually constituted. The recognition that masculinity has dominated mainstream discourse and knowledge systems since the Renaissance has been a major achievement by feminists. Today feminism itself is an established knowledge system. Minority women researchers, theorists and writers have won the right to challenge the partiality of mainstream feminist knowledge and discourse.

The establishment of feminism as a knowledge system has proven that socially marginalized groups are capable of functioning as powerful agents; their previously suppressed experiences have yielded rich cultural and epistemological resources. Today more and more minority Canadian women are fighting for the agents' role in Canadian society. Their struggle for equality has challenged and interfered with the existing systems. What has yet to happen is the transforming of their suppressed voices and experiences into cultural expressions within the dominant language. This practice will modify and enrich the existing systems intellectually and linguistically. Since agents and systems are mutually constitutive, minority women need to be constituted into the systems of discourse and knowledge in order to fundamentally alter the existing cultural institutions controlled by the white male perspective.

It is a pioneer task for women of colour to constitute our suppressed experiences as agents in modernism and its institutions. To fulfil this historic task, we will find adopting a combined strategy of the celebratory mode and deconstruction beneficial. The celebratory mode has its roots in traditional humanism, logical positivism, etc., which have been criticized by feminists for concentrating on thematic patterns or other pure textual analyses based on universalist assumptions.[11] In French feminist theory "body politics" adopts the celebratory mode to establish an essentialist female-body-oriented theory. "Body politics" is challenged by feminist cultural critics for separating women's body from the socio-historical context in which her body has been interpreted as a sexual object and for idealizing a non-existent female discourse which is not conditioned by the symbolic order.[12] The problem with this approach lies in its separation of epistemological and other textual meanings from the cultural and social institutions that have historically determined meaning. Aware of this failure, women of colour researchers can avoid the pitfall of separating our social history from the literary textual representations of our history. We should dismiss any attempt at constituting essentialist women of colour literary theories or practices through the celebratory mode. Only when deeply grounded in socio-historical reality can a the celebratory mode bring out the suppressed culture and inform mainstream discourse and mainstream knowledge systems.

In order to make celebratory art more effective, it must be combined with deconstruction. To say or even prove that modernism marginalizes women's experiences or that the existing Canadian literary canon stereotypes Chinese men and excludes Chinese women is not enough. Since modernism and Canadian literature are established academic and cultural institutions, their powerful, legitimate presence confirms and reconfirms its agents and the perspective they represent. Without the radical and systematic deconstruction of the existing systems, minority celebratory art can easily be absorbed and appropriated by the existing mainstream systems.

Deconstruction, a modern philosophy, presents a theoretical challenge to Eurocentric cultural dominance and its biases and hence an opportunity for equality and mutual respect between minority and mainstream culture. Jacques Derrida offers some preliminary reflections on the word deconstruction. According to him, "deconstruction" is a "common way of saying *construction*." (Emphasis added.) He explains how deconstruction functions:

> To be very schematic I would say that the difficulty of *defining* and therefore also of *translating* the word "deconstruction" stems from the fact that all the predicates, all the defining concepts, all the lexical significations, and even the syntactic articulations, which seem at one moment to lend themselves to this definition or to that translation, are also deconstructed or deconstructible, directly or otherwise, etc. And that goes for the *word*, the very unity of the *word* deconstruction, as for every *word*.[13]

The wide scope of deconstruction provides minority researchers and theorists with a liberating and enlightening philosophy. Deconstruction has been adopted widely by feminists to challenge patriarchy and to rewrite the male-gender-dominant ideology; it can be applied by minority researchers and writers as they attempt to rewrite the collective histories and minority women's herstories.

Chinese Canadian writer Sky Lee effectively combines celebratory art with deconstruction; she successfully creates a Chinese Canadian community which has not been represented in Canadian literature before. In *Disappearing Moon Cafe* the marginalized Chinese men and women are depicted as agents in a community that has fought against racism in Canada for over one hundred years. She also deconstructs the gender and racial stereotypes of the silent and submissive Chinese woman. Through celebratory art, Lee makes their quest for freedom and love the major events in her novel.

Lee employs the traditional narrative form of the family saga to embrace a structural irony. Since Chinatown has suffered a historical sex ratio imbalance, the majority of the Chinese labourers have never had any families. In a traditional family saga the stories are usually centred around the linear growth of the male in the family. This family-oriented narrative form is deconstructed in Lee's novel, and hence reconstructed, to represent an unusual kinship among the Chinese bachelor men in Vancouver's Chinatown. Character Wong Gwei Chang, as the community leader and one of the few successful business and family men in Chinatown, realizes that this unusual kinship among Chinese labourers has kept the community together through many years of hardship: "Year after year, right or wrong, they had always been loyal to each other. How many lonely, softhearted nights, respectfully attentive to the would-be heroics of laundrymen and gardeners, *they had all played surrogate wives to each other.*" (Emphasis added.)[14]

Disappearing Moon Cafe employs Wong Gwei Chang's memory as a structural frame: its prologue and epilogue are set in his memory before his death in 1939. This structure establishes a socio-historical background in which all Lee's characters are contextualized. Nevertheless, the focus of the novel is not on Chinese men but on four generations of Chinese women, spanning the 1880s to the 1980s. Among them are married wives, a sent-for paper bride, incest victims, servant women, a hired surrogate mother and lesbian lovers. Ironically, Lee appropriates the male-centred family saga for a Chinese women's collective saga.

Within the socio-historical framework of the community, Lee makes Kae Ying Woo, a fourth-generation great-granddaughter of Wong Gwei Chang, the narrator. Further, Lee empowers her with a first-person narrative. Kae is entitled to choose the stories from her mother's side instead of her father's and to tell the stories about her mother, Beatrice, and her Aunt Suzanne but not about her maternal uncle, John. The timing for Kae to become a storyteller is critical, coming right after she has given birth to her son. Lee uses the physical change brought on by childbirth as a dramatic paradox, for Kae sees herself becoming powerless because of the biological function of her body and confined to the traditional social institutions of marriage and motherhood. But Kae is a character capable of adapting; she sees that she can use this maternal change imaginatively and artistically, to empower herself and to free the mothers and daughters of the Wong family tree:

> Thus, the story — the well-kept secret that I had actually unearthed years ago — finally begins to end for me with the birth of my son ... It took quite the sentimental occasion for my mother to finally loosen a little of her iron grip on her emotions in order to reveal a little of her past that she thought so shameful — the same past that has shaped so much of my own life ...[15]

Lee uses motherhood extensively as a trope for the maturation and transformation of her women characters. Through motherhood, Lee's characters are transformed from silent to speaking subjects, and their suppressed, shameful experiences are finally told in her fiction.

Lee's female characters reflect Chinese Canadian women's

historical reality and thus supplant the dominant white bourgeois women's experience in Canadian literature. Her half-dozen female characters are related in two different ways: on the public or sociological level, they are divided into two classes, the rich wives and the poor servants; but in a private space, they are linked by various female gender bonds. The matriarch, Mui Lan, wife of Wong Gwei Chang, belongs to the rich class. Song An, the only female waitress in Chinatown hired by Mui Lan, belongs to the poor. But because Mui Lan and Song An came to Canada in the same boat they seem to be bonded to each other, despite their class difference. Mui Lan stood behind Song An when the latter was beaten up by her elderly husband, an old railway labourer. Mui Lan offers the abused woman a job as a waitress so that Song An can support herself. However, out of a mixed feeling of trust and a wish to exploit the waitress, when Mui Lan's daughter-in-law fails to show any sign of fertility, Mui Lan hires Song An to sleep with her son, to produce a grandson for the Wongs. Lee uses motherhood to transform the waitress to an agent for her own life; after Song An has given birth to a baby boy, she decides to raise him herself. Years later, when telling her son who his father is, Song An is not apologetic.

Another unusual female bond exists between Kae Ying Woo, the narrator, and her mother's old housekeeper, Seto Chi. "Chi, my old nanny... As a (trans)parent, she established an intractable reference point for power between the two of us right from the start. She had all, and I had none."[16] As Chinese Canadian women's subculture has never been represented like this in Canadian literature, this relationship might sound strange to a mainstream reader.

The relationships between Mui Lan and the waitress and between Kae and the old nanny illustrate two of the many situations where Lee gives a traditionally powerless woman a share of power. In this female saga power is made evident in an unfixed human relationship rather than as the result of class or gender clashes. She empowers women in a private sphere, installing personal relationships and the private sphere as equal locales in which the traditionally powerful and powerless gain the opportunity to switch their socio-historical positions. Further, the representation of the unfixed power relationship in the Chinese Canadian women's sub-culture enriches Canadian literature.

In their immediate public world, Chinatown, Lee's female characters are caught in their collective fate as Chinese women: to give birth, especially to male heirs. Their personal identities are based on their contributions to the linear male procreation. Even Mui Lan, the wife of the richest man in Chinatown, has no other identity except that of wife and mother:

> She was simply the mother of Gwei Chang's only son. Stamped on her entry papers: 'A merchant's wife.' A wife in name only, she relied heavily on him for her identity in this land, even though the hard distance remained on her husband's face. And this she could only bear in silence.[17]

Ironically, to establish her own identity, Mui Lan has to use patriarchal power to reinforce her dominance.

The dramatic conflict between Mui Lan and her daughter-in-law, Fong Mei, vividly depicts another aspect of Chinese women's sub-culture: a younger female's biological reproduction is usually reinforced by the older woman in the family. Fong Mei, a sent-for paper bride from China, is a human reproductive machine initially purchased for the Wongs. But since Fong Mei has remained idle for five years after the wedding, her mother-in-law, Mui Lan, complains of how the Wongs have been cheated:

We received her into our home in the most flamboyant
style. With the costs of hiring the go-betweens and the
negotiators; with the costs of her passage and the bribes,
never mind the gifts; and of course the cost of the wedding
itself — never mind the risks we took with our Wong name
and livelihood in a government investigation to secure *her*
immigration status ... [18]

Money is made the focal point of Fong Mei's disgrace by Mui Lan, which recreates the mother-in-law's power in the traditional Chinese family. The use of "her" instead of "you" in direct conversation between the two women posits the mother-in-law as powerful and the daughter-in-law as powerless. Lee explores this power relationship further to show that Chinese women's sub-culture has been historically conditioned by the surrounding patriarchy. She makes Mui Lan a patriarchal guardian; through Mui Lan, Lee exposes the feudal marriage practice — the selling of a woman by her own family to another family for the continuity of the male line. Failing to show any sign of fertility within a certain time, a married woman can be abandoned by her husband's family. In *Disappearing Moon Cafe*, Mui Lan gains the power to enforce such a practice:

"Go back home to your own family! You have more than
enough gold here to pawn for a passage." Mui Lan sneered,
knowing full well that a spurned daughter-in-law would
rather commit suicide than go back to her parents' home,
for all the ten generations of everlasting shame that she
would cost her family, in fact her whole village.

"I don't care where you drag your dead body. You definitely
have no right to stay in the way of my son's son. Who's
going to speak up on your side?"

"But our customs are clear and practical too. If the first wife cannot bear a son, then she stands aside for another. That way, the family is assured of a yellow, 'lucky' road. Otherwise, who will there be left to honour even you, to sweep your grave?"[19]

By making Mui Lan and not Wong Gwei Chang or their son the patriarchal guardian who wants to dismiss Fong Mei, Lee does not romanticize her female characters or exclude them from cultural affairs. Instead she posits her female characters in their socio-historical context, in which they are both agents and its products.

Fong Mei is first described as an independent and intelligent woman who is capable of self-empowerment after she is abused by her mother-in-law, Mui Lan. Once she sees that her opportunity lies in her fertility and motherhood, Fong Mei finds herself a lover, gets pregnant and gives birth to a baby daughter and later to another daughter and a son. Again, we see Lee persistently using the trope of motherhood to give her female characters an opportunity for changing identity. She dramatizes this change in Fong Mei to show that women's biological function can be used for their own self-empowerment:

> After two weeks of confinement, she came home a very nervous, high-strung woman, so any spark at all could have sent her into a fiery rage. Yet fierceness, whether she was conscious of it or not, was exactly the artillery she needed to do battle with her mother-in-law in order to usurp the throne.
>
> Fong Mei produced only a girl, who, tiny as she was, gave her mother enough omnipotence to vie for power and

launch a fullfledged mutiny (as one can do only from deep within the ranks). First, Fong Mei learned to drive a car; next, she took her share in the family business and turned it into the most lucrative one of all — real estate.[20]

The development of Fong Mei as an independent female does not exclude the sexual desire of the modern woman. Not only is Fong Mei the one who takes the initiative in approaching her lover, she also enjoys sex psychologically and physically as much as her male partner. Lee describes her character's sexual desire and physical power as overwhelming and totally feminine. Through celebratory art Lee deconstructs the stereotypical passive role of Oriental women, especially in sexual encounters.

Fong Mei, however, is just as contradictory as her mother-in-law, who is first seen as Fong Mei's oppressor. Following her mother-in-law's pattern, Fong Mei, the survivor of the feudal marriage practice, in turn becomes its agent, reinforcing patriarchal authority once she becomes a mother-in-law herself. The anti-feminine transformation of the mother-in-laws shows that women's suppressed sub-culture has to be voiced; otherwise, their struggle for personal fulfilments will fail, and their battle against patriarchy will leave them feeling guilty and further silenced. Fong Mei's hostility towards her two daughters' love affairs shows her own guilt as a survivor of the patriarchal marriage practice. Although she does not have to apologize for what she has done, as an established businesswoman she must avoid scandal. To guard her secret past, she avoids using the term "incest" to explain why she objects to her daughter Suzanne's love affair. Speaking to Suzanne, Fong Mei uses a language of human torture mixed with dogmatic social morality and a threat of power:

I'll see you dead first. You'll never marry him. You're going into Greenwood, a prison for cheap sluts like you. I've already made all the arrangements. And that thing in you is a deformed monster, so I'm giving it over to the government to raise.[21]

Suzanne is the most uncompromising female character of all the Wong women; she becomes, as the narrator puns in a title for a poster, the tragic heroine of the "*Temple of Wonged Women*."[22] Seto Chi, their old nanny, summarizes, "Suzie was one of those types who couldn't be contained."[23] Suzanne cannot survive the patriarchy; her difficult labour is told in the first-person voice of the character, the dramatic and despairing outcry of a woman deprived of her right to her body and to her newly born child, a woman whose voice has been silenced by a misogynistic environment:

You're hurting my baby! I don't have a voice. Little legs pounding against me, little hands scratching to get out. My little deformed monster, what have they done to you?

"Knock her out! Why isn't she knocked out yet?" screams the irate doctor.[24]

Medical specialists, depicted as the guardians of conservative morals and the persecutors of women who belong to sub-cultural categories, deprive Suzanne of her motherhood and destroy her feminine power. With the sacrifice of the unwanted baby and Suzanne's consequent suicide, Lee makes Fong Mei's ghost recant: "I forgot that they were my children! I forgot that I didn't need to align them with male authority, as if they would be lesser human beings without it."[25] Lee points out that women's historical bondage under patriarchy is partly prolonged by a self-imposed denial that holds that we are equal partners in marriage and parenthood. With the recantating of Fong Mei's ghost, Suzanne's ghost cries out for justice and a collective awakening of women: "All this bondage we volunteer on ourselves! Untie them! Untie me!"[26] Writing from the contemporary reader's point of view, Lee makes a moral argument for resisting patriarchy.

At this stage, Lee thematically and structurally sets the daughters and the mothers free from the Wongs. Their sub-culture has been rendered into English discourse and they have become agents who speak about their own history. The narrator, Kae, exclaims her freedom: "After three generations of struggle, the daughters are free!"[27] Lee also reveals the freedom that a minority woman writer achieves in her quest for a denied herstory, for collectively shared individual identities. The narrator's friend, possibly her lesbian lover, underscores the collectivity of women's experiences voiced in *Disappearing Moon Cafe*: "Do you mean that individuals must gather their identity from all the generations that touch them — past and future, no matter how slightly? Do you mean that an individual is not an individual at all, but a series of individuals — some of whom come before her, some after her? Do you mean that this story isn't a story of several generations, but of one individual thinking collectively?"[28]

In addition to her themes, Lee's sructure sets her characters free from the narrative bondage of the traditional family saga. She names the prologue "Search for Bones," suggesting a researcher setting off to make silent historical and anthropological materials speak the collective history of Chinese Canadians. After she tells the Wong women's stories in the body of the novel, Lee then names the epilogue "New Moon," indicating a new era for her female characters and for the reader as well.

Endnotes

[1] "The Minority Reports" published in June and July, 1992, were surveys based on random telephone interviews with Torontonians of Italian, Chinese, Portuguese, Indian, Pakistani, Jewish, Caribbean or Black background or descent.

[2] Lois Sweet, "The Chinese Community: Still Seeking a Better Life," *The Toronto Star*, July 12, 1992, pp. A1 and 6-7.

[3] Paul Yee, *Salt Water City: An Illustrated History of the Chinese in Vancouver* (Vancouver and Toronto: Douglas & McIntyre Press, 1988), p. 10.

[4] The reports prepared by the three Royal Commissions were: the *Report of the Royal Commission on Chinese Immigration* (Ottawa: Printed by Order of the Commission, 1885), the *Report of the Royal Commission on Oriental Immigration* and *Report of the Commission Appointed to Inquire into the Subjects of Chinese and Japanese Immigration into the Province of British Columbia* (Ottawa: Printed by S.E. Dawson, 1902), and the *Report of the Royal Commission Appointed to Inquire into the Methods by which Oriental Labourers have been Induced to Come to Canada* (Ottawa: Government Printing Bureau, 1908).

[5] Harry Con, Ronald J. Con, Graham Johnson, Edgar Wickberg and William E. Willmott, *From China to Canada: A History of the Chinese Communities in Canada*, Edgar Wickberg, ed. (Toronto: McClelland & Stewart in association with the Multiculturalism Directorate and the Department of State, 1982), p. 26.

[6] Lee Wai-man, *Portraits of Challenge: An Illustrated History of Chinese Canadians* (Toronto: Council of Chinese Canadians in Ontario, 1984), p. 162.

[7] Robert Kroetsch, *Badlands* (Toronto: General Publishing Company, 1975), p. 13.

[8] Robert Kroetsch, "A Conversation with Margaret Lawrence" in *creation*, Robert Kroetsch, ed. (Toronto: new press, 1970), p. 63.

[9] Winston Christopher Kam, *Bachelor-Man*. Produced in Toronto by Theatre Passe Muraille in 1987.

[10] Joan E. Hartman and Ellen Messer-Davidow, eds. *(En)Gendering Knowledge: Feminists in Academe* (Knoxville: The University of Tennessee Press, 1991), pp. 2-3.

[11.] Kathryn Pyne Addelson and Elizabeth Potter, "Making Knowledge" in *(En)Gendering Knowledge: Feminists in Academe* (Knoxville: The University of Tennessee Press, 1991), pp. 262-263.

[12.] Janet Wolff, "Reinstating Corporeality: Feminism and Body Politics" in *Feminine Sentences: Essays on Women and Culture* (Cambridge, UK: Polity Press, 1990), pp. 129-132.

[13.] Jacques Derrida, "Letter to a Japanese Friend" in *Derrida and Differance*, David Wood and Robert Bernasconi, eds. (Evanston: Northwestern University Press, 1988), pp. 2 and 4.

[14.] Sky Lee, *Disappearing Moon Cafe* (Vancouver and Toronto: Douglas & McIntyre, 1990), p. 226.

[15.] *Ibid.*, p. 23.

[16.] *Ibid.*, p. 127.

[17.] *Ibid.*, p. 28.

[18.] *Ibid.*, p. 58.

[19.] *Ibid.*, pp. 59-60.

[20.] *Ibid.*, p. 134.

[21.] *Ibid.*, p. 203.

[22.] *Ibid.*, p. 209.

[23.] *Ibid.*, p. 190.

[24.] *Ibid.*, p. 206.

[25.] *Ibid.*, p. 189.

[26.] *Ibid.*, p. 200

[27.] *Ibid.*, p. 209.

[28.] *Ibid.*, p. 189.

Veró Boncompagni / National Film Board

An interview with
DIONNE BRAND

In the company of my work

SILVERA: So, you don't want a "why do you write" question?

BRAND: No, I'm so bored with that. And I don't even know why any more. I just write because it's habit now. Necessary habit.

About what you were asking earlier — I've always been a leftist from the time I came into any kind of political consciousness. And I don't mean leftist in terms of airy ideas or something like that, but a leftist in terms of concrete work, which is why I've always had this big trouble with whether I should be writing or not — whether I should be writing, or going somewhere and doing political organizing in a Black country, or doing political organizing around labour or something like that. But I've never been reviewed that way because, I think, people are really afraid to say that kind of thing, afraid that it would be insulting.

I find nothing shameful about being leftist, and I want to state explicitly that my work is leftist work and that I've always seen my work as leftist work, as much as Pablo Neruda's was leftist work or Bertold Brecht's was leftist work. It's a strong and good tradition. My work documents not just the Grenada revolution but the events around the coup and the invasion, Caribbean life and its political context, the history of working-class Caribbean life and so on. It's always been clearly directed through the prism of leftist analysis.

And I'm not the kind of poet who thinks that my subjects should be obscure. I couldn't give a fuck about that. I'm not a white, middle-class poet. I couldn't give a damn about cats, dogs and other small things. I'm forty-one, and I really don't give a damn. I'm not saying there isn't any good white, left poetry — it's the only poetry of that kind that I've had any respect for because I think there are things going on in the world that we ought to talk about, that must be talked about, and not just our own individual well-being.

So I really didn't mind that reviewer saying that I have always been influenced by Marxism and feminist ideas. I don't see Marxism and feminism as theories I need to graft onto people, I see them as living things. Analysis is supposed to work, to be living, growing. And I don't mind saying I belonged to the Communist Party — even though certain communist states have fallen and the ideas of communism seem to have come into disrepute, I don't think there's anything different going on in the world since those communist states fell. I don't think people have stopped being exploited. I don't think poverty has suddenly disappeared. I don't think corporate capital is our salvation and answer.

I still think there is a need for a socialist vision. And I honestly do not mind saying that that is what my work is about. I think that is where my work differs — in its explicitness about that idea.

SILVERA: So would you say that this is where your work differs from other African-Caribbean poets or writers in Canada?

BRAND: In Canada, probably. I think so.

SILVERA: What are the similarities and the differences in what you have to say and what other African-Canadians and Afro-Caribbean writers here have to say?

BRAND: If I try to think of all the works that I've read, whether it's Maxine Tynes, Claire Harris or Nourbese Philip — maybe not Lillian Allen, maybe her work has been in some places specifically left. I'm not saying that their work doesn't intersect on other levels. But the difference is that I'm a lesbian. So my position vis-à-vis being a woman, I think, has sometimes been different from other women writers. It didn't appear in my earlier work because I hadn't come to lesbian consciousness then.

SILVERA: In what way?

BRAND: I think that my positioning as a woman in my work — and I can only say this now in retrospect, it's not like I was doing it consciously or anything like that — has always been to question what it means to be female. I don't mean *that* one is female, but what it means to be that. I'm remembering writing about my grandmother's life.

The poems about my grandmother's life are always poems tinged not just with her difficulties but with her departures from male life, departures from where men had a role in defining her. What I saw in her life were those departures — notwithstanding her relationship to men, or to my grandfather — and I rejected that construct that also constructs women. I read in my work my distance from certain constructs of womanhood.

And I'm not talking simplistically about asserting myself as a female. I'm talking about distancing myself as a human being from concepts or constructs of womanhood that are laid down largely through the rule of men. In *Chronicles of the Hostile Sun*, there's a poem that goes,

> I am not that strong woman on the mountain
> at Castle Bruce ...
> I cannot hold a mountain under my feet ...
> I am the one with no place to live
> I want no husband
> I want nothing inside of me
> that hates me ...
> I want nothing that enters me
> screaming
> claiming to be history.

I'm not talking about super-repressed women, I'm not talking about women who have conformed to the idea of femininity as weak. I'm talking about the strong women I saw all my life on the streets and in my house: they were buried in those constructs of womanhood. When I look back at some of the work I've written I can see myself wanting to get away from that radically, so radically as to not ever allow those constructs to determine even how I wrote a love poem. I can see myself making that distance, not getting buried by those constructs, whether it's the woman super-exploited through her femininity or the woman who doesn't conform to those rules of femininity but nevertheless is caught in them. I also didn't see myself carrying on a dialogue with men about anything.

SILVERA: You're talking about your earlier writings and your response to a patriarchal construct of woman?

BRAND: Yes. I kind of find hints of it in *Epigrams*, even as the epigrams directly engage the subject, in *Chronicles*, and even in *Primitive Offensive*—which is not a book I particularly like any more because I find it kind of young. In the first poem in *Primitive Offensive* I was writing about the memories of a woman who sees the white slavers approaching her village. I can see myself trying to trace what those recollections might have been of life and of history, if we had asked a woman who was seeing it. And why? The speakers in the discourse on this encounter are largely male and for the most part they propose country and nationhood as a male right and this invigorates the morality in anti-colonial arguments. I think this misses the point or undermines it. I've always felt in myself that a woman has another life apart from the male construct of a woman's life, that she has a derisive kind of eye, an eye of cynicism, an eye that notices its own oppression but resists it, not openly, but just by having that other way of seeing the world, a way that doesn't engage itself with the male vision. So possibly, I don't engage men in my work. In a funny way, they don't exist in my work.

SILVERA: You mean you never engaged them even when you were heterosexual?

BRAND: I think I did, but what I'm saying is that I can trace the uneasiness in my work. There are moments in all of the work where I sensed — before I came into lesbian consciousness — that I found engaging men useless *(laughter)* or unimportant. And I'm not meaning that as an insult to the women who do take on so-called male-female relationships. I'm saying there's a part of me that was also very outside of that.

SILVERA: So would you then say that as a young, heterosexual writer, your writing was somehow different from your personal life and your relationships with men? That there was a space in your life for men, but you didn't make that space in your work?

BRAND: I think that's true, but I think even the space I had in my life for men was limited space. I held back a lot of my personal space where men were concerned, and men didn't enter certain places in my consciousness. In some sense it had nothing to do with men per se, and it's only in the context of the taken-for-granted themes in women's lives that we discuss these things in this way. But if we were to look at it from the point of view of human integrity then my evolution would be perfectly coherent.

SILVERA: When did you decide that you were going to be a writer?

BRAND: When?

SILVERA: When you were growing up? Or when you came to Canada?

BRAND: At seventeen, when I came to Canada.

SILVERA: So let's talk about that. You came to Canada at seventeen. To do what?

BRAND: To run away. To escape.

SILVERA: Okay, let's talk about that.

BRAND: I left because of the really limited possibilities for me as a girl at that point in Trinidad. It was an ex-colonial country with few possibilities for anybody, truly. Especially girls. What was a girl going to do? Become a wife and mother? And mother, mostly. And then what? Or do what was called a "commercial course" and not even actually become a typist because there wasn't that much work. And some jobs were based a lot on the nexus of race and class, and I wasn't fair-skinned enough to get a job in a bank, or connected enough.

SILVERA: What kind of school did you attend in Trinidad?

BRAND: It was a Presbyterian girls' high school. I passed my 'O' Levels in five subjects — sat them twice. I'm a good thinker, but I'm not a good conformist. I was a great dreamer, but I didn't learn well by rote. I was a bright kid — I always came second or third in my class — so I went to Naprima Girls' High School. And unless you passed high, you couldn't go to high school.

SILVERA: I take it then that if your marks weren't high you couldn't get a place in the school?

BRAND: Not for dem high school. Other people might have bribed — people who passed lower, or who had money — to get into the prestigious schools. But that's not what happened in my case. *(laughter)*

But when I say "escape" I'm talking about being as young woman growing up in a country with few possibilities for young women — never mind that I had left in the fifth form one of the best high schools in the country. Later, I repeated my GCEs, but you don't go into form six when you repeat. So there was nothing else for me to do — there was no job training I could go and do. And when I talk about "escaping" I also mean escaping the history right around me, even family history.

SILVERA: Was your "escape" different from, say, the Caribbean writers of the generation before you — different from Selvon, Lamming, Naipaul and Clarke?

BRAND: Well, the interesting thing about all of them is that they're men, so I don't know where my experience intersects with theirs. I do know I was running scared as a young woman.

SILVERA: But they were also running from colonialism.

BRAND: They were also young, bright boys sent away to do better, to make country proud, to return as leaders — unlike my mother and her sister who went to England to become nurses in England's expansion of its National Health Service.

When my generation came along — when that whole exodus of people left for Canada or the United States or wherever — the stakes were smaller. They were going away to fill in the cheap labour spots. So it wasn't the élite going off to become doctors, lawyers and so forth. My generation was more of the masses — maybe lower working-class to upper working-class — and we were saving up money and going away. And going away to find a job to send back money.

And I have to say that when I left I was also running from femininity. I can't say I did that consciously, but I know I felt something on my shoulder: the possibility that staying there meant finding some boy to get pregnant for.

SILVERA: So you didn't wanna find a bwoy to get pregnant for? To maybe marry? *(laughter)*

BRAND: No! That scared me shitless. Absolutely. It was not conscious. It was just being scared — being young and very scared of that —

and it's not without foundation. I have seen all the women in my family have children and have a rough time raising those children. I was the product of a rough time. So when I saw all the women in my family having trouble I didn't wanna have trouble like them. And they didn't want me to have trouble like them either, which is why they helped to collect the money together for me to go.

I remember my aunt waiting by the electricity company for the man who was the father of her children, and it would hurt my aunt to stand there with one child on her dress and one on her hip and one in her arms.

SILVERA: But you had other choices didn't you? Other role models? There was a dancer? *(laughter)*

BRAND: Yes. I had different role models — my god, I hate that term, Makeda. It's so class-bound. One was a stripper, which nobody knew because she said she was a cabaret dancer! I had an uncle who was in and out of jail. I had an uncle who was a teacher. I had a mother who was a nurse and an aunt who was a nurse. And then I had two other aunts who did daywork. And I knew I didn't want three, four, five children. And the desperation on my aunt's face, it scared the shit out of me.

By the time I came along, education was free and the pool of people getting an education was also bigger — the pool when Naipaul and Derek Walcott got their education was small and you had to pay lots of money for your child to go to a "big" school — so the pool was bigger and there were many more of us out. And out of work and out of opportunity by the time we finished high school.

SILVERA: Who would you say had the most influence on you?

BRAND: In what sense?

SILVERA: While growing up. Your grandmother?

BRAND: Please, let's not get into my grandmother again. I loved the woman and I want to leave her alone now.

SILVERA: Do you think she had any influence on you becoming a writer at all?

BRAND: Only by being a kind of subject for notice. I loved her a lot and I looked at her a lot — and she did tell stories really well and really nice. But I suppose everybody had some grandmother who did that.

SILVERA: But was she an influence on any other aspect of your life?

BRAND: I think by the time I met her she was a loving kind of woman. That's what I remember, though her children may not remember her that way. That was her gift to me: she encouraged ambition in all the little children because she didn't want us to end up in ways she thought she ended up. So that's what I got from her. She didn't tell us we were going to suffer. She didn't like the idea of us suffering. She told us: if you don't want to suffer, do this. And it was mostly girl grandchildren that she had.

SILVERA: When you came to Canada at seventeen you knew were going to university. What were you going to study?

BRAND: English lit.

SILVERA: Was there a time you wanted to be a lawyer?

BRAND: I think that's what my family said. I thought it was an interesting idea only because that's what you were supposed to go away and do. But when the time finally came for me to make that kind of decision I realized it was not something I really wanted to do — it was something I had been told would be good to do.

And I guess I had long decided — even before that moment came — that I wasn't going to do the thing that would make me a living because making a living wasn't ever going to be sufficient. I think I was just lead by pleasure: I liked to write and I liked the idea of writing.

SILVERA: The poetry book — your last one — *No Language is Neutral*, how's it different from your other books?

BRAND: How's it different? Just maturity. I think in *No Language is Neutral* I finally caught my style. If you look at the books before *Epigrams*, say, you will find I was interested in holding form together. The easiest and the most difficult way of doing that was to find the shape of a poem — the shape of an epigram — and see how I could work it.

My poems have always been poems that document something social, something historic, so there has been a mix of documentary poems and at times more lyrical poems. Finally, I came to the point in *No Language* where I could do those two things together. In some ways I'd always thought: this subject documentary, this subject lyrical. I think what I did in *No Language* was to mix the lyricism with the documentary.

But what I also did in *No Language* was finally to find a way of writing in the language that I grew up in — not only in terms of its cadences but in terms of its syntax. Before, when I wrote I wrote in a kind of English that had Trinidadian cadences but was spelled as Received Standard English. I never wanted to write in so-called dialect — certainly not without first appreciating what I was doing, and that had a lot to do with finding myself in a country like Canada where everything can be turned exotic. Everything that is non-white, that is not standard.

I didn't want to be party to white Canadian titillation at the exoticism of a Trinidadian language. And I knew that would also limit me in what I would say in that language, given that when we arrive on these shores we are pushed aside by the way white Canadian life permeates the life. Then, it seems to me, our language too is chopped into the most exotic bits. I felt pushed to speak in that way, pushed to exoticize the language as opposed to really living in it.

SILVERA: So when did this change? When did you decide to live it and to write it?

BRAND: I didn't decide to live it and to write it. It wasn't like that, it was like this: I thought it important enough to wait until I could do something more with it than only use it for the minimal purpose of exoticizing it.

What it is, is when we land here we also only hear Canadian English. It fills up a lot of spaces. And we are also forced to live in Canadian English — whether it's at Eaton's Centre or going to the store or whatever. You spend a lot of time learning that language. You have to learn the nuances of that language — mind you, fuck, you never do because they always got some new twist for you — but you spend a lot of time doing that initially and feeling defensive about your own talk. Language becomes either degraded or exoticized. Either they tell you "now talk English," or "come now, say that thing for me." So in some senses the society does not allow the room to experience your language. And I didn't want to do the limited things that it was assumed I could do with it. I would never make the mistake of exoticizing it or degrading it. I would write it. I cannot tell you this was conscious or that at this moment it happened. What I'm saying is when I began to write *No Language* lots of things had happened, and I had also become more easy with language as a whole, more easy with literature. I'd become more mature, I'd become more versed, more clever — you know all dem shit. And I'd also come to understand that I could write anything now. And I did. So when Received Standard was adequate for whatever thought I fell into, then I wrote in it. And when it didn't, then I simply went into Trinidadian language.

I had to feel free in the Trinidadian in a lot of ways: I had to feel free in the language in terms of its elements, its own content. If you look at my country most Calypsonians are men — there are a few women Calypsonians — so those who could boast of the language being their instrument are men. I mean publicly, I don't mean in the yard and in the street. I mean publicly, where they could make decisions in it. Those who can do that are men mostly, so I had to think about all those things.

And there are so many things to think about when you use language. It is never simple. So in the beginning I refused to use it because I really didn't want any Canadian to exoticize it. And then when I finally used it I wanted to use it well. I really wanted to bring something else to it — because of its innate lyricism, somebody just hears it and they say, "ohh ... " And I really didn't want all that patronizing shit. I wanted it to be taken seriously.

SILVERA: *No Language is Neutral* was nominated for the Governor General's Award in 1992 wasn't it?

BRAND: I thought you knew that Makeda.

SILVERA: Yes, Dionne, but this is an interview. I need to ask these questions. Did you think it would win? Many of us thought that it would and that it should. It was an excellent collection.

BRAND: Are you crazy? I didn't think the book would win. I thought the book should win because I thought it was the best book. But I didn't think it would because I know where I live. I live in a white-dominated society. They are not about to let anybody of colour, at this moment, get any closer to the prizes and accolades at the very heart of their national discourse. They are not about to let anybody like me or you do that yet. They have complete control at this point over all those things.

But I think it's more than keeping people of colour out; I think it is keeping their master discourse going, a discourse of white supremacy.

SILVERA: But what is that?

BRAND: At the core of it lies the business that they are the master speakers in the society, in Canadian literature and in Canadian history — and the business that their speech is more valid and what they have to say is more valid too. And in it all is their dominance of language, the language that describes this country.

SILVERA: So basically, they don't want to enter in a discourse of 1990s' urban —

BRAND: In this country they don't want to even enter into 1970s' discourse. We were thinking much more about this in 1970 than we are now. So while I think the book should have won, it could not have won.

SILVERA: How do you feel about *No Language is Neutral* now?

BRAND: When I do a piece of work, I get a distance from it: I either feel like running from it, because I feel, oh shit, I didn't do good enough, or I can see it as if somebody else wrote it. And *No Language* was as if somebody else wrote it. I knew it was a good piece of work, and it should have won. But the establishment won out for all kinds of reasons. I think it got on the short-list because it would have been shameful if it hadn't, and I also think it got on the short-list because it was time for them to put another person of colour on the short-list, just because of what was going on: the upheavals in the society, the business about appropriation, about multiculturalism and all of that.

SILVERA: Given what you've said, do you think it would have been on the short-list if it were published by a small press, a press say, for example, like Williams-Wallace or Sister Vision Press?

BRAND: I don't know. I've been on a jury, so I know you just get a whole bunch of books, and you read them. Now me, I might look at a book put out by McClelland & Stewart a little more curiously and say, well, why am I picking this book? Because it's published by an establishment publisher or because it's good?

But somebody who's a little more slavish would probably say McClelland & Stewart are esteemed and so this book must be good. And I think Coach House Press has a certain small press cachet, and *No Language* came to the jury's notice more. They also probably noticed it more because Coach House Press had published a Black woman writer. But I can't consider myself the norm in who's looking at books. I don't know what a white man does when he's looking at books.

SILVERA: Do you think that when reading your poetry — and particularly when reading your collection of short stories — that readers or reviewers think of it as autobiographical? Have you come across anything like that?

BRAND: Only to the extent that I think people think women writers write that way.

SILVERA: Do you think it's women writers? Do you think that for women of colour writers it's even more? That readers and reviewers usually think it's autobiographical? That women of colour usually write in that way?

BRAND: I don't think that people think that Toni Morrison writes autobiographically. I don't think that they think that Toni Cade Bambara does. No, I don't think so. But we tend to get reviewed sociologically or anthropologically, as ethnography.

SILVERA: So they don't ask you, "Now did this really happen?"

BRAND: Not so far; I haven't gotten that at all. But I think the writing that comes out of feminist presses is prone to being asked these questions.

SILVERA: So why do you think that is?

BRAND: Because of all kinds of levels of misunderstanding about feminist thinking, feminist consciousness, and about the feminist principle of the personal being political and the political being personal. And also, to some extent, because some feminists have reinforced this notion that the personal is political in the narrowest sense.

And what always get popularized about radical movements is the most simplistic vision, and sometimes it happens from within too. So I think that that's the reason for that kind of thinking. I think there are also some feminist writers who really think that every word they write is sacred and that they don't need an editor to say that's not important, and so on. That's just naïveness and youthfulness — it's not feminist consciousness, it's not the personal is political. It's just naïveté.

Silvera: Let's talk about the process, Dionne. We differ on this — I love to talk process. People want to know about it and you're guarding it!

Brand: *(laughter)* I'm not guarding it. I don't think it's important. Why is it important?

Silvera: For example, I don't get up in the morning and go to my desk to write, or go to a writing place. I live in a household with people, family: my teenage daughters, my lover, cats and turtles. *(laughter)* But seriously, often I am forced to act pleasantly, and some days I don't feel like it. Some days I just want to be left alone, ignored. The phone rings ... a grandmother needs help ... a daughter needs to talk ... a lover offers you breakfast ... the cat gets sick ... it all breaks your silence. Of course, by the end of the day, I am a bitch on wheels.

Brand: I know we differ. But why so important?

SILVERA: People want to know. People who don't know you want to know how you write. Young Black writers want to know. They read the stuff, they are aspiring writers, and they just want to know how you do it because this is all such a mystery — how writer's live and work. Or, on the other hand, they think they can talk about us and not know us. *(laughter)* I think it's interesting that you don't think it is something to discuss.

BRAND: I don't think it's important because I think there's no clue, no key, to doing it.

SILVERA: But we're not talking about clues, or keys or even pointers to new writers. I am asking you about what you do — how do you do it? *(laughter)*

BRAND: I don't know how to answer that question.

SILVERA: Okay, say you're working on a collection of short stories, or a novel — what do you do? Say you're working on a novel. Do you just sit down and write or do you spend a long time thinking about it? Are there two months, three months, where you do some head things? Take me, I sleep late, I spend a lot of time in bed, and I dream about the stuff and then I start to write.

BRAND: I know we don't have no trade secrets ... I had this idea for this novel about a woman living underground in this city and I couldn't figure out how I was going to write it — whether it was going to be a long poem about identities and changes and about moving to a country and a place and a city like this and then to a street or another area in the city like this and having to keep changing identities. There were women who were illegal, and they always found themselves having to change names, places they lived, having to run away from some man. They had always to change identities and a couple of stories struck me — one about a woman working in a factory and pretending to be deaf.

She had given the factory people a certain name, and they were calling her the name one day, and she couldn't remember that she had given that name, so when the man came she suddenly got the idea to tell the man that she can't hear. So I was thinking about that, about how you lose pieces of yourself in order to fit into the identity of a new place or to fit into the stereotype that the place has of you.

You know we play the stereotype — it would be so much trouble to play our real selves. We'd really have to mow down a bunch of white people to play our real selves. We'd have to go to war with white people to be our real selves, so we fit into the little corners and spaces they allow us. And as you move through this kind of society, you are losing and losing and losing. I had seen all these women losing and losing and losing and seen myself too losing — losing the things one could have lived or having worries one would have not had — and then I was thinking: how do I do this. Thinking from the end of the last book, that's how I work: I work from the end of my last book because by the end of the last book there's the beginning of another book.

SILVERA: The end of the last book? That's quite interesting because the last book was poetry.

BRAND: I thought of how I would put it, and I thought it would be poetry. At the end of the last book, *No Language is Neutral*, there's a line that goes "In another place, not here, a woman might touch something between beauty and nowhere... back there and here." I like that line, and that line is supposed to be the beginning of something else. So I began to think about that and I thought of it as being a poem, a long poem, and this is where I made that very critical, practical judgement. For me to write a long poem, it takes me years. And I wanted to get my hands in and work faster. And for me working faster is working fiction. Mind you, it ain't turned out that way, but you just sort of convince yourself that this is going to be alright. And so I started to write that book.

Now that book is probably nothing about what I just said. But that's where it began. And I was doing lots of other things, like earning a living. I was at the University of Toronto, I think, when I started to think about it, and then when I was in England, I think I wrote the first couple pages of it, and then from there on with me and a piece of work, I work all the time. That is, I don't think about anything else but work, unfortunately for the people I live with.

SILVERA: So can you work on two or three things at the same time?

BRAND: Yes.

SILVERA: When you're working on two or three things do you work in different spaces?

BRAND: No, the same place. Space is not important to me. At the point that I have the idea to write the thing, writing it becomes the only important thing I can do.

SILVERA: So you can put down one thing and then work on the other two?

BRAND: I don't think that will happen in the same day, no. Right now

I'm working on the novel, and I'm working on some essays.

SILVERA: Do you work in the same room on these different projects?

BRAND: I work in the same room. I have a chair and a table and lots of books around. The only little quirk I've ever had was that I used to sit by the kitchen table and write, but that was because the kitchen table was where everybody passed around, and I could know what was going on, make a cup of tea or something. This is nonsense about space.

SILVERA: Excuse me, it's nonsense about space? What do you mean?

BRAND: No, no, it's not nonsense that you have to have space. You do have to have room to write and not a lot of distraction. But you know, Makeda, I've always been really ruthless about my writing. You know that.

SILVERA: Yeah, but tell us. How are you ruthless about writing? That gets back to process.

BRAND: Stop that silly word.

SILVERA: You keep saying it's not important, but it is.

BRAND: I don't think so.

SILVERA: Okay, let's forget the word.

BRAND: What I'm saying is that I don't think that some room I write in is all that important.

SILVERA: What I want you to talk about is what you mean by being ruthless about writing and about the space you need.

BRAND: It just means that a long time ago I decided — I was twenty-four — and I decided I would have no children because I thought children took the time and the same energy from the same place as writing. I decided that I loved to write, that it made me happy to write. And I would actually sit in my room at two a.m. and feel really nice about what I wrote. And it was not that I was going to get it published, but I would be in the company of my work — and I don't mean just my individual work, I was also reading. I think writing is also reading: reading massive amounts of all kinds of people through all times is necessary.

That engagement with the work in the middle of all the other work sitting around — I loved it. I felt happy. I felt happy, particularly when I wrote poetry. That's one of the moments when I feel totally blissful. I like that. And I knew I couldn't take on a whole bunch of other things that women ordinarily take on, like children, like men.

SILVERA: But you had men, what are you talking about?

BRAND: I didn't have men to take up space. No man ever took up space. The one man who kept calling me up asked me if I cooked. *(laughter)* I didn't have men like that, I had men to give whatever pleasure they could to my body but never men I had to plan my life with or pick up laundry for. I never did that.

The only thing that tore me from writing was political work, was community work, whether I was going to go and join some revolution and live by my convictions. That was the only thing that tore me. So then my whole life was then organized and geared toward how to make room for writing, where to find money or a job

THE OTHER WOMAN

for six months and then take off six months to write. I'm lucky.

SILVERA: So you never at any point felt the desire, as most women do, to give birth, to have a child, to be creative in that way?

BRAND: No. That was work. That was not joy and creativity and all that. It looked like work to me long before I ever decided to write. It looked like work to me since I saw my aunt on that corner. It looked like work and it looked like a kind of work that was tortuous. It looked unhappy and it looked difficult.

SILVERA: What? Having children?

BRAND: In my life that's how it looked. I'm not saying children don't give women pleasure. What I saw of it — the kind of burden it would seem to me that we were to my grandmother, mouths to feed and just everyday botheration — it just looked like a difficult life and I didn't want it. Gradually, as the years have gone by, I've been able to concentrate or to devote more and more time on only writing.

SILVERA: Let's talk about when you were a writer in residence at the University of Toronto and about your brief teaching job at an Ontario university.

BRAND: The teaching job was just a job. All of them were jobs. I have to pay the rent. Only community work and political activism have torn me away from writing. Anything else — whether it is teaching or doing some other kind of project for money — has always been about trying to save up some money so I can write. I am single-minded about that. Now, if you want to talk about process then that's it. I am not preoccupied with anything else.

SILVERA: So you think writers ought to be very selfish?

BRAND: I don't know. Are you saying that what I've just described is selfishness?

SILVERA: Yeah!

BRAND: That's bullshit! *(laughter)* It's self-preservation.

SILVERA: It's a very single focus.

BRAND: It is and it's self-preservation for me. I cannot say how somebody else would do it. All you asked me to say is how I do it and the choices I made given the conditions I lived in. So that's all I can tell you. I haven't sacrificed anything — it's the kind of living that I wanted to do, and in that sense I say I'm lucky. I didn't have a whole heap of other people oppressing my life to the extent that I couldn't think about this or concentrate on it. I've made a choice to forego other things that I didn't think would make me happy or as happy as writing. I get up in the morning, and I always think about work.

SILVERA: You get up in the morning. Then do you always write?

BRAND: Yeah, I have to.

SILVERA: So there's nothing that keeps you away from that? Say, for example, if you have a fight with your lover?

BRAND: No. I ask her to please stop fighting with me. I cannot do anything if you fight with me.

SILVERA: So you're saying if there's a fight or there's a conflict that you don't write? Is that what you're saying?

BRAND: No, no. It's more difficult to write if I have a fight. And after a while, if the fighting does not want to come to terms, I just go and write! *(laughter)* I also have deadlines. I work at my house. I'm always with my work. My work is physically in the same room with me all the time. It's always there for me to do. It's self-motivated and it's self-propelled.

Each piece of work is a piece of my life. It is my life's work. The writing is not a career thing. It's a vocation. It can't be put off. If I didn't do this novel this year — if I don't finish it this year or at least make a major dent in it this year, or if I hadn't started it when I did — I would forget it. I wouldn't be able to stretch my thoughts to it at any other time. I would miss it completely.

Writing is the outcome of your ruminations, your logic, your reasoning, and it reflects your growth as a person too. So if you don't catch it at the moment it comes, you're going to miss it. It's more than putting out a book, it's the possibility for growth for yourself too. With every piece of writing I can see I moved.

Bob Hsiang Photography

Sky Lee

C. Allyson Lee

SKY LEE
talks to C. ALLYSON LEE

**Is there
a
mind without media
any more?**

C. LEE: For those of you who have just joined us, this is August the 13th, a lovely Saturday morning at 11:15, we're at the On Lok, our favourite neighbourhood Chinese restaurant, and I'm C. Allyson Lee sharing a lovely lunch with Sky Lee, and we thought we'd have a little discussion. We're going to be switching the tape machine on and off ...

SKY LEE: Yeah, so we can talk about the juicy stuff "off the record."

C. LEE: There's one question I need to ask you about. Are you Sky or Sharon today?

SKY LEE: Today, I guess I'll be Sky. On the record I'll be Sky.

C. LEE: On the record you'll be Sky. A lot of people are confused about that because they don't know there are two people in one.

SKY LEE: I love confusing people.

C. Lee: I know you do. I know that sometimes you do SKY and sometimes you do S.K.Y. because at the Writing Thru Race Conference you were S.K.Y. Would you do us the honour of explaining, please, what the S.K.Y. stands for?

Sky Lee: Well, that's my nickname: Sharon Kun Yung Lee.

C. Lee: That's your nickname — not your Chinese name?

Sky Lee: Sorry, my real Chinese name.

C. Lee: But they're initials.

Sky Lee: Yes, they are my initials.

C. Lee: It's quite nice that they form into a nice little word that we can use. So we're diving into a nice little bowl of greasy donuts here.

Sky Lee: I'm a registered nurse. Thank God, eh? Otherwise I'd be awfully skinny. Oh, I'd be awfully skeletal *(laughter)* and awfully hungry.

C. Lee: Yeah. You've been doing that for sometime — it's your occupation to pay the rent.

Sky Lee: It's a great job, I really like my job. And now I'm half- time. You know I'm in my forties now. I'm becoming rapidly a woman of leisure.

C. Lee: Good!

SKY LEE: Neat, eh?

C. LEE: That's real neat, and part of your leisure is writing, is it? Or has it always been?

SKY LEE: Yeah, part of my leisure has always been writing. Coming from a working-class background ...

C. LEE: You were born in Port Alberni.

SKY LEE: Yeah. Unfortunately for working-class types like us, poetry is a luxury ...

C. LEE: When you were growing up were you brought up with Cantonese in your household?

SKY LEE: Toisan.

C. LEE: And you spoke it at home a lot?

SKY LEE: No. Enough to get by.

C. LEE: With your parents?

SKY LEE: Yeah. My parents are not very articulate. When you talk about your mother being high-school educated, my parents were illiterate, and of course the same kind of very bleak, morbid, harsh kind of village types. They were not very verbal.

C. LEE: My father was uneducated.

SKY LEE: That's why I admire people who are very verbal. And I think I also almost became a writer because I was so inarticulate. You know, verbally. It was a way of resolving that. Because as inarticulate as my background was, I still had all of that intensity, that madness ...

C. LEE: It is. When did you first start writing? Whatever that means to you ...

SKY LEE: I think my first piece was my final year of college when I started combining writing into my art teaching. So I did a series called *Iron Chink,* and in it I did little, anecdotal stories, and that was when I began. And people came along and they were impressed, right?

C. LEE: Well, then I'm to understand you were a fine arts student first?

SKY LEE: Yeah. I coined the phrase "Berry Fortunate Asian Degree" *(laughter)* No, otherwise a Bachelor of Fine Arts degree.

C. LEE: From?

SKY LEE: University of British Columbia. Back in the days when we used to have lots of grants and it was cheap to go to school, remember? Remember when we used to be able to get a student loan to go to Europe? *(laughter)*

C. LEE: I bought a car with mine ... mmmmm ... MSG.

SKY LEE: Lovely, isn't it?

C. LEE: Isn't it? So getting back to the original question — got sidetracked by the food — when you first started writing you wrote pieces to go along with your art pieces. Had you thought at any point then that one day you would be a published author?

SKY LEE: Oh, no.

C. LEE: You were just playing around with stuff?

SKY LEE: What happened soon after that, I think, is that we started the Asian-Canadian Writers Workshop. Did you ever go to any of those meetings?

C. LEE: Couple of them. Who's we?

SKY LEE: Oh, back in those days it was like Jim Wong-Chu, Sean Gunn, me, Rick Shiomi — people like that, and I remember, oh even Derrick Chu — you know, people who are long gone kind of thing.

C. LEE: What year was that?

SKY LEE: This would be about 1976 or 1977, and then we did an anthology called *Inalienable Rice*. That was a great success, actually. But I seem to be one of the lucky ones because I lived what I wrote, and I did write very few short stories back in those days. I was highly encouraged to go on by people like Jim, and whatever I did write, I also got published right away, so the *Iron Chink* series got published in a journal, and a couple short stories got published right away too. Even the rottenest short story I've ever written in my life got published. I'm embarrassed and I'm not going to mention what journal, neither, so ...

C. LEE: Why not?

SKY LEE: Actually, I only recently discovered that I'm an introvert — can you imagine? — as opposed to an extrovert.

C. LEE: Shy about things?

SKY LEE: Yeah. And very silent and very much of a loner, so I just went right into doing *Disappearing Moon*, I just launched into it.

C. LEE: Oh, but in *Disappearing Moon* you had conceived of the idea years ago and it took you sometime to actually get everything together, didn't it?

SKY LEE: What I did was — I remember after I graduated from university I started doing the research, and I wanted to focus on this murder case, the Janice Smith murder case. But I didn't have anywhere to go with it until years later, and again through the Asian-Canadian Writers Workshop — when we started exchanging ideas — I developed the venue for this murder story.

C. LEE: Was it very important for you to have that encouragement and support?

SKY LEE: Very important. It made a big difference. In fact, most of my work as an artist has been very much community-based. I mean all through University of British Columbia and the Bachelor of Fine Arts I was this woman of colour trying to be an artist in that fucking exclusive white boys club. You were actually going to get nowhere fast. I did the work of really examining what it was that I was trying to do. And I realized that you really had to go against the grain.

C. Lee: Which you did.

Sky Lee: I suppose. I graduated and the first thing I did was — well, I guess all along I'd been in that period, working in Chinatown in the Chinese community, right? And then I kind of just veered off the track from race to gender, so to speak, and I landed up on Commercial Drive at Makara Woman's Art Collective. Remember that old collective?

C. Lee: Yeah, I do.

Sky Lee: So again it was like through the encouragement of all these community artists that I started to get a solid foundation because I certainly didn't get it through a university education in art.

C. Lee: About what year were you involved in Makara?

Sky Lee: About 1976-1977. What were you doing at that time? You were still in the Prairies, weren't you?

C. Lee: Yeah, in Cowtown, Calgary, because that's where I was born.

Sky Lee: I like Calgary.

C. Lee: You like Calgary?

Sky Lee: I might be thinking of moving there.

C. Lee: Get out of here.

Sky Lee: I will. Look what's happening to the coast — like most of the world's population is living on the coast now.

C. Lee: When was the last time you were in Calgary?

Sky Lee: Just about a month ago. I got invited to go to Crow's Nest. I really like Calgary. I first got there when Fred Wah invited me. I really like the small town attitudes.

C. Lee: Yeah? Tell me, you were born in a small town. And so what does it feel like?

Sky Lee: Yeah, and as redneck as they come. *(laughter)*

C. Lee: And Calgary ain't no better.

Sky Lee: Oh no. After a lifetime of rednecks you get to know rednecks. I got along real well with rednecks. *(laughter)*

C. Lee: I remember first hearing your name when Salt Water City was happening.

Sky Lee: I wasn't really involved with Salt Water.

C. Lee: But in a roundabout fashion what had happened was an exhibition of Chinese Canadian history in Vancouver. Do you know I forget the year. It was the early '80s, I think.

Sky Lee: It was actually later. It was actually about '84. Nathan was born. I know because I was counting on when I came out, right?

C. Lee: Came out of where?

THE OTHER WOMAN

SKY LEE: *(Laughter)* When I came out of the closet.

C. LEE: Oh, that closet.

SKY LEE: I remember that was '87-'88, I think.

C. LEE: You have a better memory than I have. Anyway, I had to do this article for *Kinesis*, and someone from *Kinesis* invited me to this do, and I heard your name then. And they said, "Oh, Sharon Lee's going to be around here." And I said, "Who's she?" "Oh, she used to work for Makara." "Yeah, I know that, but who is she?" And you didn't show up, I guess, the time I was there. And I remember wanting to meet you then.

SKY LEE: I met you at the Cultural Centre, I remember that now. You were sitting in some stuffy reception. Wasn't that Paul Yee's reception, book launch?

C. LEE: Yeah. We had run into each other a number of times after that at things like Women In View.

SKY LEE: But we never had the chance to talk, right? You knew a lot of Chinatown old-timer types.

C. LEE: Only because my mother was brought up here. Because I didn't grow up here. I didn't know people personally, but my mother's family lived here for some time. I remember you coming up to me and recognizing me, but I didn't recognize you because every time, I swear, I saw you — you looked different.

SKY LEE: Yeah, I do. People say that.

C. Lee: I remember, though, one of those times when I did run into you. Particularly I remember one of those forums at Women In View — you being very vocal about something. I was volunteering that night. You were really upset, you were shaking, and I thought: well, there's a political woman. And I remember all the things you said were very political.

Sky Lee: What did I say?

C. Lee: It had something to do with racism, of course. And I think you had mentioned something in response to some woman's comment: "Hey, I experience racism too," or something to the effect. And you said, "Hey, but you don't walk down the street and have people call you names because of your visibility, because of how you look and things like that." Maybe the woman didn't even get that.

Sky Lee: Well, I've since then come to realize how much oppressors talk about being oppressed.

C. Lee: *(laughter)* Yeah, you put them in their place, and I really admire you for having done that, sticking your neck out, because I've never done that.

Sky Lee: Since then I've kind of given up that kind of polarized oppositional style in dealing with racism. I've since come to really look at the way they are oppressed too. Sometimes what I can offer them is welcome-to-the-club *(laughter)*. Make them feel better.

C. Lee: Conciliatory on your part?

Sky Lee: Well, one of the brightest things I ever heard came from an up-and-coming Asian lesbian feminist in Calgary. I just did this incredible workshop, right? And it was very strange because in this workshop it was all women who specifically chose to be in my workshop, and strangely enough it was three young, very politicized Asian babes and two older, very white middle-class women that just wanted to be non-political writers, right?

So you can imagine the clash. It was a horrific, thunderous crash between the two groups. I remember the white woman asking, "Well, why if I'm so awful, why do you talk to me?" She said to her — which was not conciliatory but very true — she said, "Because my very survival depends on connecting with yours as your survival depends on connecting with me." And I sort of thought, gosh, that's so wise for a young woman in her mid-twenties. Nowadays they seem to be born more sophisticated, more politicized.

C. LEE: Have some of this great ginger-onion oil.

SKY LEE: You're as bad as me. Every time I come here I always ask for that for free.

C. LEE: I think I admire you for your strength of convictions too. You know, so many of us either get bypassed for certain things. Or, as you say, we become tokens. Or they try to get away with paying us less. And I think I took that to heart, using your example, but if people are serious about something, they will put their money where their mouth is. So I began then to think. So many times I've been asked to do things for free, to MC things, to organize things, and people work hard and they do it willingly for nothing. I thought: why should I do that? You're going to pay other people to do it. Why can't they pay me? No more. Fees, yes, for reading. And now whenever anyone asks me I ask for an honorarium or whatever.

SKY LEE: The first thing I do is ask the group: who is your funder? And usually the people that I agree to work with are people that I know have been working in the community. They kind of have to come through a referral system. That keeps me happy. I don't feel like I'm wasting my energies going to the very mainstream events, right? Where I'm literally kind of put into a slot kind of thing. I'm good enough at doing that myself, I don't need other people to do that for me.

C. LEE: Can you tell us — when you started *Disappearing Moon,* did you approach Douglas & McIntyre? Did you know someone there?

SKY LEE: Oh yeah, with *Disappearing Moon* I actually had three publishers interested. And the reason why I went with Douglas & McIntyre is because a long-time friend, a long-time supporter of mine was there.

C. LEE: That's more mainstream, they're a bigger publishing company too. Good exposure.

SKY LEE: Yeah, they're one of the more, I guess, interesting ones out West. They're definitely a Western publisher, they disagree when you say "mainstream." They consider themselves quite the rebels and renegades when you think about Eastern style of publishing houses, and they don't really appear to be that Eastern, as in Toronto, Ontario. You know that part of the country gets all the funding. *(laughter)*

C. LEE: You have a new book coming out in the fall. Can you tell us about that?

SKY LEE: Oh yeah, *Belly Dancer,* a collection of short stories by Press Gang.

C. LEE: Has that been in the works for some time?

SKY LEE: Far too long. I meant to get that done a long time ago, but I guess after *Disappearing Moon* I kind of headed to the hills. I went to hide out. I needed it. I had so many traumatic changes, personal changes, in my life that I probably needed a few years just to consider that, never mind all the work of writing. So I actually didn't start writing *Belly Dancer* to any serious extent until I came back out to Vancouver.

C. LEE: How big will the book be? How many pages?

SKY LEE: I don't know. Two-hundred pages or so, I guess. There's about fifteen short stories ranging from five to seventeen pages. Kind of longish.

C. LEE: Would you say the content of your writing now differs?

SKY LEE: This collection is very different from *Disappearing Moon*.

C. LEE: How so?

SKY LEE: Well, in it I'm trying to do some very interesting things. I'm trying to look at what I call use of language and I think people like us who have been literally culturally marooned have a specific kind of language. And I'd like to enhance that because it's part of our reality. I guess as a text it's more difficult to read than *Disappearing Moon*. I kind of looked at it as my post-graduate course, kind of a thesis, in that I became more self-conscious as a writer.

C. LEE: Self-conscious how?

SKY LEE: In terms of use of language, in terms of ego, in terms of where the narrator comes in, where she stops, that kind of thing. It was very difficult. It was very hard to do.

C. LEE: You're getting very particular and very fussy. Or are you adhering to your own set of standards?

SKY LEE: I was adhering to my own set of standards, and it was like really trying to push literature over a kind of established edge. The funny thing was that with *Disappearing Moon* I had done that so unconsciously that I had to kind of go back and say: hey, what happened here?

C. LEE: So it wasn't simply just a chronicling for you to write all that out?

SKY LEE: For *Disappearing Moon?* Yeah, it was. It was much more of a kind of unconscious act of chronicling, right? But what had happened is that I had discovered I had a very strong style. Basically a strong reality that was going to come out in my words, in my use of language and stuff like that. So what I had to do for *Belly Dancer* was basically harness it.

C. LEE: So are you pleased with the results? Does it express what you wanted to express?

SKY LEE: I'm pleased with the second attempt at literature. It's not going to fall under a category very easily, it's not going to be kind of like a popularized novel like *Disappearing Moon* because of the content and, I guess, the spontaneity of voice. Like I said, this voice is far more self-conscious, and what it's trying to do is to push at an edge here, trying to push at the barriers, right? And that always means trouble. *(laughter)*

C. Lee: Testing limits.

Sky Lee: Yes. It means more trouble, more questions.

C. Lee: But you like, I think, living on the edge because you like confusing people about your name, and you like people to be, I suppose, startled or surprised and make them think about things. And I like that too.

Sky Lee: Well, I like the process of writing very much because it's a very arduous and very lonely process. It's very troublesome, but the whole ego-tripping around being a writer I don't need because it can be very self-destructive too. I think after *Disappearing Moon*, I guess one of the most important things I did was head out to the hills and try and work on my ego. Because the whole system of course, tries to enhance that.

C. Lee: Self-image?

Sky Lee: Yeah. My favourite question is: is there a mind without media any more? Like media is a very hungry kind of organism right now, and it's constantly needing to chomp and chomp and eat and eat. It'll consume you to death. And then spit you out, right? And since I didn't want to be chomped up and then spit out, I just kind of had to more run away from that whole bureaucracy. And it is a very established bureaucracy right now.

C. Lee: You were looking after yourself.

SKY LEE: Oh very much so. Literally, to keep my integrity intact. I can see where people really, literally, fall apart after.

C. LEE: After the success of *Disappearing Moon,* which was very successful and continues to be successful.

SKY LEE: It's still quite popular.

C. LEE: And I understand you've written a screenplay for it?

SKY LEE: Oh yeah.

C. LEE: Are we allowed to talk about that?

SKY LEE: No, not really.

C. LEE: Oh, all right, then I won't ask.

SKY LEE: Well, I can tell you basically that I've done a screenplay on speculation, and that's probably something I might go into later on. As a writer — I mean as a person — I'm politicized enough to know that I want to look into cultural alternatives, and one of the most wonderful things about the '90s is that so many people are doing it. God, it's just so gratifying. Everbody's coming out with fantastic, inspiring ideas. So that kind of leaves me free as an artist to just fly off on my own tangent, I don't have to worry about being a representative of the community or whatever any more, I'm just like an artist on my own.

C. LEE: I find that very exciting too. That people I know are actually doing things like writing plays and scripts and actually putting things into film and stuff like that. And they are not easily pegged into being Canada's answer to Amy Tan or anything like that. I hope one day to see your *Disappearing Moon* on film.

SKY LEE: I wouldn't mind. But film is such a difficult medium to work in. You know, script writing is all very fine if people have a glamorous idea of movie-making because then it seems like it should be a lot of fun and it probably is. But it's so oppressed, it's been so centred, so controlled, that what you're mainly doing is fighting against that censorship and you know it's so controlled by the white boys' club.

C. LEE: And the money associated with it. Sometimes you just can't get things done because of the lack of money and then you become compromised. It's hard to see someone's integrity go down because of the lack of money.

SKY LEE: I saw you in Karen Lee's film. You had a very dramatic presence.

C. LEE: Thank you. Oh well, it was a lot of fun. I remember walking into Ariel Books. Just looking on the shelf. Books on writing. And the woman behind the desk, an Asian woman, said, "Are you a writer?" And I said, "Hah, hardly. That's why I'm buying this book." Which is a very flippant thing to say and she did not smile. She was: if you're a writer, I think you ought to submit something. She said, "Here, I'll write this address down for you." And I thought: what the heck is happening here? She wrote the address for *Fireweed* in Toronto, and I said, "Well okay, I've never done this before, but might as well — what's there to lose?" I mean what's the big deal? So I sent the stuff in, but I used my name C. Allyson Lee, which is my second name, because I wasn't really ready to come out as a writer or anything else. *(laughter)*

Now it wasn't until a year later when someone came up to me in Santa Cruz, California, during a conference for Asian lesbians and said to me — because everyone knew me as Corinne — "Are *you* C. Allyson Lee?" And I just stopped dead in my tracks and said, "How do you know that?" She said, "Because I'm one of the editors of *Fireweed* — your piece is going in "Letter to My Mother." I was shocked beyond words. And that's the first piece that got published. And then I started getting requests from people who were doing anthologies to submit things.

Do you have a certain theme in mind before you begin a story?

SKY LEE: I usually have a concept in mind.

C. LEE: I mean you don't just suddenly start writing and then it just all comes in place? You develop it around a central theme and the characters come out? Or?

SKY LEE: Well, actually no. I just sit down and things will develop and I let it flow. But as I said, because *Belly Dancer* was a far more conscious process I had to tame it and try to harness it more.

C. LEE: How do you feel your work is accepted-not accepted in "mainstream" or in dominant Canadian literary culture?

SKY LEE: Because I'm so suspicious of mainstream and dominant Canadian literary culture, I'm rather suspicious of how *Disappearing Moon* got accepted. But, actually, when I think back I realize that when *Disappearing Moon* was rapidly on its way to being in hand I told Aretha Van Herk in Calgary — she's a colleague of Fred Wah — and she put in her two cents. She was very supportive of me and what I was trying to do, and that was when it started getting more interesting reviews. At first it seemed like it didn't fit into a category — the writing was just too unusual, the whole structure of the novel was just too confusing and unusual, not your usual, Western way of thinking, right? Not only that, I think it was a very angry novel when I think back now. That was kind of, I guess, offensive, but in the end all those points worked for the book in terms of dominant literary culture. I remember when it got nominated for a GG. The first thing I said to ...

C. Lee: Governor General's Award for those of you who don't know — she's too modest, anyway ...

Sky Lee: I said: what the fuck happened to the rest of the dominant literary culture? Like they're just like drying themselves up and boring themselves out of existence, and they were looking for new blood, they were looking for new ideas, and I found that very encouraging because all along I've always been a separatist, whether it be a Chinese-Canadian separatist or a lesbian separatist. I've always said to Jim Wong-Chu in the Asian-Canadian Writer's Workshop: don't get sucked into their bureaucracy, don't get literally sucked into writing what they want, write what you need to write, what we need to write, like build up our own strength, our own muscles, and I bet you anything, they'll come to us. And sure enough that happened.

Tell me about the Writing Thru Race Conference. Weren't you one of the organizers?

C. Lee: Okay, I confess. I confess.

Sky Lee: Let's start at the very beginning when they had this minority writers' committee.

C. Lee: The racial minority writer's committee. Yes. We met for a conference in Orillia, Ontario, just outside of Toronto a few years ago, and it was a big charge because it was all writers of colour.

Sky Lee: Oh yeah, big charge.

C. Lee: I don't know where you were at that time.

Sky Lee: I was grieving cause my partner just died and so I was like...

C. Lee: Yeah. For me it was a great gathering place to make contacts. As a result of that we all decided ...

Sky Lee: You were all inspired, right?

C. Lee: Very inspired, such talent. There was one evening on the Saturday night where about twenty or thirty writers that wanted to read were given a limit of three minutes. It was hilarious. So you had to compact everything that you had into three minutes. I tell you it was just stunning. The talent there was unbelievable. So we kept in contact and it was Roy Miki who decided we should have a conference in Vancouver. So he asked me to help plan for it and we gradually got other writers involved, like Larissa Lai, Ann Jew, Scott McFarlane. Men and women.

And, yeah, we had a lot of growing pains, as anyone would in organizing anything of this magnitude. We had funding problems because we were accused of being inclusionary to First Nations and Writers of Colour only and excluding whites. All the media could see was that we were excluding whites and being racist. Well, as a result of all that fervour, one of the Reform MPs in Calgary stood up in Parliament and said, "I object to government funding something that's racist like this."

As a consequence a big grant that was promised to us was rescinded, taken away. And that sent shock waves. But we weren't going to let that beat us because this thing's got to go on. As you say, don't let people knock you down just because you don't conform to their standards. We were gonna have this thing no matter what. If we had to have it on someone's lawn and have people sleep in sleeping bags on the ground, we would still have the conference. We sent a plea out to many organizations asking for contributions. Well, we did very well, thank you very much. We got huge contributions from private individuals, trade unions, etcetera. We needed a venue in order to work safely, free from the thought that we might be dominated by somebody or silenced by somebody who was not a person of colour. So we provided this. We got donations as well.

SKY LEE: I had a really good time. And, of course, the whole idea of the conference became very important after the little media fiasco.

C. LEE: But it was great seeing people together. I mean we're not just having a party here. We're building alliances and it was my hope that in this conference a lot of people who had never published before, who might otherwise be intimidated by the fact that people are published, would gain some kind of support and encouragement to go on with their craft.

SKY LEE: Well, I'm still kind of suspicious of that. You know, trying to gain representation in the dominant literary culture. The Asian-Canadian Writer's Workshop meeting and working together is an ongoing thing. I like that community sense.

C. LEE: That's Jim Wong-Chu's agenda.
SKY LEE: You don't have to pay a cent. All you need to do is go in there

and do your own work. And you know there's a group here, a group that's perhaps connected to another group, and on and on.

C. Lee: I must say I admire that. Encouraging people.

Sky Lee: He's one of my mentors. I call him the Grand Old Man of Chinatown ... Perfect west coast summer day.

C. Lee: And it's not even a wet coast summer day because it hasn't rained for some time.

Sky Lee: It hasn't. That makes me nervous. Does that make you nervous? No, you wouldn't be. Because you're from Calgary.

C. Lee: Get out of here ... Listen, every day is a bonus here when you come from Calgary. I tell you the only thing that this place doesn't got that Calgary has is the aurora borealis. The northern lights.

Sky Lee: I've always wanted to see the northern lights ...

Makeda Silvera

Stephanie Martin

An Interlocutor talks to MAKEDA SILVERA

The characters would not have it

INTERLOCUTOR: I want to ask you about a question you so often ask in interviews: what's this preoccupation with process?

SILVERA: It is something that's always fascinated me. Perhaps that's why I read so many biographies of writers and other artists. I know the word process often turns people off, and at times they resist the question. I don't know why — perhaps for some people it's never been a question. Perhaps they just get up and start to work. Perhaps for others process is a private act, something they do not wish to share. Maybe, instead of asking about process, what I should have asked was, "How do you negotiate time to write?" I live in a household with people who depend on me; in order to write — I must be organised and selfish with my time, and that has not always been possible. With teenage daughters, pets, lovers, a business, an extended family, it's difficult to find the time to write, and so I'm always curious about other writers and how they survive demands on their time.

INTERLOCUTOR: When you do decide to write, where do you find that peace, that solitude? Do you go to a special place, a park, say, or a get-away for a week or two?

SILVERA: More than often that is not an option for me. I am too bound to routine, to obligations, to work, to home, even when it gets crazy. So I go away in my head. It's very economical. *(laughter)*

INTERLOCUTOR: What does it mean — "to go away in your head?"

SILVERA: It's very simple, and not as crazy as it sounds. For me, going away is a clearing of the head, getting ready to write, no matter what the obstacles. I do it in two ways. I might clean house, wash, cook, rearrange furniture. I'm alone in my thoughts, making room, throwing out stuff, rearranging. It allows my mind to wonder and to wander freely and peacefully. Or I might go dancing, partying the night away, not a worry or care. Then I begin to write.

INTERLOCUTOR: Looking back on some of your earlier work, you put a lot of emphasis on history, on women's working-class experience and also on family. I am thinking in particular of *Silenced*, the testimonies of domestic workers, and of your essay "Manroyal and Sodomites" which appears in *Piece of My Heart: A Lesbian of Colour Anthology*. Could you talk a bit about these works?

SILVERA: The women in *Silenced* are Caribbean-born domestic workers living in Canada. These are working-class women who have been working in poor conditions for low wages since the 1950s. During the 1970s and 1980s, I began to work with domestic workers and found many documents written about their lives and their struggles. But these pieces were by white academics — lots about the women and nothing from them. I came to know them as bright, articulate women who perfectly well understood their conditions, women who were well aware of the sexism, racism and anti-working-class bias in their day-to-day lives. To me, they were the most logical people to tell their stories, not the academics who presumed to speak for them.

"Manroyal and Sodomites" is very much about history and family, about the search for an Afro-Caribbean lesbian presence in the Caribbean while I was growing up. When I wrote it in 1987 I knew of no other exploration of a Caribbean lesbian sexuality. I was searching and trying to make sense of my sexuality -- to connect and ground it to a lesbian/bisexual sensibility. Living here in Canada for such a long time can sometimes blur memory. It was important for me to summon memory — to place Caribbean lesbian/bisexual women in a context — to name them and their history. Again, I had to fall back on oral narratives to make sense of pieces of conversations from my mother, grandmother and women of their generation. I must say however, that "Manroyal and Sodomites" was not written as a personal confession but as a family/community coming out. I wanted to (re) search how commonplace this act was, how much a part of community it really is, how deep it is buried in people's family history, and the silence that surround this.

INTERLOCUTOR: How did this really contribute to your development as a writer?

SILVERA: It became the basis for many of my stories. It presented an opportunity to exercise that memory. It enabled me to go back to a community I had left behind years ago and to break it into different compartments; to envision characters, to get to know them as individuals and then to piece the whole cast back together again. The experience was almost like merging reality with fiction. It was my job to make these women come alive, become next door neighbours, ordinary folks, who lived in a community, had children, went to church, ate the same food and participated in that community. I believe I began to find my voice and some experience through that essay.

INTERLOCUTOR: You first started to write as a reporter in the early 1970s, and then in the 1980s you went on to do two non-fiction works, *Silenced* and the anthology *Piece of my Heart*. What made you start writing fiction?

SILVERA: I did start out on a newspaper, and in retrospect it seems that I had no choice. I was a young woman of eighteen years old, without a clue of what I really wanted to do in the world. My only skill was typing, and I loved reading and dreamed of writing. I started off as a typist-receptionist, later worked as a freelance journalist and much later was an editorial assistant at *Share* newspaper in Toronto. It was because of all this work and my life as a community activist that *Silenced* got written — some eight or nine years later.

INTERLOCUTOR: What did you do in those eight years?

SILVERA: I fell in love, got pregnant, got married, got pregnant again, was a mother, wife, housekeeper, office worker. Separated, then divorced, went back to school, worked as a typist, waitress, then as a journalist — again.

INTERLOCUTOR: Did you not write at all during those years?

SILVERA: Nope. I read when I could. But mostly I was changing two sets of diapers, trying to find baby-sitters, holding down a full-time job, cooking and all the rest of that stuff at twenty-one years old — thank god for parties and a community of friends. The idea was always there somewhere in my head that writing was what I wanted to do, but it wasn't possible then, it was crazy to want it, even to imagine it.

INTERLOCUTOR: So tell me, when was *Silenced* done?

SILVERA: Some seven or eight years later, when I had stopped being a single parent and was in a long-term relationship with a woman. I had already started work on the book and was determined to finish it, but she certainly made the finishing line faster to get to. About four years after that, I wrote "Manroyal and Sodomites."

INTERLOCUTOR: What about where you grew up — was your childhood happy? Are there special moments? Did you read a lot?

SILVERA: There isn't much to say. I was born in Kingston, Jamaica, of working-class parents. I spent my first twelve years there before coming to Canada. My early years were happy and free. I grew up as an only child in my grandmother's house, with lots of friends and cousins close by. Almost every moment was happy. I was loved unconditionally. I was free to roam where I pleased, climb trees, fly kites, play in the rain, go to the movies. I was encouraged to read and had lots of books around me.

INTERLOCUTOR: Some writers — Afua Cooper, Lenore Keeshig-Tobias, Isabelle Knockwood, to name a few — have talked about the landscape, about water; the beauty and the effect it had on them as children. What was your relationship to the land? Was it special for you?

SILVERA: No. I never had that kind of relationship to the land, unfortunately. I grew up in a city, a small place, with a big population, with rooms crowded with families and friends. The streets I travelled were always in need of repair. One had to travel on a bus to get to a park. I remember it was a long ride. Going to the sea was never a priority — we went perhaps once or twice a year. I appreciate the sea and trees and open spaces, but they hold no particular fascination for me, or let's say, they hold the same fascination that any big unknown city would.

INTERLOCUTOR: What was it like coming to Canada as a young girl? Did you find it difficult to adjust?

SILVERA: Disastrous. The cold, the stares, awful teachers, wicked classmates, no friends, no Blacks, snow, cold and more cold. And I was not impressed with the landscape, not that I saw much of it. My parents never travelled much outside of where we lived. I was in my late twenties or perhaps even early thirties when I took my first ride out to Northern Ontario and discovered there was water one could swim in, almost. *(laughter)*

INTERLOCUTOR: Did you enjoy anything here? Certainly there were more books to be read.

SILVERA: I hated everything about Canadian schools. I found them very cold and unfriendly. During grades seven and eight, I was one of two Black kids in the school, and during my high school years one of four. We were made to feel like unwelcome guests. And being so alienated 'outside' my home exacerbated my alienation from my parents. Everything was so white, the libraries, the curriculum, the bias. I don't know how some of us from that era survived.

INTERLOCUTOR: What were the first books you read as a child. Can you remember?

SILVERA: Yes ... I can remember. Fairy tales were my first introduction to the written word. I became enchanted by the lives of Cinderella, Snow White, Hansel and Gretel and the strange and wonderful places they lived in. I remember waiting eagerly for parcels of books to come from England where my parents had emigrated. But something changed as I became older and started school. I became acutely aware of the differences between my reality and Cinderella's and didn't enjoy the stories as much.

INTERLOCUTOR: Where did you find books to read that spoke to you?

SILVERA: It's too much of a long story to get into, but after scouring the library looking for other books that were closer to the realities of home and community and finding little, I somehow discovered Bathurst Street — it was the '70s and it was happening. I met other Black youths who introduced me to books by Malcolm X, Richard Wright, Claude McKay, James Baldwin, and that is where my Black Canadian education began, where I began to feel human again, where writing became a possibility.

INTERLOCUTOR: Were you encouraged to write at home?

SILVERA: Are you crazy? No. My mother thought that there was no possibility, no future for a young Black woman who wanted to write. She encouraged me to find a profession and *then* write.

INTERLOCUTOR: As you read more and became comfortable with the idea of writing, who were your role models?

SILVERA: Ah! Role models. I don't believe in role models. They can get you in trouble. Seriously, I went through a long and painful time finding that out, which has to do with what you asked me much earlier about writing fiction. Some months ago I heard an interviewer ask Ntozake Shange who her role models were, and her answer was so powerful in its simplicity, I wish I had heard her or someone else like her talk when I was stumbling and trying to find a path. She said, and I'm paraphrasing — don't look too high. If you want a role model, look at the ordinariness of life. Look at the mother that wakes up every morning, goes to work, comes home; if we need role models, they are right beside us.

I read a lot of novels and short stories by American Black women who were being published in the United States. For Black Canadian women writers, Toronto was still like a vacant parking lot. When I discovered this source of writing just south of the border, which was closer to my new North American urban experience, I took to it like a duck to water.

The first short story I ever wrote, some twelve, thirteen, years ago, I patterned off a short story by a Black woman writer whom I admired and who had become one of my 'role models'. In it I wanted to chart a time in the life of a young African Caribbean mother, a working-class woman struggling to find her voice. I wanted to put me in that story, to fashion it out of my life. Paulette Childress-White was saying the things I knew and felt and wanted to say, and in my untutored way I used her voice to speak for me. In retrospect, I know I had not found my voice, had not found a language in which to tell my own stories.

Since that time I have written many stories; the paths they took sometimes were not always what I expected, but they do mark my footsteps and mine alone.

INTERLOCUTOR: Were there no Black Canadian or Caribbean writers working at the time in Canada?

SILVERA: Not at the time, to my knowledge ... Barbadian writer Austin Clarke must have been writing then, but I was not aware of his work. I don't believe there were any contemporary Black women writers here. But it's really important to understand that period in Canada, and just how important Black America was to Black people in Canada. The culture of Black America overshadowed our reality as Blacks here in the 1970s, even those of Caribbean background. It was the time of the great big afros, the time of the Black Panthers — many of whom were in Toronto, not only escaping the draft but also running away from the FBI. It was an exciting period to be Black and we were drugged with the nectar of the time. Even when we looked at radical Black Canadians during the 1970s, they modelled themselves on Black America.

This is a part of our development in Canada that we tend to forget, but which we should resurrect and analyze. It is also important to remember that many of us left the Caribbean in the 1960s and 1970s to seek 'better' — to 'get away'. We did not see a future in the Caribbean. This journey, or self exile was not without its cost; for it separated many of us from our Caribbean 'role models.'

INTERLOCUTOR: In *Remembering G,* your first collection of short stories, you drew very much on the ordinary, and it is also clear that you had found your own voice.

SILVERA: Yes, I did. By the time I came to *Remembering G,* I had come through a whole period of searching, of finding and taking root. And that is why Ntozake Shange's response to the question touched me so. Yes, I did write about the ordinary. I wrote about the things I knew as a child. I wrote about eating cornmeal pudding. I wrote stories about a young girl coming to adolescence, about the ordinariness of a granny telling her grand-child Anancy stories. It was a place that I knew, and I could make magic and laughter out of the ordinariness. Yes, and I also found my own Caribbean voice and with it, the language that spoke for me.

INTERLOCUTOR: I want to move to the story "Caribbean Chameleon" from *Her Head a Village*. What's behind that story? And was it difficult to write it in Jamaican patois?

SILVERA: Let me first say that while the characters in the story are fictional, it is a dramatization of something that happened to me some three to four years before I wrote the story. It was a hellish nightmare at Pearson International Airport on a return flight from Jamaica. I had gone on a week's vacation and stayed in one of the resort hotels. On arrival in Toronto, I was questioned, interrogated, searched. I told the immigration officer that I found her questioning me over and over again insulting and smacking of racism. She looked at my Canadian I.D. and still wanted to know my place of birth. When I told her my place of birth — one which I had left over twenty years ago — she wanted to know why I had to stay in a hotel. Why didn't I stay with family? Immediately I was a suspect — a drug trafficker or something like that. When I refused to follow her to be strip-searched the RCMP was called in ... and on ... and on. It ended very badly, and I was angry, horrified, and wanted literally to murder somebody. Instead, I raged like a madwoman.

Still, I knew it was a story I wanted to write. Several months after the incident, I tried but the story would not come. Then a year later I tried again, and it still wouldn't come. Some time later, I went back to Jamaica on holiday and I began to see the story. I could feel it coming, it was then I knew what I had been doing wrong. I was trying to tell the story in Standard English, and the characters would not have it. They were Jamaican. The woman was angry, and her anger could not be expressed in Standard English — it didn't have the words, and the story would not make sense unless I wrote it in patwah. After *Remembering G,* writing in Jamaican patwah became easier. Although it is my first language, I was not literate in it. We were taught Standard English in schools, and patwah was never recognised as anything but the language of the illiterate masses. Of course this has changed, thanks to Miss Lou (Louise Bennett) and dub poetry.

INTERLOCUTOR: Do you write everyday?

SILVERA: Yes, letters. I write a lot of letters everyday, it's part of my work. Creative writing, no — not if writing means sitting down at a desk, but I carry writing with me wherever I go. I am most always thinking about characters, about themes. I don't have time to sit everyday writing, so I need to incorporate it in my living, in working, in doing all the other things I enjoy doing.

INTERLOCUTOR: But when you begin to work on a collection of short stories does the routine change at all?

SILVERA: Yes, that's different. Once I have decided on a project and the characters are fully with me, I know that it is time to retreat, to stay in the house. I am focused, and block out all other activities. I work very intensely. I don't go away to write, but during writing season I barricade myself from the world. I can ignore a ringing phone, a knock at the door. It has not always been like that. The phone would ring, and it would be my grandmother wanting a chore done and I would leave to attend to it. Or the school would call for the fifth time that week about one of my daughters and I would leave to attend to the matter, or a friend would appear unexpectedly to take me to lunch. I still have a hard time saying no, though I don't always say yes.

INTERLOCUTOR: What is this writing season? What do you mean?

SILVERA: It's the time that I put away to write. I'm not disciplined, so this self-imposed writing season is my way of making sure I do write. There is no other way for me to do it. Other demands on my time makes it near impossible to chart a writing schedule that begins every morning at five or six 'clock, or even one that begins after midnight. Perhaps if I were Dostoevsky, Flaubert, Hemmingway or even Virginia Woolfe I could do that.

INTERLOCUTOR: During this time, how many hours a day do you write?

SILVERA: Six to ten hours. I can go without eating, I can go without sleep too. I feel free, my characters come alive, and life outside does not seem to matter. There has been times when I consciously have had to balance that intensity and take a break, mop the kitchen floor, cook a meal, watch TV, spend time with my lover.

INTERLOCUTOR: Where do you write?

SILVERA: I like to move around. I start in bed. I love to write in bed — it's probably just a way of procrastinating, but I enjoy it. Then I might move to another room, perhaps with a desk, to do the second draft. Space has always been very important to me. I like to get lost in the house, so it's important for me to have many rooms.

INTERLOCUTOR: Can you work on more than one writing project at a time?

SILVERA: No, that's very difficult for me. I can write letters and still do fiction, or I can put the fiction aside and work on an essay, but to do two fiction pieces at the same time, no.

INTERLOCUTOR: I want to turn for a moment to motherhood. Do you feel any regrets at having children at such a young age? Earlier you said you did not write at all when your daughters were very young. You said it was not possible, even crazy to want to ... I'm asking the question within that context.

SILVERA: I have no regrets. It was a difficult period in my life. I was young, a mother of two, unsure of myself with very little support. Yet pregnancy and childbirth remain amongst my most memorable experiences and I would not exchange them for all the books I could have written. And, in retrospect, I don't really think I had that much to write about. Over the years my children have brought me much joy, some pain and much understanding. My writing is coming into it's own, and I am thankful.

INTERLOCUTOR: Are you a feminist? And if so, what impact does feminism have on your writing.

SILVERA: ... A feminist ... some days I don't know. Some days I'm just a woman trying to survive ... Yes I am a feminist. I am, because I am not satisfied with the imbalance in the world. I am sick and tired of it. Equally, I am not happy with the notion of feminine being less than masculine. As a feminist my job is to continue to contribute and struggle against gender oppression, race and class oppression, and of course heterosexual oppression. My feminism is not a banner against Black men. I struggle with them to let go of false power, to respect woman. Feminism did influence me in a lot of positive ways and did have a deep impact on me. It taught me to take care of myself, to love myself and to care for my body. The feminist writings I found in magazines, journals, books, sustained and built character during the years when I was a young mother and university student. The movement nourished and presented different ways of being in the world. One had options.

INTERLOCUTOR: What advice would you give to Black women who are writing and trying to get published?

SILVERA: I think I would say go out and buy a plain black lined note book at the corner store. Write in it everyday. Write anything. A thought, a letter to a friend you might never mail. Ideas for stories, poems even if you never write them. The purpose of this exercise is to practise, to start the active process of thinking and writing. Read. Read magazines, journals, newspapers that speak to your interest and style of writing. When you feel a bit sure of yourself send some of your work to them. This may be a particular bias of mine, but I do believe young writers should try to understand the publishing industry. Too many of us are ignorant about what really takes place, about how power is used and where and why our work get to a place or not get there. It is important to know about the means of producing these works into books. My final advice — don't rush to get published, enjoy your own work, read it aloud to yourself, friends, feel the quality of your words, know your voice. There *is* time.

INTERLOCUTOR: How do you see your writing? As a political act? Or as purely creative? Or the two combined?

SILVERA: As the two combined, which adds up to political. Every thing we create and put life into becomes political. I might not necessarily have that in mind while writing fiction, but ultimately what ever we write is a political statement. I write to understand history and family, I write to make sense out of a world that's full of nonsense, that can be vile and cruel. I write for a woman who also reads and hopes and strives to understand that world. So when I pick up my pen I must remember that the world is not a perfect place.

INTERLOCUTOR: I have a final question. Some time ago I was at one of your readings and someone asked you to comment on the violence in your short stories. What's going on here? What's behind the violence?

SILVERA: I think writing is fighting, is struggle. There are times the world is the last place I want to be. I get pessimistic, feel in a rage — not necessarily physically — and writing is a way of channelling that. So, yes, it has been noticed that sometimes there is violence in my stories. Take the young girl in *Remembering G*, for example. She is not a sweet child, and much of what happens to her is not nice. It's hard work writing about the violent emotions my characters feel. It means exposing things that aren't supposed to be exposed.

I have had to bear witness to the 'good' and the 'evil' in those we love, in ourselves and even those we despise, and to understand there is much ambiguity in this. Human tragedy has so many layers of the true story. We live in a brutal world in which we are sometimes blessed with love and kindness. We have little control over the violence that surrounds us. We must write about that.

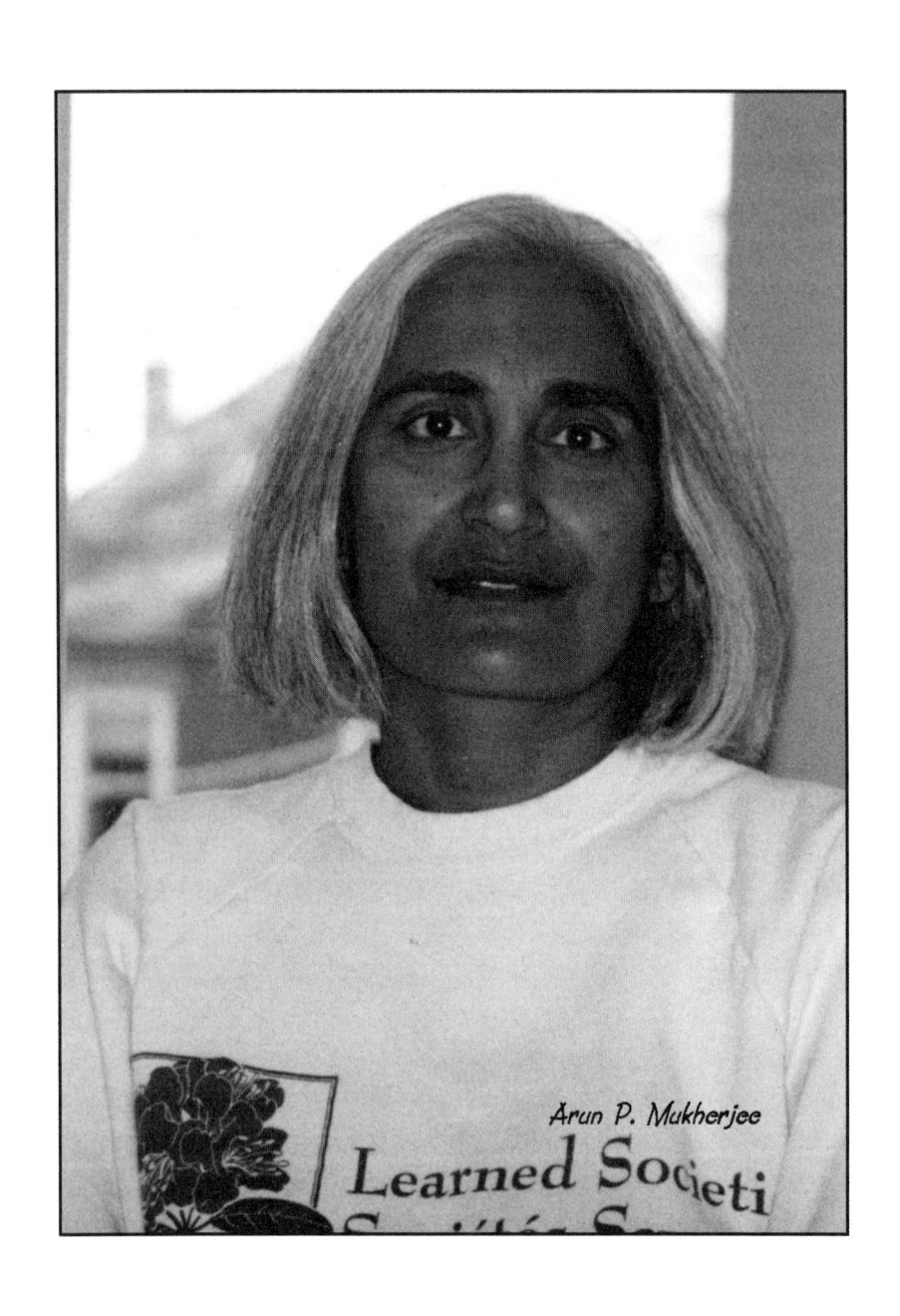

Arun P. Mukherjee

Arun P. Mukherjee

Canadian Nationalism, Canadian Literature and Racial Minority Women

AS A PERSON whose life trajectory coincides with India's independence and coming into being as a nation-state, I do not share the currently fashionable view, propagated by scholars such as Eric Hobsbawm, Tom Nairn and Homi Bhabha, that regards nationalism as a "pathology" or "dementia" (Nairn 359). The post-independence India I grew up in was high on nationalism. They were euphoric times when India was poor but proud. India and Indians had dreams of a brilliant future when poverty and inequality would become things of the past. Pandit Nehru's stirring speeches, delivered from the ramparts of the Red Fort in Delhi on Independence Day mornings, performed a national ritual that touched young school girls like me as we listened to his emotion-packed words on blaring radios while marching in the Independence Day school rallies as they wound through the bazaar of our small town. And the words he spoke in India's Constituent Assembly on the midnight of August 14, 1947 still retain their magic for me:

> Long years ago we made a tryst with destiny, and now the

time comes when we shall redeem our pledge, not wholly or in full measure, but very substantially. At the stroke of the midnight hour, when the world sleeps, India will awake to life and freedom. A moment comes, which comes but rarely in history, when we step out from the old to the new; when an age ends; and when the soul of a nation, long suppressed, finds utterance. It is fitting that at this solemn moment we take the pledge of dedication to the service of India and her people and to the still larger cause of humanity (quoted in Spear 237).

These words, whose rhetorical nature is now clear to me, still manage to touch me somehow, despite the ironic resonances that have gathered around them due to later tragedies and disappointments that have dimmed the lustre of India's democracy. They are words charged with emotion and mystery, not just the arbitrary signifiers deconstructionists say words are.

That dream of post-independence Indian nationalism that was inscribed on my consciousness through various ritualistic acts, images and cultural productions is, for me, the empowering side of nationalism. Post-independence Indian nationalism was inclusionary and empowering. Free India's constitution heroically resolved to right the wrongs of the past, for untouchables, for the poor, for women, for minorities. India, as our first prime minister never tired of telling us, in those voluble speeches he never tired of giving, was going to be a model community.

I am afraid that Western Marxists' and postmodernists' condescending disavowals of nationalism and nationalists overlook, as Benedict Anderson reminds us, that nations inspire love and sacrifice (7). Such theorists are rightly reprimanded by James Blaut for their universalist ethnocentrism that has prevented them from seeing that not all nationalisms are fascist or Nazi, that nationalisms can imagine nations that are secular, progressive, international in outlook and culturally and ethnically diverse (8-56). Such versions of nationalism have been totally ignored in Western Marxist and postmodernist theorizing on nationalism. It has thoroughly overlooked the Third World experience and theorizing which claims that the nation can be an "enabling idea" (Sangari 183).

When I come to discuss Canadian nationalism I do not want to begin with the universalist premise that *a priori* condemns and ridicules nationalism. I agree with James Blaut that we must evaluate each nationalism in terms of its aspirations and achievements rather than universalize about an abstraction which has really been derived from the European historical experience of ethnic nationalisms (33).

When I respond to Canadian nationalism I cannot help comparing it to my first hand experience of Indian nationalism. For many of us South Asian Canadians, Trudeau came to represent Canada as Nehru had represented India. A majority of the South Asian immigrants who emigrated to Canada in the late '60s and early '70s — the first batch of immigrants from South Asia who entered Canada under the post-1967 non-racist immigration policy — has felt a personal gratitude to Trudeau and continues to vote for the Liberal Party because of that bond. Those of us who entered Canada at the height of Trudeaumania felt that Canada was on a cusp of change. It was hard not to be thrilled by Trudeau's message of a "just society" and "cultural pluralism." This attitude to Trudeau is alluded to touchingly in M. G. Vassanji's *The Gunny Sack* where East African Asian immigrants begin to compare Pierre Trudeau to a "Pir," a holy man with miraculous powers (248).

Although Canadian nationalism of the '60s and the '70s is remembered for Expo '67, which was held to commemorate the nation's centennial, for the surge in anti-American feeling and the desire for Canada's economic and political independence, and for the institutionalization of Canadian literature in schools and universities, it is the opening up of Canada to non-white immigration that registered most strongly for Canadians of colour. The striking down of racist immigration policies of the past was experienced by us as the most promising manifestation of the vision of the just society.

So why is it that racial minority women have expressed such negative views about Canada? If nations, according to Benedict Anderson, are experienced as "imagined communities" and evoke discourses of kinship and home (143-44), why does the narrator in Dionne Brand's short story, "At the Lisbon Plate," describe herself as "A woman in enemy territory"? (1988 97). Himani Bannerji's tropes of "prison" in her long prose poem "doing time" similarly challenge the notion of Canada as an "imagined community" (1986 9-11). "Doing time" depicts Canada as a prison house for those who are "not white, and also women" (9). And in *Chronicles of the Hostile Sun*, Dionne Brand uses the trope of homelessness to describe her relationship with Canada:

> I am not a refugee,
> I have my papers,
> I was born in the Caribbean,
> practically in the sea,
> fifteen degrees above the equator,
> I have a Canadian passport,
> I have lived here all my adult life,
> I am stateless anyway. (70)

Such alienation from a national entity called Canada and from "Canadians" is quite commonplace in the writings of Aboriginal and racial minority Canadian women. If Canada is "enemy territory" for

Brand's Black female narrator and "prison" for Bannerji's poetic persona, it is occupied territory in the writings of Aboriginal women. For Mary Panegoosho Cousins, an Inuk, Canada is a totally arbitrary colonial construction:

> I am concerned that Inuit, who have an amazing history of Arctic living, have been nationalized under the flags of the U. S. A., Canada, Denmark, and whatever country is across the Bering Sea from Alaska. We Canadian Inuit are then sub-divided by the borders of Labrador, Quebec, and the Northwest Territories. The "outsiders" seem obsessed with drawing lines on maps, and they really believe these lines appear on the earth. What strange thinking! ... These boundaries are the first signs that the "outsiders" decided to dominate, operate, control, and generally run people called Inuit ...
>
> I am concerned that these well-meaning but misguided "outsiders" did more than mess up the land. They also occupied much of the land in all these artificial communities they created. Once again they drew lines on townsite plans telling us where to live and where not to trespass (52-53).

Mary Cousins and other Inuit women writing in *Sharing Our Experience,* an anthology of epistolary writing by Aboriginal women and women of colour, identified themselves as Inuit first. Similarly, Patricia A. Monture-OKanee sees herself as a member of the Mohawk nation:

> I am a Mohawk woman. I am a citizen of the
> Haudensounee Confederacy (the Six Nations Iroquois

Confederacy) ... My woman's identity comes from the fact that I am a member of that Confederacy, that I am a member of the Mohawk nation. You cannot ask me to speak as a woman because I cannot speak as just a woman. This is not the voice that I have been given. Gender does not transcend race. The voice that I have been given is the voice of a Mohawk woman and if you must talk to me about women, somewhere along the line you must talk about race. ... I cannot and will not separate the two (194).

Ever since I heard Patricia Monture-OKanee say those words at a feminist conference in 1989, I have thought of Virginia Woolf's famous statement differently. Woolf's "as a woman I have no country" adorned Women's Day posters in Toronto a couple of years ago. Perhaps our white sisters thought they were denouncing nationalistic jingoism and promoting sisterhood by disclaiming their Canadian citizenship. However, Monture-OKanee's words help me understand the "white privilege" hidden in such gestures of denunciation. White women remain British or Canadian or American and enjoy the privileges of that status however much they claim they are just women. Women like Dionne Brand or Mary Cousins or Patricia Monture-OKanee, on the other hand, cannot be unproblematically Canadian — or "just Canadian" as those with privileged ethnicities claim to be — because their other identities put them at a disadvantage in a racist nation-state. I, similarly, cannot speak of gender and nationalism when I speak of these women's response to the nation-state because it is their race that sets them apart in this country and denies them the status and privileges that white Canadians enjoy. It was because of these considerations that Jeannette Armstrong chose a male protagonist for her nationalist novel, *Slash*, a choice many white feminists criticized her for.

The racial minority Canadian women's and Aboriginal Canadian women's discontents against the Canadian nation-state are based on different grounds and I would not like to lump them together. Both Mary Cousins and Patricia Monture-OKanee belong to First Nations whose borders do not match those of Canada. In their eyes, Canadian border and Canadian culture are exercises in genocidal domination. The following words of Monture-OKanee eloquently express the First Nations point of view:

> What needs to be understood is who has done the defining. It has not been First Nations. Many of us do not accept this great lie any longer. We understand the solution lies in our inalienable right to define ourselves, our nations, our governments, and in protecting the natural laws the Creator gave us. Nor has the restructuring of law and government on Turtle Island to conform to European norms been achieved with the expressed or implied consent and/or assistance of First Nations (196).

While 125 years of Canadian nationalist discourses have proposed a distinct Canadian identity, their explanations ranging from pure Viking blood of northern races and the salutary effect on the same pure Viking blood of Canada's harsh winters, from Canada's cultural duality to Canada's geography (Berger), the words of First Nations women point out how exclusionary and racist these nationalist agendas have been. The Aboriginal peoples' coinage of the term "First Nations" to describe themselves is a brilliant rhetorical intervention to counteract the racist nationalist discourse of "two founding races," a discourse which undergirds the Canadian state and all its social and cultural hierarchies. It exposes the glaring omissions in the legitimizing fictions of white settler Canada.

The texts of Aboriginal women disturb the normalcy of Canadian literary and cultural understandings. The canonical works of Canadian literature, barring a few exceptions where Native characters are present as ghosts provoked by guilt (Fee 1987), are oblivious to the Native presence in Canada. According to Marjorie Fee, "Both general books and survey courses on Canadian literature ... promote master narratives of the nation that ignore regional, ethnic, Native, and female difference" (1993 33). These master narratives are framed in terms of Canada's two founding races, refigured as two founding peoples to suit these politically correct times. English Canadian literature courses, therefore, begin with Susanna Moodie's *Roughing It in the Bush* and not with Native orature.

Canadian literature — created, published, taught and critiqued under the aegis of Canadian nationalism — promotes the settler-colonial view of Canada. The nationalist critics like Northrop Frye, Margaret Atwood, D.G. Jones and John Moss produced an essentialized Canadian character that, according to them, was discoverable in the literary texts of canonical Canadian writers. Canadians, these revered critics have told us, suffered from a garrison mentality because of their intimidating physical environment. They developed a victim complex, aiming only for survival rather than grandiose achievements, unlike their neighbours to the south.

Although these environmentalist explanations of a Canadian identity, as well as the very obsession there with "a" Canadian identity, have been challenged often enough, they have not been replaced yet by more inclusive theories of Canada and Canadian literature. Now we hear talk about postmodernist irony and dominants and marginals, but we do not hear any concerted responses to what Aboriginal and racial minority writers tell us about Canada and Canadian literature. Like our political leaders who virtually ignored Aboriginal and racial minority Canadians' concerns when they came up with their Meech Lake and Charlottetown Accords, much critical theory continues to be churned out in Canada that is premised on notions of Canada's duality and remains profoundly oblivious to Aboriginal and racial minority voices.

A stunning example of this exclusionary critical work is Sylvia Söderland's *Margin/Alias* where the terms "colonized" and "postcolonial" are unproblematically appropriated for Canadian (read white) and Québécois literature and vast generalizations made about nation and national identity based on the work of five white male and Québécois writers.

The enormous gap between white and Aboriginal Canadians can be gauged by white cultural establishment's response to Aboriginal spokespersons' demand that white writers and artists stop telling Aboriginal stories. These demands were immediately branded as censorship. All the old nostrums about the freedom of the artistic imagination were trotted out and replayed over and over again. While to the Eurocentric mindset, freedom of imagination may seem a universal, self-evident truth that has nothing to do with white skin privilege, Aboriginal writer and storyteller Lenore Keeshig-Tobias suggests that white writers' appropriation of Native stories is of the same order as white settlers taking away Native land (175).

The point is that seemingly universal, "purely" aesthetic ideas are not really universal but culture-specific. White Canadians, however, have employed vocabularies that claim universality, despite their exclusionary nature. Thus what seems universalist and apolitical on the surface often turns out to be a Euro-Canadian conceptualization. What I would call the nationalist-universalist tradition ensures that it is white Anglo writing or Anglo-conformist writing that gets the lion's share of attention. It is they who speak as Canadians. It is their experience, their version of history, their notions of literature, their vision of Canada that dominates. As Dionne Brand says, "Canadian national identity is necessarily predicated on whiteness" (1993 18).

Many Aboriginal and racial minority women writers have spoken eloquently about how their writing has been turned down time and again because it was not deemed "Canadian," but "ethnic," that is emerging from and speaking to a minority group. When published by small, usually "ethnic" presses, the establishment — reviewers and academics — othered it in multiple ways: it was exotic; it was "Black," or "Native," or "South Asian"; it was about "immigrant" experience. The category Canadian has been denied to these writers, their work seldom seen as contributing to "Canadian" life.

The canon of Canadian literature in English, formed according to the common-sense notions of Canadian nation-state and Canadian identity, is, not surprisingly, devoid of "regional, ethnic, native, and female difference" as Fee has argued. This canon, according to Robert Lecker, who did not seem to notice its whiteness or its Angloness, valorizes works that are "ordered, orderable, safe." He suggests that these texts have been read and promoted as "an expression of national self-consciousness" (658). The preferred texts of the canon makers, he says, are those that are "set in Canada" and focus on Canadian events and issues" (687).

Although Aboriginal writers' works have not got into the canon even though they *are* set in Canada and focus on Canadian events and issues, such nationalist criteria have had an extremely negative effect on the production and reception of writings by writers of colour. The following words of David Staines are quite representative of the criteria that have been applied to devalue the work of racial minority writers:

Resonances are the intangible traces of a country and its people that haunt, unconsciously and unobtrusively, the pages of the country's literature. Resonances can be heard only by those from wherever here is, or by those exceptional artists, such as Michael Ondaatje, who seem to sense instinctively and naturally the meaning of these even though they are not from here. But the Ondaatje sensibility is rare. Too common are those transplanted writers, however gifted their writing, who try to show their Canadianness by placing scenes on Sherbrooke Street (West, of course) or Bay and Bloor, who introduce obtrusive references to Marshall McLuhan or the Canada Council, who struggle to impose references that are unnatural in their context. The truly Canadian writer writes out of his or her own world, making resonances without ever knowing it (66).

Bharati Mukherjee was told by an eminent Canadian critic that she could not be a Canadian writer because she "didn't grow up playing in snow" (quoted in Parameswaran 86). Similarly, Margaret Atwood, explaining why she had excluded some writers in her discussion of Canadian literature, said: "It seems to me dangerous to talk about 'Canadian' patterns of sensibility in the work of people who entered and/or entered-and-left the country at a developmentally late stage of their lives" (quoted in Metcalf 11). According to nationalist critics, in order to be considered a Canadian writer, one does not just need Canadian content in one's work; only "birthright Canadians" can be considered Canadian writers.

Such criteria have meant that non-Canadian-born writers' work has been slotted as "immigrant writing." Immigrant writing supposedly comes in two kinds: if it deals with subject matter that alludes to where the writer came from, it is perceived as nostalgic. If, on the other hand, it has Canadian content, it is automatically considered to be about an immigrant's struggle to adjust to new realities. As M. G. Vassanji has pointed out, white immigrant writers have not had their writing branded thus (2). Their works were judged according to universalist criteria of merit and quickly found their place in Canadian literature anthologies. The immigrant label, then, is coded racially. The danger of such labelling, according to Vassanji, is that the writing deemed "immigrant experience" begins to "seem irrelevant to the ongoing dialectic" (2).

Too many racial minority writers have had their work turned down by Canadian publishers either because, according to publishers, it was not Canadian, or because they felt that the Canadian readers would not identify with it. As Cecil Foster told my students during his visit to my class, a major Canadian publisher informed him that his company's criterion for accepting a work for publication was whether "the bored housewife in Mississauga" would be interested in reading it or not. Minority writers who have used non-Canadian settings have been rejected on the pretext that their work was too distanced from the Canadian reader's experience.

It is not too hard to see that the Canadian reader here is presumed to be white and incapable of taking interest in the realities of places like Barbados or South Africa, let alone to have come from there. Claire Harris, in response to a comment by Brian Fawcett about the economic difficulties of publishing minority writers' works, says, "This is an absurdity that presupposes that Canadians are all so racist and so provincial that they would refuse to read the books of minority groups" (1990 140).

Minority writers' works set in other countries have either been published abroad or by minority presses until very recently. Farida Karodia has lived in Canada for the last twenty-four years, and yet few Canadians have heard of her because all three of her books are set in South Africa, and, consequently, she could not interest a Canadian publisher. This writer's work is being marketed by Heinemann in its African writers series, and I doubt that it will be put on Canadian literature courses or critically responded to in the near future.

There are many ways of othering racial minority writers. A hallowed critical tradition has developed in Canada around the term "regional." So we have anthologies of critical and creative writing devoted to "Prairie writing," "Maritime writing," and "West Coast writing." But looking at these volumes, one would assume that no racial minorities live and produce work there. Claire Harris has spoken in detail about her struggle to get recognized in Canada: "Since I'm writing on the prairies, it seems to me I have a place in books on Prairie writing. Whether mine is the received wisdom on the Prairies or not!" (1993 117). To all intents and purposes, the category "regional" has been as exclusionary of Aboriginal and racial minority writers as the category "Canadian."

The construction of "Canadian literature" by powerful professors, bureaucrats, editors, publishers and reviewers — the majority of them white males — has been carried out under the aegis of 19th century European notions of nationhood which proposed that a nation was racially and culturally different from other nations and uniform at home. A nation's literature, according to such theories, has to reflect the "soul" of the nation, its history and traditions, which are also conceived in terms of a nation's unified "spirit." Canadian literature was constructed in the service of a Canadian nation conceptualized in terms of these ethno-cultural theories of nationhood. These critics believed that reading Canadian writing would lead Canadian readers to develop into a distinctive national type, to discover the "soul" of the country, to become united as Canadians. Writers like Hugh McLellan came to believe that their job was to produce works of documentary realism wherein Canadian readers would recognize themselves and their land. These ideas about Canadian literature have a century-long history and have dominated the theoretical debates in the 60s and the 70s, the time when minority voices were beginning to emerge. Such views have stood as impenetrable barriers against minority writers in getting their works published, acknowledged and taught as part of the curriculum.

As many non-white men and women have said in many places, Canadian is a code word for white. Camille Hérnandez-Ramdwar, born in Winnipeg in 1965, grew up being called by every racist epithet: "nigger," "paki," "injun," "bogan," "chink," "spic." She writes:

> The experience of being labelled at so young an age has deeply affected my feelings of being a Canadian, of "belonging." My general feeling has been that I do not feel like a Canadian (despite being born and raised here) because I am not accepted as one at face value. People, upon meeting me, still open conversations with "And where are you from?" as if a person of my complexion could not possibly be born here. I blame a lot of these continued misperceptions on the media, who seem satisfied with presenting an all-white Canadian face in advertising and television shows (61).

Dionne Brand says "all Blacks are always suspected of being recent immigrants" (1993 16). Such assumptions on the part of the dominant community result in our unfriendly treatment at border check points, attacks and abuse on the streets, and isolation in the work place. However, complaining against such treatment, Brand says, brings only retorts like: "'Oh no, we're not like the United States,' be grateful for the not-as-bad-racism-here" (1990 45).

These minority perspectives on Canada are seldom deemed

Canadian. The hegemonic view of Canada, the view presented at home and to the outside world, is the white (middle class?) Canadians experience. A recent special issue of *Massachusetts Review*, for instance, trotted out the familiar comparisons and contrasts between "Canada" and "America," of course predicated on white experience. How removed this Canada is from the experience of racial minority and Aboriginal Canadians became evident for me when I read Ian Angus describing his experience of crossing national borders:

> If one is crossing back into one's own country, even these questions [by customs and immigration officers] are the beginning of an embrace, a belonging made richer, more palpable by absence. Inflated, so that even official inquiries seem benign since one is forearmed with all the right answers (32).

He has obviously never heard of the treatment accorded to racial minority and Aboriginal Canadians at these same borders. Yet it is his experience that is deemed "the Canadian experience," silencing, no, obliterating other Canadian experiences.

In her recent article in *Brick*, Dionne Brand uncovers the racist agendas of this business-as-usual attitude of the white Canadian cultural establishment which manufactures and promotes a perfect fit between whiteness and Canadianness:

> Assumptions of white racial superiority inform the designation of formal culture in this country and the assigning of public funds. Culture is organized around whiteness through various "para-statal" bodies including the Canadian Broadcasting Corporation, the National Film Board, the Canada Council and other provincial and metropolitan arts councils

and through private media and cultural and educational institutions.

In film, radio and television, all one has to do is listen to the voices, watch the faces, note choices of themes and point of view to get it. Simply, who is reflected there? This same "common-sense" racist ideology interrogates the production of any cultural work by artists of colour and that interrogation ranges from dismissal to anointment — and far more dismissal than anointment. These works are "placed" by their relationship to and relevance for the dominant cultural form. Reviewers always comment on the "anger" in my work for example (anger having been categorized as a particularly "Black" emotion), and its portrayal of "the Black experience." White work on the other hand is never interrogated for its portrayal of "the white experience" (1993 17).

According to the "common-sense racism" Brand is talking about, "the white experience" equates with Canadian experience. Other experiences, if they get noticed, are dubbed "Black," or "ethnic," or "immigrant" experience, depending upon the mood of the namer, who is usually white and often, though not always, male.

Canadian nationalism, for us non-whites, is a racist ideology that has branded us "un-Canadian" by acts of omission and commission. Its proponents determined what is Canadian culture. Only two cultures were considered officially Canadian, although the Québécois don't feel they are treated equally — equal to the Anglos I presume. Aboriginal cultures and Aboriginal rights were denied and continue to be denied. Minority Canadians were treated as second-class citizens, allowed in Canada only as beasts of burden. Canadian nationalists of the '60s and '70s seldom pondered on these aspects of Canadian history. They did not produce an ideology of national liberation that would include all Canadians on an equal footing. Instead, they constructed a Canada that was being savaged by American domination and used tropes of rape and seduction to speak about it. Their Canada was an innocent victim. These Canadian and Québécois nationalists appropriated anti-colonial vocabularies to speak of themselves as "the colonized" and, in the case of the Québécois, as "the white niggers of America." In positioning themselves as victims, they forgot that they, too, had victimized and needed to make amends.

In the absence of an anti-racist, egalitarian ideology, Canadian nationalists of the '70s created an all-white canon of works about small towns and wilderness, about white settlers pioneering on the frontier with the RCMP maintaining law and order. This canon was taught and written about in universalist terms, thereby discounting its whiteness.

The work of Aboriginal and racial minority writers has challenged these constructions in several ways. By positioning themselves as Aboriginal or Black or South Asian or Chinese or Japanese Canadians, by writing from the specificity of their community's experience, they have called into question the universalist stance adopted by white Canadian writers. As Dionne Brand says, from non-white readers' perspective, white writers' works deal with "white experience" and are therefore as hyphenated as the works of non-white writers.

Another strategy they have adopted is to insist on the relevance of their so-called non-Canadian experience by pointing out that Canada has participated in the spoils of imperialism and colonialism. Dionne Brand and Makeda Silvera write about Caribbean domestic workers in Toronto. They write about the children of these workers left in the Caribbean. Non-white writers often challenge Canadian insularity by imbuing "Canadian" signifiers with non-Canadian connections. For example, where native-born Canadians might see only a neon sign brightening the Toronto skyline, Brand sees centuries of colonial exploitation in which Canada has participated:

> When I come back to Toronto from the Playas del Este, I will pass a flashing neon sign hanging over the Gardiner Expressway. 'Lloyds Bank,' it will say. Lloyds, as in Lloyds of London. They got their bullish start insuring slave cargo (1990 52).

Non-white writers' texts challenge Canadian nationalists' claims to Canada's unique difference from the US and Britain by exposing Canada's participation in the networks of international capital and colonialism. They call into question the benign Canada that nationalists like Margaret Atwood and B.W. Powe have spoken about, a Canada that unlike its neighbour to the south is not supposed to have a history of violence. By writing about the Aboriginal peoples' colonial experience, the Chinese Head Tax and the *Chinese Exclusion Act,* the Japanese internment during the Second World War, the voyage of the *Komagata Maru,* and about slavery, these writers rewrite Canadian history, thus exposing the lie about the innocent Canada of white Canadian writing. Because racial minorities' experience does not respect Canada's borders and because they have global links, diasporic for racial minorities and political for Aboriginal peoples, their writing necessarily brings in these other places and their histories. Diana Brydon's comment about Brand's poem, "Blues Spiritual for Mammy Prater" is generalizable to other minority writers as well. She suggests that boundary-crossings in Dionne Brand's poetry question the systemic pressures that shape and mis-shape our subjectivities as people defined through categories such as gender, ethnicity, class, or nation. Her poetry, whatever its subject matter or setting, explores questions of crucial interest to Canadians today. Although ostensibly addressing what some might see as an American (that is, US) topic, "Blues Spiritual for Mammy Prater" speaks directly to our Canadian obsessions with cultural continuities and identity formation, refusing simplistic embracings of "essence" in favour of more complicated explorations of subject construction (86).

As Paul Gilroy has suggested in *The Black Atlantic,* Black experience cannot be separated and discussed as specifically African, American, Caribbean or British. He claims that a Black Atlantic culture has developed whose expression exceeds the categories of ethnicity and nationality. I think that a similar analytical grid can be applied to the diasporic cultures of Chinese, Japanese and South Asians.

I teach a third-year course on Aboriginal and racial minority Canadian writers. One of the most frequent comments my students make during the class discussions is, "Why didn't I know about this?" They are angry that their education kept hidden from them the history I mentioned earlier. The texts of non-white writers are teaching them things about Canadian history and Canadian people that they did not learn in their Canadian literature course.

Along with Canadian history and society, they are also learning about oral and literary traditions that are not Eurocentric. Native writers, I believe, are the most challenging in this regard when they question things such as the primacy of "print" and "literature" (Brant 357). By speaking of the "healing" function of writing, by substituting the concept of storytelling for "literature," Native writers force us to rethink the nature of literature and the literary institution in fundamental ways. In both their literature and theoretical writing, Aboriginal women writers have thrown challenges to predominant modes of thinking that have yet to be acknowledged.

Both Aboriginal and minority women writers have rejected the notion that Canadian writing must follow "a" Canadian tradition, which, of course, has been exclusively defined in Eurocentric terms. Dionne Brand, for example, has said that she does not write from the margin of the Canadian tradition but from the centre of the Black tradition, which she defines as African Caribbean, African American and African (1990a 273). Himani Bannerji, similarly, writes about the "gaps" and "holes" a non-South Asian reader may experience while reading her texts because her allusions are not to Greek, Roman and Biblical sources but to Indian texts such as Hindu scriptures and the Bengali writers she grew up with (1990 33). These texts, then, need to be decoded and interpreted by paying attention to their cultural contexts, a process which, according to Claire Harris, requires education (1990 307). That, at the moment, is not the case. As Minnie Aodla Freeman says, "We do not sit with each other long enough to understand each other. We do not educate each other enough to understand each other's cultures" (188).

I cannot forget an exchange that occurred in my class last year while studying M.G. Vassanji's *No New Land*. A South Asian student addressed a group of white Canadian students and said, "I am glad that this text will make you do the kind of work I have to do when I read the Western texts and have to learn about all those allusions by doing some legwork." That the remark provoked laughter and not anger suggests to me that we may be going through an exciting transition to a new literary paradigm here.

Claire Harris suggests that her use of African and Caribbean themes and styles "interrupts and moves beyond Canadian literature as it has been defined, as in Anglo-Saxon, male. Canadian literature is not defined along the lines of the population" (1993 121). Harris's reference to changing demographic patterns of Canada is really a call to discuss how we are going to define the Canadian reader. The writings of racial minority writers have effectively pointed out that "the bored housewife in Mississauga" stereotype needs to be retired on account of its obvious sexism and covert racism. We have certainly reached a crisis of legitimation in Canada. The old paradigms of nationalist criticism and the white-only canon no longer convince all Canadians. Nor does the master narrative of two founding races/peoples/cultures.

The old Canadian nationalisms, founded on racial purity and cultural duality are being challenged by those who have long been excluded from the tables of deal makers and dice rollers. Canada needs a new nationalism, a nationalism whose grounding premise will be Canada's heterogeneity. In Claire Harris's words, we need "a new vision of Canada ... one that includes all its people as full and legitimate citizens" (1993 116). Whether that Canada of our dreams will come into being or whether the force of old ideologies of race and culture based nations will fragment the Canadian nation-state remains to be seen.

Bibliography

Anderson, Benedict. *Imagined Communities: Reflections on the Origin and Spread of Nationalism*. London: Verso, 1991.

Angus, Ian. "Crossing the Border" in *Massachusetts Review*, No. 31, 1-2, Spring-Summer 1990, pp. 32-47

Bannerji, Himani. *doing time*. Toronto: Sister Vision Press, 1986.

> "The Sound Barrier" in *Language in Her Eye: Views on Writing and Gender by Canadian Women Writing in English*. Libby Scheier, Sarah Sheard and Eleanor Waachtel, eds. Toronto: Coach House Press, 1990), pp. 26-40.

Berger, Carl. "The True North Strong and Free" in *Nationalism in Canada*. Peter Russell, ed. Toronto: McGraw-Hill Company of Canada Limited, 1966, pp. 3-26.

Blaut, James M. *The National Question: Decolonising the Theory of Nationalism*. London: Zed Books, 1987.

Brand, Dionne. *Chronicles of the Hostile Sun*. Toronto: Williams-Wallace, 1984.

"At the Lisbon Plate" in *Sans Souci and Other Stories*. Stratford: Williams-Wallace, 1988.

"Bread Out of Stone" in *Language in Her Eye: Views on Writing and Gender by Canadian Women Writing in English*, Libby Scheier, Sarah Sheard and Eleanor Waachtel, eds. Toronto: Coach House Press, 1990, pp. 45-53.

Interview by Dagmar Novak. *Other Solitudes: Canadian Multicultural Fictions*, Linda Hutcheon and Marion Richmond, eds. Toronto: Oxford University Press, 1990, pp. 271-277.

"Who Can Speak for Whom?" in *Brick*, No. 46, Summer 1993, pp. 13-20.

Brant, Beth. "The Good Red Road: Journeys of Homecoming in Native Women's Writing" in *And Still We Rise: Feminist Political Mobilising in Contemporary Canada*, Linda Carty, ed. Toronto: Women's Press, 1993, pp. 355-369.

Brydon, Diana. "Reading Dionne Brand's 'Blues Spiritual for Mammy Prater' in *Inside the Poem: Essays and Poems in Honour of Donald Stephens*, W. H. New, ed. Toronto: Oxford University Press, 1992, pp. 81-87.

Cousins, Mary Panegoosho. "A Circumpolar Inuk Speaks" in *Sharing Our Experience*, Arun Mukherjee, ed. Ottawa: Canadian Advisory Council on the Status of Women, 1993, pp. 52-56.

Fee, Margery. "Romantic Nationalism and the Image of Native People in Contemporary English-Canadian Literature" in *The Native in Literature*, Thomas King, Cheryl Calver and Helen Hoy, eds. Oakville, Ontario: ECW Press, 1987, pp. 15-33.

"Canadian Literature and English Studies in the Canadian University" in *Essays on Canadian Writing,* No. 48, 1992-1993, pp. 20-40.

Freeman, Minnie Aodla. "Dear Leaders of the World" in *Sharing Our Experience,* Arun Mukherjee, ed. Ottawa: Canadian Advisory Council on the Status of Women, 1993, pp. 186-190.

Gilroy, Paul. *The Black Atlantic: Modernity and Double Consciousness.* London: Verso, 1993.

Harris Claire. "Ole Talk: A Sketch" in *Language in Her Eye: Views on Writing and Gender by Canadian Women Writing in English,* Libby Scheier, Sarah Sheard and Eleanor Waachtel, eds. Toronto: Coach House Press, 1990, pp. 131-141.

"Mirror, Mirror on the Wall" in *Caribbean Women Writers: Essays from the First International Conference,* Selwyn R. Cudjoe, ed. Wellesley, Mass.: Calaloux Publications, 1990, pp. 306-309.

Interview with Janice Williamson in *Sounding Differences: Conversations with Seventeen Canadian Women Writers.* Janice Williamson. Toronto: University of Toronto Press, 1993. pp. 115-130.

Hernández-Ramdwar, Camille. "Once I Wanted to Run Away from Canada" in *Sharing Our Experience,* Arun Mukherjee, ed. Ottawa: Canadian Advisory Council on the Status of Women, 1993, pp. 61-63.

Keeshig-Tobias, Lenore. "The Magic of Others" in *Language in Her Eye: Views on Writing and Gender by Canadian Women Writing in English,* Libby Scheier, Sarah Sheard and Eleanor Waachtel, eds. Toronto: Coach House Press, 1990, pp. 173-177.

Lecker, Robert. "The Canonization of Canadian Literature: An Inquiry into Value" in *Critical Inquiry, No.* 16, Spring 1990 pp. 656-671.

"Response to Frank Davey" in *Critical Inquiry, No.* 16, Spring 1990, pp. 682-89.

Metcalf, John. *What is a Canadian Literature?* Guelph: Red Kite Press, 1988.

Monture-OKanee, Patricia A. "The Violence We Women Do: A First Nations View" in *Challenging Times: The Women's Movement in Canada and the United States,* Constance Backhouse and David H. Flaherty, eds. Montreal: McGill-Queen's University Press, 1992, pp. 193-200.

Nairn, Tom. *The Break-Up of Britain.* London: New Left Books, 1977.

Parameswaran, Uma. "Ganga in the Assiniboine" in *A Meeting of Streams: South Asian Canadian Literature,* M. G. Vassanji, ed. Toronto: TSAR Publications, 1985, pp. 79-93

Sangari, Kum Kum. "The Politics of the Possible" in *Cultural Critique,* No. 7, 1987, pp. 157-186.

Söderland, Sylvia. *Margin/Alias: Language and Colonization in Canadian and Québécois Fiction.* Toronto: University of Toronto Press, 1991.

Spear, Percival. *A History of India: Volume Two.* Harmondsworth: Penguin Books, 1965.

Staines, David. "Reviewing Practices in English Canada" in *problems of literary reception/problèmes de réception littéraire,* E. D. Blodgett and A. G. Purdy, eds. Edmonton: Research Institute for Comparative Literature, 1988, pp. 61-68.

Vassanji, M. G. "Introduction" in *A Meeting of Streams: South Asian Canadian Literature,* M. G. Vassanji, ed. Toronto: TSAR Press, 1985, pp. 1-6.

The Gunny Sack. Oxford: Heinemann, 1989.

The Contributors

LILLIAN ALLEN moved from Spanish Town, Jamaica, to Canada and the United States in 1969. After studying at the City University of New York and York University in Toronto, she became the birth mother of dub in Canada, performing alone and with *de dub poets*. She has three albums for adults, one for children, two books for children and young people, and performs locally, nationally and internationally. A cultural strategist and long-time cultural worker and arts activist in Toronto, Allen's also a writer of plays and short fiction and has recently ventured into film-making.

HIMANI BANNERJI came to Canada in 1969. She teaches at York University in the Department of Sociology. Her research interests feminist theory and the sociology of culture and politics in the areas of gender, colonialism and nationalism are equally divided between Canada and India. Her writing is also equally divided between the creative and the critical.

DIONNE BRAND is a Toronto writer. She was born in the Caribbean and has lived in Toronto for the past twenty years. Brand has published six books of poetry, two works of non-fiction and a collection of short stories. Her work appears in several anthologies.

MARIA CAMPBELL is the author of *Halfbreed*. She teaches writing at the University of Saskatchewan.

FREDERICK CASE is a professor of African and Caribbean literatures at the University of Toronto and Principal of New College, University of Toronto.

LIEN CHAO came to Canada in 1984 to pursue her M.A. at York University. Her doctoral thesis, "Beyond Silence: Chinese Canadian Literature (in English)," introduced this literature into mainstream Canadian literature. For the Toronto Board of Education, she teaches English to new immigrants and English literacy to mentally challenged adults. She is also writing a novel, *My Mother and Her Daughters*.

AFUA COOPER is a doctoral candidate in the Department of History at the University of Toronto, where she is doing research on Ontario Black women's history. She has done extensive research on Black teachers and Black education in 19th-century Ontario. Cooper's lectures on Canadian Black history have taken her throughout Ontario. Her poetry has been published in several anthologies in Great Britain, Canada, the United States and the Caribbean.

BEATRICE CULLETON is a Métis writer from Winnipeg. She is the author of *April Raintree* and also wrote a revised edition of that book for use in the schools. She now writes under her birth name, Beatrice Mosionier. She lives in Bracebridge, Ontario, and in Toronto.

BETH CUTHAND was born in northern Saskatchewan. She is a poet, educator and activist of the Little Pine Cree, Scots, Irish and Blackfoot nations. Her short stories and poems have appeared in Aboriginal and feminist journals and magazines. The mother of two grown sons, Beth earned a Bachelor's degree in sociology from the University of Saskatchewan and an Master's in creative writing in Penticton, British Columbia. She lives in a log house looking over Lake Okanagan with her two cats, her dog and an intriguing cast of house mates.

RAMABAI ESPINET was born in Trinidad and Tobago and has lived in Canada for many years. She is a writer of fiction and poetry, a critic and an academic. Her research interests lie in post-colonial literature and Latin American and Caribbean studies. Her work as a community activist includes a bi-weekly column, "Focus on Women," for the community newspaper *Indo-Caribbean World*. She is a professor of English at Seneca College in Toronto.

LENORE KEESHIG-TOBIAS is an Ojibway storyteller and writer from the Neyaashiinigmiing (aka Cape Croker) on the Bruce Peninsula. Her children's stories have been published in the CIRCLE program, an integrated primary English-as-a-second-language program for Native children. She shares the 1993 Living the Dream Book Award with her daughter Polly for their book *Bird Talk*.

ISABELLE KNOCKWOOD, born in Wolfville, Nova Scotia, attended the Indian Residential School in Shubenacadie from 1936 to 1947. She is the mother of six children and has fourteen grandchildren. At the age of fifty-eight, she enroled at Saint Mary's University in Halifax, to work on a major in anthropology and a minor in English, and graduated in 1992. She lives at the Indian Brook Reserve, Nova Scotia. At a special sunrise ceremony at Indian Brook, Isabelle was given her spirit name, Maqmikewe'skw or Mother Earth.

JOY KOGAWA was born in Vancouver in 1935. Like other Japanese Canadians, she and her family were persecuted and interned during World War II. She lives in Vancouver and Toronto and has almost finished a new work.

KARLYN KOH is a graduate student living in Vancouver, for the moment.

C. ALLYSON LEE has been published in various anthologies and journals, including *The Very Inside: An Anthology of Writing by Asian and Pacific Islander Lesbian and Bisexual Women* (1994), *Piece of my Heart: A Lesbian of Colour Anthology* (1991), *Outrage: Dykes and Bis Resist Homophobia* (1993), *The Capilano Review*, and *Fireweed;* and is the co-editor of *Pearls of Passion: A Treasury of Lesbian Erotica* (1994). She has a smouldering passion for guitars, primates and WET Coast Womyn Warriors.

SKY LEE was born in Port Alberni, British Columbia, and holds a Bachelor of Fine Arts degree from the University of British Columbia as well as a diploma in nursing from Douglas College.

SALONI MATHUR is a doctoral candidate in the Department of Anthropology at the New School for Social Research and is a part-time visiting lecturer in the Women's Studies program at Rutgers University.

AHDRI ZHINA MANDIELA is noted for her dynamism in dub, both in performance and on paper. This Toronto poet and director is taking a *step/in poetry*. Applying step dance in the same way jazz instruments create improvisation, *step/in poetry* integrates the word-sound musical power of dub poetry with the total free-styling instrumentation of the improvisational rhythms and patterns of step dance. She has a CD release planned for spring 1995 and a winter single and video pre-release of "in the canefields."

ARUN PRABHA MUKHERJEE was born in 1946 in Lahore, India. With the 1947 partition of that country, her parents fled to India, and she was raised and educated in Tikamargh, Madya Pradesh. After doing graduate work in English at the University of Saugar, she came to

Canada as a Commonwealth Scholar to do graduate work at the University of Toronto. She has taught at several universities in Canada, and is an associate professor of English at York University, Toronto, where she teaches courses on Post-colonial Literature and Women's Studies. She is the mother of a seventeen-year-old son, Gautam, and is working on a study of Canadian perceptions of India. A new collection of her essays, *Oppositional Aesthetics: Readings from a Hyphenated Space*, is to be published shortly.

UMA PARAMESWARAN is professor of English at the University of Winnipeg, which she joined in 1967 and where she initiated Women in Literature courses in the early 1980s. More recently, she led a three-year project on women-focused research. Her present research is on South Asian Canadian literature and the literature of the Indian diaspora. She has published extensively on post-colonial literatures.

CARMEN RODRÍGUEZ was born in Valdivia, Chile in 1948. Since being forced into exile by the 1973 military coup, she has lived in the United States, Bolivia, Argentina and Canada. Her poetry, short stories and articles have been published in *Paula, Aquelarre, The Capilano Review, Fireweed, Norte-Sur, Prison Journal, West Coast Line* and *Kinesis*. She has a collection of short stories soon to be released. Rodríguez is also an adult literacy consultant, teaches at Simon Fraser University in the Faculty of Education and is a member of the *Aquelarre* magazine collective.

ELAINE SAVORY formerly wrote as Elaine Savory Fido. She taught at the University of the West Indies from 1974 until 1990 and was part of the faculty team which established Women's Studies there. She has written widely on African and Caribbean women's writing and is concluding a study on cultural complexity in African, Indian and

Caribbean women's texts. Savory worked in feminist theatre in Barbados and is working on a play about Jean Rhys. Presently, she divides her time between New York and Barbados.

MAKEDA SILVERA is an African-Caribbean-Canadian writer who has lived in Canada for over twenty-five years. Her writing explores identity and language from a lesbian feminist perspective. She lives in Toronto.

CAROL TALBOT was born in Windsor, Ontario, and teaches English in London, Ontario. Talbot received a new playwright's award from Theatre Fountainhead for *The Gathering* and an Excellence in Education certificate and pin from the Ontario Secondary Teacher's Federation in London for her book *Growing Up Black in Canada*.

RITA WONG was born and bred in the Prairies and is at school in Vancouver. She has worked in China and Japan and is very interested in livable communities where women of colour can flourish. Her writing has appeared in *Fireweed* and in *Contemporary Verse 2*. She is on the editorial collective of *absinthe*.

Selected Works by the Contributors

Lillian Allen

Rhythm an' Hardtimes. Poetry. Domestic Bliss, 1982.

If You See Truth. Children's poetry. Verse to Vinyl, 1987.

Why Me? Children's poetry. Well Versed Publications, 1991.

Nothing But A Hero. Children's poetry. Well Versed Publications, 1992.

Women Do This Every Day. Selected poems. Women's Press, 1993.

Himani Bannerji

doing time. Poetry. Sister Vision Press, 1986.

Coloured Pictures. Young people's fiction. Sister Vision Press, 1991.

The Writing on the Wall: Essays on Culture and Politics. Non-fiction, TSAR, 1993.

Unsettling Relations: The University as a Site of Feminist Struggle. Non-fiction. Co-editor. Women's Press, 1991.

Returning the Gaze: Essays on Racism, Feminism and Politics. Non-fiction. Editor. Sister Vision Press, 1993.

Dionne Brand

Earth Magic. Children's poetry. Kids Can Press, 1979. Republished by Sister Vision Press, 1993.

Primitive Offensive. Poetry. Williams-Wallace Publishers, 1982.

Winter Epigrams & Epigrams to Ernesto Cardenal in Defense of Claudia. Poetry. Williams-Wallace Publishers, 1983.

Chronicles of the Hostile Sun. Poetry. Williams-Wallace Publishers, 1984.

Rivers Have Sources, Trees Have Roots. Non-fiction. Co-ed. Krisantha Sri Bhagaiata, Cross Cultural Commmunications, 1985.

Sans Souci and Other Stories. Fiction. Williams-Wallace Publishers Inc., 1988. Republished by Women's Press, 1994.

No Language is Neutral. Poetry. Coach House Press, 1990.

No Burden to Carry: Narratives of Black Working Women in Ontario, 1920s to 1950s. Oral histories. Women's Press, 1991.

Bread Out of Stone: Essays on Sex, Politics and the Imagination. Non-fiction. Coach House Press, 1994.

Maria Campbell

People of the Buffalo. Co-author. Douglas & McIntyre, 1975.

Riel's People. Douglas & McIntyre, 1978.

Halfbreed. Goodread Biographies, 1983.

Achimoona. Fifth House, 1985.

Stories of the Road Allowance People. Theytus, 1993.

Give Back: First Nations Perspectives on Cultural Practice. Co-author. Gallerie Women Artists Monographs, 1993.

Afua Cooper

The Red Caterpillar on College Street. Children's poetry. Sister Vision Press, 1989.

Memories Have Tongue. Poetry. Sister Vision Press, 1992.

Beatrice Culleton

In Search of April Raintree. Novel. Pemmican Publications, 1983. Republished by Peguis Publishers, 1992.

Beth Cuthand

Voices in the Waterfall. Poetry. Lazara Press, 1989. Republished by Theytus Books, 1992.

Horse Dance to Emerald Mountain. Chapbook. Lazara Publications, 1987.

Ramabai Espinet

Creation Fire: A CAFRA Anthology of Caribbean Women's Poetry. Editor. Sister Vision Press, 1990.

Nuclear Seasons. Poetry. Sister Vision Press, 1991.

The Princess of Spadina. Children's story. Sister Vision Press, 1992.

Ninja's Carnival. Children's story. Sister Vision Press, 1993.

Lenore Keeshig-Tobias

Bird Talk. Sister Vision Press, 1991.

Joy Kogawa

The Splintered Moon. Poetry. University of New Brunswick, 1967.

A Choice of Dreams. Poetry. McClelland & Stewart, 1974.

Jericho Road. Poetry. McClelland & Stewart, 1977.

Obasan. Novel. Lester and Orpen Dennys, 1981. Also published in the US, Japan and Germany. Republished by Penguin Canada, 1983, Quebec/Amerique, 1989, and Anchor Books, 1994.

Woman in the Woods. Poetry. Mosaic, Canada, 1985

Naomi's Road, Children's Fiction. Oxford University Press Canada, 1986.

Naomi no Michi. Young adult fiction. Shogakkan, Japan, 1988.

Itsuka. Novel. Viking Canada, 1992; Revised, Penguin Canada, 1993; Anchor Books, 1994.

Isabelle Knockwood

Out of the Depths: The Experiences of Mi'kmaw Children at the Indian Residential School at Shubenacadie. Roseway Publishing, 1992.

Sky Lee

Teach Me How To Fly, Skyfighter. Illustrator. Lorimer, 1983.

Disappearing Moon Cafe. Douglas & McIntyre, 1990.

Telling It: Women and Language Across Cultures. Co-ed. Telling It Book Collective, Press Gang Publishers, 1990.

Belly Dancer. Stories. Press Gang Publishers, 1994.

ahdri zhina mandiela

speshal rikwes. Poetry. Sister Vision Press, 1985.

dark diaspora... in dub. A dub theatre piece. Sister Vision Press, 1991.

Arun Prabha Mukherjee

The Gospel of Wealth in the American Novel: The Rhetoric of Dreiser and His Criticism and Cultural Imperialism. Croom Helm, 1987.

Towards an Aesthetic of Opposition: Essays on Literature, Criticism and Cultural Imperialism. Williams-Wallace Publishers, 1988.

Sharing Our Experience. Editor. Canadian Advisory Council on the Status of Women, 1993.

Uma Parameswaran

Cyclic Hope Cyclic Pain. Writers Workshop, 1974.

Trishanku. TSAR Publications, 1988.

Rootless But Green Are the Boulevard Trees. TSAR Publications, 1989.

The Door I Shut Behind Me. Affiliated East/West Press, 1990.

Carmen Rodríguez

Guerra Prolongada/Protracted War. Poetry. Women's Press, 1992.

Elaine Savory

Out of the Kumbla: Caribbean Women and Literature. Co-editor. Africa World Press Inc., 1990.

Makeda Silvera

Silenced: Talks with working-class Caribbean women about their lives and struggles as Domestic Workers in Canada. Williams Wallace Publishers, 1983. Republished by Sister Vision Press, 1989.

Fireworks: The Best of Fireweed. Editor. Women's Press, 1986.

Growing Up Black: A Resource Manual for Black Youth. Sister Vision Press, 1989.

The Issue is 'Ism: Women of Colour Speak Out. Co-editor. Sister Vision Press, 1989.

Remembering G and Other Stories. Sister Vision Press, 1991.

Piece of My Heart: A Lesbian of Colour Anthology. Editor. Sister Vision Press, 1991.

Her Head a Village and Other Stories. Press Gang Publishers, 1993.

Carol Talbot

Growing Up Black in Canada. Children and young people's book. Williams-Wallace Publishers, 1984.